DAYLIGHT

DAYLIGHT

Elizabeth Knox

Ballantine Books ✦ New York

I would like to thank
Sarah and Michael Brewer—
cavers and cave rescue volunteers.

A Ballantine Book
Published by The Random House Ballantine Publishing Group

Copyright © 2003 by Elizabeth Knox

All rights reserved under
International and Pan-American Copyright Conventions.
Published in the United States by
The Random House Ballantine Publishing Group,
a division of Random House, Inc., New York,
and simultaneously in Canada by
Random House of Canada Limited, Toronto.

Ballantine and colophon are registered trademarks of Random House, Inc.

www.ballantinebooks.com

Library of Congress Cataloging-in-Publication Data
is available from the publisher upon request.

ISBN 0-345-45795-1

Text design by Liney Li

Manufactured in the United States of America

First Edition: April 2003

1   3   5   7   9   10   8   6   4   2

The light which puts out our

eyes is darkness to us.

—Henry David Thoreau, *Walden*

Contents

〜

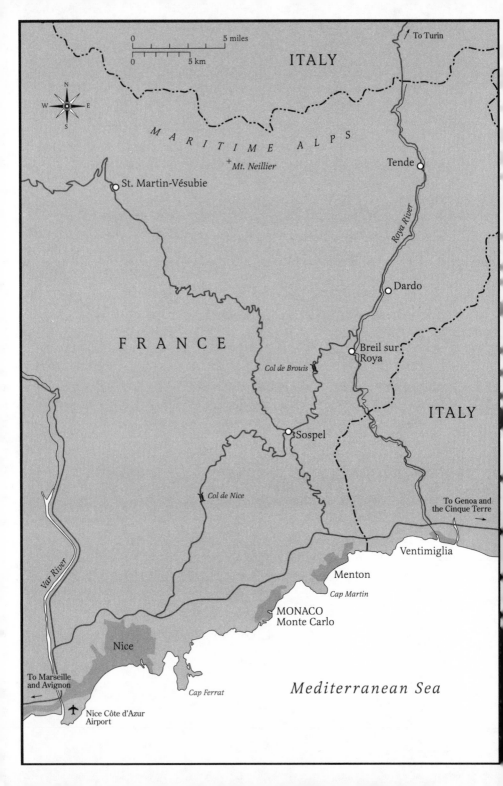

Chapter 1

A BODY RECOVERY

*R*iomaggiore Railway Station stood against a coastal cliff face and between two tunnels. The station's platform was covered in tourists, perched on their packs as though hoping to hatch them. The trains were on strike.

Bad's pack bristled with steel climbing equipment so it couldn't be used as a cushion. He was tired—his room the night before had been above the rail line, where the trains, then running, had passed all night at twenty-minute intervals. He had slept finally, but his dreams were in Dolby and threatened monsters, trying to account for the funneling roar from the wings of their stages.

Bad was sleepy and homesick. The Cinque Terre's beautiful landscape chafed him—like clothes he hadn't tried before buying, chosen for him by someone else. His girlfriend had organized the trip, had sat, her laptop on the kitchen counter of their Sydney apartment, paging through tourist sites and

2 ～ Elizabeth Knox

timetables, while Bad tried to get comfortable in his untethered parts, between a padded plastic neck brace and the cast on his right leg.

Bad wondered where Gabrielle was now. He was following the itinerary they had planned. She had left him, but he stuck to their path. He put himself in her way, not because he wanted to hook up with her again but because he wanted to present an obstacle to her usual positive momentum.

They had parted ways a few days before, in Genoa, after squabbling their way through the first three weeks of the trip. Most of their arguments were about money, their budget. Gabrielle earned more than Bad, and, as she'd willingly admit, she liked to spoil herself. Bad resented being coaxed into spending more than he should and was only annoyed by her offers to treat him. But more than that, he resented the occasions on which she felt moved to reassure him that she *respected his job.* It was a statement he'd always hear followed by an unspoken *but.*

After what Gabrielle liked to call his "work-related accident," she had taken care of him. She'd helped him live on his insurance payout without dipping into their vacation fund. She'd put in time, energy, and resources. She believed she'd earned her right to try to make him "consider his options."

Gabrielle was a management consultant, her speciality human resources. She'd moved up to analysis and planning and now only had to deal with management, behind their own closed doors or in the big seminar room of her company—a room that looked out onto Circular Quay, its traffic like an executive toy in perpetual hypnotic motion. Because in the past she had "project-managed" restructuring and had had to talk to employees, Gabrielle knew how to represent change as challenge and setback as opportunity. When she and Bad got to Europe it became clear that she'd decided the vacation was his chance to take stock, since he hadn't begun to in his months laid up. She began to talk to Bad about his future. She wanted to make him see that while it was good to give *part* of life to work that was altruistic, there came a time when . . .

Her campaign reached full intensity at Bad's birthday dinner in Genoa. By the time coffee came, it was clear to Bad that Gabrielle had exhausted and excelled herself in laying out his options. She'd worked up the next five years of his life, twenty-nine to thirty-four, years he should invest in seeing just how far his brain and balls could take him *in his own interest.*

Gabrielle put down her coffee cup, folded her hands, and said, "Well—that's my pitch, Brian."

Bad said that his pitch was different—any vertical face too high to climb without a rope. Bad's favorite sports were caving and climbing, and he'd just spent a few days with his friend Gino at the Site Bernhard Gobbi in the Mercantour.

Gabrielle sighed. Despite the convivial-looking table, with its shot glasses of warm grappa, its coffee and tray of six sugars, she looked sour and out of sorts.

Bad picked up the smaller of her two presents and rattled it. He could see that the other present was a book, and he was already regarding it with polite tolerance and the faint sense of entrapment he'd always had at the sight of a flat package of a certain size under the drooping baubled pine trees of his childhood Christmases.

"Go on, then," she said.

The little package contained a Mamout, a knife with everything, except that on its handle, instead of a gold cross, was a woolly mammoth. Bad admired his Mamout, spread it into its full scintillating glory.

The other present was wrapped in sober blue and threaded with gold ringlet ribbons. Bad pulled at its knot with his teeth; he made a demonstration of eagerness and got the wrapper off.

The book was a hardback—*The Great Beyond: Is Your Outlook a Closed Curtain?* His girlfriend had given him a motivational book. On its cover a man and woman, shoulder to shoulder and touching only fraternally, were staring into a mirror, to one side of which was an open window and a landscape like a map.

Gabrielle said, "Brian, look, you're better than anyone I know at recognizing opportunities for adventure. But life isn't an Outward Bound course. And sure, there are dirty jobs someone has to do, but that someone doesn't always have to be you."

Bad thought of a man he knew, a miner for fifteen years and a mine rescue captain. He thought of the man's explanation of how he became a rescuer. "I'd been working underground for only a year when there was an explosion in the mine and some men were trapped," he'd told Bad. "Most of the guys around me couldn't get out of there fast enough. But for some reason I found myself going the other way, into the smoke."

Gabrielle was staring at him. "Brian, I don't want to see you hurt again," she said.

Bad gave the book a decisive little shake. "Right," he said. "This can be my—what do they call it?—my *vade mecum.*" (They had visited a library of illuminated manuscripts in Florence and had admired the incunabula.) "This can *go with me,*" Bad said. Then, "But perhaps you shouldn't."

On the path opposite Riomaggiore's station something was happening. A crowd coalesced, a crowd comprised of figures in suits or uniforms, some in high-visibility vests. The alert bustle gradually took on the appearance of an incident. Bad watched men in suits shake hands with men in uniforms. Several paramedics appeared with a stretcher they wheeled on the straight and carried around corners. People spoke into mobile phones and radios. The only thing the scene lacked was a base-line of rotating lights. But there were no good roads into four of the villages of the Cinque Terre, and the path on which the crowd had gathered was narrow. The path ran at the rear of houses whose walls were practically continuous with the cliff on which they perched, a cliff at one side of the cove one over from Riomaggiore's port. The path was narrow and, in places, cantilevered out from the cliff face.

(Bad had taken a walk around the headland the previous evening, in the company of a young Swiss woman he'd met in a bar. He'd had some hopes of her—of her bed and her room, which had to be quieter than his. But he was feeling too baf-fled and angry to turn on his charm. And, in the end, he'd done something that made her call him—in English—a "nanny," or possibly a "ninny." Bad hadn't liked the look of the path and had hesitated at the corner, taking hold of the Swiss girl by jamming his hand down the back waistband of her sweatpants. She didn't mistake his tackle for a pass—not for a moment. And she sneered at him when he thrust his head through the guardrail to inspect the bolts in the stone—fresh paint over bubbles of rust. She walked on, shaking her hips and shrugging her shoulders as if he still held her. He followed, and the path felt solid after all. The girl picked up her pace and went on her way. She left Bad standing for a time watching the swell roll into the narrow cove and turn white, then gray in its groin, a scummy stew the same color and texture as wet kapok.)

There was still no sign of a train, so Bad decided to inves-tigate. He picked his way through roosting backpackers and clambered down from the platform. He stopped only a few feet short of the several uniforms and suits who were on the edge of the cliff opposite the cantilevered path. Bad let his gaze follow the direction of theirs.

The waves in the cove were high for the Mediterranean, a comparatively narrow and shallow body of water, whose waves were "fetch limited," never towering, like waves on an open ocean, but tricky, sometimes steep and close together. That morning the V of the cove was completely white, a white like oversugared meringue mix, neither a stiff foam nor fully liquid.

Bad saw a body heaved about behind a rock in the pitted cliff. For a few minutes he watched it, pushed down by waves coming and going, borne up against the roof of an embryonic sea cave, dropped and dragged, but never floating free of the rock at the cave's entrance. The force of the waves entering the cave had carried a corpse there—corpse or drowning person—and the backwash wasn't enough to carry it out again.

Bad edged closer to eavesdrop on only one side of a conversation—for distortions in the radio's transmitted voice robbed him of even the little he would be able to follow. He gathered that the locals were very reluctant to take a boat into the cove in that sea.

One man was clearly in charge—a police detective perhaps, a man in a good suit that hung poorly because he carried too much in his pockets. His hair was groomed in defiance of the elements, and the sea wind had only managed to unpick a few strands from its bonded surface. He kept looking out to sea, was perhaps waiting for a police launch.

Bad studied the sea: waves and reflection waves. Water piled against the cliff, rebounding from either wall and meeting in the middle, where it made an ugly scar. The waves produced a pattern of predictable forms, but in a complex sequence. Where the cliff was notched the waves reflected back at several angles, the whole cove heaving and roiling with white water, water that was sliding, layer over layer, in every direction.

A Jet Ski appeared at the head of cove, its rider in a wet suit and life jacket. It began to move cautiously in. The police, paramedics, and civic authorities leaned over to watch. On its way in, the Jet Ski was overturned and swamped. Its engine died. Its rider clung to its handlebars, shaking water out of his ears—performing a pantomime of discouraged discomfort, Bad thought. The guy seemed embarrassed. He was taking his time.

Bad was afraid for the man as, the night before, he had been for the Swiss girl. Bad was concerned for the man's safety, and furious with him. The man reminded him of himself as a self-conscious seventeen-year-old, taking his time, taking three backward steps off the viewing platform above the glacier on Dart Ridge Track, his body having made its own estimation of the platform's soggy give. (It gave rather than bounced when his friends began to jump up and down. "Hey!" someone said, delighted. "This thing springs! It rocks!" And Bad said, from the shingled track, where he'd stopped, "I don't like the way it feels"—apologizing for his timidity. Some of them laughed at him. They were laughing, then their hands flew up, lunging for a hold above them in the air, as the platform collapsed, and they fell. All but one, the quick one, who launched himself off the platform's receding solidity and into the safety of the thornbushes at the edge of the precipice.)

Bad closed the blast doors in his head. He shut out the past and didn't hear the crash—the platform exploding on the ice field below Dart Ridge. Instead he said, succinct and scornful, "Him, too." And, when the detective turned around and looked at him, Bad pointed with his chin at the Jet Ski. "Dead in the water," he added.

But the skier was up again and struggling to start his engine. After a time it caught and he sped out of the cove. Bad turned to one of the tourists who had joined him. "They are going to go in with a boat and gaff, and it won't work."

"Remind me not to order the fish," said one girl to her boyfriend, then flinched faintly as the detective came away from the edge of the cliff and stopped before Bad. The man asked, in English, what Bad would do.

"A land-based recovery," Bad said. "You'd have a fire truck

and crane over there if the terrain could support it. What you need instead is a couple of men in protective gear, helmets and wet suits, on two rope rigs, ascenders with a two-thousand-kilo body strength—because you have to consider the pressure of the sea—descenders in line, pulleys and carabiner for human cargo, a Stokes basket, a couple of hauling and belay teams, and a progress capture device at the edge of the drop behind all the action."

Bad shut his mouth and he and the detective peered at each other. Then the detective touched Bad's sleeve to coax him away from the other tourists. He gave Bad a notebook and had him make a diagram. Bad drew his rig, labeled in a mix of English and French, from the three-wrap prusik hitch to the *descendeurs* on the cliff men's *baudrier*. He turned the notebook and they studied it together. The corners of its pages vibrated in the breeze.

"You want a mountain rescue club," Bad said. "The *Corpo Nazionale Soccorso Alpino*. I can give you the number of the local *stazioni*."

"We are in a hurry," the detective said.

"You can't hurry," Bad said. "You're not heavy rescue capable, so you have to go easy. And the guy's dead." Bad imagined the police, keen to preserve any evidence, wanted the body out as soon as possible. He watched the corpse alternately tossed up and buried by foaming water. Bad asked the detective, "Were you waiting for this body?"

The man shook his head. He certainly hadn't been, he said. He'd been in Portofino on another matter. He turned and signaled one of the uniforms closer, relieved him of his binoculars, and passed them to Bad, who stepped closer to the rail, where the spray came up like smoke and shrank the tissues in his nostrils. Bad put the binoculars to his eyes and fell into a swooping blur of wet rock and bright, beaten water. He searched and saw the head, facedown. He saw long light brown hair and that her parting was paler, fair for a good five

centimeters at least. You didn't often see that—hair that graduated to transparency from ends to scalp.

"I could do this," Bad said to the detective.

But *this* was an itch he shouldn't scratch. It was adventure
and danger and an eventual probable destination, a place he'd
reach with all his skin torn off, and cold, like the corpse in the
sea cave.

Bad could see that the corpse's arms, exposed by a pale
sleeveless top, weren't spongy, macerated by long immersion
or abraded by rocks. Nor was her flesh plump and smooth still.
It was dark rather, blistered and stippled with holes.

At Bad's ear the detective said, "There may have been a fire
at sea." There were numerous unreported marine disasters, he
said, boatloads of illegals crossing from Africa to Europe.

Bad returned the binoculars and looked at the detective,
waiting for more. "I guess you have a helicopter coming," he
said. He followed the detective's gaze to the horizon and a
band of fawn haze in the sky. Mistral or sirocco—Bad wanted
to ask which it was; he could only remember the names.

The detective was waiting Bad out. But they both knew
the trick—if you stay quiet, people talk. Bad realized this was
a strategy he used and that, for months, he'd practiced it on his
girlfriend—he'd waited her out. His silence urged her into
speech, and he took offense at what she said.

"Look," Bad said. "I'll give you a number." He retrieved
his diagram from the detective. "This is my friend Gino Viani.
He's a firefighter and involved in mountain and cave rescue.
He lives in Genoa. Cavers are now the only real masters of
vertical rope rescue—thanks to helicopters." Bad held out the
paper and after a moment's hesitation the detective took it
from him. "I have my doubts about your helicopter," Bad said.

"I have doubts, too. Thank you, Mr.—?"

"Phelan. Brian Phelan."

•   •   •

Bad walked back up through the village. He bought a *macchiato* and an almond pastry. He kept an eye out for the man who had rented him the room above the railway.

In a piazza by the highest houses of Riomaggiore Bad met an old woman, tiny, white-haired, shawled in black, who directed him to a top track through the vineyards. The track ran along a terrace with vines above and below it. It was lined with blue borage, tight trumpets of purple sweet pea, poppies, buttercups, and clover with long dusky blossoms. Far below Bad, on a broad path by the rail line, were other walkers, daytrippers, in a thick ambling stream. Bad had decided not to walk on to the next village. He found a seat, a flat stone on the wall of a terrace, and sat with his legs dangling, waiting for the helicopter to arrive. Waiting to see how it would do.

The helicopter was too far above the action and not in a direct line with the cave. It couldn't come into the cove because of the wind, and because of the gusts its pilot didn't dare lower a man right down beside the cliff face. Bad watched the man winch in again, the helicopter rise and dip its nose and dart away. For another half hour he watched a big launch and an inflatable standing by at the mouth of the cove, both vessels tilting and twisting in the steep swell.

His phone rang. It was Gino. He said, in English, that he was gathering the necessary experienced bodies and their gear. "You put this detective on to me?" Gino said. "*Mr.* Phelan? Did you tell him you are with the police also?"

"No," said Bad. "There's a question mark over that."

"He said you gave him my number and then disappeared."

"I'm above Riomaggiore, keeping my eye on the action. I volunteered *your* expertise, Gino, not my own."

"When we arrive will you be there?"

"Sure."

"Are you going to want to be on a rope, Bad?"

"Yes."

"Hauling or in the surf?"

"I was on a rope last week, Gino. I'm completely fit."

Gino changed tack. He said that, earlier in the week, Bad's girlfriend, Gabrielle, had been by his apartment to collect the bag she'd stored there.

Bad asked if she'd said anything.

"She said she wasn't your ideal audience." Then, "Bad?" said Gino, into his friend's silence.

"Okay, mate, I'll meet you there," Bad said. "At the edge."

Before Bad's work-related accident he and Gabrielle had been "going out," to parties, movies, barbecues, her colleagues' polo games. She stayed over at his place, he at hers. They took a friendly interest in each other, and pleasure. They would agree that they'd had some important talks, several about the sad neediness of other couples they knew. These conversations were a kind of orientation exercise: they worked out where they were in relation to their expectations of themselves. They discussed dependence and independence—but never considered interdependence. Bad once overheard Gabrielle saying proudly to her friends, "Brian and I don't like to live in each other's pockets."

After Bad's work-related accident he moved in with her and she declared that she wanted to get to know him—*really*. "Remember *Woman of the Year*?" (They had seen a new print at the film festival.) "Well, unlike Katharine Hepburn, I *do* know how my man likes his eggs. But I don't really know what makes him tick."

"Am I ticking?" said Bad.

The bomb that had injured Bad had been under a car in a garage beneath a concert hall. Two cardboard pizza boxes had been taped together, one on top of the other, with a visible timer attached. The police emergency ordnance disposal team

X-rayed the package at different frequencies before detaching the timer and freezing the whole thing with dry ice, in order to retard its detonation time. They guessed that there was probably another detonator concealed underneath it, on anything from one to five seconds—five to ten at minus ten degrees Celsius. Bad's colleagues did what they could, then moved back. Bad was told to take in his Predator robot to pull the package out and turn it over. As Bad maneuvered his Predator, he thought about his psych instructor, who used to say, about bombs costumed in dummy timers, "If terrorism is a theater of war, then bombers know the bomb squad are theater critics. They are going to want you to know, if only for an instant, how artful they've been."

The garage was still. There was a static cough from a radio. Red and blue lights bounced off the clean glass and paintwork of the concertgoers' cars. Bad, blinkered by his helmet, entombed in his armor, performed the *tai chi* of a robot controller. He got the Predator's arms in under the car and inched the box out. The reading by his left eye said the box weighed twenty kilos. More than it should. (That was the lead plate, millimeters thick, shielding the detonator from prying X rays.) Camera two, on the Predator's antenna, showed no wires running from the box, no mooring of booby trap to explain the resistance. Bad had time to say, "I've got a weird figure on its weight. Is there any known ordnance . . . ?" Then he saw that the cement was rougher in a patch under the box. That it wasn't cement but packed sand. And he thought he saw the shining blister of a switch on which the twenty kilos of lead sheeting—and nothing else—had pressed. A small antipersonnel mine was embedded in a sand-filled hollow under the car. The emergency ordnance disposal team had thought that the car was the target, but the car was the bomb itself, and loaded with explosives.

A shock ran along the umbilicus from the Predator, a burst

of feedback. Static, then blackness, no signal. A brutal concussion wave threw Bad ten meters backward. The fire followed him, bright even through his blast shield, flames accelerating toward him, unstoppable—till a lid slammed down on them, a concrete slab, part of the floor above, five by five meters and twelve centimeters thick. It landed at an angle, its lower edge against the sole of Bad's right boot, its upper edge wedged against one of the garage's main supporting pillars, on which there was a poster for an exhibition of European Modern Masters. Bad saw sparks, and the cement chipped by shrapnel. He watched the band of yellow and black paint on the pillar's edge blistered by heat. The poster was on the pillar's sheltered side, but the air got under it and made it pulse, then billow free and fly at him, its edges catching fire and burning in toward the pure heart-shaped face of Jean Ares's *Eve in a Gaucho Hat.* Bad saw Eve consumed by a closing iris of fire. Then he lifted his head and looked for his hands.

His hands were whole, and holding his girlfriend's motivational book. He was up to chapter 3: "Solid Approaches to Infirm Positions."

The afternoon light was changing color now, slanting down the terraces above Riomaggiore, touching their tops but not their steps. It was, Bad thought, the kind of light that seems to look over your shoulder, like sunlight in a church. It made him feel embarrassed by the book, so he closed it, put it in his pack, got up, and went back along the top path and down into Riomaggiore.

When the sun was only its own depth above the mountains everything was finally ready. They had three rigs, and Gino and Bad were on separate lines, with the battered chicken-wire

Stokes basket on its own line above them. Gino had brought Bad's caving gear and his wet suit. Only he and Gino had wet suits—all Gino's cave-diving friends were down a system in the Dolomites, helping out on a mixed-gas dive.

The cove was entirely in the shade. Beyond the station and the resurgence of the rail line between two tunnels the rock face was a darkness checked by gray vapor, a chain-link fence put up to catch falling rocks. Above this the terraces were sun-striped, the golden air grainy with insects working spring flowers. In the light even the businesslike regularities of laid cordage—prusik hitch and alpine butterfly—were all magically vivid. The jumars and the worn rollers of the brake bar racks were all objects the climbers took good long looks at and, not believing their eyes, rattled and wriggled and yanked.

Gino switched on his helmet lamp. He said that all he'd told the detective, concerning Bad, was that he knew what he was doing. "And nothing about your injury."

"I've been climbing," Bad said. "You were there."

Yes, Gino said, and Bad wasn't on the same rope as him, and the woman in the water was dead. "So." Gino shrugged. "And I told him you were police. That made him happy. But here he comes." Gino climbed over the fence. Bad turned on his own headlamp and looked up at the detective, who blinked in its beam. Bad crossed the fence, too, and clipped his jumar onto the lines coming under its rails, lines that ran over the padded edge of the path and the rollers of stainless steel racks. Bad took off his sunglasses and passed them to the detective, then let himself down, caught the lower edge of the concrete path in one hand, and pushed off. The rope ran out three feet and Bad swung into the shadow. His boots connected with the cliff face and he bounced out again and began to abseil quickly down.

Bad glanced up once to see that Gino was well over to one side, dislodging a litter of pebbles from the cliff, but none that fell anywhere near. High above them Bad could see the underside of the path, its straight edge interrupted by several craning heads and the lit transparency of smoke from the brake bar racks, heated by friction.

Bad stopped within two meters of the surf and braced his legs against the cliff. Gino appeared beside him and they watched as the Stokes basket was lowered, revolving slowly. Gino gave Bad a thumbs-up—they were using hand signals, unable to make themselves heard above the surf. Gino raised his arms to catch the basket, clipped himself onto its line, made an OK with his gloved hand, and spoke into the radio on his harness. Bad tightened the strap of his helmet and let himself down into the water. He felt the confused pressure of a boil, then the drag out and, in the next instant, the push in. His feet sought and found the rock at the cave mouth. The tread on his soles caught on its surface, rough under a soft layer of seaweed. Bad looked into the cave, saw that it was around three meters deep, with a small water chamber, its roof higher than its opening. Bad's taut rope and braced legs kept him outside, but the seaweed provided lubrication between his feet and their foothold. He looked up at Gino, who had his ear down to the radio. Gino began to relate information from the people above, about the waves. Bad was to wait for a low set. He waited. Then, on Gino's signal, Bad let out his line enough to crouch on the rock. He found a handhold seaward and reached his other hand back to the body as it rolled his way in the slow drain of a backwash. He slipped his hand into the waistband of her trousers. As he did he remembered the previous evening, his anxious reflex snatch at the Swiss girl as she set out along the cliff path. Bad bent both elbows, his upper body a closed spring, and hauled the body partway up onto the rock. Her rigid legs still pointed back into the cave.

A wave went under Bad and he felt it refloat the body. He gave a hard tug and she slid closer, emerging from the foam, her skin blistered, not by bursting bubbles but blister upon blister, some still full of straw-colored lymph, some open and red, with filmy white skin at their rims.

Bad waited out another wave and then looked up, gave Gino the nod. The basket began to descend. Bad put his head down to hold on through another wave, this time focused on the pulls on the fabric of the victim's knit top.

This woman's long hair, paler at its roots, didn't look like a dark dye job and regrowth. The color was blended gradually from roots to ends, gold to brass to amber to brown. The hair was a mess, a matted mass after her time in the sea, but the color was memorable. Bad had seen a similar unlikely high-maintenance dye job once before—a woman with blond roots graduating to brown ends, her face in a blur of pallor, as if a light shone out of her scalp. He remembered her because there had been weeks when he'd hoped he'd see her again or hear she'd been found. She was never found. That was nine years ago, but for a crazy moment Bad thought he'd found her in the sea cave at Riomaggiore. Found her finally, dead, as he'd expected her to be.

The basket lightly tapped Bad's helmet. He freed a hand to pull it down onto the rock, then clambered over the body and dropped down into the water inside the cave. He took shelter behind the rock from the full horizontal force of a slightly bigger wave. The wave formed an eddy behind him, rolled against the roof, turned wholly white with trapped air, and pushed Bad under. He waited for the pressure to diminish, and gripped the woman's ankle in one hand. When he came up for another breath, he found the basket above him and wrestled it down into the water. Before the next wave swamped him he saw Gino abseil down and set one boot on the back of the corpse. Bad closed his eyes and held his breath. The wave relented, but rather than letting him up it thrust him onto the rock. The basket surged up too, and punched him in the armpits. Then it dropped into the water behind him, disappeared, and reappeared, a sieve for foam.

Gino got his attention, gave his shoulder a soggy slap. The

body was rolling across the rock. Bad lifted his feet and let her roll under him—then he jerked the harness on the basket. It scooted toward him, and the body tumbled into it.

Bad fumbled for the straps. Gino shouted at him—then shrank from Bad, grew smaller, rappelling out from the rock and hauling himself up a number of feet. Bad saw Gino wrap his leg around the slack rope on the Stokes basket. A big wave came at the cave mouth, broke, and poured only part of its volume into the hollow. As it hit, Bad saw Gino buried and pushed against the cliff face. He saw Gino's rope-wrapped leg emerge from the white wall and into the cave. Then the cave filled and Bad was thrown up against the top of its water chamber. His helmet hit the rock roof with a crack. He was spread-eagled, and the Stokes basket rose diagonally on its taut rope and pushed against him. Bad put his gloved hand against the corpse's neck and held her down, held her in place. He felt the basket pulled sideways, but the water wasn't withdrawing yet. Bad clung to the corpse and basket and put his head down so that he could clear the cave mouth as, with the help of the hauling team above, Gino—acting as a human redirection pulley, his wet suit puckered and stretched, his leg rope-burned beneath it—pulled Bad and the Stokes basket right out of the cave. They poured out with the wave.

Bad was again suspended; he and the basket swung dripping for a moment; then the big following wave covered them and Bad kicked out to fend off the cliff face. The sea had his legs. Then it didn't have them, and he was making slow but steady upward progress, the hauling team hard at work far above him. Gino swung toward him and together they got the body's right leg and arm back in the basket and closed the remaining straps.

Gino joked that he now had one leg longer than the other. The beams of their lights crossed and parried as they peered at each other's faces, arms, and legs. The sun had gone behind the mountains and, in the dusk, the water below them glowed, a blue-shadowed white. It crashed and raved and Gino remarked that *these* waves were the big set; the one that carried Bad into the cave merely came in at a difficult angle. "Fifteen seconds more," Gino said, and smashed his fist into his palm.

Gino was exhilarated, Bad could see. As for Bad, he felt as he had hoped he would, finally thoroughly cleaned of something—something dimming rather than dirty—as if the pizza-box bomb had filled his soul with gloom, a shrapnel of small shadows.

Together Bad and his friend turned their faces and head-lamps down to the basket's load. Water dripped from the rim of their helmets and Bad could hear, against the surf, small *puck puck* sounds of drops on taut cloth. They looked at her face; then Gino's light moved and let Bad see where Gino was looking. Her shirt was rucked up, and the skin on her midriff was innocent of blisters.

At the top of the cliff the paramedics bagged the body. Bad showed them his hands, the palms of his wet gloves to which matter had adhered. He was asked to take them off and saw them bagged, too. Then he went and shook hands with the hauling and belay teams—Gino's caving friends and some fire-fighters from La Spezia. Gino asked him how his neck was. He'd noticed that Bad's helmet had taken a bit of a beating.

Bad said, "My neck is fine."

Gino was smoking, which always amused Bad. He was used to Sydney firefighters, who, for the most part, were dis-inclined to smoke.

The body was carried off and the rig dismantled and packed.

"This will need cleaning," said someone, about the basket.

"I'm going to act helpless at this point," Bad whispered to Gino, who glanced at him, then turned fully and came close to

Bad, excluding everyone else. "We both did several stupid things down there," he said.

"Yes, I know."

"So long as you know."

Gino had come with as much gear and as many hands as could be spared, though he hadn't been able to muster many off-duty firefighters—with the trains on strike the region's emergency services anticipated problems on the roads. Still, Gino's van was filled to capacity, so Bad caught a lift back to Genoa with the detective.

The detective complimented Bad on his French. Bad said thanks, but he was sure it didn't pass muster with the French. All credit was due to his grandmother, who had grown up on Jersey Island. But Bad had been in this part of the world before. Nine years ago. He'd met Gino then. Gino had rescued him from a flooded cave. He'd stayed at Gino's parents' place in Dolceacqua. Still, his Italian wasn't a patch on his French.

Bad was sleepy. He slid down in his seat.

The detective overtook a truck in the tunnel and surged out into the open air. The detective's phone rang. A hands-free car phone, thank God.

Bad yawned. His jaw clicked. He listened to the detective ask questions, heard the detective use a name he'd been idly trying to recall—the name of the village at the lower end of the big cave system in which he'd met Gino. The whole system had flooded in '92, and Gino's *zona* had been looking for trapped cavers.

"Dardo," said the detective. Then, "Martine Dardo."

They went into another tunnel. The truck overtook the detective.

"I hope you won't mind if I drop off," Bad said. "My room last night was above the rail line."

The detective told Bad that the woman had a credit card

in the back pocket of her pants, which greatly simplified things if it was *her* credit card. They had an address already, financial records, the name of a lawyer and next of kin. She'd have to be identified, of course. "Martine Dardo," the detective said. "It sounds very familiar."

Bad felt rather clever. He told the detective that Dardo was the name of a village just across the border. "A French village with an Italian name."

"An Italian village that chose with its head, not its heart," said the detective. "But it's the whole name—Martine Dardo—that is familiar."

They emerged from the tunnel.

"Tell your guys to put it into Google," Bad said.

The detective got his subordinate's attention and asked him to put "Martine" plus "Dardo" into a search engine.

GENOVA, said a sign—without a distance. Bad hunkered down and closed his eyes. He thought of the air mattress on the floor of Gino's living room.

The detective was talking; then his phone blipped as he broke the connection.

Bad opened his eyes and raised an eyebrow.

The detective said there were many hits on "Martine" and "Dardo" together. He said, "The Blessed Martine Raimondi of Dardo."

"A saint?"

"So, you are not a Catholic, Mr. Phelan?"

Bad told the detective that while his grandmother was Catholic, the rest of his family were "don't know and don't care" and "not at the dinner table, dear."

The detective explained that "Blessed" meant that Martine Raimondi, a nun, born in the village of Dardo and murdered by the Nazis in 1944, was *beatified*, but not yet canonized.

"And our floater?"

"Our floater, as you so delicately put it, might have been

named for the martyred nun and her village. We will no doubt discover that when we speak to her next of kin."

Bad said good, he hoped the detective wouldn't mind if he gave him a call in a few days. He'd like, at least, to know what had happened to her.

Chapter 2

THE POSTULATOR

One morning in May, twenty minutes before the bells rang for Matins, Father Daniel Octave's phone began to shiver. Daniel was sleeping with the phone curled in his hand and his hand against his sternum, the exact position in which, in childhood, he'd held Donkey, a knit toy, a present from his cherished grandmother. The phone was a prepaid mobile and only two people had its number: Martine Dardo and the old man in Montreal.

Martine had given Daniel the phone nearly a year earlier. She'd said he must keep it charged, topped up, and switched on. "No one need know you have it," she said. "It vibrates." She had given him the phone because—Daniel surmised—she felt she might need a priest at the end of it. He had waited to hear her confession. Sometimes the phone would quake and it would be Martine, testing him. Sometimes it would be Father Neske in Montreal, wanting to talk about John Paul II's "purification." The old man would say that without Purgatory they might as well all be Protestants. He'd say, "I still pray every day for the souls of the dead. Daniel, you're the only living soul for whom I say a prayer."

Daniel sat up, pressed a button on the quaking phone, and put it to his ear.

Martine said she was in a boat.

Daniel reached behind him to pull the cord on the holland blind. The blind snapped up and wound around its cylinder. "Are you alone?" Daniel said.

"It's a small boat, with an outboard. Or . . . it *had* an outboard."

Daniel scrubbed a hand across the top of his head. His hair stood up. "What happened to the motor?"

"I loosed it," Martine said, "and I let it go."

Daniel asked Martine why she'd ditched the outboard.

"I'm waiting for the sun to come up," she said. "Though if I was truly resolute I'd have thrown the oars away as well."

Daniel looked over the top of his headboard at sunlight shining on the eaves of the roof across the courtyard. The sun was up in Rome but not yet on the Riviera dei Fiori. He said, "And then what?"

Martine began to talk. She said it had happened—the thing she was unwilling to face. She had finally infected someone. Infected, and killed.

Daniel was surprised. He hadn't known that Martine was HIV-positive. She'd talked about "health problems" in the past but had given the impression that they were related to allergies.

"I don't want to infect anyone else," Martine said. "Or kill again."

Daniel didn't know what to say. He was a scholar, not a parish priest. And he was having trouble imagining Martine's behavior—the behavior that had brought her to her troubles. Still, he suggested that she *change* it.

"Oh yes," she said. "I could carry needles, and a cannula, and a plastic tube as a drinking straw."

Daniel was sitting up now. He was tugging at his hair—which was why he wore it short, so his fingers couldn't get purchase and pull. His hand slipped and went back. He was patting himself on the head.

Daniel said, "I don't understand what you're talking about."

Martine said that for years she'd looked east only at evening. She hadn't seen the dawn in full color. Dawn and dusk were like festive aprons, like the costume of the Arlesiennes. Martine said that her friend Eve Moskelute had met her husband, the artist Jean Ares, at the festival in Arles. Eve was unhappy before she met Jean, so ever since associated certain things with her reprieve, like the smell of fresh horseshit and the costume of the women of Arles. To watch what happened on the horizon opposite a sunrise or sunset was like looking only at the strings of the festive apron. "I've looked after myself, you see," Martine said, "and I've starved myself."

Daniel knew he must make Martine state her intentions. How could he argue with her if she wouldn't admit what she planned? First he should help her think about her beliefs. Help her remember them. He asked her, "Why is Judas in Hell?"

"Oh, Daniel," she said, "this isn't despair. This is a decision."

Across the city, bells began to ring, high and low, neither happy nor solemn, only summoning bells. Daniel put a finger in one ear and pressed the other to the pierced black plastic behind which this woman waited for him to save her, no matter what she professed. He told her that people only imagine they are making a rational decision to end their lives because they believe that their lives are their own.

Martine said, about the dawn, "It always looks as if it's about to happen long before it does. I've had about an hour of its advance publicity. I have seen this, looking back over my shoulder and running for my life."

"Martine—" said Daniel.

"I would run for my life now," she said, "if I could." Then, conversational, "It's so clear, and I'm so far out that I almost imagine Corsica is visible. There's no haze, and no wind."

"I should end this call," Daniel said. "I shouldn't listen to you. This isn't your transfiguration, Martine; it's just a miserable, lonely act." Then, *"In a minute!"* he said, to whoever was knocking on his door.

Martine said that she would love to know what he went on to do. What he eventually decided. "Because you do have to make some decisions, Daniel. You've broken a vow. You've been disobedient. You made choices you should have left to the bishop. I read your *Life of the Blessed Martine Raimondi*. I recognized much of it from the Process. And I read the Process when it was published. You left out your doubts, Daniel. And you left out the evidence that cleared them up. You didn't want anyone else to ask the questions you'd asked."

Daniel's Martine was the Blessed Martine Raimondi's namesake. At one stage in his investigation of Raimondi's virtues Daniel had thought that his friend Martine Dardo might be the martyred nun's daughter. He'd only confided his suspicions to the people whose testimony proved them false.

"I'd love to know what you are going to do," Martine said again. "I loved your *Life*. You're in love with her story. You're in love with the testimony—Grandfather Raimondi saying that he saw her following 'a bird' through the cave. A bird like the Holy Spirit in the old mosaics. 'A bird like a beckoning hand.' You know, Daniel, that there's God—but there are also the glories of nature."

"Martine—"

"Here it is," she whispered. "It's about to boil over."

Daniel supposed she meant the sun on the horizon.

"I always wanted to show you," Martine said. "I wanted to show you the Island."

Was she talking about Corsica? Daniel's hand was slippery. He swapped hands and put the phone to his other ear.

Martine was speaking again. She hadn't been talking about Corsica or the sun. "The Island is a glory of nature," Martine said. "A dust devil who dances forever."

Daniel heard a sound, like the instantaneous ignition of a patch of spilled gasoline, a short, fierce exhalation. "Martine?" he said. But she had dropped him in the sea. He heard himself go under, the splash, and the phone sinking away from its splash. He heard the water by the air rising through it, the air pulled under with him. He heard the phone malfunction, then nothing.

After a total of eleven years of study—punctuated by a two-year stint of teaching high school history—Daniel Octave gained his doctorate at Louvain in France, and after a final year of theology in Rome he was ordained at the age of twenty-eight. Father Daniel Octave, S.J., took up a lectureship in his hometown, Montreal, at Loyola University, in the History of the Modern Church. Then, in 1990, on a warm day after the spring break, Father Octave was summoned into the office of the rector of his house and told that he was to go to the bishopric in Nice. Daniel went without knowing what was expected of him. When Daniel met the bishop the man had on his desk a copy of Daniel's book based on his doctoral dissertation: *Those Things That Are Caesar's: The Society of Jesus and the Vichy Government*. It was Daniel's own French translation—he'd written it in Italian, his fourth language, if you counted the familiar skeletal conversational Latin he'd had to acquire as a novice. When he saw his book Daniel began to see that the house rector's "Go there" had some discernible chain of reasoning behind it, not just the vague sense Daniel had had since his undergraduate years of being watched in a kind of relay—by Father Ministers in his Jesuit houses, by professors, by superiors in Quebec, all the way up to the Father General in Rome. It was clear that Daniel had been chosen as the man for a job. He was to help the man who had the job—a Marist brother—in "this matter." He was given a thick file to read, a protean Process, a collection of testimonies concerning an Italian nun, who had already attained the status of "Venerable." Daniel took the file and opened it when he was alone in his room in the convent. Daniel read and, for the first time since the Regular Order of the Novitiate had performed on him the change it was designed to perform—a kind of preparation of the ground by its complete defoliation, then sterilization—for the first time since those early years some kind of disorder looked back into Daniel's mind. Opened its eyes and gazed back at him from the undergrowth of evidence. It was that first miracle—an act of God that looked like the work of another artist. Or like the Great Artist Himself—and great artists are often great mimics—composing a picture in some style He admires but that isn't His Own.

Daniel had met Martine Dardo in 1990, over some letters she had in her possession. Daniel had been employed for several months as assistant to the postulator appointed by the Holy See to investigate the theological and cardinal virtues of the Venerable Martine Raimondi.

Mother Pauline of the Order of the Daughters of Grace—the Venerable Martine's order—told Daniel that there was "a woman" who had a collection of the Venerable Martine's letters. The Process the postulator and Daniel were working on so far lacked *writings* as proof of Raimondi's theological virtue. The postulator told Daniel that if the letters were authentic, they must have them for the Process.

Mother Pauline was vague about the woman—Martine Raimondi's namesake. (Mother Pauline always called the Venerable Martine merely "Martine." They were near contemporaries and it was Sister Pauline to whom the Germans had released the martyred nun's body after her execution in

September 1944. And it was Sister Pauline who had traveled beside Raimondi's coffin on the train from Dardo to Turin and who had seen Martine Raimondi interred in a tomb in the gallery of the round votive chapel of Santa Maria della Fiori.) Mother Pauline told Daniel that she had no idea how the letters came to be in Martine Dardo's hands. Yes, Martine Dardo was Martine Raimondi's namesake, an orphan, raised by the sisters of the order and named for the martyred nun's village. But there was no birth certificate for a Martine Dardo—the order had neglected to keep records at that time. "We were hiding children," Mother Pauline said. "We were deliberately forgetful—because of the racial laws. You must understand, Father."

Daniel understood, but he didn't like it. He liked documents behind his documents.

Mother Pauline gave him Martine Dardo's address. "We only have it because she wrote asking for a copy of a photograph—a group photo of the 1929 Tricentenary of St. Barthelemy's in Dardo. A photo which shows Martine Raimondi and her family. The fathers at St. Barthelemy's told me that Martine Dardo let them know she had some letters."

Daniel wrote to Martine Dardo. He included a number at which he could be contacted.

She spoke Italian, her voice slight and hoarse. She said that the letters were from Martine Raimondi to her grandfather and were full of inquiries about aunts and cousins and requests for stories about her little goats. "She was only a girl, and homesick. The letters don't have anything in them remotely resembling theological musing. They're not what you want—the thoughts of a fine soul in troubled times. They're not even of any real historical interest. She does once mention the curfew, but only because she has to catch an earlier tram home from the hospital."

"Nevertheless, I'd like to see them," Daniel said.

They arranged a meeting. Daniel was to come to her house in Genoa.

It was a summer evening when he visited. She'd said to come late, for she worked late. Daniel found Martine Dardo's front door along a dingy *sotto passagio* and under a permanently lit silvery street lamp. There was a folded newspaper over the drain by the door, to dampen down the smell.

When Martine opened her door to him Daniel looked into her face and saw the end of everything he and the postulator had worked toward. He took in Martine Dardo's dyed hair—brown with a lighter regrowth—and her plain, shapeless clothes. She was thin. Her complexion was dilapidated; her flesh firm, but her face glossy and a mass of fine lines, as though her skin were coated in dried egg white. She asked Daniel in, and as she walked ahead of him down the narrow passage to the living room, he saw that she limped. Limped like Martine Raimondi, who as a child was known by schoolmates as "Martine Malavise"—Martine the clumsy. Martine Dardo appeared to have a clubfoot. She seemed to have inherited everything: her mother's face and physical impediment as well as her letters.

Martine left Daniel while she made coffee, and he prowled about her small living room inspecting the spines of books—many medical texts—and her ornaments. She owned some intricate old enamelwork, including a crucifix with the entombed Christ on its horizontal and risen Christ on its vertical. At the axis of the cross was a round medal showing a rabbit, its ears back, sniffing a fallen arrow. This artifact hung on the wall under a reproduction of a photo of the Tricentenary at St. Barthelemy's in Dardo. The old church appeared dwarfed by the cliff behind it. In the foreground stood a group of men and women and children—all in their Sunday best—and two priests in soutanes and hats.

Martine Dardo came back into the room with a tray. She

said, "Raimondi is the chubby girl in the front on the right. The one wearing a built-up boot."

Daniel looked closer and identified Martine Raimondi from other photos he'd seen.

Martine Dardo put the tray down on a low table and came to stand beside Daniel. She leaned in to the picture, her face tender, and said, "This funny-looking man is her uncle."

The man had oiled hair and a walleye.

"The photographer had instructed all the men to look to the left, toward the church. The uncle obeyed the photographer with his right eye but swiveled his left back to watch what the photographer was doing. The whole village told him off for spoiling the picture."

She pointed again. "This is Grandfather Raimondi, to whom she wrote her letters. These villagers are mostly all four families—Truchi, Raimondi, Vail, Villouny."

Daniel asked if Alberto Vail was in the picture. Alberto Vail was the leader of the partisans with whom Martine Raimondi had spent the final three months of her life. (Daniel had interviewed Vail, who was scornful about the postulator's project. Vail was a communist and an atheist. Vail had said to Daniel that there was no God, the Virgin and the saints were no better than Hindu idols, and the Church was a thief. "However," he said, "I will not misrepresent the character of a comrade. Martine Raimondi was brave. She was pious and chaste, but not proper or precious. She got her hands dirty, but didn't carry arms. She was a good, brave girl, and true to her faith. You know what that SS man, Giesen, said about her, after he'd had her shot? He said, 'She went to her death bravely and I honor her as a hero.' But I'll tell you, Daniel, Martine didn't want to be a hero. She didn't want to be a martyr and remembered. She said to her confessor, 'I want to live on and fight them.' ")

Martine Dardo told Daniel that Alberto Vail could be seen at the left-hand edge of the group. "He's the big boy trying to include his bicycle in the picture."

Next to the photograph was a map of Corsica made with shells. It was a vulgar thing, a kitsch collectible, and Daniel eyed it, faintly offended by its close proximity to the photo. Beyond the map was a print—a reproduction, Daniel assumed, till he saw the numbers penciled in one corner. Seven of twenty—he read—below a famous dashing signature.

"You have an Ares." Daniel was very surprised.

"His widow, Eve, is my friend. That's Eve as Persephone."

Martine told Daniel to come and have some coffee. They sat down, and, as she poured, Daniel saw the skin on her hands, too, was dry, mottled, and damaged. He asked her where she worked.

"I don't. I only wanted you to come late because I keep irregular hours. I have health problems."

Daniel said that he had thought that perhaps she was a nurse or doctor. He gestured around him at the books.

"The books are part of a private project," she said. Then she gave him the letters, a bundle of papers in a folder. She said, "I have these because I stole them. Or perhaps *pilfered* is a better word. The Order of the Daughters of Grace raised me and named me after Raimondi. And I didn't have a mother."

Daniel put his cup down to pick up a folder. "Martine Raimondi is not your mother?" he asked. He asked and sounded calm but found that he felt desolate.

"No, she isn't." Martine Dardo didn't seem at all surprised by his question.

"We do have to delve deep, and dig up any indiscretions. Everything is gone into, and tested." Daniel said that he had talked to all the living witnesses, the people the Venerable Martine had lived among—the sisters of her order, the people of Dardo, and the surviving partisans. There was nothing to suggest—"But you look like her," Daniel added, interrupting himself.

Martine Dardo waited.

"It's a problem," Daniel said. He had to deliver the letters to the postulator—and with the letters he must deliver his suspicion.

Martine Dardo asked him what *he* thought of the Venerable Martine's Cause—he, personally.

"Her first miracle," he began, then hesitated, remembering his earliest impression of that first miracle—that it was the work of God, the Great Artist, imitating the style He admires but that isn't His Own.

Daniel continued. "His Holiness is very interested in the Venerable Martine's Cause. His Holiness is a saint-making pope. He thinks that the Venerable Martine's first miracle is the most persuasive verified miracle of the modern era."

"And her second?"

The second—still under investigation—was the cure in 1955 of a sister of the Order of the Daughters of Grace of her tuberculosis of the bone. Daniel knew that the postulator believed this miracle wouldn't finally pass muster. It was a difficulty for them, and for the Church, because the Venerable Martine already had a steadily growing local cult, a cult the Church couldn't recognize, for Martine Raimondi must be beatified before the Church could issue a Concession of Public Worship. Bishops in two nations—in Nice and Turin—looked warmly on the cult, which wasn't, in fact, officially entitled to their warm regard.

Daniel said that about the second miracle he couldn't say.

"How coy," she said. She refreshed Daniel's cup. Daniel watched her face, the fragile, sore-looking lids of her downturned eyes. Martine Dardo was entitled to personal remarks after his question about her parentage, but Daniel felt uncomfortable. For the first time she seemed considerable in herself, not just as the custodian of the documents he wanted or as the Venerable Martine's possible daughter—and she must be, somehow; she *must*. Martine Dardo had considerable *nerve*, despite her shaded lamps and fastened shutters, her shut-in's house and hypochondriac's library. She had nerve, so Daniel told her what he thought. (And he made a friend by doing so, he was later to realize.)

"The second miracle looks like someone else's work. If I was writing a story, instead of investigating a life, I'd be disappointed by the mismatch. Of course they don't have to match. If Sister Ursula sent up her prayers to Martine Raimondi, and her prayers were answered, then it was by Martine Raimondi's intercession. And, naturally, the suffering Sister Ursula was asking for the intercession of a woman she'd known personally. Someone she believed had already performed a miracle. Nevertheless—"

Martine Dardo smiled; she leaned back on her sofa cushions, as relaxed as someone relieved of a worry. Daniel was provoked to ask her what *she* thought of the Venerable Martine's Cause.

She said, "I think no. No beatification, no sainthood. Raimondi wanted the soldiers in Castel Abelio to be killed."

Alberto Vail had talked to Daniel about Castel Abelio, a ruined Savoyard fortress that stood six hundred feet above Dardo and overlooked the pass into Piedmont. During the occupation there were always fifteen men posted in the fortress. Fifteen men, their dogs, and a radio. Only two days after Martine Raimondi's execution the soldiers at Castel Abelio perished in one night's fighting.

(Alberto Vail had told Daniel, "It wasn't my people who killed them. We heard gunfire and made our way up to the Castel. When we came along the ridge we could hear a loud, devilish howling. When we arrived in the fortress we found all the Germans dead. Their attackers had escaped unscathed, or carried their wounded away. The Germans' dogs were alive. There was a dry well in the courtyard of Abelio, and three dogs were in the well, standing packed in the dust at the bottom and barking. It was the most eerie thing. My people went straight down to Dardo to attack the remainder of the garrison. We had no choice. Because of the reprisals. The soldiers were on their way up. I lost twelve men. The villagers ran away. It was coming on to winter and some of them starved. The whole of Dardo scattered, down to the coast, into the mountains, across into France. You know, Daniel, I think it was the Maquis who attacked Abelio. The French were in touch with the Allied armies—we weren't; the Allies only dropped things from the sky, like motor scooters. We didn't have a radio. I think someone ordered the Maquis to take out the watch on the pass. But I don't understand why. It was weeks before the Allies arrived, and when they did they went around Sospel and the Roya, trapping the Germans, who did more terrible things in their desperation." Vail had shaken his head and poured Daniel another glass of his sulphurous homemade wine. He'd said, "I still can't imagine why the dogs were in the well.")

Daniel told Martine Dardo that if Raimondi had wanted the soldiers dead it had been a *thought*, not a plan. The Maquis killed the soldiers. Besides, the Old Testament would have praised the Venerable Martine for being able to call down God's wrath on her enemies.

"And to think your Vichy book was so temperate," Martine said.

Daniel blushed. He hadn't imagined she'd read it.

"Did the Maquis ever lay claim to the killing?" Martine asked. Then, "It did no good," she said, of the soldiers' deaths. "And it was an evil wish."

"How do you know what she wished?"

"Ask your witnesses. Ask Alberto Vail."

Daniel reported to the postulator. He said that he was very sorry to say it, but he believed that Martine Dardo was Martine Raimondi's daughter. There was no birth certificate for Dardo, though, and no hint of Raimondi having concealed a pregnancy. And Alberto Vail, when asked, had said, "How would she have concealed it? When would she have given birth? She was in a convent school, then a convent. Yes, she attended classes at Turin University. Yes, she worked in the hospital pharmacy. But she lived in a convent. Later she lived in the hills—but only for three months. *When* did it happen?"

The postulator told Daniel that Rome had to consider all the evidence. Martine Dardo's name and face and limp were as much evidence as the testimonies of the people who had lived with Raimondi. "Write it up, Daniel," the postulator said. "It must all go in the Process."

Several days later the postulator suffered a sudden fatal heart attack.

The Congregation for the Causes of Saints recalled Daniel to Rome. He was told that another postulator would be appointed in due course. He should organize all his material in readiness.

Before Daniel left for Rome he met with Martine. She came all the way to Nice to see him—scotching a suspicion he had entertained, that she was an agoraphobic as well as a hypochondriac.

They met at dusk in a café on the Promenade Anglais. She bought wine and water, then leaned over the seawall to call to a man who was trudging up and down the beach selling bottles of Orangina. Martine bought his remaining stock and then mollified the waiters by giving it to them. "For the bar," she said. Then, to Daniel, "I just wanted to let the poor man go home." She looked after him. He was making off toward the glowing headland of the castle, his shoulders straightening, his whole body lifting with relief.

Daniel told her what had happened. That the postulator had died and that he was waiting for another appointment. He gave her back the letters, which he had copied and added to the mass of papers that constituted the Process.

"Stalled," she said.

Daniel didn't tell her that he had neglected to add his doubts to the evidence. He left out his questions, to her and to Vail, about her parentage. The postulator had said, "Write it up," but the postulator had died.

Daniel didn't want to be the one to bring it all to an end. His life had been one of thought, research, travel, of taking the testimonies of the faithful, whose faces often seemed to shine with the reflected glory of a revealed God. But Daniel had never before encountered what he felt in the shrine and caverns of Dardo—a sense of absolute certainty that something miraculous had happened there.

"Stalled, for now," Daniel said. He told Martine that the Bishop of Nice was still pushing for an exhumation. They were waiting for permission from the bishop in Turin. Successive bishops had been reluctant, since the village Dardo claimed Raimondi's remains and Dardo had been French since 1947. "Negotiations are in progress. We have proposed that certain relics be sent to Dardo—in France—while Turin and Italy retain the body."

Martine Dardo leaned back in her cane chair and sipped her wine. She was looking healthier that evening—rejuvenated, almost pretty.

Along with the permission for relics to be removed from the body Daniel said he hoped to be allowed to collect a tissue sample. "I'd like to know whether you're prepared to let a DNA test settle the question of your parentage?" Daniel left his mouth open. He was a little breathless, both embarrassed and excited by his question.

Martine said, "All right. I'll supply my sample once one is retrieved from Raimondi's remains." She smiled at Daniel, blithe and secretive.

A cavalcade of Rollerbladers poured past them along the broad pavement of the promenade. Martine started to say something else, but her voice was overwhelmed by this noise.

She leaned forward. Daniel thought for a moment that there was something wrong with her mouth. It looked awkward, as if she had something growing inside it. She said, "You took a good look at my things the other day."

"I looked at the photograph. And, naturally, I was impressed by your Ares."

"What did you think of my crucifix?"

"It's unusual."

"The rabbit sniffing the arrow represents God's Grace. God's *best* Grace. The best Grace is giddy innocence—a rabbit sniffing a spent arrow, ignorant of the deadly intention behind the bowman's poor aim."

Daniel hoped she didn't think *he* was a rabbit. He said, "So . . . 'As I walk through the valley of the shadow, let me at least not know it'?"

Martine nodded.

"But that isn't something we can take comfort in. The innocent aren't always spared, and if they are, and they haven't apprehended any danger, how can they use comfort?"

"You're being Jesuitical," Martine said.

Daniel said it was in his job description.

Martine said that perhaps it wasn't the rabbit who was to take comfort but whoever had aimed the arrow. Perhaps the *dangerous* were to take comfort in the assurance that God will sometimes turn their harm harmlessly away. Then she said, "Did you ask Alberto Vail about the soldiers in the Castel?"

Happy to find an excuse to visit the old man, Daniel had seen Alberto, one of the few people for whom Daniel felt affection. Daniel had tried to ask Alberto in a way that wasn't too leading if Martine Raimondi had ever spoken to him about the soldiers posted in the Castel Abelio.

Alberto had given Daniel a searching look out from under his bird's nest eyebrows. "Martine was killed two days before them," Alberto said, guarded.

"Nevertheless," Daniel said.

Alberto told Daniel that there were things he'd thought about harder and more often than anything else in his life. For longer than the obsessive wondering he'd done when he was in love. Deeper and more constantly than the thinking he'd done about politics—and he'd thought a lot about politics. Alberto told Daniel that the months between June and December 1944 were a lifetime for people all over Europe. He said that in July of that year he'd had a man blinded by gunfire. For three weeks Alberto's partisans had nowhere to leave the man. They took him around with them, concealing him in hiding places for hours at a time. Alberto said that what he remembered was the way the man looked every time they left him— a look of wrapped-up resignation. And Alberto remembered the look on the man's face when they'd come back, a look of relief that was somehow frightening and pitiable to see. That had stayed with him. What he and his men found in the Castel Abelio had stayed with him, too.

Alberto would not say more. Daniel asked him why was it different. Different from other actions. And Alberto only shook his head. Then he said that Martine Raimondi had said, of the soldiers posted in the Castel, "They can be killed. We can have them killed."

A strange way to put it, Daniel thought. For if by "we" Martine meant herself, Alberto, and the partisans, and her "we" was to *have* someone killed, then *who* was to do the killing?

Martine had pursued and maintained their friendship. Daniel hadn't reciprocated, only graciously gone along with it. They'd stayed in touch—though she made all the efforts— even after the exhumation and its unsatisfactory result. Even after Daniel was appointed postulator—much to his surprise— and a third, more persuasive miracle revealed itself and his

Process carried Martine Raimondi's Cause as far as it was able. Martine Raimondi was beatified in 1995, at a ceremony in the Basilica of St. Peter's in Rome. His goal achieved, Daniel was, thereafter, in Nice and Dardo only for the first two weeks of June each year, to attend the pilgrimage that commemorated the Blessed Martine's first miracle. Still, each year Martine Dardo had made an effort to see Daniel and two years before she had given him a phone. A phone and instructions.

Daniel had kept the phone charged and waited to hear her confession.

In the days following his friend's call from the boat, Daniel rang her home number three times, thinking, *Perhaps she didn't do it, after all. Perhaps she was picked up.*

Twice he left a message: "Martine, it's Daniel; are you there?"

Silence, spooling.

"Martine, it's Daniel again; are you there?"

It was like a séance. *"Is there anyone there?"* Table rapping.

The third time he called, the phone was answered.

"Martine!" Daniel said in a rush of relief. He felt blood flood the roots of his hair.

"No." It was a man.

"Is Martine there?" Daniel was hopeful.

"I'm looking for her, too. I have a bone to pick with her." The man was an American.

Daniel told the man he had fears for her safety.

The man asked Daniel why he hadn't called the police.

Time had passed, Daniel said, and it had become less and less possible.

"And who am I talking to?" the American asked.

Daniel gave the man his name.

"The Father Octave who wrote *A Life of the Blessed Martine*

Raimondi?" The man seemed amused. "I haven't read it, but I had a friend who had a very personal attachment to it. To its tales of people lost in caves."

"You mean our friend? Martine?"

"No." The man laughed, an idle, ruminative laugh. Then he said, "I hope you like surprises."

Chapter 3

A CAVE RESCUE

ad's girlfriend had happily owned the story of the concert hall bomb, his work-related accident. Gabrielle seemed to see the story as the dramatic culmination of Bad's colorful career in what she called "the hero business." To Bad, however, the concert hall bomb was only the most recent, and most *manageable*, of several traumas. Several stories.

Dart Ridge, *as a story*, was so good that it had silenced Bad. For it was a story he couldn't tell without the support of his hearer's prior knowledge. Gabrielle was an Australian and would need the whole thing explained. He couldn't just say to her, "I was there, in 1991, when the Dart Ridge viewing platform collapsed. You know me—I'm the one who ran to get help." Bad wasn't injured at Dart Ridge, but Dart Ridge was his life's great singularity, a cairn, a heap of stones like the terminal moraine left by a glacier that has shrunk back up its valley and waits—with all its cold power to move—for the climate to change again.

After Dart Ridge there was a commission of inquiry, which paralyzed the survivors by fixing events in everyone's minds, particularly in the minds of their parents. Bad's parents had happily sent him to board at Collegiate when he was thirteen, but after the accident they seemed unable to let him out of their sight. He couldn't walk out of the house without one or the other consulting his or her watch and saying, "Be sure to be home by . . ." It was as if he were a young child again and straying near the edge of a drop. They wanted to warn him but not to call him back, scare him, trouble his tender confidence. Bad saw his parents' fear and their self-restraint. But he couldn't think of any way to help them.

It is in the nature of inquiries to leave no one entirely happy about their results. It was felt by some that the wrong heads had rolled. There was a great deal of talk about accountability. People lost their jobs.

Everyone concerned expressed sympathy for the families of the dead teenagers and their teacher.

Three days after the commission's report was released, the boy who had saved himself by jumping into the thornbushes turned up at Bad's place, in an old camper van. He wanted Bad to share driving. They would collect two other survivors, a boy in a wheelchair and the girl who could no longer drive herself because of her headaches and visual difficulties—the two who, as the girl told reporters, had "surfed" the platform down, landing on it, rather than on the glacier. The survivors planned to take the van and go around to all their friends' families.

Bad went with them. He watched them reach out and touch their dead friends' mothers, fathers, brothers, and sisters, touch because they needed touching back. They slept in the bedrooms of their dead friends—some packed up and some preserved—or in the van in driveways. They filled in the broken palisades of family dinner tables, the boy in the wheelchair always at the head of the table. They made sure the girl got to bed early, before tiredness brought on her headaches—the bright birdstrike, the flocks of color that blinded her and brought her crashing down. They looked out for one another and fine-tuned the channels of their shame.

The two who fell were lucky and were learning to live with it. The boy who jumped saved himself by his competence, his decisive speed. Whereas Bad, who played center in rugby and played hard, who had been known to throw a punch after six cans yet had always shown the odd intelligent hitch of caution in his headlong boyishness—had shown it often enough to have earned one of the several obvious nicknames that went with Phelan—Bad had saved himself by an exercise of good judgment.

"But I didn't speak out," he said to his friends one morning as they were on the road between Kaikoura and Christchurch. "I didn't shout, 'Get off the fucking thing before it breaks!' I thought I was being a nervous ninny. You did, too; you were laughing at me."

"Are you mad at us for laughing?" the girl asked.

"No. But it's—it's like it's the last thing I saw. Can there be a last thing you see if you go on living?"

"You were smart." The girl turned to the window, keeping an eye out for the rest stop above the seal colony. She didn't tell Bad, "There's no shame in that." They were tired of saying it to each other and tired of hearing it said. It was rational but felt untrue. After all, the only other survivor wasn't with them—she was in care, unable even to dress herself. But she *hadn't fallen*. She'd been behind Bad, farther back along the track, shaking a stone out of her shoe. When the platform collapsed, Bad, faster and fitter, ran to get help. She had climbed down the long way to the glacier and went from body to body, took turns sitting by the four who were conscious, while the boy who had jumped and was trapped in the thorns just under the edge of the drop called down tearful questions. He needed more than her first report, her shrieked, "They're not breathing! They're not breathing!"

After the trip, Bad's parents told him he shouldn't enroll at the university until the following year. They wanted to send him off traveling. He could go to Europe with his cousins who were off on a working holiday. His parents were happy to pay. They felt he should get away.

Bad went to England. He parted ways with his cousins when they were camping in Yorkshire. Someone offered him a job pulling pints in a pub on the moors. On weekends the pub was full of potholers. A group of them eventually offered to take Bad down, deeper than novices usually got to go. He borrowed gear and made a trip. And he loved it, the muffled silence and water noise, his light working its way through darkness, a world where the air was shaped and his view constrained.

Six months later he was in a cave system inside a mountain on the border between Italy and France. He was wise enough to sign in with the local *zona*—"Brian Phelan: a two-day transverse trip *souterrains* from the entrance at Passo del Abelio to the Grotte de la Hermit at Dardo"—his message a typical example of the mix of languages on that border.

During his two days underground Bad hoped to sleep in the big cavern called the Salle de la Nef, in one of the sleeping bags that had been there for twenty years and whose zippers had become a dust of rust, their teeth locked fast. Much of the system was dry, but Bad took his wet suit, because he wanted to go up through Le Lien Vert, a series of caves with waterfalls. None of it was close—Bad didn't enjoy tight caves. There was nowhere he had to go pushing his pack before him. He was traveling light but could carry some bulk, his roll of foam, and his rescue blanket.

Bad enjoyed the trip. He passed through sections of composition cave, formed by water but dry for thousands of years and full of unimaginably slow growths of minerals, ramps of

translucent flowstone, stalactites in tallowy streamers, and sta-
lagmites in sturdier amber columns. There were cave floors
covered in calcite snow and passages like greenhouse gardens,
hung with gypsum flowers, with rigid petals and curled tendrils. Bad was hot and cold, damp and parched. He conserved
his light, lay in the gritty damp sleeping bag in the Salle de la
Nef submerged in a quicksand of night, his ears stoppered,
stuffed with silence.

Early on his second day, only an hour after he'd started out,
he had to back into a funk hole as another party passed him.
They talked for a time, established that he was alert but not a
native French speaker. They shone their lights into his face,
impolite but concerned. They gave him some noodles to eat.

Neither he nor they knew that outside it had begun to rain
heavily. It was July, and a deluge wasn't seasonal, wasn't part of
the forecast.

It was hours before Bad first became aware of the rain. His
map had said, of the duck near the bottom of Le Lien Vert,
that the water was usually two feet from the ceiling. Bad was
in his wet suit by then, and he found himself wading and swimming through the duck with his helmeted head tilted up and
scraping on the rock, while his chin was underwater. Bad felt
tiny; he became the size of the habitable world his sight
showed him, flashlight bright between a pinkish rock roof and
the satiny black water—six inches of air. Bad splashed and
clambered up into the next chamber, then straddle-walked a
stream up a short passage to the first wet pitch—the first of
four pitches from that end. Together the pitches represented
around seven hours of caving.

It was forty hours back the way Bad had come, but still he
should have turned back straightaway, gone through the duck
before it filled. But he was tired and his traverse was almost
complete. He wanted to finish it.

Bad clipped his cow-tail onto the line attached to the rock
face. He climbed the first pitch. The line—a semipermanent

fixture—had been rigged out from the waterfall, from the best hold that allowed it to dangle beyond the normal course of the cascade. But the cave was flooding, and when Bad was at the bottom of the pitch he was under the water. He began to ascend.

He had expected to get wet, to be in the waterfall's full force for a few meters at least. Instead he climbed for five. The water pouring off his helmet made his light dim but living—it flashed and rippled around him. In the thick of it, Bad had to hold his breath. Then his head was free, his light settled, and he dragged himself up the rope and out of the cascade, husked of its weight.

The art of every pitch is to get on and off it. That first pitch was very difficult to get off. The cataract was thick and had filled the whole horizontal opening of the pitch. Bad had dragged himself up through it. His hands and face were very cold, so he took a rest to revive them. He ate a handful of nuts and ran his light up and down the lower ten meters of the next pitch. The cave was cacophonous, its flooded river hosing through a confined tube of rock. He decided to climb up just this next pitch, where his map showed that the cave above, with its long fall of crester run, was broader, and possibly still dry in places. Just one more, he thought, then he'd make camp and climb under his rescue blanket.

Bad repacked his food. He got up and began to edge around the stream to the bottom of the pitch. It was fifteen meters high, and the rope was under the fattened cataract for half the height. The din of water was terrible, tiring. Bad tugged at the rope to test it and shook splinters of water out of the cataract.

He clipped his cow-tail on the rope, then the first of his foot loops. He stepped into a loop and under the water. His headlamp went yellow. Water thumped on his helmet. He was compressed by blows. He hooked on another foot loop and stepped up, reached back to retrieve the last, and was nearly washed off the rope. It swung and he tangled. He had to take his foot out of the second loop in order to free himself. Even with the background roar, the splashing on his helmet and the shoulders of his polypropylene suit was piercing. Splashes like someone breaking dry sticks right by his ear. For a moment Bad struggled to sort himself out, then his strength went, and he simply hung, only two meters up and right under the waterfall.

And then the waterfall moved. Or Bad believed it moved. He was under its edge; then he was out of it altogether, with the volumes of water that had washed down the neck of his wet suit already beginning to warm between his skin and its insulation. Bad began to climb, steadily and quickly, taking advantage of this inexplicable respite. The rope quivered as though it were attached to something flexible, a tree branch, not bolts in a rock face. When Bad was near the top of the pitch the rope moved—this time he believed it was the rope, not the cataract. He came closer to the falling water but was still clear; it only hammered at his shoulder. Bad concentrated on his climb. He got to the top of the pitch, where there was the usual obstacle, a jutting lip he'd have to haul himself over. He caught his breath, put his arms over, and began to kick and wriggle up. Then someone took hold of his harness and hauled him up and across the rock. Bad came to rest on his stomach, his ascender jamming into his ribs. He looked up—a quick crane just to catch the eyes of the other cavers, before he worked himself away from the pitch into whatever space there was near them. It was a polite, instinctive, economical glance—they would all shake hands once he was clear of the drop. But when Bad looked he saw bloodied knees, the torn hem of a long summer skirt, a blouse of some silky stuff, very much the worse for wear, bare legs, and sandals. Bad rolled over onto his back, still gasping from his climb.

The woman stooped closer, her face in a pale halo, her hair lighter at its roots. She unclipped his chin strap and removed his helmet, then came nearer still, so that Bad imagined she would kiss him. He felt the rock cold through the hair on the back of his head—then he lost consciousness.

When he came to he'd been dragged away from the top of the pitch. He was detached from the rope and his foam was under his shoulders. She had unzipped his suit and was lying on his bared chest, her shirt open and her damp skin against his. They were both covered by his rescue blanket, his helmet and headlamp under it with them, shedding its small warmth and reflecting magnified in the blanket's creased silver fabric.

Bad's mouth was full of blood. He'd bitten his tongue. It felt fat but numbed, as though by Novocain. When he turned his head a slime of congealing blood oozed from his mouth and across one cheek. The woman had her hand under that cheek, her face inches from his, a face with high cheekbones, a smooth forehead, creamy skin, and a narrow undershot jaw with a pointed chin. Her mouth was the most determined Bad had ever seen, her lower lip jutting from a habit of effort, from pulling her lower jaw forward so that her teeth could comfortably meet. She kept that lower lip in place by hooking it over her top teeth, which made her look defiant, jaunty, and haughty all at once. Her eyes were long, calm, and a light brown.

Bad was then nineteen—but he'd never lain quietly breast to breast with a woman. For a time he blinked at her, groggy. Then she moved his arm and her own into the helmet's light. She consulted his watch—she had none. "*Neuf-vingt,*" she said, "*mais lequel?*" Nine-twenty, but which? Bad translated. He watched her put out her tongue to groom the grazes on her right hand, skid marks of flayed skin, the flesh around the wounds painfully pulled and puckered. He wanted a better look at the injury, so took her wrist in both his hands. The cold came under the blanket between them. He felt her nipples then, like bony fingertips, one pressed into his chest and the other against his forearm. He began trying to guess her age—

anywhere between five and ten years his senior. He frowned at her hand. "How—?" he said, but there was too much to ask. She was at least a hundred and fifty meters underground and dressed for high summer. She didn't even have hiking boots.

"Do you have a flashlight?" he said.

"It ran out," she said. Her English was scarcely accented.

"How long have you been sitting in the dark?"

She shrugged, and the bony fingertips trailed caressingly across his skin. She pouted at him, rueful. He was surprised she understood him. His tongue was so swollen that it pushed about in his mouth against his cheeks like a young reptile about to tear its way out of the skin of its egg. He had to speak, though; she had to be brought to an appreciation of the gravity of the situation. A WIGU situation—as the cave rescue amateurs in Yorkshire would say, as they clustered into booths in Bad's pub, waiting for a call-out on a wet Sunday. WIGU— When Idiots Go Underground.

She was grooming her hand again, her tongue keen, as though she liked the flavor of her flesh in its dressing of cave mud. She stopped to say—as though explaining something— that she thought his hitch had locked and he didn't have a load release hitch.

She was a caver, after all, or a climber—but her clothes made no sense.

"Nine A.M. or P.M.?" she asked, and tapped the face of his watch with one torn but glossy fingernail.

"P.M.," said Bad, and she sat up, shook off the silver blanket, and began to button her blouse. Bad saw that her breasts were small and beautiful.

"Why are you dressed like that?" Bad said. He had to shout now, to penetrate the water noise that filled the cave and thrust itself into the few feet of air between their faces.

The woman looked thoughtful, then sly and amused. She said she'd been at a party.

"In a wet cave?"

"In a dry one." Then she said she was going. She pointed up the long slanting fall of the crester run that led to the chamber above and the penultimate pitch. There was no rope rigged on the crester run, which in normal conditions would entail only a long scramble to ascend. Now it was 80 percent covered by water in a thick, steady stream, with shallow spilling edges of mud-greased rocks. Bad believed *he* could climb it, but he had the right footwear.

He sat up, shawled in the rescue blanket, and unzipped his bag. He pulled out his Corduren overalls and threw them at her.

She caught them, stood holding them against herself, her form eclipsed by their silt-smeared vermilion, the ends of the legs trailing on the ground. Bad thought he heard her say, "Very fetching." Then she stooped and stepped into them, stuffing her skirt down each loose leg, shrugging on the arms, gathering the dark ends of her particolored hair so that it wouldn't get caught in the Velcro. She knelt to help Bad back into his wet suit, raised it from his waist, and guided his arms into its sleeves.

Bad had begun to shiver. "Why aren't you cold?" he said.

She said, "Isn't that better?" Then she gave Bad a quelling up-from-under look. She got him up and put his helmet back on. She fastened its straps and gently settled the plastic cup on his chin. Then she drew him closer to the bottom of the crester run so that his light shone on its speedy ripples. Bad took hold of her and began to explain. They should stay put and cuddle up. He was due out at one, but the people he'd left his intentions with wouldn't come looking till the morning. If it was raining outside they might know to come sooner, might already be on their way, but they'd have to rerig those last two pitches—if it was still raining outside. And if it was still raining outside, then the cave would continue to flood, which meant that they would be pretty damp and deaf if they stayed put, but, since caves never flooded steadily, they'd be much safer *staying put*. The cave would pulse flood, Bad said. Somewhere above them a pool would fill to capacity and overflow and the flood would suddenly double.

The woman put up her uninjured hand and gave his cheek several slow pats. "I'll lead the way," she said. She walked to the foot of the crester run. Bad stumbled after her, off-balance—he'd had a good grip on her, he thought, but she'd stepped away and nearly pulled him over.

She began to climb. Bad saw her feet come clean in the little eddies of shallow water at the edge of the run. The flimsy sandals were gold, flat-heeled but gold—evening wear. Bad shouted at her and went on shouting as she receded in the light of his quaking headlamp. She was turned his way now, her back pressed against the wall as she edged around a jutting wet rock. She was making very good progress. Bad gestured at her, hooked her back, slapping both hands into his chest at the termination of each hook, desperate and imperative. Then the flood hurtled his shouts back into his face. They came back with a wave of air. The stream on the crester run doubled instantly, and the woman looked at Bad. Or looked toward him. He thought he saw her gaze measure the air between them. He saw her hands turn white, each knuckle and ligament standing out like an X ray. She rose a full foot out of the water, as if she'd jumped as the flood scooped her off the rock face. Her legs were swept out from under her and she fell on her back in the shallow cataract and tumbled, twisting, all the way back down the crester run. Bad lunged at her as she passed him. His fingertips scraped the fabric of his own suit; then she was gone, before his head had turned to see her go, over the edge of the waterfall and down the pitch. He didn't hear her land but *felt* it through the rock under his feet.

Bad wrenched his arm out of the water and scrambled back from the stream. For a moment he stared at its airy white sluice. For a moment he listened to an echo, a crash and complicated syncopation of flesh and bone—the sound of the collapsed platform hitting the glacier below Dart Ridge. Then he came to and, howling, crawled over to his pack to fetch his bolt kit. He went back to the pitch and, despite his trembling hands and the high-pressure hose of water at the pitch's edge, spent the next hour hammering in bolts. He bolted out beyond the waterfall and rerigged the rope, then stuffed the rescue blanket back in his pack, put it on, and abseiled down the pitch.

She wasn't there.

He couldn't find her, so he found the driest spot, climbed between foam and rescue blanket, and sat in a silver tent, with his helmet in his lap, sobbing and nodding off.

A long time later he became aware that someone was singing rounds at him. *"Dormez-vous? Dormez-vous?"* Lights flickered and swelled around him. Above the flood he heard boots in soggy gravel; then someone shook him. "Are you Brian Phelan?"

"Bad. I'm Bad," said Bad.

They were speaking a mix of Italian and French. Bad remembered that he had passed under the border. He was asked, in English, what day it was. They were checking for hypothermia—was he in the gray zone? Usually the first question anyone was asked was, "What's your name?" But they'd given him his.

"Great," said Bad, mocking them. "Hey, Brian, what's your name?"

Someone said, in French, that he wasn't making any sense.

He told them about the woman. "An idiot in street clothes. She's down there. Perhaps in the flooded duck. The duck is a sump."

The blond Italian who was trying to feed Bad soup from a thermos said they would look—but what was this "duck"? The nearest sump was at the bottom of the Passage of Time.

Bad explained his terminology, sipped soup, and answered further questions.

The rescuers had run a wire through the cave and were talking to the surface on a phone. Bad gathered there had been an unseasonal deluge, a number of parties were trapped, and one other person had been swept away.

The rescuers split up; some went on down, to look for a body. The rest took Bad up. The crester run was low again, and they had rigged a Tyrolean. Bad, restored by several hours' rest, was actually fitter than his rescuers. He soon took the lead, hurrying to get out of that horrible hole. He'd gone under in Italy and came out in France, near one of those French villages with an Italian name. He was followed closely by the blond Italian, Gino, who dried him off, fed him up, and drove him back down to the camping ground to gather up his mashed, sodden tent.

Bad jumped out of sleep. He shoved himself back against the seat and stared at the narrow stone streets of Genoa's old town, painted by the mixed light of the detective's head- and fog lamps.

"You were asleep," said the detective.

Bad had been asleep, but as he'd come out of it he was fully conscious—his mind more alert than awake. And in that state he'd made a connection. He already understood that, on seeing the body in the sea cave, he'd done more than just venture an opinion—he'd gone down a rope and into the sea cave because of the sight through borrowed binoculars of the drowned woman's hair.

The match of the dead woman's surname with the name of a village near Le Lien Vert wasn't a coincidence—if she was named for the village. And it wasn't coincidental that Bad sought to *make* a connection, because one reminded him of the other. Martine Dardo's particolored hair was like that of the woman he'd found and lost again in Le Lien Vert. But there was another connection, another reminder, another coincidental correspondence that Bad hoped like hell meant—what?—nothing, or something?

Because it *must* mean something. It was a connection that Bad felt should have a mathematical expression, like those of explosions, whose formulas express the conversion of one chemical to another, change accomplished in microseconds, with a release of great force. Bad thought of the chemical expression for the detonation of RDX—hexamine hexamethylenetetramine with legs, a chemical with all its nitritized molecules hanging out. The connection *felt* like a detonation: it blew Bad right out of sleep and followed him, billowing and burning.

Nine months earlier the pizza-box booby trap had set off its fertilizer bomb and blasted a hole through the ground floor of a concert hall, throwing cars around its basement and tossing the nearest living being ten meters through the air although he was wearing forty kilograms of body armor and was twenty-seven meters away from the blast. When the bomb went off, Bad was transfixed by an exhibition poster on a concrete pillar, seared by the sight, not just because his heart was pumping or because he was flooded with adrenaline and imprinted by every terrible second of time, but because Jean Ares's *Eve in a Gaucho Hat*—Eve, with her long calm eyes, undershot jaw, pout, and bunched maxillary muscles—was a portrait of the woman Bad had met and lost in Le Lien Vert.

And, Bad realized, perhaps it was this recognition that had led him to nudge Gabrielle's vacation planning toward this part of the world. Perhaps *this* was why he was here.

Chapter 4

EVE

*I*t was mid-afternoon when Eve Moskelute got back from Genoa. She had been to the Questura, where she had spoken to the police, and the morgue, where she had identified the body of her friend Martine. She drove into the courtyard of her Ventigmiglia house, got out of the car, and automatically opened its trunk to look for shopping bags. Then she remembered.

She went indoors and stood for a time, subdued, in the dead air of her dark atrium. Eve found she was rubbing her fingertips together, her hands before her at the height of her waist. She could still feel the powdery interior surfaces of the plastic evidence bags she'd handled, picking them up and rubbing over what they held: Martine's credit card and keys.

She went on down a short passage into the living room, opened the doors onto her terrace, and went out.

The sun was overhead and there was smoke like cement

dust hanging over the tangled interchange of the autostrada.
The rail lines were showing bright, like dots and dashes of sol-
der in a circuit board. The greenhouses on the terraces at the
head of the valley caught sunlight and blazed like banked
stadium lights. The rest was hazy, semisolid mountains and,
darker than the mountains, a forest fire of thunderclouds
rolling down the valley.

Because she'd been out on business Eve had on high heels,
and as she went back indoors her heels' determined noise
masked the bright utterance of the one loose tile her foot
touched. She crossed to the dresser and tilted a framed photograph to the light. A chain of girls danced, in diaphanous shifts
and crowns of flowers, behind them a stone wall, prickly pears,
and umbrella pines. The photo was of Eve, her twin sister,
Dawn, and a friend, in a garden on Cap Martin. The year was
1954; the photo was of a pageant the children had put on—*The
Judgment of Paris*. It had been the last summer Eve's Russian
father had put in an appearance.

The first time the twins saw M. Moskelute they were five. He
turned up late one evening with a bag of quail and a bicycle.
The girls came out in their nightgowns to find a new bicycle
on the tiny terrace of the family's Menton apartment. In the
morning the bicycle was gone, though their father wasn't. He
didn't go till he'd run through their mother's money, in one
night at the casino. The twins' mother stored the bicycle with
a friend at his garage on the Avenue Sospel. The girls had to
pretend they hadn't seen it while their mother pretended to
purchase it from the garage a piece at a time—one week the
front wheel, next the rear, and so on, ending with the bell.
Nothing good could be seen to come quickly—that would be
bad for their character. And no good was to come from their
father.

The Moskelute twins' mother was English. And they were

always told that they were English, too. Their mother would tell the girls to think of themselves as English almost as often as she'd remind them to brush their teeth. However, their names were their father's idea. He *did* consult their mother before he went to the Hotel de Ville to register their births. She was still in a dusky state of anesthesia and gave him a choice of two—she hadn't grasped what he'd said, that there were two babies. "June or Evelyn," she said. "Either will do." The twins' father got drunk and sportive. He registered his twin girls as "Eve" and "Dawn." Perhaps the registrar spoke no English and only wrote down what M. Moskelute spelled out, without understanding the words. He hadn't asked, "Are you *quite sure?*" Or perhaps it was just that at that time the town was rather sloppy with records, as a form of passive resistance. The year was 1942, the Italians had withdrawn, and the Germans had entered the Free Zone.

Eve opened the cabinet that stood on the sideboard among the photographs, in pride of place. It was a gilded oak case, like a portable icon. Inside and under glass was a single illuminated page. The page was crowded—tiled—with illustrations of artifacts. There were clothes, empty but animated, as though puffed up by the limbs of ghostly mannequins. There were tools pictured, too. A paving hammer with a long curved handle. A water carrier's velvet-covered container. A surgeon's instruments, among them the long tweezers used to give communion to those suffering La Peste. The page was the work of an eighteenth-century artist influenced by illuminated books in the collection of Marquis Guy de Chambord, who was the subject of a biography Eve had published when she was twenty-seven.

Chambord was an eighteenth-century collector and a dabbling dilettante. Chambord acquired whole volumes of illuminated manuscript books with locks, books that clasped darkness between each page like protective tissue. If he couldn't get whole books, the marquis had acquired bits of books—the capitals from the chapter headings in early incunabula, illustrations cut from manuscripts in unguarded libraries, beauties that were only then beginning to find their way out of the night between covers, into frames, and under glass. He collected other things, too—had his cabinet of curiosities, his babies in jars of ethanol and dressed in coral bracelets, his Amazonian butterflies and sloth skeletons and stuffed giraffes posed with the male mounting the female.

The artist of Eve's single page had had access to Chambord's manuscript collection and had chosen to imitate. The page had found its own way into Chambord's library decades after the marquis's death, when it was somehow recognized and secured by the library's custodian.

Eve had acquired the work in the late seventies, a month before the death of her famous husband.

Eve met Jean Ares in July 1971, when she was away from home, inland at Arles. It was her birthday, an anniversary that found her in flight from the familiar. It was the second birthday after the death of her twin sister, Dawn. She had passed the first in the hospital, had *barely* passed it. The birthday was five weeks after Dawn's accident—and her own admission to St. Roch, in her bloodied nightdress, with a towel wrapped around her punctured wrist. Those five weeks were a pinched place in Eve's life. That first birthday had gone by without Eve knowing. She'd sat in a chair in the dayroom or walked along the hospital corridor, her balance so impaired by tranquilizers and antipsychotics that she'd had to walk with one hand against the wall. She didn't know what day it was. Her mouth was dry. There were days and nights but no dates.

A week before the second birthday after Dawn's death, Eve went to Avignon. She knew the town well, had lived there for a time while she was researching her biography of Chambord. But Avignon was no good. At a certain time each evening Eve would remember phone calls she'd made to her sister, just checking in or excited by her research. She remembered how everything had seemed to lie before her, how she was coming down into her life with a stately hydraulic progress, it seemed, in a movement like an extension bridge. Her roadway would meet another, with the strong machinery of her family behind her and publishers' contracts and academic appointments before her. Roads would join; she would get off and go on. Eve had felt this in Avignon only three years before—but Dawn had been on the other end of the phone then.

So Eve left Avignon for Arles. It was the week of the festival of the Arlesiennes. The town was full of costumed women, with embroidered aprons, black patent-leather boots, and lacquered hair. It was hot and the streets smelled of fresh horseshit. Camargue horses, their black-flecked white hides polished smooth, were parading under the plane trees on the town's avenues. All the leaves of the trees were burned brown at their edges and made a constant rattle in the wind, so that the streets were loud although the traffic had been diverted.

It was very hot. Eve wore a sundress with chains of embroidered daisies for straps. She stopped at troughs and fountains to dampen her chest and face and arms but felt as if she were walking through warm water wearing a pressure suit and weighted boots. In shops the freezers had given out, and the pavements were slicked by rivulets of fluorescent syrup from melted Popsicles.

Eve moved from one café to the next, resting, drinking water or pulpy orange juice. Between stops she inclined with other onlookers against walls on the shady sides of streets, with the heat from the nearest patch of sun reflecting up into their faces.

Eve didn't want to go back to her hotel room and wait out

the day on her plastic-wrapped mattress. She didn't want to think what day it was and *how strange*, how castaway she was in this parched, dusty, tumultuous celebration. She felt more estranged by the festival and heat wave than she had by her previous birthday's Thorazine.

She didn't know Arles well, so it was by chance that she found the coolest place in town. She visited the cathedral, and there she saw a sign directing tourists to the Roman storage cellars. She found their entrance, paid her fee, and went down. After two turns of the stairs, she had shaken off the wind. She couldn't hear it anymore. At the bottom of the steps Eve opened her bag, took out her white cotton cardigan, and put it on.

The cellars were vast, a square of low, vaulted ceilings and columns, of arcades in receding ranks. The space was poorly illuminated by fluorescent lights, tubes behind greenish plastic, and recessed, so as not to spoil the contours of the arches. The floor was wet in places, its surface sometimes corrugated clay, sometimes paving stones sunk in dark silt.

Eve wandered about in the gloom and lost sight of the entrance. The space was huge and—although it was the only habitable place in the whole town on that hot day—empty. All other tourists were out watching the festival, packed into patches of shade.

Eve was alone for an hour and remained in motion, walking off her anniversary as one walks off an overdose. The joints in her jaw ached from keeping her mouth closed, her lower lip anchored on her top teeth, till she could almost hear her mother telling her—or possibly Dawn—that she was "frowning like a puppet." Eve thought of their orthodontist: "It isn't an overbite, and I can't correct it, Madame Moskelute. Your girls simply have underdeveloped lower jaws."

After an hour another party arrived in the cellars. Eve stopped still in the dimness partway along the central arcade and waited for them to appear. They were making a circuit of the outer walls, as she had. They were a family group, with children, some costumed—the girls in white aprons and puffy-sleeved shirts, the boys in black waistcoats and breeches buckled at the knee. Some of the adults were in costume, too, the women fanning red faces and sighing as they let the cold air in under their skirts. A family—a solitary grandparent, his children and their spouses, and their children.

The old man was wiry, bald, and bandy-legged. His children surrounded him in a phalanx, most heads turned his way as he talked, waved his brown arms and big, long-fingered hands. None of the grandchildren were infants; they soon left the adults and exploded into the dark, running and shouting. Two boys passed Eve, the tassels of their waistcoats flying. They jumped when they saw her and veered away, looking back to ascertain that she wasn't a ghost, only a woman in a white dress. Eve could see it in their eyes, fear for a moment, then indifference. She vanished for them, was only an obstacle, like the columns.

The girls found her next. They made a few passes around her, to check her clothes. Eve was young and stylish enough to excite their curiosity. When the adults eventually strolled by they, too, were startled but recovered quickly, the women inclining their sleek, dressed heads.

Eve heard the family gather at the back of the cellar, the children dropping pebbles through a grille that covered steps down to another level, only partly excavated. She heard stones clink on steel and rattle on stone, then the children called away by their mothers.

Two women were talking about a trip they planned to take to the States. The men were discussing public access to a beach below a property one of them owned. They talked about the mayor (of Nice, for one named him: "Médecin") and of "pressing their advantage."

There was talk about Paris and "another show." One man said he hoped his father realized that there would be *more* advantage in scarcity of supply. He was answered instantly: "I cannot play shopkeeper with God's gifts."

"Must you always be so high-handed, Papa?"

The group passed Eve again, several hesitating, then looking more closely. The women nodded again and went on.

They were talking about the time now and the tables that would be laid along the road to the necropolis. "I want to be quite sure it's cooler before I set foot in that street," someone said.

A few minutes went by; then the grandfather came back and stood beside Eve, as if the arch she was under were a bus shelter, beyond which was a rainy night. He waited, not looking at her.

Eve knew he was concerned about her, and felt embarrassed. She cast about for something to say, a polite reassurance or a plausible excuse. She said she had feared the heat would result in a migraine.

He said he'd had the same thought—though his migraines were sometimes worth it. He wouldn't be willing to trade in the aura with the headache. On the last occasion he'd had one he said he'd seen a sort of sketch—black figures on the kind of white surface to be seen in the cinema when the film breaks, leaving projected white light. In black on white, a row of swings, animated and swinging out of sync. The swings' seats were the lash-fringed upper lids of shut eyes.

Eve said she always had her best ideas in the days before a migraine. She'd solve problems in her work.

He said he knew his own mind—he should, at seventy—but his migraines weren't his mind, as such; they were more like dramatic mental weather. A divine light that turns into sunstroke.

"My auras are sometimes silly," Eve said. "I see that diagram from school textbooks, of an ape evolving by increasingly hairless stages into a man."

"Ah," the old man said, "that picture. My grandchildren have it, too. One of those creatures looks at the viewer—does he not? It isn't 'modern man' who is stoutly striding off, out of the right edge of the page."

Eve finally looked directly at the man she was talking to. She saw that he was relaxed and animated; she saw that his eyes were a paradox: black yet as bright as lamps. "It's Cro-Magnon man, I think," Eve said.

"Yes, Cro-Magnon man. Grimy and sullen and patient. Like a refugee."

The old man said that at each festival there was an alfresco meal set out on the shaded way to the necropolis, at the end of the Via Appia, the great Roman road. Would Eve care to join him and his family? He held out his hand. He hadn't introduced himself or asked her name—they were somehow already on a more intimate footing.

Eve hesitated. She thought of her mother's cautionary stories about "strange men." If her mother were still alive she'd be younger than this man. Then Eve thought, *But this is Jean Ares.* She recognized him as she said his name to herself. Eve even knew the names of his former wives and his famous lovers. In the same instant that she realized who he was, she had his life—or the myth of it—the flash of a shape anyone would immediately recognize. This *wasn't* a strange man; this was the artist Ares.

Eve gave him her hand.

Ares had three great periods. In his first, 1925 to 1939, it somehow seemed that the way Europe saw itself altered in answer to his vision. His and others'—but it did seem that it might be possible to tell the story of Western Europe between the wars with one illustrator, Ares. There were collectors and art historians who favored his next great fertile period, 1950 to 1960. His decorative, celebratory, sensual works. It was a period during which he did little painting but produced etchings, sculptural works, and designed the stained glass in a Modernist church in Marseille.

In 1971 Ares was still working and selling his works, but it could be said that he had devolved into an *honorable presence*. He had commissions for public works. He collaborated. He played with new technology to make prints and print books. Then—said the historians, the curators, and the author of his first biography—Ares met Eve Moskelute. Eve was Ares's Eurydice, said the biographer; Ares had to play his best, his most heartfelt, in order to move Hades, win death's clemency, and lead Eve out of the underworld. A picture caption in the biography read: "*Eve under the Arches,* oil on canvas, 1972. Again and again Ares would try to capture his Eve in the moment he first saw her, in the Roman Storehouse at Arles. Here Eve is a ghost, a quenched soul, a votive candle Ares must light."

("A ghost he must lay," Eve wrote, in 1983, on her copy of the proofs, before posting them back to the biographer.)

With Eve, Ares had six more great years before the obstruction, the operation and chemotherapy, the relapse, the good "managed" death in his own home.

A month before Jean died, Eve went to an art auction. Jean asked her to attend because one of his famous early works was going under the hammer. He was curious, he said. Everyone knew he was ailing—"on my way out," he added, in English. (It was one of Eve's mother's sayings. They would occasionally come into her mouth, and Ares would repeat them in affectionate imitation.) Jean said he wanted to get an idea of what would happen after he'd gone. "Some clue. My career is one of the stories I've been following—like the lives of my children. How *vexed* I am not to know how it all turns out."

Eve went to the auction and sat at the back of the room. She watched the bidding on her husband's painting. She wrote the figure on her wrist. She was forgetting things—drained by the deathwatch and by the effort of retarding her anxiety, not thinking about her future alone until she was alone to think. Eve wasn't fearful—she'd survived losing Dawn, with Jean's help, and there was something about Jean's help that had provided lasting survival training. Eve wasn't distraught, only tired and forgetful.

In an interval between lots 15 and 16 the owner of the auction house brought Eve a glass of wine. They talked about Jean's health. Then the man said, "You'll be interested in this, Eve." He picked up the catalog from the chair beside her and found the page where a work was reproduced in black-and-white. "Never mind the murky picture—read the description."

The work was an illuminated picture from the library of the Marquis de Chambord, Eve's biographical subject.

The auctioneer said that the flood in '65 had done some lasting damage to the building in Avignon that housed Chambord's collection. After much discussion and several unsatisfactory interim remedies it had been decided to sell some items to pay for the repairs to the building. The illustration was by a contemporary of the marquis but had been acquired after his time. The library had decided to let it go.

"It's an unknown artist," said the auctioneer. "But it's of interest. Would you like to take a closer look at it?"

Eve said yes, thank you, she would, and followed him out the back.

The illuminated page was crowded—tiled—with figures, rendered with great intricacy. Or, at least at first glance, that was what Eve saw. In the next moment it seemed to her that the figures were deformed. Then she saw that what she'd taken as people were clothes and empty. The page was filled with clothes and tools; it was a kind of catalog, of a time and place, of life revealed through human artifacts—the things that survived their owners and their owners' bodies.

It was then nearly ten years since Eve had published her biography of Chambord, but no other subject had come along and taken her up. (There was a subject threatening, though—her husband was about to become her subject, even if she didn't write about him. A letter had come, to Jean, from Flagstaff, Arizona, and a young man with a doctorate in art history. Tom Hilxen wanted to write a biography of Ares. "But I understand that your wife Eve is a biographer herself, and I wouldn't like to tread on any toes or poach a cherished subject. . . ." Jean was ill already and he passed the letter to Eve. "You deal with this," he said. "You'll have to make these decisions. But you must promise not to waste your time with drones. No lazy people with tape recorders.") Eve's loyalty to her first subject, Chambord, was unchanged, and her acquisitiveness about him. She looked at the intricate catalog of objects from Chambord's time and wanted it, for itself and for the sake of her subject.

The auction house was very interested in keeping Eve happy—after all, she would soon be in possession of a healthy proportion of Jean Ares's estate. When Eve expressed an interest in acquiring the picture, the auctioneer withdrew it from sale and fetched papers for her to sign and packers so that she could carry it away with her.

Eve sat in the auctioneer's office and had another glass of wine. She kept an ear on the room next door and registered when it was announced that lot 18—"a curious example of illumination, circa 1775, artist unknown"—was withdrawn from sale.

Eve finished her wine, collected her package, took her leave.

She paused on the steps, tucked the package under one

arm, and drew on her gloves. Her breath caught green fire from the lights under the fountains in the Espace Massena—an extensive plantation of tall white jets.

Eve heard someone running lightly down the steps behind her. "Dawn!" someone said, at Eve's ear. "Why are you out on your own?"

A woman stopped beside Eve. A woman in a long, yoke-necked, drab brown velvet dress. A young, malnourished, dry-looking person.

Eve just stared. Then she lunged forward, tried to seize the woman's arm. It should have worked—Eve had the advantage of surprise—but her hand closed on nothing. The woman was several paces off now. Her expression was puzzled. She said, "You're not yet up to speed. You should eat."

Eve dropped her package. It wouldn't have come to any harm—braced as it was in layers of cardboard and a frame clamped with wing nuts at all four corners. But it didn't hit the ground. The woman reached, her whole body darting out before she threw a foot forward to catch herself. She snatched the package in midair, perhaps eight inches from the ground, shot her foot out to balance, and froze, balanced. Then she straightened slowly, Eve's package in her hands. She tilted her face and sniffed the air. She considered. "You're Eve," she said.

Eve said, "You said 'Dawn.' "

"Sorry, my mistake. I forgot at which end of night your name came." The woman returned the package.

"Do we know each other?" Eve said. This must be someone from her school days.

The woman was fishing in the pockets of her imposingly drab garment. She handed Eve her card. She said, "I'd like it if you called me sometime."

The card said: "Martine Dardo, 5 Vico della Torres, Genova." And a phone number.

Martine Dardo was fussing with her pockets now, as

though she had to rearrange everything around her card case. Her shoulders were hitched up near her ears.

"Why should I call you?" Eve said.

Martine Dardo stopped fossicking and took a deep breath. "Well. I can tell you about the so-called anonymous artist. Who is—" She smiled suddenly and her face became beautiful. "Who is not unknown to God," she said. "Or to me. His name is Ila. Lou Ila."

In Provençal *Lou Ila* was *the Island*.

Martine Dardo tapped a crooked finger under one eye. She said, "Those auctioneers don't know everything." She bid Eve good night and walked away, not responding to questions called out after her. ("Were we at school together?" "Did you know my sister?")

Jean was delighted with the Island's picture. "The world of humans with human individuals exorcised," he said.

Eve propped it up on the big dresser opposite Jean's bed, where he could see it. It covered the mirror so that when Jean was sitting up in bed he was no longer faced with himself, his face falling away, a dull skin forming over the hot oil of his eyes. Eve let the light shine on the picture, although Jean and she both knew that she should protect it, that light was the enemy of paper, cotton, linen, wood pulp, an enemy of skin and of the pigments in ink.

Sometimes Eve carried the picture to the bed and she and her husband would study it together. Once she fetched a magnifying glass to read the inscription in the bowl of an enameled spoon. "It's Provençal," she told Jean. "It says: 'Many people are rather wicked, even those that hate pleasure.' "

For weeks Eve treated the illumination like a vase of cut flowers. But it didn't wilt and she didn't have to change its water and—after weeks—it seemed undamaged, unaltered, even though she discerned that its skin was warmed by the sun on the day she finally removed it from the dresser opposite the empty bed and slipped it back between its covers of acid-free cardboard.

In the twenty-two years since Ares's death Eve had entertained or corresponded with dozens of art historians, collectors, curators, and biographers. The important one was Tom Hilxen. When Tom came into Eve's life Jean had been dead two years and Eve was still periodically in a rage of grief. Grief, not misery, a kind of exultant fury at Jean's children, who'd had enough of him; his first wives, who'd had more than enough of him; smug collectors, the values of whose collections were now soaring because of limited supply. Alive, Jean was the antithesis of scarcity. Jean was busy and quick; he even listened like a dancer, with action behind his still attention. No one could possibly understand what Eve had lost. Lost *again*. Eve remembered trying to tell Tom this—that no one knew what she'd lost. She had shouted at her husband's biographer. In this very room. A safe room, with sunshine in it. Tom had gathered his papers. Then Tom was at the door. Then Tom came back and put his arms around her, whispering the title of a painting he'd first seen as a slide, in an art class, at the University of Flagstaff, Arizona. *"Drunken Eve,"* he whispered.

Eve sat at her table for so long that the tide of afternoon sunlight reached her folded hands, took them in its watery warmth, then began to climb to her downturned face. She looked at her hands in the soft light and felt weak.

She went out to buy bread—went down the Scala Santa, the long shallow-stepped ramp to the river, across which was Ventimiglia's modern town, with its banks, beach, shops, and apartment houses. She bought bread at a bakery near the station and walked slowly back. Halfway up the Scala Santa, Eve finally felt the baker's brief warm clasp of her wrist. She stopped in surprise. She must be showing her distress. The baker had put out a hand to offer her comfort.

Eve was angry at Martine. And her anger felt like anxiety, as if there were still something she could do. She *had* worried about her friend. She'd never felt comfortable with the risks Martine had taken in pursuit of knowledge—of answers. Eve knew that—for instance—Martine had been e-mailing a doctor at a teaching hospital in the States. Martine didn't just want to *know* about her condition but was looking for a cure. Martine presented her investigations as altruistic, but Eve had always thought they were selfish and self-hating and dangerous.

Now Eve felt that Martine had got herself into trouble. That she'd courted disaster and disaster had responded with amorous violence.

No one desires the death of a criminal who has evaded justice. They always hope that the person—however altered by age or senility—will be found, extradited, tried, brought to account, which, since criminals had to defend their innocence, had come to mean to *pay*, not to explain. But, on the other hand, people often do wish, with shame, that death will release those they love from suffering. Eve's friend Martine Dardo was an uncaught criminal and a sufferer both. But Martine's death wasn't part of her penance. And Eve had loved her.

Eve realized she was thinking about Martine's death as Martine might have. She was making up a moral ledger, her red pen poised to write: "Payment overdue." These weren't really her feelings, surely. Had she grown hard of heart? Or was she only waiting for one of her remaining intimates—two now, with Martine gone—to tell her how to feel?

Eve went back under the arch at the top of the ramp and along her street. She waved at a waiter across the way, on the terrace of a restaurant, and punched her code at her gate. She went into her courtyard, and the gate hummed and rattled shut. She turned to her house.

The humming stopped, but the gate continued to rattle. Someone said, in guidebook Italian, "Excuse me, one minute, if you please."

Eve turned but didn't approach the gate. She could see that if she went in either direction, toward the button or toward her door, he'd follow her along the bars, hunching and hand-over-hand. He had to hunch to see her; if he stood straight his eyes would be masked by a band of fishnet filigree supporting the long iron spikes that topped her gate. He tried French next, better than phrase-book but full of classical formalities. "Madam, if I might pose a question," he said. He looked urgent, but that might be only his hunched posture—this big stranger to whom Eve was very unwilling to open her gate.

He was tall but built like an aerialist, his arms and shoulders powerful. He had dark eyes and curly hair, the hair and eyes no novelty in these parts, but his complexion was sanguine and Celtic, his brow pale but his flat cheeks and neck and knuckles blushing mulberry. Eve, looking for a moment with the eyes of her unappeasable friends, thought—on their behalf—that he looked appetizing, a pleasant prospect.

The stranger at Eve's gate said that his name was Brian Phelan and that he and the friend with whom he was staying—Gino, a firefighter in Genoa—had recovered Martine Dardo's body from the sea cave in Riomaggiore. He had been talking earlier that day to the detective Eve had dealt with, the man whose job it was to decide if Martine's was a suspicious death.

"Yes?" said Eve, in English. She wondered if he had more up-to-date information.

"I'm not a civilian," Phelan said, reverting to English. "But

I still couldn't guess what that detective is going to decide. I mean . . . some of it depends on how you push. You—her friends."

"Why are you here?" Eve asked. "What do you want to ask me?"

Phelan said that after the recovery he'd asked the detective to call him. "I said I'd like to know how Ms. Dardo died, if letting me know didn't compromise any investigation. It's my search-and-rescue background, you see. Search and rescue is more concerned with causes than results. I mean, statistically and anecdotally. We like to know what went wrong—how the victim got into trouble."

Eve began to tap her foot. She wanted to see how easy it was to disrupt his signal—a strong signal on a narrow band. His easy athletic posture was a kind of supplication. "Go on," she said. She wanted to let him in but thought she shouldn't.

Phelan said, "So I called the guy and he gave me what he could and asked me for my opinion about something—never mind what—but it was all the encouragement I needed. Through the phone I could hear a church bell striking the hour, at the same time and in the same pitch as the one down the road from Gino's apartment. He was calling from Martine Dardo's place, and I figured that her place was near Gino's. So I hopped on Gino's scooter and buzzed about till I found the cars parked on the pavement. Police, right?"

"Very clever," Eve said, without encouragement, as she would to a boasting child.

Phelan tapped himself under one eye with a forefinger, a local gesture and one he must have picked up from his friend. "I still had to try three different buildings. I was looking for an apartment, but of course it was that whole house off the skinny passage between two streets. Our detective was on the *primo piano,*" Phelan said, pleased with himself and his little scraps of Italian.

"Yes," Eve said, urging him on.

Phelan told her he had stood out of the way till the detective had done being piqued and trying to hide his pleasure at seeing him. The detective couldn't see any case shaping up. He kept coming up with questions that weren't obviously related to—"Well," said Phelan, "to the circumstances of your friend's death."

Eve said, "I told the detective that Martine had a couple of serious allergic reactions to things she ate when she was traveling. Breathing difficulties, a rash, and unconsciousness." Then, just as she had when speaking to the detective, Eve added, "That's what Martine told me. She was into alternative medicine, and the police will have some trouble turning up her medical records."

Phelan nodded. "That all works for me," he said. "And I think it worked for him, too. But I'm sure you want to know what he's interested in."

"I want to know what *happened*," Eve said.

The young man made a low rough sound in the back of his throat. It was supposed to be an affirmation but was almost a nervous purr. He said, "But do you want *him* to know what happened?"

For a short while Eve said nothing.

Phelan stretched his long legs, adjusted his position, then fixed his eyes on hers again.

"Why are you interested in all this?" Eve asked.

Phelan said, "Did you ever lose someone in a cave?"

Eve thought he must be talking about the Blessed Martine Raimondi and her miracles. That would make sense. This young man had lost someone—in a cave perhaps—and had chosen to take the Blessed Martine as his saint. He had only just learned about her cult. For some reason his role in the recovery of Martine Dardo's body from the sea cave had raised the ghost of an old failure, an old loss. He was looking for something, a sign or an altar on which to lay down his trouble. *That* made sense. All Eve had to do was treat him gently, take his helm and navigate him back into the public waterways.

Eve said to Phelan that she guessed he was talking about the Blessed Martine Raimondi's first miracle.

"Am I?" Phelan unlocked his arms from the gate and sat down on the road, one shoulder to the bars and three-quarters of his face toward her. "Tell me about that."

Chapter 5

THE BLESSED
MARTINE RAIMONDI'S
FIRST MIRACLE

*I*n early June 1944, a young nun, Martine Raimondi, returned from Turin, where she was a
pharmacist in a hospital, to her village, Dardo, in the Roya
Valley. She came to help her grandfather bury her aunt. Martine helped sort her aunt's house. She visited cousins and
friends, dandled babies, and talked to her former teacher, Father Paolo. She had her papers inspected by the Germans—in
a fairly cursory way—when she first arrived.

In 1944, the mountain village of Dardo was as permeated
by partisans as any other mountain village—but had so far ex-
ported its resistance, individual men and boys, into the surrounding mountains. The village supported the partisans with
sacks of bread, olives, wine, and vegetables, which were carried
to the top terraces at evening and left. Toward the occupying
forces the villagers were wary and cold and uncooperative. By
1944 the village's few Fascists were, for the most part, trying
to reshape themselves as patriots unwelcoming to any foreign

army. Of course there were always some *more* friendly—like the girl who entertained the handsome German corporal.

In May 1944, in Turchino, near Dardo, partisans bombed a movie house, killing six soldiers. The Führer had a standing order for reprisals—ten for one. Frederich Engel, the man who enforced the Führer's rules in Liguria, executed fifty-nine civilians, men and boys. Engel earned himself a title: the Butcher of Genoa. Two of his victims were a brother and nephew of *another* butcher, Dardo's, who—in better times— would slaughter and dress one or two animals a week in his narrow flag-floored house beside the hotel. This man was a peasant landowner, like every other person in the village, ex- cept for the priest, Father Paolo, and the schoolteacher. The butcher owned four terraces under the long slanted escarp- ment that hung above the valley. A narrow path ran on from the cemetery above the town and passed the butcher's gate. The foothills of the Maritime Alps are seamed by paths for foot traffic and mule trains, for centuries kept clear by local travelers, now by hikers on walking tours. This mule track ran from the cemetery, through the butcher's property, and on up to the Castel Abelio.

Three days after the execution the butcher saw, from his window, ten soldiers set off up the path to relieve part of the force at the Castel. This was their normal practice, and the butcher knew that, by dusk, the ten men they had relieved would pass down the path to the town. Or, rather, nine men would go all the way down to the stone bench under the morello cherry tree by the gate of the cemetery, where they would wait for just under an hour before being rejoined by the handsome corporal. The corporal would visit his girlfriend, whose father's property was immediately adjacent to the butcher's.

Once the nine soldiers went by his house, the butcher went down his path to wait for the corporal. By dusk he was hidden in a bay in the path. It was a place where walkers had to go slowly, even by daylight, because an old cypress tree had ruptured the paving stones and scattered its rolling bearings of seed everywhere. It was fully dark under the cypress and dim anyway on the path, the sun behind the mountains and the moon nowhere near the horizon. Everything was set, and the butcher waited, holding a billhook and his breath. He had stolen the billhook from the corporal's girlfriend's father. This butcher was a little simple, so sincerely believed that the Germans would take the murder as the act of an enraged father, not partisans.

The corporal eventually appeared. The butcher tensed, readied himself—then the soldier stopped on the path above the leaning cypress. He stopped and stooped and looked at something.

On those terraces there was always someone watching, if there was any light at all. On those perpendicular properties you were always in someone's line of sight. Someone had seen the butcher go in under the cypress and not emerge. Someone had followed the soldier and seen him pause to appreciate the sight of a thin grass snake winding its way down the slope, in the pale dust beside the paving stones, like a quick rivulet of some black, mercurial liquid.

The butcher was troubled. In motion the soldier was merely a figure; still, he was a man, bent at the waist, hands spread at his sides, and smiling at the ground. The butcher surged out of his hiding place and swung the billhook. The soldier looked up and lifted his hands to fend it off, and the hook cut his throat and partly severed several fingers. The soldier fell face-first on the path and slid down into the dark beneath the cypress. The butcher flung the billhook away and ran.

The following morning the Germans rounded up the first ten men they could lay hands on—including the butcher, who was in his shop cutting up a chamois he'd found on his step at dawn. The chamois's neck was broken. He had assumed it was a gift from the men in the hills. That the partisans knew, and approved, of what he had done.

The Germans marched the villagers to the Church of St. Barthelemy and locked them in. The local SS officer, Hauptmann Giesen, gave the village two hours to tell him where they could find the persons—the partisans—responsible.

Martine Raimondi was at the church, in the confessional, when the men were pushed inside. Father Paolo came out of the confessional and remonstrated with the Germans but was thrust back into the church and told he could hear the condemned men's confessions.

Martine didn't emerge till the doors were barred. Then she went to comfort her grandfather, who was among the men. It was Martine's grandfather who suggested to the priest that he should begin to hear their confessions. They should consider Turchino, the old man said, and abandon any hope of rescue or of mercy.

At this the butcher burst out crying, and when he could be soothed into coherence he told his story. Then he rushed to the church doors and beat on them, calling out that he was the one and that the soldiers should open up and take him away. Eventually they did open the doors, to find the priest beside the weeping, wildly gesticulating butcher, a huddle of men in the pews, blinking and glaring, and a nun wearing the pale fawn habit of the Order of the Daughters of Grace. For a moment the Germans looked at Martine Raimondi as though she were an apparition, polished plaster come to life. Then the butcher flung himself down the steps and confessed. He confessed, and since in his state he was only able to muster Ligurian, Father Paolo translated for him. Giesen, who had till then been rather more predictable than some SS officers, abruptly exploded. He hauled the butcher through his men and drove him off with punches and kicks, then rounded on the priest and said, Was there only one hero among them?

Had they drawn lots and sent out that little imbecile hoping to save themselves? Well then, he'd spare the villagers' chosen sacrifice but shoot their priest instead, just to make up his ten. He ordered the doors closed again—for one more hour. He didn't even acknowledge the nun.

No one knows quite what happened next, what decided Giesen on his following actions. He had a meeting with Dardo's mayor. He had an espresso. He telephoned his superior in Breil and then Engel in Genoa. Neither Engel nor the man in Breil are likely candidates for Hauptmann Giesen's inspiration. What he chose to do was untidy, *un-German*, and dependent on local knowledge, on local dread. It is possible he may have acted in what he saw as the spirit of clemency or with an inquisitor's sense of malice or perhaps merely from fastidiousness. For if Martine Raimondi hadn't performed her miracle, Hauptmann Giesen would have gone down in history as a murderer and a grave robber. Because Giesen had meant to rob Dardo's men of their graves, and the family plots—Truchi, Raimondi, Vail, Villouny—of the bones of their men. Whatever his motivation, on that day, June 1, 1944, somewhere between mayor, espresso, and telephone calls, Hauptmann Giesen came up with the idea that damned him. He went back to St. Barthelemy's and had his men open the doors. He sent his men into the church and had them carry out all the candles. Then he dispatched some down into the crypt and had them unseal the passage he had ordered cemented up when he and his men first arrived in Dardo. The soldiers broke the cement with hammers and pushed the grate in. Beyond the grate—as everyone local knew and as the valley's guidebooks will tell you—there lay a cavern, a long sloping tube of rock that led up to the Grotto of the Hermit where, centuries before, a famous holy man had lived and fasted and prayed. The grotto looked down fifty meters of sheer cliff face—the spur on which the village was built—to the Roya River. The grotto was also the only known outpost of a great unexplored cave system. No one then knew how extensive the system was or where it came out. (Thanks to speleologist cartographers, it is now known that its nearest exit was two kilometers away through caves that were dry, yes, and never so tight that a person had to crawl but were nevertheless narrow, labyrinthine, and utterly dark.)

"There is your hole," said Giesen. "Go down it."

He went up into the body of the church and, before leaving and barring the door for, he said, another hour, he stopped by Martine Raimondi, touched her sleeve but didn't meet her eyes, and said that, naturally, if the sister was found in a hour *alone* and at her prayers she would be spared. "*Ten*, not eleven," he said.

Martine held her grandfather close to her. She whispered to Giesen, "Eleven, not ten. The eleventh commandment is: *Love one another.*"

Giesen and his men went out, and the door was sealed.

Father Paolo took Martine aside and showed her where he kept the oil for anointing—for extreme unction. He decanted half from the jar into a cup and Martine made wicks from twists of silk. The priest then told the villagers that he would say mass, then they should go into the cave and put their trust in God. Perhaps they could hide for a time, he said, tentatively, then, rallying his faith, "God will provide."

Martine had taken communion that morning and had confessed, so, before he began, she said to Father Paolo that she would like to pray in the Grotto of the Hermit. Father Paolo blessed her and she climbed up to the grotto, which looked out into blue air, and at the interleaved slopes south. Martine Raimondi got down on her knees on the smooth place in the rock where the hermit had knelt to pray six times daily every day for twelve years. She made her appeal to God.

Saints are saints because God answers their prayers.

In 1965, when the testimony of witnesses was first taken

officially, Father Paolo testified that, when he'd finished giving communion, he found Martine Raimondi before him at the rail. She was white and, he said, she seemed to have grown. She was, he said, a tall taper, a candle in the dark church. Martine told the priest, her grandfather, and her neighbors to follow her. She took up her cup of oil, and her grandfather lit its wick with one of the ten matches he carried. Bearing the single floating flame, Martine led them away through the crypt and into the caverns.

The caves were such—tilted, winding, pinched, fringed with flowing rock—that the men even three back from the light could only see its glow receding, funneling along the rock walls. Martine Raimondi held her grandfather's hand, and he for the most part watched his feet, watched where he placed his stick. His testimony—in a letter to a nephew written in 1947—said that he had looked up once, and swore he saw a white bird flying through the cave ahead of his granddaughter's feeble floating candle. A bird like a beckoning hand.

The first jar burned down. They lit the second. Martine Raimondi hurried them on. Eventually that light, too, burned blue, then shrank to nothing. The men clung together in a blackness like blindness, like the lives of creatures who haven't ever had eyes. It was a dry cave, and there were no sounds other than those they made.

Martine's grandfather lit a match.

He saw the faces of his neighbors, the black eyes like opened mouths blowing his match out. It burned his hand. He dropped it. He lit another. Someone said, "No, you fool, don't waste them." But then whoever it was thought better of it and let the old man go on lighting them, one by one—flare, fail— against the dark. At the seventh the old man turned to look once more on the granddaughter he loved. But he saw her veiled head turned away toward the darkness. She pulled at his arm. "Come on," she said.

The match went out.

Grandfather pulled at the man behind him and said, "She's walking. Martine is going on. Follow her."

She said, "Come." Sometimes she said, "The roof is low here," and raised her grandfather's hand to show him—and he raised his other hand to show the next man, who showed the one following, and so on. Sometimes she said, "Ah, I see," breathless with awe or fear and as if she could see and hear something the men were unable to. And, after six hours in the cold and dark, Martine led the men out of the cave at a gorge two kilometers above the top terraces of Dardo. It was dusk. They sat down under the trees, while the one who knew where to run ran to find partisans.

Eve Moskelute finished her story, and Bad got up and stretched. He stood and rested his forehead against the gate's iron filigree.

Eve Moskelute said that there was a shrine in Dardo, at St. Barthelemy's. "Martine Raimondi was beatified in 1995. There's now a 'Concession of Public Worship'—though the people of the parish have been praying to her since she died."

A man in an apron bustled up behind Bad and asked Eve Moskelute if the stranger was troubling her.

"No." She pressed a button and Bad pushed himself back from the gate as it began to move. The man—who had come from the restaurant across the road—stood ostentatiously wiping his hands on his apron and looking at Bad with a narrow gaze.

"Thank you," Eve told him. "I'm quite all right."

The restaurateur shook his shoulders and head gently in opposite directions, signaling his dubious concession. He went back over the road.

Eve Moskelute invited Bad to follow her into her house.

There she gave him water and told him she was going into her garden to pick some fava beans.

Bad went out onto her terrace and watched her climb down to her garden and cut a head of broccoli, gather a handful of young fava pods, and pull some leaves from a pale, frilly lettuce. She placed the vegetables on the step in the shade. Then she disappeared into a small shed and emerged with a ball of string and some green plastic stakes. She began to restake the blue-green thicket of favas. She was trying to construct a flimsy fence to contain the stand, which had begun to lean, but the plants kept jostling in the wind and making the stakes bristle out at all angles. Bad watched Eve push her gray hair back and curse quietly. He went to help her.

He knelt on the ground beside her and scooped the mass of plants back with his arms. Eve fastened the string in a tight double row from stake to stake. "Thank you," she said. Then, "I'm going to make you something to eat."

Bad looked up the valley. He asked her what wind this was.

"It's from the northwest, moving ahead of that storm, which might only travel along the mountains and not come down here," Eve said, then added that she thought it would, though, by its persuasive piled blackness and the way the leggy smoke bush at the edge of her terrace was whipping about. She picked up the vegetables and led Bad back indoors.

They had the leaves dressed in olive oil, lemon juice, and thin shavings of pecorino. Eve grilled several *cicolini* and let the favas simmer for a minute before tossing them with olive oil and black pepper. She put out a loaf of bread shaped like a crown of thorns.

Bad ate and looked at his hostess from time to time, abashed and appreciative. Eventually he wiped his hands on his napkin but then went on pulling off little lumps of bread and sopping up the oil from the dish of beans.

He told Eve Moskelute that while he was in Martine

Dardo's house in Genoa the police had an expert looking at the contents of her computer. "Martine Dardo was conducting a few correspondences, the detective said. That's when he mentioned your name. That's when he said you'd identified her."

Bad's hostess waved her hand at him, asking him was this going anywhere.

Bad told her he was only passing on what the detective told him. "For instance, Martine Dardo was writing to a Father Octave."

Eve Moskelute made a little noise of encouragement. Then she just stared at Bad over the remains of the meal, like a poker player over a fence of fanned cards.

Bad said, "Do you *know* Father Octave?"

"I know who he is," said Eve. She told Bad that Daniel Octave was the postulator. Father Octave wrote the Process for the Cause of Canonization. He was present at the exhumation in 1991. The village of Dardo had pushed for an exhumation for some time. It was argued that Martine Raimondi's body really belonged in the crypt at St. Barthelemy's. But Raimondi's open tomb did not exude the fragrance of "little fennel-scented apples." In fact, her tomb was occupied by another body. The exhumation was an obstacle on her journey to sainthood. However, in 1992 there appeared a very persuasive candidate for a second miracle—after an earlier proposed second miracle had been disproven. Father Octave's Process picked up momentum again, and the absence of a body was, in the end, not an obstacle that was insurmountable to the saint-making John Paul II. In 1995, Martine Raimondi was beatified.

Eve Moskelute said to Bad that in the early nineties her friend Martine had been in touch with Father Octave, who was hunting up the last of Raimondi's small body of writings. "Martine turned over what she had," Eve said. "Twenty letters to Grandfather Raimondi. The letters were lively and sweet-natured—my friend said—but not exactly heroically virtuous." Eve Moskelute shrugged. "I didn't know that Martine had remained in touch with Father Octave after giving him the letters. But then I didn't always know who Martine knew, or who she was seeing."

Bad said that he guessed the detective would get on to Father Octave. Then he said that, despite being "into alternative medicine," Eve's friend was writing to a microbiologist in the States.

"Not a hematologist?"

Bad cocked an eyebrow at her. "Did I say a hematologist?" Eve didn't answer him.

"They were swapping pictures of slides," Bad said. "Microscope slides."

"Coffee?" Eve inquired, getting up.

He nodded, said, "Please." He had the impression she'd turned her back on him to hide her expression. He said, "I looked over the computer guy's shoulder. Your friend had e-mailed the microbiologist the image of a slide, the microbiologist returned it with a question, and she answered his question."

Eve Moskelute loaded her already steaming machine. She said, "I suppose you'd like this diluted?"

"I come from Sydney, not Salt Lake City," Bad said.

She laughed.

"There was the slide, right?" he went on. "A picture of pink-stained cells. The microbiologist sent back, asking: 'What *is* this?' And your friend answered him: 'This is a single-cell parasitic organism mimicking a human stem cell.' "

Eve shut off the valve when the cups were half-full. She brought the mere mouthfuls of coffee to the table. She said, "It doesn't mean a thing to me. I'm not a biologist."

Bad watched her face, looking for daylight. The clouds had come down the valley and the room was twilit, its colors under dusk's dark filter. Bad asked, "Was your friend sick?"

"She had health problems," Eve said. "Tell me, Mr. Phelan, are you going to communicate with the detective again?"

"I don't know."

"So . . . you came to tell me what the detective is up to?"

Bad told Eve why he'd come. He said that, ten months back, he'd been injured by a bomb. "I cracked a couple of vertebrae and broke a leg. I had a near miss with a concrete pillar in a collapsed underground garage. On the pillar there was a poster for an exhibition of European Modern Masters. Jean Ares's painting *Eve in a Gaucho Hat.* Your face," he said. Then, "Did you have a daughter? Do you? By the way, that's only my second real question after, 'Did you ever lose someone in a cave?' "

Bad watched Eve Moskelute's face lose all expression. She got up from the table again. She opened a drawer and came back with paper and pen. She sat down and began to write. She told Bad that this was a note of introduction to the caretaker at Jean Ares's house on Cap de Nice. The house was right beside the sea. There was a short escalade down to a summerhouse, and a small apron of pebbles on the water. "The clear turquoise water," she said. "It's a beautiful place—open to the public in the high season, from the second week of July to the end of August—but you can have four weeks there before it opens. There's a market nearby. The caretaker will show you," she said. "Go; enjoy yourself. It'll soon be swimming weather." She slipped the thick textured white sheet into an equally crisp envelope. "You'll never get another offer like this. This is for fetching my friend's body out of the sea. Thank you. Take it, Mr. Phelan, and go."

Bad took the envelope, then her thin-skinned hand, and retained it. "You didn't answer me," he said. "I don't mean to cause you any pain."

Eve stood. The table was between them. She edged away so that Bad was obliged to release her.

But Bad persisted. He apologized and explained. "I'm sorry that it was me there both times. In Le Lien Vert and at Riomaggiore. That's why I'm here. Because it's the strangest chance. I know I wouldn't have muscled in on the recovery at Riomaggiore if it wasn't for the way your friend wore her hair. I took one look at her hair and said to the detective, 'I can do it, I can get her out of the water.' Because the only other person I'd seen with hair like that was your daughter—the girl who died in the cave near Dardo in 1992. I never did hear whether they found her body. I wondered why no one called to hear my story. I'd given my name and address to the rescuers from Gino's *zona*. I expected to hear from her family. But no one wrote. I never knew if she was found, or who she was. But she wore her hair the same way as your friend Martine." He shook his head, dazed. "Not that I understand why she would have done that. But, at Riomaggiore, I had a crazy feeling—I thought it was *her* in the sea cave. And it turned out there was a connection, between her and Martine Dardo. *You.* I remembered the face in the exhibition poster—it looked like her, but it was you."

"I had no daughter," Eve said. "It was my sister."

Bad frowned at Eve. He made calculations, counted the years back to '92. The woman in the cave would be in her mid-thirties now. That still left a twenty-five-year age gap between the sisters. What he was hearing didn't make sense. He said, "What was your sister's name?"

"Dawn Moskelute." Eve pointed at the envelope. "You know, Mr. Phelan, that's a dream offer."

Bad folded the envelope and slipped it into the inside pocket of his jacket. He waited for Eve to ask him questions. He waited for permission to ask his own. But Eve Moskelute remained silent. She held his gaze, friendly and calm. She wouldn't allow any mutually satisfying confidences.

"I wish you'd explain it to me," Bad said.

Eve Moskelute shook her head.

After a long, discouraging silence Bad gave up. He said that he'd go brave the austrostrada on Gino's Vespa. He was sorry for bothering her.

Eve Moskelute saw him to the door. "Thank you," she said. She put her hand in the small of his back, gentle and managing, and propelled him into her atrium, then out into her courtyard. She pushed the button on the gate. She said, "I'm grateful for your efforts."

Bad thanked her for the meal.

"Have a lovely time, Mr. Phelan," she said. "Send me a postcard."

Chapter 6

AN EXHUMATION

*A*week after Martine Dardo's call from the boat and several days after Daniel's phone conversation with the American in Martine's apartment, one of Daniel's brother Jesuits appeared at the open door of his room, where Daniel was busy packing a bag. He was on his way to Dardo to attend the pilgrimage commemorating the Blessed Martine's first miracle. Daniel's brother Jesuit said that there was a call for him, from a detective in Genoa. "I said I'd see if you were in. If you take this call you'll miss your train."

Daniel put Father Roderigo's *Manual for Preparing the Processes of Canonization* in the top of his bag and closed its zipper. He went into the library to take the call.

The detective told Daniel that Martine Dardo had been found drowned. Until then Daniel had entertained a faint hope that, although Martine had followed her phone into the water, she'd thought better of it, had climbed back and used the oars she'd not had the resolution to abandon.

Daniel told the detective that he had last heard from Martine Dardo only a few days ago.

"How did she seem to you?"

"Troubled. She was in poor health."

"Father, do you think it's possible she was troubled enough to have done something desperate?"

"I couldn't say."

"Have you tried to call her again since you last spoke?"

"Yes. I got her answering machine."

The detective was silent for a moment, and Daniel waited to continue parrying questions with politeness. He was aware that he hadn't yet lied, only made omissions. He didn't want to lie, but he knew he would.

"Isn't there anything you would like to ask me, Father?"

Daniel said that he'd appreciate it if the detective could give him the address and phone number of Martine's friend Eve Moskelute. He would ask her about Martine's funeral.

The detective said, "I think we have to conclude that Martine Dardo took her own life."

Daniel shook his head, at the phone, the book-lined walls, the time on the library clock.

"We've been distracted by the presence of a severe contact rash on Signora Dardo's upper body. We've speculated more than we need have, apparently."

Daniel said, "Did she have a clubfoot?" He was surprised by his own question.

"Yes, she did, but it didn't kill her, Father."

"I wish I could offer you more help," said Daniel. "But I'm in the dark."

Each year, on the anniversary of the day that the ten villagers were locked in the Church of St. Barthelemy, then led by a young nun to safety through an absolute and unmapped dark, a group of people made the same journey. Every year more pilgrims participated, and the two-kilometer underground route was now illuminated for its full distance by electric light. The pilgrimage was, in fact, more a commemorative journey with rituals. For five years Father Octave and the three priests of St. Barthelemy's had performed those rituals, with the attendance each year of a group of sisters of the Order of the Daughters of Grace, including their current Reverend Mother, who had known the Blessed Martine. Other contemporaries of the Blessed Martine were also in regular attendance. Three of the people who made that first journey were still alive, men from Dardo, all in their teens in 1944. Then there were the partisans—war veterans—among whom every year Father Octave would hope to see Alberto Vail. Vail made the pilgrimage but kept his hat on. All the pilgrims wore helmets, but Vail made a point—a *show*—of fastening his helmet over his cloth cap. He'd make sure to do it in Daniel's sight, his eyes gleaming at the priest from under the shadows of his prodigious eyebrows.

Alberto Vail would not remove his hat in church. He was a communist and atheist. He was also responsible, in a way, for Martine Raimondi's beatification. Sometimes Daniel would entertain the thought that God had sent him this atheist in order to make up his mind. Vail's testimony did not appear in Father Octave's Process of Canonization, but it was what Vail told Daniel that led him to leave certain things out of the Process, things concerning the Cardinal Virtues of the Blessed Martine. Alberto Vail's vital testimony was this: "She had no child."

In 1991 the bishop in Turin gave permission for an exhumation. Father Daniel Octave was present. Along with the permission for the removal of relics, he had permission to collect a sample of hair or tissue for analysis. He had persuaded Martine Dardo to let a DNA test settle the matter. She said she'd supply her sample once one was retrieved from Martine Raimondi's remains.

Martine Raimondi had been captured by the Germans at

the beginning of September 1944. "She was ill and wasn't able to stay on the move," Alberto Vail had told Daniel. "She was in bed, and in the care of an old woman, the only occupant of an all-but-ruined farm on the path to St. Sauveur above Tende." ("And you needn't arch your brows at me, Daniel," Vail said. "She *wasn't* lying in, about to deliver. I thought we'd done with all that!") Martine was exhausted, depleted, not sufficiently robust for life in the hills. Vail visited her only two days before she was caught. "She was running a fever, covered in a rash, and she couldn't keep anything down. She wouldn't have been able to escape the soldiers, even if she had a warning," Vail said. "And she was troubled."

"Troubled?" said Daniel.

"About St. Barthelemy's, and the men she'd saved."

"About their future?"

Alberto shook his head. Then he shrugged and said, "She told me that their lives had come at a price."

Martine was captured and executed in September 1944. Her grandfather and a sister of the Daughters of Grace (who later became Reverend Mother) received Martine's body from Giesen's men (with his remark about honoring her as a hero). A carpenter in Dardo made her coffin, placed her in it, and sealed its seams with lead. The sister accompanied the body on its journey by train to Turin. The order was then without its own church, St. Marguerita's having been bombed, so the young nun—already seen as a martyr—was interred in the great round votive chapel of Santa Maria della Fiori, in a marble sarcophagus in the gallery high above the octagonal nave and under the dome.

The exhumation took place in March 1991. Cold radiated from the frescoed plaster of the dome and from the tessellated mosaic on the floor of the gallery. Daniel couldn't seem to keep his feet warm, no matter how he shuffled and stamped.

In the gallery with the churchmen and -women were a pathologist and stonemasons and laborers. Some stood out of the way above the trestle where they would lay the lid of the sarcophagus once it had been raised from its place. Others worked to tighten elasticized straps around the lid. Far below in the nave a service was under way. Mass was being said, a booming murmur in which words were indistinguishable.

The workmen didn't prize at the lid and risk chipping it. Instead they got a good grip on the stone with the straps, which were coated in latex. They took hold of the handles attached to the straps and hauled. The heavy lid came up a little. The men were panting, and the air filled with their breath. It billowed, a visible cloud for a few feet above their heads, solidifying further in the glancing light from one of the small windows at the apex of the dome, then vanished in the gloomy space beyond.

Daniel thrust his hands into his armpits to warm them. He watched the workmen maneuver planks beneath the rocking lid. Once the planks were secure and their hands were free the workmen crossed themselves. The planks protruded from either end of the lid. Between the planks and the edge of the sarcophagus was a black crack. Daniel wanted to step up and apply his eye to the crack. Lifting the lid seemed too swift a transition. They were all nervous. Daniel's arms were sore, though he'd done no lifting. His chest was tight and his eyes were watering.

The workmen rested for a minute, then went back to their places around the lid and, in a concerted effort, lifted it off the sarcophagus. They shuffled over to the trestle and set the lid down. They watched what they were doing, where they were putting their feet, didn't risk even a sidelong glance. Daniel respected this practical pause; he followed the lid with his eyes till it was securely on the trestle. Then he looked back at the tomb.

The Reverend Mother's hands were lifted to her head. She looked horrified but at the same time began to blush deeply.

Lying curled among shards of smashed wood was a mummified corpse, its flesh a dark leather torn in places or worn down to bone. The mummy was wearing black, the deflated uniform of an officer of the SS.

"It's Giesen," Daniel said. But, of course, it needn't be Giesen. It was six hours by train from Dardo to Turin, and who would take the kind of trouble needed to get the man here—dead or alive—even to arrange this dramatic, symmetrical revenge? The partisans may have killed Giesen—who had disappeared when the Allied armies bypassed Sospel and the Roya, trapping all the occupying Germans—but who would exchange Giesen's body for his victim's? It didn't make any sense.

For half an hour Daniel stood listening to a stunned circular discussion by the clergy while the coroner and his assistant removed the mummy from the tomb. As they worked, it was revealed that, at the back of the sarcophagus, where it stood hard up against the wall of the dome, there was a hole. A hole smashed through the marble tomb and the brick wall behind the tomb. Where the bricks had been removed was a gap-toothed darkness.

Daniel told the others he was going in. He borrowed a flashlight and climbed into the sarcophagus. One of the workmen asked if he wanted company.

"If you like," Daniel said. He didn't care—his curiosity felt like a fit on him.

He switched on the flashlight and shone it into the gap. He couldn't get onto his knees to look—the litter of smashed coffin and most of the broken bricks were on the bottom of the sarcophagus. Just inside the hole Daniel could see a pile of stacked bricks. The tomb had been broken into from inside the hole, the bricks wedged out of chipped mortar and piled up in the dark, then the marble attacked and chipped and eventually penetrated.

Daniel said that it appeared there was a space between the inner and outer walls of the dome.

"The inner one is mortared brick and braced with iron hoops; it goes up in steps from the bottom, only its interior is smooth," the bishop explained. "The architect's plans are in the library here. The cupola is marble slabs laid over support beams. Can you see the timber bracing?"

Daniel said he could. He had climbed into the hole.

The dark space curved away from him, broken by a nest of timbers criss-crossed between the inner and outer walls to make a kind of rigid maze. It confused the beam of Daniel's flashlight. The space was all gaps and blockages, some solid, some shadow.

The workman followed Daniel. Their breath hung in the air around their heads.

The man tapped Daniel on the ankle and held up a rusted chisel. "I didn't find the hammer," the workman said. "But this was what was used." Daniel nodded and went on, stepping over some beams, ducking under others. The air was musty, the timber cold under his hands, so cold it stung, as though the wood were live and conducting the cold of the marble.

Daniel saw a smudge on the outer wall and held his flashlight to it. It was a handprint—someone had put out a hand. Daniel suspected the smudge was blood. He went on. The workman moved delicately behind him. Both were mindful of the age of the timbers and the weight of the masonry they supported.

Daniel had realized that the inner wall was a series of steps, the internal dome built like a rough hive. The wall was climbable. He asked the other man to turn off his flashlight and switched off his own. At first the space was black, the darkness a heavy gas that seeped into them at the eyes. Then Daniel saw a smear of light above him. He turned his flashlight back on and began to climb the stepped inner wall, squeezing between timbers. As he got higher up the curve, the gap between the two domes narrowed, for of course the walls were designed to incline together for support. The man below called up to Daniel, "Come back, Father. It can't be safe!" Daniel waved to show he was all right and went on out of the man's sight. At the end Daniel was slithering, pushing himself up the now shallow slope with his hands and soles against either wall. There were no timbers to impede him now; the walls were tied together by bolts, the gilded studs of which showed on the cupola in the church interior as a crude constellation. Daniel was nearly at the top of the arch, within sight of the rotunda that pierced the apex of the dome and tied it all together. The rotunda had windows giving onto the inside of the church, Daniel recalled. Only an hour before he'd been watching a condensation of breath materialize in their light.

Daniel reached the rotunda. Through the few centimeters of free space under his chin Daniel saw that he was above the lower set of windows, those visible from the church, and that the inner wall ended against the rotunda, which these windows pierced. Above these windows, at a ninety-degree angle, was another set, between the top of the rotunda and the outer dome, through which the sun shone, dazzling and distorted through thick, flawed old glass. Daniel forced himself up another few feet and into the space between the two sets of windows. He examined them. He looked down and saw, below, the tiled floor of the central nave and the ends of pews. He looked up and saw that the lead had been picked away from three sides of one exterior window and only pushed back in places so that the glass was held like a gem in claw clasps. The heavy glass shivered in the wind. Daniel spotted a wad of cloth dropped into a gap beside one of the lower windows. Fawn and white cloth. He lay on his stomach and stretched for it, caught it with two fingers, and lifted it into the light.

It was dusty and faded but recognizable as the white cowl and fawn veil worn by sisters of the Order of the Daughters of Grace.

Daniel had taken this latest revelation into his final interview with Antonio Vail. He told Vail how it seemed to him. The theft of Martine Raimondi's body was bizarre, and its replacement with her executioner's was an absurdly dangerous and strenuous task—so covert an act it could be said to have originated at a level below secrecy. "There's too much poetry in its justice."

Vail laughed at Daniel and called him "Father Jesuit." So Father Jesuit imagined there was a realm *below* secrecy?

Chapter 7

DAYLIGHT

*E*ve was parked on a narrow street in Nice, facing the Rue d'Angleterre. She could see there was still a line to the club whose entrance was just around the corner. She'd allowed herself to close her eyes once and had gone to sleep. When she woke, disoriented and unable to judge the duration of her nap, she was reassured to see that the line was only a little smaller than when she'd last looked.

It was nearly two when Eve saw the couple appear from behind the line. As they appeared, the line shuffled forward and two more bodies were admitted into the club, which was observing fire safety rules and counting heads, not imposing a dress code on its clients. It wasn't that kind of club. The couple, a man and woman, stepped off the curb. He turned his ankle and the woman caught him. He was dizzy drunk but not otherwise inebriated, Eve thought. She understood the woman's preferences—knew that she liked clubs where people drank and those with "encounter spaces," low-lit rooms with padded benches and toys. The woman didn't like big dance parties where people took the kind of drugs that made them stay on the dance floor and pour sweat. She didn't like to be surrounded by the ecstatic—it was unflattering, she said; their attention was superficial, skipping like flat stones tossed glancingly at smooth water. The woman preferred the muddled malleability of drunks or the mesmerized seriousness of the stoned. She was, she'd say, old-fashioned.

The couple crossed the street. The man had one arm around the woman, but she steadied him as they went, heads together, into the narrow Rue Victor Juge and out of sight.

Eve waited only ten minutes.

The woman reappeared, bounded across the intersection, her high-heeled sandals in one hand and swinging by their straps. She came to the driver's door and opened it for Eve. They swapped places.

Eve's sister reeked of pastis. She put a small bundle of banknotes into Eve's lap and started the engine.

"You robbed him?" Eve said.

"He'd expect me to rob him," said Dawn, practical.

Eve Moskelute's English translation of the Marquis Guy de Chambord's romance, *Daylight*, was published in 1969. Eve was in London for its publication. The book had caused a small stir in France, where it appeared the year before, also in translation, for the marquis had written it in Provençal. The text itself was of considerable interest. The marquis was a sophisticated and cosmopolitan man, who in his fifty-something years traveled as far west as Dublin, north and east as Riga, and south as Syria. He wrote poetry in French but chose to write his one work of fiction in the local "dialect"—although in a letter to a friend he claimed that its "legitimate inspiration" was a German text, Goethe's *Sufferings of Young Werther*.

In her introduction, Eve argued that the heroine of the

romance, Grazide, was represented as speaking an aristocratic version of the peasant tongue. She was like Arnaut Daniel in *Purgatorio*; her Provençal had an antique nobility.

"Grazide tells the hero that matters of the heart cannot be communicated in a language that is strange to the land," Eve told an interviewer in London. "I realize that it is difficult to ask modern English-language readers to take on faith what this twice-translated text has to say about language and authenticity. In France *Lumière du Jour* is published with its verses in Provençal and French, the two versions on facing pages, so that scholars can make a comparison." Eve said, "The thing that Chambord does so well—and we must remember that his is a minor work; it *isn't* Rousseau or Goethe or Kleist—is create a heroine whose sensibilities are utterly foreign to the hero. Strange and transporting—so that gradually in the course of the story the hero finds that his beloved's appetites and values have completely replaced his own. As this happens, the hero moves fully into a world that, since childhood, he's only *inhabited*, not *lived in*. Grazide both seduces and converts him, so he feels that his ancient, unhealthy provincial home—Avignon—has become a kind of paradise, a paradise of the senses. So much of this depends on the heroine's fluency in Provençal. Chambord gives Grazide his best lines. His choice of Provençal is clearly intended to be an homage to his heroine. Scholars have so far failed to identify a historical figure with Chambord's Grazide, but I am sure that Grazide is a portrait of someone the marquis knew and loved.

"The book," Eve said, "was clearly as influenced by Rousseau as it was by Goethe. It takes pains to create an alternative reality where family fealty and citizenship are illusory—false laws. The book advocates instinctive feeling; its ideal life is alert and sensual but also infantile and self-gratifying. Unlike in Rousseau, however, there is little discussion of social organizations. The work has nothing to say about the monarchy, or the Church. It is interested in being *alive*, not being human; in consciousness, not moral agency."

Eve wasn't particularly surprised by the attention both her biography and her translation received in France. The success was a matter of timing, she believed—of fashion. It was an intriguing work, but it had been around for some time. Her translation had the luck to coincide with the aftermath of '68 in Paris and America's Summer of Love. The Marquis de Chambord was something of a libertine, *Daylight* a romance with a touch of the infernal. *Daylight* was also fashionable in its ambiguities. For instance, the heroine's manservant, an enameler's journeyman whom Grazide lures away from his trade and day job with public promises of patronage and private promises of pleasure, was, in the book, less a rival to the hero than a figure the hero both hates and covets. The hero is equally happy to pay the manservant to leave Grazide and work for him or to pay him to go away altogether. In the romance it is the journeyman who inspires the heroine's more sinister sensuality. At one point Grazide assures the hero that he is her love, while the journeyman is only her *larder.* She tells the hero that she treasures the journeyman for his vigor and the hero for his finesse; the journeyman for his brawn, the hero for his imagination; the journeyman for his brute ignorance, the hero for his erudition.

"A fascinating triangular relationship," said Eve in interviews.

It was when Eve was on her promotional tour that her twin sister died.

Dawn Moskelute was living in a commune on a farm near St. Agnes. Every few days Dawn took the bus from the village down to Menton to check on their apartment, the apartment the twins' Russian grandfather had bought in 1919 and had left to his daughter-in-law, their mother.

Eve and her sister were close despite their different lives. They saw each other frequently, usually spending one or two days of every week together—often doing a little work on the interior of the apartment, unimproved since the thirties, when the family last had any money. Dawn had been down more often while Eve was away. She had been collecting Eve's mail.

The day Dawn died she had just come back up to St. Agnes from the coast. She'd taken the bus up the road with its hairpin bends. She was expected—a friend from the commune was in the village, waiting in a café in the lowest piazza, near the place where all heavy traffic stopped and turned. The friend saw Dawn's bus arrive and its passengers disembark. Dawn was the last off. She remained by the wall on the far side of the road while the bus turned to park facing downhill and its driver got out to amble up to the village and have his midmorning coffee and marc. The friend saw that Dawn was draped across the wall, catching her breath, perhaps queasy from the trip up the twisting road. After a time she straightened and turned. Her friend stood and waved to her.

There was a truck near the bus stop. Its driver had finished his deliveries and had waited for the bus to get out of his way; he was leaning out the open door of his cab, his foot on the running board, preparing to reverse. He *was* looking where he was going. Perhaps Dawn saw her friend waving to her—but her friend believed she saw nothing. She seemed dazed, faint, disoriented. She started across the road—and walked right into the path of the backing truck. She was only two feet from its flatbed as she stepped in its path. The truck driver saw her and moved his foot to the brake. But his foot slipped, and the truck stalled. And as it stalled it lurched and struck Dawn. A bolt that closed the back gate of the truck's bed hit her hard a few inches under her ear, breaking her neck. When her friend reached her, seconds later, he found a pulse, but in the next half hour, while they waited for an ambulance, her heart stopped.

Eve was called and came home.

Together she and the commune arranged Dawn's funeral. Eve did allow a blood test—which showed only the tiniest amount of alcohol. "She was always moderate," Dawn's friend said. An initial examination also found a bandage on Dawn's right wrist and a short, deep cut beneath the bandage. This was a shock—the twins had been together only two weeks back and Dawn had seemed perfectly happy. Her friends agreed with Eve, then said, "Dawn was fine, as far as we knew."

Eve told the coroner that the cut could have been an accident—it was on Dawn's right wrist and she was right-handed. "Surely accidental?" Eve said. "We were doing some carpentry."

The friend said that when he'd phoned from the village the night before to fix a time to pick her up Dawn had seemed quite normal. "She was tired, she said. A little off-color. Perhaps coming down with something. Perhaps a little sick from the paint fumes." (Dawn had been painting a wardrobe. Eve found the wardrobe, finished but still surrounded by paint-spattered newspaper.) "It might have been an infection, or fumes, or car sickness, or drowsiness, or simply inattention—how will we ever know?" Dawn's friend said.

Eve wouldn't allow a full autopsy, and Dawn was interred in a shroud, in keeping with the commune's beliefs. Dawn was laid in one of the big lead-lined stone sarcophagi in the Moskelute family mausoleum in the old cemetery at Menton—the most impressive real estate the Moskelute family had left to them. The mausoleum was a marble building with an onion-shaped dome covered in faded ceramic tiles. Dawn's friends from the commune carried her temporary hardboard coffin from the hearse at the gates and up to the top terrace. Eve unlocked the tomb's bronze door, and the mourners opened the twins' grandmother's grave. It took ten people to raise the lid and carry it two feet to rest on another sarcophagus. They lifted Dawn out of her coffin and slipped her into the tomb on her side and curled around her grandmother's slight, dry skeleton. Then they replaced the marble lid.

Eve shone her torch around the tomb, at the memorials. The oldest were in Cyrillic script, which she couldn't read. She noticed the corner where the floor was broken by cypress roots, and the long crack in the wall above it. Eve didn't like to leave her sister in the dark. She remembered how distressed they had been when their mother finally died—confused, exhausted, unwilling—in a ward of the Hospital St. Roch. The twins had confided to each other that for months whenever they went within sight of the hospital they would be seized by an impulse to go in and find the mother they felt they had forgotten and left behind. The hospital was the last place they had seen her alive, so they felt they might still be able to find her there, waiting for them to come.

Eve had last seen Dawn when they'd had a scratch dinner together after finishing laying a timber floor over the tiles in one bedroom. They'd sat at their table on the terrace, while in the room behind them the displaced bedroom furniture loomed like a forest. There was light on the sea still, and warmth radiated from the concrete face of the apartment building. When it was dark Dawn had plugged in the outdoor lamp for the first time that summer, and its light shone softly, diffused through an accretion of dusty spiderweb.

Eve closed the door on her sister.

Several days later, at five in the morning, Eve woke her nearest neighbor by leaning on their doorbell. The neighbor came to the door to find Eve in her nightdress. She had one wrist wrapped in a bloodstained towel.

A doctor on the psychiatric ward at St. Roch said to Eve that it was unusual for anyone contemplating suicide to get ready for bed before making the attempt, even more unusual for someone to try it first thing in the morning. What was in her mind? This was an impulse, but what was its trigger? Her own face in the mirror? Not self-loathing of course—but her *sister's* face.

Eve could remember what had happened but wasn't clear in her mind, and it didn't make sense. She felt dead already—her life taken—so why would she try to do what had already been done? She remembered that she'd been up in the night. She'd had a dream in which Dawn was calling her from another room, a room Eve couldn't find no matter how hard she looked. She thought that she perhaps had wandered about from room to room in her sleep, looking for her sister. She remembered that, in her dream, she found herself standing at the marble-topped vanity in the bathroom. Someone stood behind her, holding her wrist and letting her blood—so that it trickled to form a silky red pool on the marble. The person—a man—was already inside the apartment but kept asking for the key. He persisted: "Where is the key?" He walked her around the apartment opening drawers. Then he wrapped her wrist and sat her in a chair in the entrance hall, under the portrait of her mother. The door was open, so Eve staggered out and leaned on her neighbor's bell.

"But none of that can be true," Eve said to the psychiatrist. "I know it was a dream, because the man was speaking Provençal."

Eve and Dawn went over the Col de Nice—that crumbling country—then through Sospel in the dark, then over the Col de Brouis and down through a forest of ash, and limes in feathery bloom, to the Roya. Dardo appeared, on its spur of rock, the river swinging wide around the base of the spur and its half-moon river meadow. They drove on, crossed the bridge, and circled back. The sun was up over the sea already, but sun and sea were hidden behind the peaks to the east, back toward Ventimiglia. It was a clear day and the sky above the mountains was an airy, voluminous blue.

They drove up the avenue of plane trees, whose mottled trunks made a regular paddling swish as the car passed. They parked in the first space on the wide end of the Avenue 19 Septembre 1947. Eve's sister jumped out of the car, leaving the door open. Eve took her time. She got out and watched Dawn sprint up under the plane trees. Dawn ran fast, her hair gleaming, fair and dark. She disappeared around a corner.

Eve followed slowly. No one was up, it seemed. In the silence the fountain by the Hotel de Ville was making an emphatic water noise. It was surrounded by buckets full of wild broom. There were broom flowers in wreaths outside the Hotel de Ville and in the porch of the smaller church, St. Eloi's.

Eve went on and up. She paused again at the escalade that went down to a landing paved not in pale cobbles but in green schist, a landing like a gallery above the sheer cliff and the river meadow. Someone had cut and stacked a first crop of hay in the meadow. There was a wind pushing up the valley, a warm wind—another change in the weather. As Eve waited, the wind carried a dry smell to her, and some glossy hay stalks flew, funneling up the cliff face and the spiral of the escalade. The stalks circled above Eve, then, moving out of the channeled current of air, fluttered down onto the cobbles.

Eve waited; she knew when to wait. The sun reached the rim of the mountains. She heard the bell of St. Barthelemy's begin to toll and finally went on, out of the sun and into the Rue Oscura—or, as its resident called it in Provençal, the "Carriera Scura." She passed under suspended iron cages that had once held oil lamps and now contained low-wattage bulbs. She came to the house with barred windows, the iron woven bar through bar. The door was open a crack and Eve went in, switching on lights as she went.

She unfastened one shutter on the windows in the wall of the house that was continuous with the spur on which Dardo was built. Eve looked down on the crown of an ash growing on an outcrop, then farther, to the meadow, from which the smoke of chaff still went up in the wind.

Cold air breathed out of every room in the house, the cold of several months past, an April chill, not fierce but persistent—spring had seemed to take its time that year. The house had been shut up all that time—closed but not unoccupied. Eve listened and thought she heard a whisper, an endearment, as of a person soothing another who has had a bad dream.

She left the window and switched on the halogen lamp over the tilted plan table. She studied the parchment pinned there, the vivid intricacies of an illuminated picture. In the picture everything was in focus, a city escape piled up into a foreground, building on building like tiles. There was no air in the picture. Eve looked at the collapsed concrete slab construction, the rags pinched between masonry; spilled intestines of electrical cord; dangling nodes of a fuse box, an electric jug, a television; the whole structure oozing matter like an overfilled burger bun. Above the tiled cityscape was a row of hanging empty body bags. These were the nearest thing to bodies the artist had drawn in a long, long while.

Out of the corner of her eye Eve saw a foggy shape in one of the black doorways. Then he was standing beside her, looking at her with his clear, giveaway eyes. Eve could see that his skin was still papery and powdered-looking. He wasn't yet up to speed. He looked sleepy but sane.

Lou Ila pointed at the window. Eve went and pulled the shutters closed and stroked their slats down. "Churr," said Ila, imitating a shutter. He wasn't really with her yet. He padded into the kitchen and she heard his long nails clicking together as he turned the tap. He came out a moment later with his face and hair damp, said hello to her in Provençal, and gave her a pair of nail clippers. They sat down and she trimmed his fingernails. After she'd done his hands he lifted his feet and held them steady, and at the right height, while she did those, too.

She finished and he took her hand, kissed it, and slipped its edge into his mouth. Eve felt the spines on the roof of his mouth lift against the ball of her thumb. They flexed but didn't pierce. She remained quite still while he tasted her, breathing softly, his eyes closed. After a time he released her hand, glossy with spit and thin strings of congealing blood—not her own. He smelled of pastis.

"I'm awake," he said in Provençal. "But Dawn must sleep." Then he said, "Tell me about Martine."

Eve Moskelute's translation of the Marquis de Chambord's romance, *Lumière du Jour*, commences with these words, Chambord's epigraph: *"Whoever comes to these pages looking for illumination will find it in the form of candles, floating wicks, pitch-soaked link lights, moonlight, starlight, and fire suspended in fountains of crystal—but never the light of day, so-called cold."*

Chapter 8

FATHER OCTAVE'S PARABLE OF THE ALBINOS

At Ventimiglia, where he had to change trains, Bad put his pack on and trudged out to the *tabac* at the station entrance. There he found two maps, one of Nice showing the major streets on the Cap de Nice and the one Gino had said he'd need, a map of the Vallée de Roya showing the main routes into the Parc Mercantour, where they planned to meet in two weeks and do some rock climbing. Bad paid for the maps, then went back into the station to change his lire for francs.

Bad bought his ticket—Classe 2, Nice Ville—and found his platform. It filled gradually with people carrying bags, boxes, and even suitcases full of clinking bottles.

Bad's map of the Roya didn't have the Parc Mercantour in any detail, but he opened it to take a look at the topography. The chart was framed by photographs of the rock paintings on Mont Bego, hikers on sunny summits, and wildlife—*le loup, le boquetin, le fier chamois*. Bad stared at the chamois and thought of the butcher from Dardo, who had taken the chamois he'd found at his door with its neck broken as a gift from the partisans. He thought of the glow on Eve Moskelute's face as she said, "Someone had seen the butcher . . ." "Someone had followed the soldier." "There's always someone," she'd said. The butcher killed the soldier, and *someone* broke a chamois's neck and placed it on the butcher's step, as though in payment. Bad wondered, *Who was "someone"?*

Bad left his pack and ambled over to the edge of the platform. The rails and ties had been sanitized, sprinkled with quicklime. The lime was yellow already and melted over lumps of toilet tissue and other matter that had fallen from the bowels of trains. But Bad saw the lime as snow. He saw the slope of a mountain, a narrow path down which *someone* was walking, the chamois across his shoulders, its hooves gathered in his hands.

Bad took up his pack, went back down into the underpass and up into the station—where he purchased another ticket, to a different destination.

The train was elderly and each carriage had its own engine. Beyond Airole the gradient increased and these engines "put their shoulders to the wheels." Bad was in the smoking section of one carriage. The train was full and he'd been lucky to get a seat. His pack was in a rack at the end of the compartment, beyond a partition of tinted glass. Bad kept his eye on the rack, though he couldn't distinguish his own pack from the mass. The glass partition partly reflected the landscape so that the view in the window beside it seemed to pull away from itself. There was a line at which the image appeared and bled, the landscape apparently generated at the line as if it were pouring through a hairline crack and into the train from a place where all the colors and shapes of the outdoors were stored in a compressed form.

Thirty minutes out of Ventimiglia the air in the smoking compartment was at full saturation. Bad's eyes were stinging. He chose to sacrifice his seat and went out to the noisy compartment beside the carriage doors, caught hold of a pole, and turned to face his pack again. He planted his feet and practiced patience. A few minutes later, through the window, the river widened and became a small aqua lake with one straight shore, where there was a dam. On the shore of the lake was Breil-sur-Roya, a town with red-roofed buildings and extensive rail yards, built on the last flat land before the Col de Tende.

The train pulled into the station and most of the people by the doors got off.

There were police on the platform. They waited for the doors to clear to board and, while they were waiting, a couple of young men slithered out windows on the train's far side and pelted away along a fence whose barbed-wire top angled out over the carriage roofs. Several police went in pursuit. Bad saw a young man flash past the window. He put his face to the glass and watched the young man overshoot a gap where wire had been prized away from the foot of the fence. The man skidded to a stop, spraying gravel, then crammed himself through the gap, scrambled up, and pounded away toward a collection of engine houses, their cement streaked with black mildew. The officer who followed him was fatter and had a gun belt and buttoned epaulets to catch and slow him as he, too, squeezed through the gap. Bad craned his neck to follow the chase out of sight.

"Algerians," said the only person left in the compartment by the door. "Illegal immigrants."

Breil-sur-Roya was the first stop along that line across the border. The train, bound for Cuneo, would leave France again beyond Tende. This section of the rail line was in a little hemorrhage of the richer country into the poorer. Since the formation of the European Union the border itself was no longer patrolled, but Gino had told Bad and his girlfriend that they should always carry their passports when traveling anywhere within a hundred kilometers of it. Bad had forgotten his once, on a day trip between Genoa and San Remo. The police got on the train and asked for Bad's passport, and there was an uncomfortable moment when they were hardening into severity and signaling him up out of his seat. But when Bad told them he was from New Zealand they relinquished him—a time-wasting person of irrelevant and inconsiderable origins.

The train was slow to leave Breil but departed with a group of police on board. They eventually appeared and Bad gave them his passport. They looked at its cover and gave it back.

They stood over the other passenger, a slight, dark-skinned man perched on one of the fold-down seats with his bag tucked back behind his feet. He unzipped his jacket and handed his passport up to them. Bad peeked and saw a maple leaf. The police positively softened; they were deferential, hushed, and meek. They gave the passport back, touched their caps, and departed—didn't even begin to swagger till they had passed through into the smoking carriage.

Bad flipped down the seat opposite the Canadian and sat, his arms folded, eyeing the man. He made a description: male, Indian or Eurasian, early forties, medium build, medium height, graying black hair, dark complexion, brown eyes.

The train turned a corner; sunlight struck down through a crevice in the cloud.

Green eyes. Dog collar. It was the dog collar that had inspired deference in the police, not the passport.

The tourist assessed Daniel point by point, as though he were thinking of buying him. The tourist was big and took up space beyond his skin; he shone with vitality. He leaned forward, rested his elbows on his knees, and pushed up his sleeves, his palms rasping over the thick hair on his forearms. He looked *into* Daniel, and colored, so that Daniel could actually see the pulse pressing in his lower lip. "You're Father Daniel Octave," he said.

"I am," said Daniel.

The tourist sat straight again. He looked immensely satisfied. He told Daniel that, before getting on the train, he'd bought a book about the Roya Valley. For the pretty pictures, of course, and the map with camping sites marked. But he had also wanted a brief history of Dardo. He'd heard a little about that saint, Martine Raimondi, and wanted to read up on her.

The tourist had a casual manner and a pleasant smile.

"Is my name in the guidebook?" Daniel was incredulous.

"No. Your name is on the Web site where I learned the little I know."

The tourist was smooth. He had a kind of practiced plausibility but still gave off smoke, like a buried fire. He said, "The book is in French, and my French is pretty bad."

Daniel asked the tourist what he wanted to know.

"I'd like to know about Martine Raimondi's second miracle. From what I can make out the book talks about a boy, Jacques Palomba, age fourteen?" The tourist waited, then said, "It's very convenient you're here, Father. You don't mind, do you? I've been in Italy for weeks, and a native English speaker is a bit of a treat for me."

Daniel said that he wasn't a native English speaker. He said he'd be brief.

In July 1992 there was an unexpected deluge in the Maritime Alps. It was a civil defense emergency and caused a number of deaths. "Twelve in total. Six in car accidents. And a couple were swept into the Bevera when they went down in the dark to inspect something at the edge of their property. And there were three fatalities in the mountains. Two climbers were knocked off a rock face by a hailstorm. Then there was Jacques Palomba. He was with a school party in a large cave system. He was carried off by a flooded subterranean river and swept deep underground. Every experienced caver from Milan to Marseille went into the caves once the water receded. There were other people trapped—the whole school party and other cavers. Six days later they'd gone over the whole system, rescued forty-five people, and recovered one body. Jacques Palomba was nowhere to be found. His family were from Dardo—though they lived in Monaco. His mother and his sisters and his mother's sisters went to pray at the then unofficial shrine in the Grotte de la Hermit—a cave above the Roya River. They prayed to Martine Raimondi, for her intercession. They prayed for Jacques's safety. Eight days after he was sucked into a flooded hole Jacques Palomba was found, damp and very hungry but intact, by a party of cavers whom his father had paid to continue to search for his body. The boy was scarcely dehydrated and was only two hundred meters from the surface, in an easy passage. He was wrapped in an ancient sleeping bag, one of a number usually kept in a huge cavern called the Salle de la Nef—the Nave. Palomba was very confused but did say later in the hospital that he had been asleep in an 'underground chapel.' There was a lot of traffic through the Salle de la Nef, but Palomba hadn't been seen there. Still, he was asked if he meant the big cavern, and he said no, it was a small, warm cave with lights and paintings, like a church.

"When I interviewed him six months later he was able to tell me that he first regained consciousness, half-drowned and in the dark, and when he'd come to an exhausted end of his bout of panicked calling, he prayed. He prayed to God and to Mary; then he remembered Martine Raimondi's first miracle, and he asked her for her help."

Daniel finished his account as the train, engines making a determined clatter, came out of a tunnel on a narrow stretch of track, a flume of green-and-white rapids in the gorge below them and the cliff looming above, screened by a fence of steel cable, already bulging with trapped rubble. Horizontal cables lay across the uphill view like staves on sheet music, behind them a sparse tune of broken stone, broom flowers, and the rose-brown of blooming smoke bush.

It began to hail. The gorge went black, its rock instantly soaked. The hail cracked on the reinforced glass skylight on the carriage roof, and lightning flickered like a welder's torch.

The tourist said something Daniel couldn't catch above the rattle of the hailstones. Daniel saw him laugh and shake his head. The train went into another tunnel, and even above the echo of its engines on the tunnel's walls Daniel could hear a mushy dripping as melted ice slid down the curve of the carriage roof.

Daniel looked hard at the tourist. If he could hear the water, even judge its composition, why couldn't he hear the tourist? Daniel was *not hearing things*—which was a difficulty he sometimes had, to do with his mother, who was only ever silent when she was sleeping.

Daniel asked the tourist what he'd said.

The train came out of the tunnel and into the hail again. Pebbly ice was piled on the track. The train's wheels hit the hailstones on the rails and began to slip, to revolve without catching. The engines surged, but the train was still; then it began to slide back downhill, and into the tunnel.

"Jesus!" the tourist said. He'd gone white.

The train stopped sliding. It idled, vibrating in the dark.

"Okay. He's waiting," the tourist said, of the driver. He looked into Daniel's eyes. "I said that I was trapped in a cave, Le Lien Vert, by the flood in '92."

"How strange," Daniel said. His ears were full of all the ambient sounds. He could hear the steel slats of the engine's vents tinkle as the engine shook them—a high, glassy tinkling above the bass cacophony of the engine and its echo. But the tourist's voice was muddy, his words scarcely distinguishable. Daniel frowned and tried to follow what was said.

"There was someone with me for a time," the tourist said. "I lost her. She was the sister of a woman named Eve Moskelute, whom you might know. The widow of the artist Ares."

"We haven't met, but I know who she is," Daniel said. "But I don't know about her sister. . . ." He felt the blood leaving his head. This conversation was too strange, too much in accord with Daniel's own, private, thoughts.

"That's not all," the tourist said. "Four days ago my friend Gino and I helped recover a body from a sea cave in Riomaggiore. The body of a woman. A friend of Eve Moskelute. You knew her, too."

Daniel said, *"Who sent you?"*

"To Riomaggiore?" the tourist said, then, "I was just there. But do you mean who sent me to you? People don't get sent, Father. I should know." The tourist was shaking his head; the fluorescent lights behind their greenish plastic were cold on his glossy curls. "I should know," he said again. He was a healthy young man, but for a moment his face, long and pale with feeling, looked like that of a corpse.

The train moved; it began to creep out of the tunnel. The hail had stopped and water was gushing down narrow flues in the cliff face. The wheels gripped and the train picked up speed.

"Something funny's going on," the tourist said.

Daniel shook his head.

"They had the same hair—Martine Dardo and Ms. Moskelute's sister. That sounds silly, I know, but you've presumably noticed Ms. Dardo's hair. That isn't a style people choose; it's not what hairdressers *do*. Even with a dark dye job and blond roots there's a clear demarcation in the colors. . . ."

"You're being absurd," said Daniel.

"Look," said the tourist, and Daniel leaned in to listen to more testimony but got something else instead.

The tourist said that when he was a kid he was a real ratbag, always making his dad go apeshit. So Pops—his mother's father—who had the family farm, and money, sent him to boarding school. He hated it and ran away all the time. The prefects used to hunt him down, beat him up, and haul him back, but he kept doing it. Eventually one of them said something to him, something that made sense. The school wasn't the world, the prefect said, and he should be patient and wait to get out and in the meantime make something of the opportunities it offered him. The school wasn't the world, but it was *like* the world in that its rules weren't going to just go away. "He said, 'Where were you running to anyway? What else is there?' Which could just about be the motto of my life." The young man frowned, thinking.

"My point is this," he said. "I'm not religious or superstitious. I walked into all this with the lowest possible expectation of anything significant happening here. I mean . . . huge things have happened to me, but they didn't have any *significance*. But now I know something funny is going on."

Daniel watched the tourist. He saw the young man's throat moving hard as he swallowed. Daniel thought of his friend in Montreal, who had once accused him of only being able to show affection to the elderly. Father Neske had taunted Daniel, accused him of gerontophilia, and then said, "But I'm putting your lacks in a far too loving light. If it was gerontophilia, at least it would be some kind of erotic instinct, but you don't feel anything; you don't even feel—as I did when I was a young priest—afraid of beautiful young people. No, you're unmoved and fastidious and . . . and I pray for you, Daniel."

Daniel gave his hand to the tourist, who took it. Daniel asked him for his name.

"Bad," the tourist said, then laughed. "My girlfriend once pointed out that I introduce myself to women by my given name, Brian, and to men by my nickname. Brian 'Bad' Phelan." The tourist pumped Daniel's hand. "But, Father, what do you think? Tell me—isn't something *funny* going on?"

Daniel said that it did look that way, but he thought that it lacked conclusive evidence—not evidence that would prove that things really were "funny" but evidence that would finally let Bad conclude that these strange events made sense of a *statistically unusual* but otherwise normal sort. Then Daniel told Bad a story.

A few years earlier, Daniel had been fortunate to be in Paris and to have a few hours free. He had taken a walk to Notre Dame, passing through the Marais, where he happened to see an albino, remarkable in itself, but what was even more remarkable was that in the next street he saw another. "A coincidence, I thought. Then, a few minutes later, I saw a *third* albino. This shook me. Three albinos in one day, in one hour! It felt like a sign, something God was showing me. I walked on wondering what it all meant when—lo!—another albino. *Oh*, I thought, coming down to earth. *It's a conference.* So you see, at this moment you're sure that you're facing a conspiracy, you're seeing signs, but it'll turn out to be a conference."

Bad Phelan sat blinking at Daniel. Then he asked, "Was it?"

"Actually, I don't know. I didn't find out."

"So perhaps it *was* a sign," Bad said. "Only God overplayed His hand." Bad sat smirking for a moment, then blushed and said, "Sorry, Father."

Daniel was amused and showing a friendly face but was thinking of Thomas à Kempis: *"Be rarely with young people and strangers."* He didn't say anything to encourage the young man to talk more, and they sat in silence for the rest of the journey. He took refuge from intimacy in Thomas à Kempis. But Daniel knew that his detachment was less a product of his reverence for the life of the mind or of the novitiate's process of emotional sterilization than of his childhood and its strange difficulties.

Daniel's grandmother had run a boardinghouse in old Montreal—which was, in the mid-sixties, a grimy ill-lit area nibbled by demolition, a moth-eaten map of historical ruins and rubble-filled lots, their redevelopment stopped by timely preservation orders. In 1965, when Daniel was six, the restoration hadn't yet begun. His grandmother was charging what she could for her rooms, but the wharves were already being slowly depopulated by the fast turnaround times on the new container ships. Half the boardinghouse was empty and succumbing to the diseases of old age, its pressed tin ceilings covered in sores and weeping rusty water, its wallpaper coming away in air-filled blisters. Daniel's grandmother explained to Daniel why he couldn't have *one of those*—whatever it was he fancied, a packet of balloons or a nodding dog or a new bookbag: "We're living hand to mouth." But she was always pulling his hands down from his mouth, saying, "You don't want to be like your mother."

Grandma looked after Daniel and his mother. Daniel's mother talked all the time, so he wasn't good at listening. Grandma was always having to lead him to the basin to wash his hands. "Didn't you hear me?" she'd say. Daniel did try, but he had trouble hearing adult voices, and before he went to school, when Grandma was busy and the house was well populated, he was confined to the top floor with his mother. Then sentences with "you" or "I" in them would begin to sound odd and striking to him. It was a strangeness he was able to recognize as a strangeness in himself, even as a small child. His mother had her ways, but they didn't seem to work for him. Grandma's ways worked, and when he went to school he was shy but compliant, because it was all right, because Grandma made his lunch and when he reported to her to receive it she would give him "a lick and looking over" before he went out the door. Daniel was good at school and from the start always did more than he needed, forged forward through textbooks and assigned reading and revised his spelling. After school he'd settle with his homework in his grandmother's big back kitchen. Grandma didn't want him bothering the lodgers. She wanted him where she could see him. She'd take his hands off his face or out of his hair if he started to scratch. She threatened him with his mother—who was in the attic at that moment, in her "studio," making lampshades from papier-mâché. She'd made five already, but for each Daniel and his grandmother had endured three days of talk on technique. Daniel's mother's imagination was ambitious and planning and populated by practical solutions to perceived problems. But Grandma had learned long ago, and Daniel was to learn, that whether you listened or not, advised or not, it was with the same result—that is, no result. Daniel's mother would simply rather tell people what she planned to do than do it. She wanted to be admired. She needed a go-ahead like others needed air, a whole hermetic green-lit environment, in which she was told, "Yes, do it," in which she had endless encouragement, and in which she would never advance. While Daniel did his homework and more, his mother planned and pottered and pulled out her eyelashes and ate them.

"You don't want to be like your mother," Grandma said. "I'm sure she has a ball of hair inside her."

But Mother didn't eat the *whole* hair, said Daniel, only bit off its root. He picked up the scallions and showed his grandmother how his mother bit off the bulb of each hair she pulled. And she was systematic, would never denude her browbone and eyelids at the same time. It was as if she were rotating crops.

Then Grandma would give him a sharp look and say,

"You're very clever, Daniel, but too cold. You shouldn't *examine* her like that. You must try not to mind her . . . because she's afflicted."

Daniel did try. It was his first exercise in "Custody of the Senses." He put his mother out of his mind—he was able to tune out her loud, toneless, repetitive talk, unless he was trying to read. He gave up reading. He sat idle. Or, sometimes during the day, he'd stand on a chair on the table in their sitting room and take out the lightbulb, give it a sharp shake till the filament broke, then replace it. When evening came and the light wouldn't work he could go to bed early. He'd pull the curtains around his bunk and listen to his mother wind down in his absence—silence alone wasn't enough.

They all went to church. Daniel's grandma was religious—she enjoyed her faith. Mother went to church, too, and Grandma and Daniel would try their best to impose stillness on her. She could stay still if she had to, if she could be made to recognize the necessity as a necessity and not a meaningless imposition. The old woman and child would sit, absolutely still and straight-backed, facing the front and would *will* her into silence. It would work, for most of the service, and when Grandma was still alive his mother wouldn't do things like get up out of the pew to get more comfortable by pulling her perishing underpants out of her crack. You didn't want her stirring herself like that. She claimed to have "no sense of smell," certainly couldn't be made to see the virtue of a regular wash. In fact, Daniel's mother couldn't be made to see the virtue of anything. What others did, and expected her to do, was all tyranny and imposition.

Daniel had confided all this, finally, to the old man, his only real friend, a month after his ordination, when he had visited the seminary at Saint Paul before taking up his position teaching at Loyola. Father Neske was then nominally employed minding and mending the seminary's sports equipment and skimming its pool. Father Neske had taught history at Daniel's high school, but he'd had a breakdown and had retired from teaching. He was Daniel's inspiration, and it was his terminal initials, S.J., that first made Daniel hanker to join that family, that brotherhood. The old man was charming, sardonic, at ease. Daniel chose him as a model, and after his twelve years' training it was to Father Neske that Daniel came to check himself, to check his appearance. The old man was a mirror—Daniel felt—in which he might finally admire himself.

Daniel talked to Father Neske. He took off his jacket and helped Neske move the vaulting horse and parallel bars. He told the old man about the boardinghouse and the back pew of Notre Dame de Bon Secours. He explained what had *formed* him. He said that Father Neske mustn't imagine that they'd had no friends. Grandma had friends. She cultivated the people who had shown her daughter kindness, her daughter's former schoolmates, old neighbors, other "artists." These were the people who would drop in and swallow a small dose of Daniel's mother's choking output of talk. They came and sat, eyes glazed, over Grandma's cakes and tea while Daniel's mother told them what she was up to, up to despite the hindrance of superficial people and silly social institutions. "Most people think . . ." she'd begin; then, twenty minutes later, "It's true, isn't it?" she'd conclude, without any modification in address between different listeners, sometimes even producing exactly the same speech, the same words, in the same word order. When her program changed it was on its own timetable. Those who came learned not to interrupt. They were kind and quiet; they helped Grandma wash up (Daniel's mother never did, never thought to, never saw what others did for her, and, ever consistent, never missed it when it wasn't done). The visitors bore it; they put in an hour or two for the sake of some life or charm or possibility they'd seen once in Daniel's mother. Or, perhaps, because of erroneous beliefs they had, about giftedness and eccentricity, genius and egocentricity.

They *kept faith;* they said to Daniel's grandma, "Someday she'll surprise you. There's so much she can do." As if Daniel's grandmother hadn't already been greatly surprised to see her funny, gnomic, inventive child become diffuse, defensive, slovenly.

Daniel's mother moved to the beat of a different drum, the friends said, in congratulation and in consolation. And— when Daniel's grandmother died—the same friends were considerate of Daniel's mother's rights, her independence. They didn't interfere. They stopped visiting—wouldn't come to clean up after her or to have their advice go unheard, their concern met by hostility. They told themselves that Daniel was decently fed and she never hit him, that he didn't need to be rescued from a parent who was, after all, only unconventional.

"They were good liberals," Daniel said to Father Neske's turned back as the old man plied a wide bristle broom across the scuffed gymnasium floor. "Child Welfare wasn't to be trusted; they were an extreme measure—something like 'armed force'—only for *abusive* parents, not loving, eccentric, incompetent ones."

"Yes, I see," Father Neske said.

Daniel's grandmother died when he was eight. His mother thought that there were things the doctors could have done and hadn't. She went to the library and took out books on her mother's condition. She made notes and formulated arguments. She rehearsed her arguments on Daniel. She made photocopies of pages from pharmacology books; she interloaned books from other libraries; she requested her mother's medical records under civil liberties laws. She told everyone she saw about her research. She found patient advocacy groups and subscribed to their newsletters and carried them with her on these visits—or into Daniel's room to show him what she'd found. The newsletters had passages in emphatic italics. They capitalized "Western Medicine" just as Restoration writers had capitalized "Wickedness" and "Folly." Daniel's mother would underline the italics, would underscore certain words once, twice, or even three times.

Grandma's friends stopped coming—her best friend after an evening when she came and listened to Daniel's mother's summary of her research, a cyclone of indignation and resentment. The room got dark and no tea was offered. Daniel sat beside his grandmother's friend. He wanted to support her, to help her through this. After an hour or so of unheard interjections, questions, soothing noises, the friend began to cry. She didn't hide her tears but fished in her sleeve for a handkerchief and applied it to her eyes, blew her nose. Daniel's mother went on, imperturbable. She didn't see the tears—wasn't prepared for them. Her mother's friend wasn't another person with feelings, grieving, too, but only the blur of a face in the dark kitchen turned her way.

Daniel put his hand into the hand of his grandmother's friend. She held him hard, squeezed his hand to show she knew he was there. Her touch—her cold, clammy hand and swollen knuckles—was to Daniel a sensation of magnificence, like a first sight of a mountain range or sunlit sea. It filled him up, inflated a space inside him to its full size. But she let go and went home and didn't come again, and nothing else ever appeared to fill the space that the old woman had made with her touch and her tears. In time a shell formed around that space, and it became something like one of those glass buoys found in antique shops. It was hard and empty, but it kept Daniel afloat.

When Daniel's grandmother died, Daniel's mother turned the lodgers away. Mother and son lived in the whole house. Over the years the house filled with things Daniel's mother might need for her artwork. Daniel would come home from school into darkness and dust, flammable staleness. He'd edge down the hallways sidelong, his back to the stacked newspapers. In the kitchen his mother would recite the best bits from the day's paper. She might have shopped but not put the shopping away. Daniel would try to remember what he should do. Sometimes his mother would cook; sometimes he would. He forgot that dishes had to be done. The washing machine stopped working. Daniel's mother washed his clothes by hand, but it was hard work and Daniel had to make his clean clothes last. His whites went gray or yellow. Kids at school moved their desks away from his. Daniel couldn't smell himself; he went about in a capsule of his home: a musty, musky smell of sweat and piss and rancid food. The filth only became a problem when it moved, like the fat lice crowning his forehead at the end of their life cycle and falling out of his hair. His mother wept over the medicated shampoo. She wept over the Roach Motels, their poisonous litter—till they became part of her everyday, filled to capacity, no longer effective, brittle with age. She didn't throw them away but simply bought more. She bought warfarin for the rats but was distressed by it. She saw the poison as a cloud in the house, an intelligent powder that would smuggle itself into their food. She washed her hands so often her skin cracked, and she locked Daniel in his room. The rats were supposed to run outside to die, driven by their thirst. But the house was sodden and there was always laundry left soaking for days in a soup of fermented soap, so the rats stayed indoors. They plunged in agony through the walls. One managed to run into the circuit behind an outlet and died there, died and cooked. Daniel and his mother went about for weeks with rags filled with powdered herbs pressed to their noses. The lights went, one by one, their Bakelite collars cracked and unable to hold the bulbs anymore. Daniel made his way about in the dark, his hand running across the fibrous, fraying walls of piled newspaper.

Daniel had no peace at home, so didn't mind that in the playground he was left to his own devices. He had a library card and borrowed as much as he was able to, meekly accepting the limits imposed. He read on the bus, using his bus pass as a bookmark. No one much bothered him. He read when his teeth kept him awake at night. He read under the desk in class. The teachers let him read, because he wasn't disrupting the class and his grades were good. He was a puzzle to them but no trouble, the egg-stained boy by himself at the back of the room, his head and jaw wrapped in a double thickness of dirty scarf, armored in his sour miasma. For Daniel his smell was silence, a barrier of bad air. Daniel's eyes moved; he traveled the page. His mother had gone to the same school seventeen years before. And the community remembered her. No one asked the questions they should have. ("Why do you tear up your bread into tiny pieces? Why do you chip at your apple like a rodent, instead of chewing it?") They turned away, blinded by disorder—the *shame* of it—and did nothing.

Daniel's mother didn't stop talking. But one Saturday, when the library had closed, Daniel found a quiet, warm place near his home. A dark corner. He found the back pew of Notre Dame de Bon Secours. He would read there, on Saturdays and after school, till he got hungry; then he'd go home to see what he could find. Daniel came and went at Notre Dame de Bon Secours. No one spoke to him or asked him what his business was. Daniel might—he sometimes thought—have gone to the church throughout the winter and never been noticed and his whole life would have taken another turn—if it hadn't been for the conjunctivitis.

For weeks Daniel's mother practiced her own remedies. She boiled water on the gas range to help bathe Daniel's eyes open. Every morning he woke to find that overnight his eyes had been mortared shut with yellow crusts of what his mother called "sleepy dirt." She tried the remedies she remembered her mother using—two eggcups full of Epsom salts dissolved in warm water and held in his eye sockets. Daniel opened his eyes each morning and got himself off to school. But his teacher eventually sent him to the school nurse, who gave him a talk about hygiene and germs transferred from hands to nose to eyes. She wrote a note to his mother. At home his mother railed against the note and spent much of the night writing her own note in reply. She gave it to Daniel in the morning, a fat roll of pages fastened with a length of un-bleached string, ends feathered and its knot covered by a blob of wax. She was showing off. Daniel didn't want to deliver this missive, so for the first time he skipped school. He went to church and sat in his pew trying to read, trying to see the page through the cables of mucus strung between his upper and lower eyelashes.

He sat through the celebration of mass. Afterward, he listened to the door of the confessional creak open and shut a number of times, with a hushed space between each movement. The church emptied; then one of the priests came to ask Daniel what he was doing there during school hours.

Daniel said the nurse had given him a note for his mother.

"And your mother is out?" the priest said.

Daniel nodded.

"That's a very bad case of conjunctivitis."

"I can hardly see," said Daniel.

The priest was sniffing his knuckles. Daniel had noticed how many people had that habit. They began to talk to him, then covered their mouths and stuffed their knuckles into their nostrils. The priest said, "The note from your nurse tells your mother to take you to a doctor, I presume?"

"Yes. It's contagious. But my mother says the school once sent me home with spots they said were measles when I'd had the measles and it was just a virus."

"Is this what you *anticipate* your mother saying or what she has said?"

"She said it. I don't want her to get into another argument with my school."

The priest asked Daniel what his name was. Then, "*Will* your mother take you to a doctor?"

Daniel said that his mother didn't trust doctors because the doctors at St. Vincent's killed Grandma by what they omitted to do.

The priest told him to please get out of that corner. He took Daniel by his dirty hand and went and made his excuses to the older priest. Then he walked Daniel to the bus stop and went with him to his school. As they rode, the priest asked Daniel questions—for instance, was he a Catholic?

Yes, Daniel said, he'd been baptized at St. Surplice's. When Grandma was alive they would get on a tram to go across town to St. Surplice's. They went all that way because, before Daniel was born, Grandma had had an argument with a priest at Notre Dame de Bon Secours. An argument about Daniel. About Daniel's father, who was an Indian grocer with a family of five who had given Daniel's mother an after-school job.

The priest looked at Daniel closely. He said, "Ah, yes." Then he asked Daniel who'd told him this story.

"My mother. She isn't a prude." (Daniel's mother thought most other woman were prudes. She'd say, "They're always going, 'Shh, shh,' at me about sexual matters. What's the good of that, eh? How are young people supposed to learn what's what?")

"Evidently not," the priest said.

At Daniel's school the priest asked the school secretary if he could speak to the principal. They got in in under five minutes, which impressed Daniel—the few times he'd been sent there he'd invariably kicked his heels for twenty minutes before being called in and told that he had some problem that needed to be "addressed immediately."

The priest explained to the principal that Daniel often sat in his church for an hour or two after school. "He's very good. And we're hardly packed to capacity. Today, however, I looked out after the midday mass to find him in his after-school spot. He has a problem with his eyes, certainly contagious, but could you not *check* that his mother is at home before sending him home?"

The principal sent for the nurse. She explained that she'd sent Daniel home *yesterday* with a note for his mother. Furthermore, he'd stayed in the sickroom and had gone home *at the usual time.*

They all looked at Daniel.

The principal looked at Daniel's file. "His mother doesn't have a phone."

"Did you give your mother my note, Daniel?" the nurse asked.

Daniel nodded. He was wondering how long this interview would take if he was quiet and compliant. How long before these adults lost interest in him?

"Have you been to the doctor?"

Daniel lied. He nodded his head. He knew he could talk his mother into taking him. What had upset her was the nurse's recommendation that she wash all the towels and bedding.

The nurse folded her arms. She asked, "What did the doctor give you for it?"

"Medicine."

"What sort of medicine?"

"It has a long name."

The nurse, principal, and priest exchanged looks. Then the nurse pressed on. "But how is it administered?"

Daniel didn't panic—he pondered—then his head cleared and he felt happy. "Liberally," he said. "It's sprinkled, liberally."

The priest coughed—or laughed. Then he asked Daniel to please go and wait outside.

Daniel went out, took a seat, closed his eyes, and swung his legs. The school secretary went into the principal's office. She came out and made murmuring phone calls. The nurse came out and asked Daniel to go with her. She took him to the nearest medical center and he saw a doctor. The doctor gave him medicine. Drops! Drops for his eyes and for his sinuses, ointment for the cracks between his toes, and painkilling pills for the trouble with his teeth, but he'd have to see a dentist.

Daniel was taken back to the church, where he helped the priest remove a litter of old notices from a notice board.

"What was his name?" Father Neske asked.

"Father Gaston Groux—a Surplician." Daniel told the old man that after that day the agents of change entered his life but didn't invade or overthrow it. Welfare was accustomed to protecting children from parents who were child beaters or substance abusers. The school informed them that Daniel was not immediately at risk—only needed looking into. His personal hygiene was bad but his grades good. He was dirty, infested, and his teeth were full of cavities, but his bones were straight and he was well nourished.

The people sent to investigate Daniel's home did so sensitively. Daniel's mother was defensive but showed them around. She explained all their odd arrangements. They had, for instance, abandoned the bathrooms on the top and ground floors when the toilet cisterns came to the ends of their natural lives. Daniel's mother would say to Daniel, "We're now using the second-floor bathroom," and she'd close the door on the mess. They were nursing their last toilet, which no longer took paper, she explained, but was flushed twice a day with a bucket.

"My mother was so blind to what others saw that she didn't even attempt to conceal matters. So . . . though we weren't flushing the toilet paper, we did use it. When Welfare came there was weeks' worth of balled soiled toilet paper beside the pan, in an overflowing wastepaper basket. My mother wasn't conscious of the impression this made. I was there— Father Groux had tried to tempt me away to the movies, but I stuck with my mother. I followed her and the Welfare people

about, adding my excuses to her explanations. I hadn't thought
about the toilet paper, or the potato peelings adhered to the
kitchen floor by their own starch—but I watched those people's faces. I read in their expressions the real meaning of the
arrangements of my home. My mother seemed unable to interpret their stares, silences, covered mouths. She just went on
explaining all our catastrophes, articulate and knowing, but
helpless about it all. I think it was the spectacle of my bedroom
that finally decided them on what they would do about me—
what they *did* do, which wasn't to pluck me up out of the dingy,
dirty bedlam of my mother's house, but to send in help—
health inspectors to condemn and seal parts of the house, City
Council cleaners to remove the litter from others, and, on a
grant from Welfare, a new washer and dryer."

"What was in your bedroom?"

"Jungles, forested chasms, farmland, meadows with earth-
works, rivers, rocky coasts. Castles and cathedrals and villages.
Over a number of years my mother had created landscapes for
my plastic animals and soldiers. She'd hung whole dressed,
painted papier-mâché cliffs and buttes from shelf brackets on
my walls. She'd covered tabletops, and had made a rag rug
with grassland, and forests, and scrub cover. My bedroom was
dusty, and littered with crumbs and crockery, but it was also a
dream room, and lovingly done.

"Between them, Child Welfare, the Department of Health,
and Catholic Social Services sorted us out. I saw what I had to
do, and every Saturday morning I'd set to and clean the rooms
we used, whether or not the dirt was visible to me. My mother
borrowed do-it-yourself books from the library and built us a
couple of cabinets and put up hooks on which to hang things.
For a time she followed the diagrams; then she began to plan
innovations on paper and the building stopped. My mother
chose to see only a few of the new requirements of our lives as
unreasonable and representative of the tyranny of convention.
She spent some time campaigning to change a bylaw about

how many doors must be between toilet and kitchen. Then she
went back to her papier-mâché, and Father Groux drove her
and her creations around the craft outlets. And, over that first
summer, he worked on her, trying to persuade her to have me
change schools. She'd gone to my state school and Father
Groux's argument was that, remembering her as 'the girl with
odd habits'—he was very discreet—the school had viewed my
difficulties as 'oddities,' too. He was quite right—my school
had remembered my mother and condemned me. Grandma
had sent my mother in clean clothes, but she'd sat pulling her
hair and picking her nose. Like me my mother was academi-
cally gifted, but my school knew that her gifts had come to
nothing. She was a solo parent, a propertied derelict, a paranoid shut-in. Despite my grades, they had no great hopes of
me. Groux didn't need to elaborate, only convinced my mother
to feel that I'd been shortchanged as she'd been slighted. The
following year she—and Father Groux—sent me to the nearest
parochial school."

Daniel held the top of the paper rubbish sack closed while
Father Neske stapled it. The old man said, "You see . . . I've
become a lay brother rather than a scholar father." It was raining, and Daniel could see two of the seminary's real lay brothers, shadows beyond the condensation-covered glass of the
greenhouse in a garden where black earth was beginning to
reappear from under a slushy crust of snow. Father Neske was
not a lay brother; he was a highly educated teacher who had
had a breakdown, whose name appeared in the *Society of Jesus
Catalog*—a publication that kept track of North American Jesuits—followed by the phrase: "Praying for the Order." "Praying for the Order" was a resigned and respectful code for
"defeated, disgraced, depressed, ill, or mad."

Daniel and the old man each carried a bag to the plywood
box near the seminary gate. They unbolted the box and put
the bags inside. Father Neske asked Daniel if he'd kept in

touch with Father Groux. He didn't remember meeting a Father Groux at Daniel's ordination.

"Gaston Groux went to work in a mission in El Salvador. He was murdered in 1982. Murdered or martyred—it's still being looked into. His family and the Church are at loggerheads. His family want it to be murder because they would like to bring a certain El Salvadoran officer to justice." Daniel mused. He said he thought that it was what had happened to Gaston Groux that had sparked his interest in the modern martyrs.

"Interest?" The old man was sharp. "Was that all your response to the death of this man? A man who would patiently ferry about the loud, redolent woman and her papier-mâché lampshades?"

"Masks," said Daniel. "She'd moved on to masks."

"*She* was at your ordination."

"Yes. That was her. No eyebrows."

"She was on crutches, as I recall."

"Yes. Nerve damage. Complications of diabetes. She's in a retirement village. She clung to Grandmother's house despite mounting pressure as the old town was restored. The council couldn't get her out. Grandma's liberal friends rallied enough to help her pay for the mandatory repairs so that it wouldn't be completely condemned. They could make sense of *that* scenario—defending the underdog from civic cupidity. The city paid to have the building's exterior done, its stone cleaned and patched, so that it at least blended in with all the galleries and cafés. When she found she couldn't manage the stairs anymore she finally let it go. It was auctioned off. It had to be gutted inside, but even so it fetched enough to keep my mother in gracious, orderly old age for longer than she's likely to last. And if there's anything left over, and if Gaston Groux's family is still chasing their cause through the courts, I'll give it to them."

Father Neske smiled. "Daniel, you're a delight to me."

They were walking back toward the gymnasium, but Father Neske stopped. He said he'd run out of chores. So they remained standing on the asphalt in the rain, where they could be alone, Father Neske squeezing Daniel's arm—the nearest he'd ever come to bestowing a blessing.

On the June evening in Dardo, when it had stopped raining, Daniel went for a walk. He followed the road along Dardo's ridge and came onto the path up to the cemetery. The pathside foliage was sodden and drooping, and the legs of Daniel's trousers grew wet as he swiped by. The morello cherry at the gate to the cemetery was in fruit, cherries ripe and black in the dusk. Daniel picked some wet fruit; their skins squeaked as they came together in his hand. He put one in his mouth, cracked its taut, cold skin. A spurt of juice broke through the seal of his lips and he was forced to stoop to spare his suit from the drips. When he looked up he found that he was not alone, that someone was climbing the hill—a man with ghostly hair and skin. A fifth albino, Daniel thought. Daniel said good evening. He said it to throw a line over the man, to slow him for a moment so that Daniel could get a better look at him—and see if he *was*, really.

The man stopped and peered at Daniel. His eyes were streaming—were they irritated? Or was he weeping? He said, "Good evening, Father." His wet eyes were pale, the pupils evident in them, even in the failing light. The man took Daniel in, top to toe, then apologized for something. He said he was sorry about the body in the tomb. Giesen's body in Raimondi's tomb.

"You're sorry?" Daniel said. Was this sympathy—long delayed and exaggerated—or a claim of responsibility?

"Yes. You didn't like the surprise."

Though the man didn't have an American accent, Daniel

ventured to ask him if he was, by any chance, the person who had answered Martine Dardo's phone. The person who'd said he hoped Daniel liked surprises.

"Someone answered Martine's mobile?" the man asked.

"No. He was in her house. An American," Daniel said.

The man was still for a beat; then he said, "Oh." He walked on past Daniel, ending their conversation.

Daniel dropped the remaining cherry, followed it with his eyes as it tumbled down the path. Then he raised his head to call out after the man.

The mule track was deserted.

Chapter 9

THE UNDERGROUND
PILGRIMAGE

ad stood at the thin end of a sunny wedge of piazza that terminated in the facade of St. Barthelemy's. The church's doors were wide, its steps crowded. The people were dressed in warm clothes—scarves, polar fleeces, down jackets. Many were kneeling with these top garments puddled around their legs. The sun was high, and of the church and its interior all that was visible was candle flames, points of faint orange, a sparse foliage of light. Most of the worshipers spilling out of the church and into the piazza had already collected hard hats from the nested stacks of Small, Medium, and Large. These hard hats did not have headlamps.

Bad was at the back of the crowd with those who weren't celebrating mass and taking communion. His was a small group, comprised of several solemn and self-conscious German tourists, an American couple who were checking the lights on their video camera and explaining to Bad that they were there because they thought Martine Raimondi was wonderful, but he was Jewish and she was a Methodist. Behind Bad were a municipal engineer and two men in the uniforms of park rangers.

Near the church door, at the edge of the crowd, a collection of camp stools had been set up. These were occupied by old men and their younger minders. Several of the old men had lapel badges—Italian Communist Party insignia and French military honors. By St. Barthelemy's doors were two more local officials. These two were making a head count.

At some sign from within the church the crowd rose to its feet and began to move, very slowly, up the steps. The head counters joined their coworkers, the engineer and parks people. One said that the count was a hundred and fifteen up on last year and if the weather had been better the day before there would have been more. The pilgrimage was becoming a *Feste de Nice*, one official remarked. The engineer expressed worries about the quality of the air in the crypt—the caves were well ventilated, their jumping-off point less so. He'd already been into the caves earlier that morning, he said, to do a final check on the sound system and video monitors. One of the parks people asked whether there were cavers already on the route of the pilgrims. The previous year the cavers were waiting for the pilgrims in the cavern called the Salle de Salvati. The cavers were spectators, like some in today's crowd— he glared at the couple with the camera—but they'd been obstructive, territorial. The bishop wasn't happy.

The old people were assisted up off their folding chairs. A priest appeared on the church steps and summoned them, gesturing to the crowd to let them pass.

"The surviving partisans of the commune of Dardo," said the American, confidingly, to his video recorder. "The Blessed Martine's contemporaries." The Americans insinuated themselves into the space behind the partisans and rode their wake into the church. Bad and the Germans followed.

In the church the aisle was full but the pews empty.

Everyone was on the move. At the rail people were kneeling in rows three deep while the bishop and his helpers gave communion. Each celebrant supped and sipped, then got up, genuflected, and joined a line disappearing through a doorway to the right of the altar—the door to the crypt.

The surviving partisans and their hangers-on were conducted down the right aisle. They passed a series of paintings of scenes from Martine Raimondi's life—recent works and, to Bad's eye, more in the style of seventies fantasy book covers than religious art. The nun appeared with thrusting breasts and a tumorous light growing out of her forehead. Bad was disappointed by the paintings but not surprised. He and his girlfriend Gabrielle had found several similar in Padua, at the shrine of Saint Anthony, including a late-twentieth-century Last Judgment with a bodybuilder Christ posed against the fires of explosions, like the hero of an action movie.

The elderly nonbelievers and video-making non-Catholics were conducted through the door that led down into the crypt. They went in ahead of the last big group of communicants. Bad went with them. He offered an old man his arm. They filed down the stairs, two turns, into white-wine-colored candlelight and the murmur of orderly assembly. The crowd in the crypt had formed a single-file crocodile that wound back and forth in the aisles between tombs. A park ranger was directing the crocodile and urging everyone to put on their helmets. He looked like a flight attendant making the safety demonstration.

Father Octave was at the end of the crypt, by the door that opened onto the cave system, a door twice as wide as it was high. Father Octave was, Bad thought, dressed with no thought for the filth and variable temperatures in caves. Though, Bad recalled, Eve Moskelute had said that Martine Raimondi's way was never close, that there were no climbs or small crawl spaces—only a steady, serpentine, uphill route. Daniel Octave looked the part of priest *and* stage manager; he was wearing a suit, black and well pressed, a white helmet, and a headset with a tiny black microphone positioned a centimeter from his lips. For a brief moment Bad held up the crocodile's progress to help the old man beside him adjust the strap of his helmet. Bad said the helmet would fit better if the old man removed his cap. His advice was ignored. The man's minder thanked Bad, and the old man pointed at Bad's helmet and said something in a voice ruined by cigarette smoke. His minder translated, "Alberto says he's envious of your headlamp."

As Bad came to the low door Daniel Octave smiled at him, then gave an even warmer smile, and his hand, to the old man. "Alberto," he said, and handed the old man through the low door to the crop-haired, casually dressed religious sister waiting on the other side of it. Bad paused to tell Daniel Octave that he had found a dry place to spend the night but had been diddled out of 25,000 lire by the man at the hotel desk just for the storage of his pack.

Father Octave answered him by a touch on the top of his helmet that seemed to both bless Bad and hurry him along through the doorway—minding his head—into the caves.

Bad had seen his own country's famous tourist caves. In Ngarua Caverns and Waitomo some thought had been given to the light scheme. Both were beautiful, ancient, limestone composition caves, passages with stone-toothed valves and splendid chambers, their lighting designed to show off their architecture. Martine Raimondi's pilgrims' route was lit for safety, not dramatic effect. It didn't have big, beautiful caverns or arresting sights. Electrical cables had been bolted to the rock at the top of the passage, and the passage was lit from above. Earlier pilgrims hadn't been discouraged from touching the walls, so that the naturally gooseflesed translucent stone coating the passage had, at hand-height, been smoothed into a kind of dirty toffee texture. In several places, where the passage was wide enough for groups to gather, there were speakers and video monitors suspended from the cables. The pilgrims' passage was not a mysterious place. Bad—to whom caves were so familiar that he sometimes felt a spurious safety on entering and sinking himself into them—was sorry for the pilgrims. The passage should either inspire or frighten them but had been too processed to perform either task.

Bad had been on solitary trips through caves of all kinds: spacious and splendid caves; tight pull-through caves; quiet, untouched caves where his careless feet might first mar the thousand-year falls of calcite snow; caves that glistened or were loud with water. These caves were ideal places for quiet contemplation of self and the limits of self. They were not distracting. The scenery was striking but seldom mobile or changeable, and they had no long perspectives or voyeurs' views, no distant figures or dust trails on invisible roads—no distracting human narratives. To Bad, the Pilgrims' Way wasn't a cave *proper.* It was nasty—an invasion of an interior space for ulterior reasons. Bad was reminded of medical im- aging technology, a light and camera on a probe, probing—a colonoscopy.

But—Bad conceded—perhaps for people who never went into caves this tramp through a stone passage stinking of car- bon dioxide and electricity was enough of a unique sensory ex- perience to strike them as mystical.

The pilgrims were asked, in French, over the sound sys- tem—its intimate, disembodied voice—to stand to one side of the passage to let the bishop's party go by. Bad settled the old man in a hollow in the wall and inclined back himself, switched off his lamp when he saw how it flashed white in the squinting eyes of the bishop—who was the only person in the cave not wearing a helmet. The bishop went by in his white lace surplice, his gold vestments and mitre. He was followed by several of the sisters and priests, including Daniel Octave. In passing, Father Octave again touched Alberto's hands.

The pilgrims waited for another few minutes and then shuffled on, until the ranger who seemed to be assigned to the group of old people told them to stop in a slightly larger cavern where there were canvas-covered fiberglass camp chairs set up. The old people sat, and the cavern filled, the crowd facing a video monitor that showed *another* crowded cavern. The old man, Alberto, looked up at Bad and said something, then swung his head toward his minder, waiting for a translation. The minder asked Bad if he had been on the pilgrimage before. Bad said no, this was his first time. Bad looked at the old man as he rasped at him, and tried to make sense of Alberto's Italian—then realized that it wasn't Italian, exactly, but was some kind of dialect. The minder translated. Alberto wanted Bad to know that what they were looking at, on the television, was *the place where they all stopped.* That bald man they could see at the top left of the screen was *there*—was there *then*, 1944. Soon the lights would be switched off. Alberto hoped that the young people with the camera would also turn out *their* lights. He was pleased to see that Bad had already.

And, indeed, with some warning in French and Italian, that temperate, bodiless voice told the pilgrims that the lights would now be switched out. They were to stand still, please.

The cave went dark. Around Bad the pilgrims sighed. Bad could still see the red running light on the Americans' video camera. And he could see thready gray-white flashes of static on the monitor. Then, on the monitor, an image appeared. A circle of faces in the light of a single struck match. The flame was reflected and magnified in the bishop's cloth-of-gold.

The first match went out. The crowd was being led in a prayer by that calm flight attendant's voice. Bad finally recognized it as Father Octave's. On the monitor, faces and flame appeared again. Those faces, the heart of the crowd, leaned into the tiny light as, in Christmas pictures, the faces of the faithful bend to the lit crib.

Darkness. Another match, like a faltering heartbeat.

Between each struck match the cave was a cave—closed lightlessness, as caves are—as Bad knew them to be. But it was a cave that murmured and breathed and whose sour air bit at Bad's throat.

The pizza-box bomb had cracked Bad's cervical vertebrae and broken his left leg. He had also received a mild concussion—mild because he hadn't lost consciousness. Although the concussion hadn't lingered like his other injuries, it had troubled him more while it was with him. He could cope with the pain in his leg and his neck and with his bruises. But for two weeks the concussion had colonized his vitality, choking him up, as exotic waterweeds—*introduced species*—choked some lakes at home. Bad had slept, but even his dreams had suffered from impaired concentration. He'd felt as if his whole potential dream life had pressed in on him, a crowd of phantoms like a corridor full of petitioners, each one asking for his attention, all standing in the dark, as the pilgrims stood in Dardo's hot, overpopulated cave.

The crowd followed Daniel Octave in prayer. An organized murmur filled the air in its stiff casing of rock. Then the lights came back on. People sighed or giggled, nervous, and there was sporadic applause. The line faced front again and, after a time, began to move. Alberto's minder helped the old man to his feet and they walked on. Alberto was shaky, still warming up his joints.

Bad waited against the wall behind the folding chairs. He let others go by, watched each person who passed, as if looking for someone he'd lost in the crowd. Only the rangers were interested in the fact that he'd stopped. They asked him why he wanted to linger. And Bad asked them whether it was farther to go on than to go back. Bad said he'd had enough of the stuffy cave. He'd like to go back—since that was simpler. Was it permitted?

They told him to take care, all the while eyeing his caving helmet. They said that if he was thinking of cutting down into

the *other* cave off the Grotto of the Hermit he should tell
them. He should always let someone official know his intentions.

"I know the drill," said Bad. "As you can see, I don't have
my pack. I didn't plan on any trips."

The rangers nodded and went briskly on. As soon as they
had passed around the bend and out of Bad's sight he could no
longer hear them. But their disappearance left none of a cave's
customary silence. The monitor hummed faintly. And, now
and then, Daniel Octave could be heard, speaking in his
serene, calming voice, about the cave's few obstacles. Bad knew
that the priest, the other clergy, their flock, and the camera-
carrying tourists were all moving away from him, but the
sound system faithfully delivered Daniel Octave's words into
the deserted overlit chamber and Bad's expectant silence.

What was he waiting for? Bad believed he was waiting for
the passage to clear. He wanted to inspect it on his own,
wanted to appreciate its unpeopled artifice. He was thinking
how he'd describe it in postcards home.

Bad sat down in Alberto's chair. He didn't get up again
until he was sure that the pilgrims' party was at the very end of
its route. He heard Daniel Octave making a muster like a tour
guide. He heard the oxygen, the *happiness* in Octave's voice. In
that voice Bad heard a person who didn't like close, dark places
coming into the light and the open air. Bad imagined he heard
a channel close when the sound system was switched off.

After another forty minutes the lights went out. Bad sat in
the blackness and tasted breath, sweat, cosmetics, textiles,
electricity, holy oils, and the candle smoke conducted through
the caverns from the church—the air was flowing that way.

He got up and switched his headlamp back on. It gave him
the cave in correct perspective, the visible world in a cone of
light. Bad began to walk, watching his feet and his hands, ha-
bitually careful of the stone surfaces. The cables along the cave
roof were even stranger now in the light of Bad's lamp. It was

as though the stone were a patient on life support, who had only just died and was still covered in tubes, cables, and clips anchored to silent monitors.

Bad came to the place where they had all stopped. He knew it by the thin pall of incense smoke against its roof and the patch of seven spent matches on its floor. Bad noticed a plastic wrapper from a chocolate bar had been poked into a crack on the cave's wall. He supposed that someone would come to clean, that, in the days following the pilgrimage, the video and sound equipment would be dismantled and removed until next year's ceremony. Bad fished the crumpled packet out of the crack and stuffed it into a pocket. He raised his hand into the cone of light to stir the smoke; he saw it part and eddy.

Someone was coming, was close already, because the rock muffled any approach. Bad scarcely had time to register that he wasn't alone before she came into sight. She came at a run, carrying a long-barreled flashlight. Bad caught only a glimpse before she vanished behind her light. Her flashlight had a stronger beam than Bad's headlamp. His light could not penetrate hers.

She stopped and shone her light straight at him. Bad saw an arm emerge from the circle of radiance, into the gauzy darkness around the circle. He saw her put one hand behind her back.

He was never sure why he did what he did next—why he unclipped his chin strap, pulled his helmet off, and set it on the floor at his feet, headlamp facing the wall. Perhaps he meant to let her get a good look at him. Perhaps he expected her to recognize him, as he had recognized her. But he wasn't *thinking*, as such. He considered making an excuse but could only think of the old one, *I don't like the way it feels.* Bad had walked backward off the platform at Dart Ridge—now he found that, in removing his helmet, he was stepping up to something, putting himself forward. He moved out from the wall and set himself in her path. She drew back, still blinding him, but he could see she meant to skirt around him. She said, friendly, "Pil-grim"—breaking the word in two, she drawled, doing John Wayne.

Bad reached for her.

She struck his arm with her flashlight, then dropped it. The flashlight rolled, swept in a half circle as neat as a compass. Bad saw that it *was* her. He saw her pale roots, the light shining out of her head.

She'd dropped what she held in her other hand, too, an object that made a pure metallic clink on the cave floor. Bad's attention was momentarily diverted. He made out a smooth gold box with a glass face, like a very expensive clock.

The woman jumped at him, speedy and abrupt, then came to a halt before him. He had no time to flinch back. He saw it all happening, like an accident, but she moved too fast for his reflexes. Her hair, under its own momentum, flicked the front of his jacket. She had her fingers inside his jacket collar and wrenched its zipper open. Bad felt the top of his T-shirt cut into the back of his neck, heard its stitches pop and the fabric part. She yanked the torn neck down to trap Bad's arms against his sides. He reeled, and he felt her leg cross behind his calf. She tripped him, and he sprawled on the floor. His head didn't connect with the rock but with her hand, its spread fingers cushioning his skull. Bad felt her breath moisten the skin of his chest; then her mouth, lips, blunt instrument of chin, her hard teeth, touched him. Something sharp pierced him. The pierced place went numb. The light was drawn out of him. Bad saw stars and swarming colors, as though his blood pressure had plummeted. He lay back, shocked—then intoxicated, weak, amorous. He touched her hair. It felt silky, unspoiled by color treatments or cosmetic preparations. He was dizzy, but he didn't lose consciousness. Instead, he lost his *self-consciousness.* He was not ashamed of himself, his submission, or of his gradually stiffening imposition into the space between their bodies. He was hard and moaned when she moved—moved her mouth and climbed his body to look into his face.

Her eyes had changed. He'd remembered them as clear and light brown. They were clear still, but one was the color of unwhipped honey, and its eyelashes were pale. She stared at him, her mismatched eyes warm, assessing, and sane—while her mouth dripped blood, *his blood*, onto his mouth. Bad saw the moment in which she recognized him.

She apologized, "You frightened me."

"You bit my tongue," Bad said.

She studied him, and as she did she slipped her hand out from under his head and hitched his torn T-shirt up again to free his arms.

Bad put his arms around her.

She smiled. "I remember its taste—your own taste, and chicken noodles. It was a smooth, pink, succulent tongue." She moved one hand to cup his groin. She said, "Would you like me to deal with this?" Kneading him through two thicknesses of cotton. "It's the least I can do." She laughed softly.

Bad said he would rather she did the *most* she could do. He craned up to set his mouth against hers. The blood, tacky already, was quickly diluted and liquefied by his saliva. Bad put his tongue into her mouth. He gave her his tongue.

He was falling. Finally, he was falling.

On the roof of her mouth Bad felt a patch of short spines bristling. Some snagged him. Again he had the sensation of being drawn up and of amorous intoxication. She was trying to move away but couldn't; he had trapped his tongue in her mouth. He was hooked on her barbs. She tried to push against him to get some slack, to release him, but he pulled back and stayed caught. He felt his tongue strain at its root and salty saliva mix with coppery blood.

She gave in and sucked at him. He heard her swallowing,

felt her growing pliant and sleepy in his arms. Their hands tangled trying to find each other in their clothes. She unzipped him, arched her back, set her pelvis against his, and put him inside her. Only then did he press forward to release his tongue from the barbs on the roof of her mouth. She sat straight and his blood ran down her chin and neck and dripped onto her shirt. She moved against him, her face blank. She seemed to be listening, trying to gauge something. Perhaps it was his strength she meant to get the measure of. But when he rose in a surge to hold her and push and push, she took his hand and slipped his wrist into her mouth. Bad again felt the barbs bristle and pierce and a local numbness, then a blast through his body of some narcotic toxin. She sucked, and they moved, and Bad came—and then dropped back gasping against the rock and the small litter of spent matches.

He stroked her hair while she continued to suckle, playing now, the spines loose in the small holes they had made, her tongue scooped to make a trough for the trickle of blood. Bad was still inside her, and attached to her. They were connected, together, a closed system, and he wanted to stay that way forever. But she released his wrist, then began grooming him with her tongue, clearing the blood from the other tight patch of thorn wounds beside his right nipple.

"You didn't die." Bad's voice was thick.

"I broke my leg and my pelvis, and this eye"—she touched the eye with the paler iris and lashes—"this eye popped out, and I had to put it back in."

"You're Dawn Moskelute."

Dawn Moskelute retrieved her flashlight and shone it into Bad's face. She wanted to know how he knew her name.

Bad told her she looked like Eve in Groucho's Hat.

She frowned at him.

"Or whatever," he said. Then, "You pulled me up that pitch. I think I've always known that, only it wasn't possible."

He thought some more. He ran his hands down her slight, firm arms. He lifted her a little to weigh her—found that she weighed like a size 10 of medium height.

Dawn Moskelute let him heft and manipulate her body. She relaxed, and her hair flopped and swung. He moved her and they smeared each other's skin and clothes, but all the time she watched him, her expression serious. After a time she said, "I can't wait to get a look at you in good light."

Bad took her flashlight and, to conserve its battery, turned it off. His headlamp, facing the wall, cast its light up in an arc that visibly dissipated at the ceiling. The shadows crowded in. The cave set its black paw down upon them.

"That's better," Bad said.

Did he feel it at all? Dawn asked. The blood loss? He scarcely seemed to. "You're perfect," she said, and dropped her head to rub her face against his throat.

"You're as full as a tick, aren't you?" he said, tender. Then, "What will happen to me?"

"Nothing."

Bad fished in the inside pocket of his jacket and found Eve Moskelute's letter to her caretaker. He gave the letter to Eve's sister. Dawn planted her elbow on his chest and tilted the page to the light. She laughed. "She didn't mention anything to me," she said. "Tell me—you saw Ares's portraits of Eve, then went looking for her because she looks like me?"

"It's more involved than that. Involved with *you*." Bad told Dawn about the body recovery, the detective, his Google hits on "Martine plus Dardo." Bad said that he was in Italy on a vacation paid for by an insurance claim. He'd been injured in a bomb blast. He was a bomb tech with the New South Wales Emergency Ordnance Disposal Unit. "There was a concert for a singer from Sarawak. The bomb was in the concert hall garage. On the garage's pillars were posters advertising an exhibition at the State Gallery, an exhibition of European Modern Masters. The image on the poster was Jean Ares's *Eve in a*

Gaucho Hat. When the bomb went off Ares's Eve flew toward me, burning. Months later, the picture was still in my head—though if I'd only seen it pasted up on a fence I wouldn't have taken it in. *Years* later you were still in my head, too—you, and Le Lien Vert. The day I recovered Martine Dardo's body I happened to connect the two memories. I saw her hair, thought about you, then realized that the woman in the poster had your face. The day after *that* I met the detective again and he told me that a woman called Eve Moskelute had identified Dardo's body. He told me that Eve was the artist Ares's widow."

"What did you make of that?"

"I thought I'd finally found your family, because I'd been able to make all these connections. It felt like a gift. As if the universe was finally making up to me for the thing it did to friends I had—for the disaster at Dart Ridge. So I went to see your sister. I thought that she might like to know about your last hours. I wanted her to help me understand why you were in the cave and dressed for a night on the town. But your sister only told me tales, and then bribed me with a free stay at Ares's house in Nice. That's when I knew for sure that there was something funny going on."

"Going on *without you,* too," Dawn said. She made a sad face, her chin wholly dimpled as she thrust her lower jaw forward to form a pout.

Bad frowned, but not at her. He was following his own story—running it through his hands and checking its knots. He went on. "I met Father Octave yesterday, on the train. I aired my suspicions, and he fobbed me off."

"Obviously *in on it,*" Dawn said.

Bad and Father Octave hadn't parted ways at the train. They had walked up to the village together and stood for a time on the Avenue 19 Septembre 1947. Bad was in an alcove by a fountain, Daniel Octave on the street, his feet by a clump of dandelions and poppies, which were prostrate and sodden with rain. The priest had seemed reluctant to leave Bad, perhaps regretting his Parable of the Albinos. He'd lingered in the drizzle and his black wool suit was silvered. Father Octave told Bad he was sorry he hadn't believed him. And Bad said, "I thought you imagined I'd made a mistaken interpretation—not that I was telling unbelievable stories."

The priest stared at Bad, and his eyes in his dark face were a cold green, like the water of the Riwaka Resurgence, a pool with an embossed surface and deceptive transparent depths, the place where the Riwaka River emerged from the base of Takaka's marble mountain, icy, after its weeks underground.

Father Octave said to Bad that he hoped Bad would join the pilgrimage. "Then you can tell me how you feel about the saint's story. Because I think you've received her story with your *head*, not your heart. And it's heart's sense you need to make of your experience in the caves during the flood of '92."

Bad told Dawn that Father Octave's "heart's sense" seemed like an *indulgence*—an easy option for the laity, the ordinary folk. "Your sister bribed me. The priest offered me a parable, and an indulgence. But I'm not going to be bought off—and I don't want to be one of the ordinary folk."

"Is this an application?" Dawn said.

Bad's breath caught. The light was shining through the amber of Dawn's damaged—and magically repaired—right eye. Its eyelashes were the color of corn silk and as thick as fur. The lower half of her face was masked in smeared blood, her mouth open. Bad could actually hear the spines stirring there. When *she* was stirred they rose and touched her tongue, checked its movement, making her lisp as she spoke.

"Yes," Bad answered her. "Yes, please."

"Come with me," Dawn said. She said she shouldn't have stopped. She'd stolen something. She climbed off Bad and retrieved the object she'd dropped. She gave it to Bad. It was very heavy. Bad sat up, reached for his helmet, and turned its light to look at what he had in his hand. It was a container, solid silver, its seams sealed with strips of gold, its front a crystal panel. It was lined inside with red velvet and contained a match, which stood, its sandy pitch and sulphur bulb upward, in a slot in the velvet. Dawn put out her hand and Bad returned the reliquary. He got up. He felt light-headed and leaned on the wall. Dawn tucked herself under his armpit and wrapped his arm across her shoulders. She asked him if he could walk. Should she give him a minute? She could give him a minute but not much support. The cave was narrow from here on, and they must go single file.

Bad drooped and dropped his face into her hair. Then he let the helmet fall again, turned in to her, took hold of the tops of her thighs, and lifted her up, up onto him, onto what came up the instant she offered her minute. He wasn't a weakling. He'd show her he wasn't. She was laughing; then she grunted. Bad put her back against the wall and her shirt rasped on the rock. He grazed his knuckles. He held her with one arm and opened her shirt to look on her, her body a lithe bow, her small breasts, flat stomach, creamy skin mottled white, in places its pigment utterly gone. These weren't scars; they were like the grain of polished stone, as smooth as the skin surrounding them. Not scars but skin, sweating and telegraphing her muscles' happy spasms.

They left the caves at dusk. The exit was under the escarpment whose overhang had sheltered Bad the night before. The grass beneath the fruit trees was flattened and littered here and there by aluminium foil, food wrappers, paper cups. Apparently some of the pilgrims had had a picnic when they'd emerged into the late-afternoon sun. Dawn took Bad by the hand and led him along a shallowly sloping track beside the escarpment. The goats who had kept Bad company the night before were sheltering already, lying on the gritty ground beneath the overhang, their legs folded under them. They eyed Dawn and Bad but didn't startle.

Bad found himself on the mule track he'd gone down that morning. Dawn led him through an apple orchard, past a haystack under a pup tent, past a springhouse built in a cleft in the escarpment and enclosing the constant resonating gurgle of working water. Dawn led him onto the steeper stepped track. Before them was the village, on its spur. Bad could feel his eye measuring the air between the mountains. The valley was like a room roofed with high cloud, a church with numerous side chapels. To Bad his eyes' measuring felt physical, as though he had a rod and line and was casting, stroking the surface of a pool. His focus moved, went out from tree to tree and slope to slope.

The track came to the cultivated terraces. Bad brushed by artichoke flowers, purple onion flowers, and stands of robust twitch weed.

That morning he'd gone down past the old cypress whose roots broke the path. He hadn't any trouble seeing then, for the sun was up over the slopes to the east and shone into the place, to show haphazard paving buried in a fall of brown jointed needles and round cypress seeds. Now, at dusk, it was very dark under the cypress—and Bad saw that someone was waiting there. Dawn drew her hand from Bad's and went forward. Her fresh paleness was eclipsed by hands and hair so white that Bad—light-headed—imagined that he was looking at one of Daniel Octave's albinos. The man raised one of Dawn's hands to his lips and kept it there. The man was biting the base of Dawn's thumb. There was space between Dawn and him—it was an intimacy, but unlike the intimacy Bad had just enjoyed. The two seemed frozen in a pose of courtliness, their faces showing no strong feeling, only absorbed placidity. Then the man's eyes closed, and she put her free hand on the back of his head. Bad could still see the air between their bodies. They didn't incline at the hips; the man touched her only with his mouth. It wasn't like anything Bad had seen before, this prolonged chaste contact.

Bad finally said it to himself, aloud but in a whisper. He spoke, and felt that he was *telling* someone—perhaps trying to convey a marvel to Pops, his mother's father, whose interest in Bad was loving and unfaltering. Or perhaps he was saying, "So there!" to Father Octave and his "sense of a *statistically unusual* but normal sort." Bad said to himself, *These are vampires, and she is feeding him from her hand.*

Chapter 10

DAWN

Bad was taken to a house on Dardo's Rue Oscura. Dawn and her friend went into the house ahead of him and didn't switch on the lights. Bad stood for a moment on the threshold and brushed his palm down the wall within the door. His fingers found a switch and flipped it. Nothing happened.

Dawn said, from the darkness, "That light is controlled from here." She didn't turn it on. Bad heard her kick off her shoes, the soft thud of each solid hoof of sole against something hollow. Beyond the street door the lamp in its web-encrusted cage was a hindrance; it shone into the house and showed Bad only a sharply illuminated patch of flagstones and nothing further. He crossed the threshold and pushed the door closed, shutting out the last thread of light. He set his back against the door and waited. A room away, around a corner, a light appeared, low and yellow. After a moment the refrigerator began to hum. Dawn's shadow moved in the light from its interior. "Eve's still here," she said. "There's milk, cheese, and salami"— her shadow grew taller and turned—"and orange wafers here on the table. I expect you'd like some salami?"

Bad asked if Eve could hear them.

"She'll be in bed. The doors in this house are solid, and kept closed," Dawn said.

Another voice echoed her. "Closed," it said—a reminder, a limitation, the law being laid down. The voice, however, was slight, a dry gauze of sound.

Bad saw the light from the refrigerator pinch and hurried toward the kitchen before Dawn closed it. He came to a stop in the dark and gasped when he saw a shape moving against the parallel scratches of moonlight through slatted shutters.

"It's early for you," Dawn said—not to Bad.

"I've no reason to stay awake," said the voice.

Bad heard a drawer being pulled out. The squeak of bad joinery. Dawn was rummaging among kitchen implements. Then she stopped, stepped away, and turned on a light. "I can't see to slice," she said to the other vampire, who, without another word and without looking at them, raised his arms, caught hold of the edge on a kind of shelf formed by the carved ceiling that covered only part of the main room. The wood creaked as it took the vampire's weight, as he closed the hinge of his elbows, lifted his legs over his head, doubled up, and flipped smoothly backward into the slot of blackness above the ceiling. He withdrew from sight, his disappearing face a smudge of pallid smoke. Bad heard him cross the ceiling, the sound seeming to progress into the wall above a padlocked door.

Dawn had found a knife and was slicing salami. She spread it out on a plate and poured a glass of milk. "Come on," she said to Bad.

Once he was up at the table she dragged her chair over to

his so that they sat hip-to-hip. She watched him eat up close, touching his chin when he was chewing and his throat as he swallowed.

Dawn's bed was a nest, a big box in a room without windows. When Bad woke he checked his watch in the light shining through the lattice of the box bed's sliding doors, radiance from a bead-fringed bedside lamp. It was mid-morning. Dawn was difficult to rouse, hot, sleepy, and pliant. Bad opened one door on the bed and pushed down the quilt to examine Dawn's scars—ordinary skin, extraordinarily white, follicles of normal appearance but sprouting tiny glassy hairs. Dawn stirred and opened her eyes. She saw what Bad was studying and told him that they weren't really scars. Scars were signs of mending, like mortar in a crack in a wall. "My patches have no edges," she said, and flexed her full length, so that every white stripe or dusting of freckles-in-negative showed, blood shining through the uneven color of her smooth body. "I am expertly patched," she said; then she pushed herself, curled up, against Bad's thighs. She flung her arms around his waist and set her open mouth against the skin over one of his hips. Bad felt her mouth's spiny interior—but she didn't bite him. Dawn ran her tongue around inside the tent her lips had made, then broke contact. She pulled him down, so that they lay chest-to-chest and face-to-face. She began to tell Bad her story.

In 1969 Dawn was living in a commune near St. Agnes, a perched village eight hundred meters above the sea. Each week she'd catch the bus down the road's many hairpin bends—past terraced farms and shady gorges full of fig trees and stands of green bamboo—to Menton. She would get off at the Gare Routière, shop at the market under the railway, and then climb the steep street at the end of which stood the crumbling, cream-plastered, Eastern-domed Palais Lutetia, where she and Eve had a first-floor apartment.

Eve was away in early July, and Dawn made the trip more often to collect her sister's mail. Eve was in England promoting her books—her biography of Guy de Chambord and her English translation of Chambord's romance, *Daylight*. The books had come out two years before in France and had made a bit of a splash.

"You mustn't imagine this is only incidental to my story," Dawn told Bad. "Nothing is, not even the weather."

On that July day Dawn climbed up the steep street from the market, creeping from one patch of shade to the next. She stopped to make conversation with a neighbor, one of those old people who pause at every encounter on the slope to shake hands and save face, to catch their breath without having to do it standing alone. Dawn helped the man with his shopping. They paused together to make kissing noises at a canary in a cage hung out for some fresh air in a street-level window.

As soon as she was in the apartment she took off her dress and shoes. She spent the afternoon in her petticoat, with the windows open and shutters closed, their slats sifting some of the heat out of the wind.

At four the sun had gone from the front face of the building and she could open the shutters. Dawn spent the remainder of that afternoon painting a wardrobe. She ate dinner at the kitchen sink, standing by one of the barred windows at the back of the building, where a fig tree's leaves were making polite applause in the breeze. She ate—then tapped the barometer, hoping for change.

It was thirty-eight degrees, though the sun had gone behind the mountains. She decided to treat herself, to go to one of the cafés on the promenade, where locals usually don't go, knowing better.

The air was cooler by the water. Dawn sat at a table on the sea side of the promenade and under a fringed cabana, one of a whole hissing strip. The breeze had increased, and the raffia on the umbrellas made a noise like small surf on the sandy beaches farther east—Cannes, Antibes—the sound of foam sinking through sand's fine filter. Dawn sipped wine and water and watched waiters dash back and forth across the road through the July traffic of Vespas and convertibles. There was a haze over the sea, of its surface evaporation. The sea was all one color, lavender, from shore to horizon. It had no perspective, looked vertical, not horizontal, and full to the brim. As night came on, the lavender grew slowly gray, then the sea vanished altogether and the stones on the beach began to glow under the street lamps, white and set in a resin of black shadow. Dawn was a little drunk. She wanted to swim but didn't have her bathing suit. St. Tropez was topless then—but Menton was a quiet town, full of retired people.

Dawn had a friend with a boat. She decided to walk along to the boat harbor and borrow it, to row out a little way, then swim beyond the reach of the lights.

The boat was a clinker-built squid boat, with seats for two oarsmen and a high prow from which hung an oil lamp. Dawn's friend lit the lamp and helped Dawn cast off. She rowed out beyond the first quay and the sheltered swimming beach, out of sight of the fortress on the mole. Then she pulled in the oars and let the boat drift.

There were no waves. Dawn stripped and jumped into the sea, surfacing to lie in the water and watch the swinging lamp gradually settle again. The boat drifted gently, and Dawn followed it. She cooled down; the sea soaked into her. The water was salty, and she was buoyant, able to lift her chest and knees up into the lamplight to scrape with her thumbnails at her freckles of white paint. She cleaned herself, then climbed back into the boat and got dressed. She blew out the lamp and rowed in closer to the shore, back past the arched doors of shops on the Plage de Sablettes, and into the mouth of the boat harbor between Quays Napoléon and Eugénie. Then she slowed, shipped her oars, caught her breath, and watched the town, the people on the promenades, the girls in sleeveless dresses eating ice cream, the boys with their shirts open, sitting along the seawall or clustered together, on scooters, holding themselves in place with their braced legs, front wheels at a right angle to backs and headlamps downcast. There had been a wedding, Dawn saw, for a cavalcade was making its way, speeding in spurts, along the Bas Corniche. Horns sounded, and the bride and bridesmaids sat in the open car windows hanging onto their roofs.

In looking at the spill of town lights on the sheltered water, Dawn first saw the person swimming toward her boat—a face, haloed white and streaming silver, moving at the point of an arrowhead of ripples. Dawn saw the head go under and the ripples change, close, and rebound. She craned over the side and caught sight of a form, a shape in water so clear that the streetlights shone through it in bright bands—water like smoked glass, the shadows of its surface ripples like flaws in glass.

He reached her boat. He came up through the water, his face raised and eyes open. His head broke the surface. Dawn watched water run from his face, pour out of his eye sockets. He kept his eyes on her the whole time, blinked only once to squeeze free a few final drops. He flung his pale arms over the stern board of the boat and hung there, top half out of the water. He said her sister's name. "Eve?"

Dawn, curious about this acquaintance of Eve—someone *she* hadn't known about—said, "Yes?"

He smiled—a brief soberly satisfied smile. He let go of the stern board and dropped back into the water—but only to transfer his hold from his armpits to his hands. He surged up out of the sea, without pausing to balance his knees on the stern board or swing a leg into the boat. He came straight up, shedding seawater, landing crouched on the plank seat. Then he rose again, off his two distinct wet footprints, and threw himself against Dawn, wrapping himself around her so that his arms protected her spine from the edge of the rower's seat and his hands cupped the back of her head. He closed her in a wet, cold embrace. He put his mouth against hers, pulled her tongue forward and into his mouth by suction, so strong a suction that Dawn felt her nostrils pinch closed as the air rushed through them, as her whole respiratory system—lungs, trachea, larynx, nose, and throat—tried to equalize pressure. Her ears popped painfully, and her tongue was pierced by something he had in his mouth. Dawn felt her body straighten in a spasm and *herself go out of herself,* roaring, like a powerful aria.

Bad interrupted. "So . . . when you really mean business you bite a person on the tongue?"

Dawn peered at him through sleepy slitted eyes.

Bad felt he must remind her, "In Le Lien Vert you bit me on the tongue."

Dawn said she hadn't wanted him to know he'd been bitten. Ila, on the other hand, wanted no one *but* Dawn to know he'd bitten her.

Bad shook his head. He didn't get it.

"He *chose* Eve, but he took me. In a moment of curiosity, of impulsive mischief, I gave her name instead of mine. Or, at least, I said, 'Yes' to someone asking for my sister. He'd seen her photo on the dust jacket of the biography. Her author's note neglected to mention an identical twin. And the joke was that I hadn't even *read* Eve's books properly. They were less familiar to me than they were to their many appreciative readers. People would try to talk to me about them and I'd just smile patiently. But with him I went further. I didn't just smirk and pretend to have read my sister's books. I said, 'Yes,' to someone *in her name*."

Ila rowed to shore, lifted Dawn onto the quay, got her onto her feet, and supported her across the road and into the warren of the old town. There he stood her up against the wall in one of those dark corners where the cobbles are set in silt from overflowing drains. He asked her where she lived.

Dawn, intoxicated, gave him her address, and he leaned in to her, took her tongue again, and drank, then let go and, with his lips, caught the drops that spilled from her slack mouth. He slipped the chain that held her key off over her head, then tilted her chin to clean her face and neck with his tongue, his lick thorough and caressing. They left the dark passage, and he took her home, matched his walk to her weaving one, supported her when her ankles and knees wouldn't lock. He carried her up her street. Semiconscious, she registered that she was cold where, that morning, she'd been hot.

He used her key to let them in, locked the door again, left the windows open but pulled the shutters and curtains closed. He put her down on a rug in the only room without windows, the entrance hall, with its five doors.

Dawn was panting; her hands and feet were freezing. She looked up into his eyes, whose huge pupils were rimmed with an iris of a pale, pinkish gray. She said, in her only attempt to defend herself, that her friends expected her. She spoke in a slur, her tongue full of deep, oozing perforations.

He replied, but she couldn't understand what he said, though she recognized the language from her sister's studies.

Dawn sat up abruptly and snatched at the quilt bunched at the bottom of her bed. She hauled it up and around her, eclipsing her glossy, dappled body. "Ila said, in Provençal, 'Stay with me.

And when I am old and forgetful you can teach me my own grammar again, and remind me who I love.' He was quoting Chambord's romance, the heroine, Grazide, addressing the hero—who *doesn't* stay with her.

"I hadn't properly read Eve's books," Dawn said again, and looked at Bad for extra emphasis. "I didn't like *Lumière du Jour.* I merely lived with Eve's enthusiasm. I felt that I was being indulgent—that I was the worldly one, and she was my bookish sister. I had the boyfriends. She shut herself up and worked for two years on her translation. I read it and I thought, *All this effort for a stilted, marginal work.* But Eve had put *Daylight* back in a living language. She'd reanimated it; she'd brought it back into the world. Eve got her face in the papers, got her column inches. And I thought, *Oh well, it takes all tastes.* I said to her, condescending, 'Good for you. Though, you know, *Daylight* isn't really my cup of tea.' Then the biography appeared, and she gave me my signed copy— rather diffidently, sensing that she wouldn't get the response she wanted and deserved. I read it and I was shocked—because Eve was so much smarter than I knew. With a pen in her hand she was another person altogether—judicial and passionate, shrewd and thoughtful. I read the book inattentively, in a haze of envy. I *resisted* it. And look." Dawn discarded the quilt and, shivering, pressed herself against Bad, strong and supple and, he sensed, almost ill with solitude. "Chambord's Grazide is—well—my grandmother. In a way. Ila is the enameler's journeyman in *Daylight.* You can ask him about it if you like. He might tell you." She smiled. "He might tell you *his* coming out story, as I'm telling you mine."

For the remainder of that night, Dawn said, she was semiconscious and partly paralyzed. She voided herself, emptied her bladder and bowel. Was indifferent to being sat on the toilet, her drooping head resting against the vampire's stomach, while her other end gushed, then dribbled. He ran her a warm bath and she drooped over the sink and vomited. He washed her, and her nose ran. Dawn wasn't distressed; she was jacked up on the vampire's venom and was in a crisis of delight.

At daybreak—which she sensed through curtains and shutters and the thick cement of the apartment building, *felt* as if the world beyond all those barriers were a highly flammable medium into which someone had dropped a match—Dawn began to seize, to quake and foam and bite on her shredded tongue. The vampire forced the blade of his hand between her jaws, and she tasted him: spicy, medicinal, a tang of iron, a smell she knew from standing in the shallows and opening the gut of a fish, freshly caught, stunned but not yet done dying, a billowing scent of cool, ferrous blood.

Later, Dawn came to in her own bed, under the covers but swathed in damp towels. She was alone. She'd been sick, she decided. Clearly, it was all a dream. She knew she must make the 8:15 bus. That a friend would be waiting for her at St. Agnes, on the terrace near the church probably, his eye on the bus stop. Dawn remembered that she had spoken to her friend the previous evening, before she went out to cool down at a beachfront café, to nurse a glass or two of its house wine, a dusty gray rosé. Dawn dressed, found her spare key, and went out.

The vampire was asleep in the back room where the sisters stored ladders and trunks and the rust-speckled bicycle their father had bought them. The vampire was happy to let his victim wander—after all, the apartment was her home; her author's note said "Eve Moskelute lives in Menton." She wouldn't run—if she was even aware of what had happened to her, her body's sudden dedicated loyalty to his venom would draw her back. She had shaken and oozed and gasped in a way that was wholly satisfactory to him, and secure in the knowledge that she was his, complacent and well fed, he slept.

Eyes covered from brow to cheekbone in the graduated

shade of her sunglasses, Dawn went out and made her bus. She made the journey, her head wobbling and eyes watering.

"When I got off at the top," Dawn said, "I lingered and looked about me. I'm so glad now that I stopped and looked both ways. Not at the traffic, not at the truck that hit me, but over the wall at the slopes northeast. Pointe du Siricoca and Razet."

Dawn saw their naked crests, short slopes of white shale, the brush and forest, and the benign blue sky. And the other way, over the sea, she saw heavy cloud with worn spots that let through patches of milky sunlight on the landscape, spotlights showing treasures without prejudice: the loopy exit from the autoroute, bare terraces, apartment houses. The whole coastline was in a capsule of mist with no horizon, no place where it came to an end. "I'm glad I looked. Since then I've had daylight in views out windows, full color to the edge of the frame, but I've lost the outdoors really—its color, which you take for granted, Bad, when you walk out the door in the morning and push your head into the day, immerse yourself in its thousands of possible points of focus and points of interest, right to the periphery of your vision, and wherever you direct your gaze." Dawn sighed and stared at Bad, or dazedly at the air around his head, as though she saw a residue there, a halo made of all the detail and volume of daylight in the open air.

Bad said that he thought she could see in the dark.

"Even lemurs can't see unless there's some light," Dawn said. Then she said, "The truck hit me, and my neck broke and over the next hour bleeding and swelling together finished the work of the first damage, cutting the signals from my brain to my heart and lungs. But I didn't die, because it was only an accident, and Eve didn't let the coroner keep my body, and my friends in the commune had strong beliefs about the cere-

monies of interment, which were made too much of in our culture, they thought. Eve put me in the Moskelute tomb. Left
me in a dark place, covered in cloth like dough left to rise. And
I did—I'd changed already, had gone over even as I climbed on
the bus and rode up to St. Agnes. I already had my aversion to
sunlight—but was months away from my allergy to it. I lay in
my tomb and *repaired.*

"On that first evening Ila woke and found me gone. The
apartment was empty. He went out looking. My friends had
collected Eve from Nice Airport and had taken her to the
communal farm. And the following morning was my funeral.
Eve came back to our apartment in the late afternoon of the
day of my funeral. She took tranquilizers and lay down. She
woke up hearing her name called. It was Ila, but of course
she walked about looking for me. Ila watched her and took in
her scent and knew she wasn't the woman he'd had. He listened to her call my name, listened to her speaking to me, and
then he asked—from the shadows—where I was. She told him.

"Ila went out, down to the sea, up through the old town to
the cemetery. He found that the Moskelute tomb had a bronze
door, with a hole for a big key that moved a thick bolt, and that
its hinges were on the inside. He ran back to the apartment
and, hungry, cut Eve with the little knife he carried, and
lapped up her blood from the marble top of the vanity in the
bathroom. He wrapped her wrist and walked her about
the house opening drawers and asking where the key was. He
spoke Provençal and Eve understood him. But she couldn't
understand what key he meant, nor—in her state—could she
find the words in his language in order to ask him what he
meant. He sat her down in our entrance hall. She escaped.
He found the key, ran back to the cemetery, putting on one
burst of speed to intercept a cyclist in the pedestrian tunnel.
He hauled the cyclist off his bike, knocked him senseless, and
employed not his knife but a needle and cannula and a length

of plastic tubing as a drinking straw. He topped up, then ran on to the cemetery, outran the sun, and shut himself in the tomb with me."

Dawn was quiet. Bad lay holding her. Her stillness was emphatic but not expectant. She wasn't waiting for a reaction, his verdict on her story. He wanted to ask her—but didn't want to spoil a moment as uncluttered and easy as waking on a day without plans. Bad felt as he had once before, when he was alone in an apartment recovering from thirty-six hours of air travel. His hosts had left him provided for and had gone out. He had gone to bed at nine in the morning, without having spoken to anyone he knew. He had slept, then got up and stood at the window, a tall seamless sheet of soundproof plate glass, and watched the rush-hour traffic. He had slept again, and when he woke to hear someone in the shower he found he was finally back *in time*.

Dawn's heart was beating. She was beautiful. There was *no bad news*. Bad asked her again, "What will happen to me?"

She didn't respond.

Bad detached himself from her and sat up, leaning over her.

Dawn was asleep. He shook her, and her head flopped.

"What happened to you after that?" he said. He needed to know now, before he slept again, committed himself to sleep in her presence, in *this house*. Dawn stirred, opened her eyes a little, and put up her hands. She pushed at the air above her as though there was a weight there. Her arms trembled against an invisible pressure.

"What happened next?"

"Corsica," Dawn said. "We went there."

"Why?"

"It's an island," Dawn said. "And I wanted Eve. I would have tried to take her."

Her arms relaxed and eyelids drooped. "Later," she said. She was asleep. Bad jostled her again, but she only moaned and lolled as though heavily sedated. Bad drew nearer, bewitched and inquisitive. He stroked the fine blond hair behind her ears and peered into them. He made a more thorough examination of her scars, checked for calluses of different tissue, and found only what he could see—an uneven coloration. He touched her scars, then licked a nipple, watched it glisten and stiffen in its goose-bumped aureole. He turned his attention to the other nipple—then stopped. It didn't seem right. Despite the intimacy she'd shown him, he knew he was taking liberties.

Bad looked at his watch. It was midday. The invisible weight Dawn had failed to raise with her trembling arms was the sun above the roof of the house. Bad got out of the bed, put his clothes on, unlocked the door, and went out into the main room.

He found a lamp lit on the table and, in the circle of its light, a note.

"*I see you got the relic,*" Bad read. "*Good. Don't forget to bring it with you. I've left you and Ila the car. I had to go back to Menton early to finalize a few things for the funeral, at which it seems I might not be the sole mourner. Eve.*"

Bad left the house to buy himself lunch and to retrieve his pack.

The day was hot and his pack heavy. The four glasses of water he had had with lunch hadn't quenched his thirst. He stopped by a covered *laverie* to dangle his hot hands in the piped spring. The water was cold and milky blue. Underwater, Bad's skin paled and smoothed out, his corded veins contracting. He inclined, elbows on the stone coping, and looked over his shoulder at a tree, a tree like an exhibit, protected by a low stone fence. The elm's trunk was partly hollow and canted like a broken column, the spread of its limbs slight in proportion to its trunk. It was in leaf late, still a tufted, tender yellow. Bad read "1713" on the stone fence.

He took his hands from the icy water and shook them. From somewhere hidden, above the sunny piazza, a bird began to sing, its voice like glass marbles shaken in a bag. Then in his pocket, his phone played its speedy tune.

It was Gabrielle, his girlfriend. She said, "Brian . . . look . . . this is crazy."

Gabrielle said that she knew now she'd been thinking in the wrong way about their relationship. Thinking of room for improvement as a personal challenge when the operative word was *room.* The space she should give him, should trust him with. "These days we're all just a different *sort* of risk-averse. We've gained some insights but lost others. We'll take short chances but not take on the long. We look at one another and wonder whether we're getting the best deal we can. We forget to factor in how things are on a day-to-day basis. The *value* of that."

"Things?" said Bad.

"This is difficult for me," said Gabrielle. "I miss you, Brian, but I'm staying away from places I might find you because I know you're mad at me."

"I'm not mad at you."

"You ended it, Brian. You were *that* mad."

"I couldn't see a future for us." Bad hoped that, put this way, Gabrielle would understand it.

"But you don't see futures, Brian—that's the issue I have with you. You wait for problems to present themselves to you. You even go looking for them—big scary problems like bombs to disarm."

Bad thought that it would be unnecessarily provocative to point out that it was his job to do so.

Gabrielle asked him if he had ever seen himself growing old with anyone.

"I see myself *not* growing old with someone," Bad said, then laughed. He was feverishly happy.

"*Brian?*" Gabrielle said.

"Yes," Bad said. "I'll go into hiding with someone. We will hide from time, together."

"But, Brian," Gabrielle said, "it's important to *spend* time together. We had that covered. I think we did. That's what this trip was about—spending time together."

Bad was laughing.

"Brian, please. Where are you?"

"A piazza off 19 Septembre 1947."

"Please, Brian! I'm trying to make contact, to make peace, and you rebuff me with nonsense."

"I'm sorry." Bad said. He told his girlfriend that *he* was their problem. "You *can* get a better deal."

"I'm not looking for a deal." Gabrielle was crying. "Or a return on my investment. I care about you, Brian. I want you to talk to me, to tell me what I can do to fix things between us."

It was his fault. Bad knew he should try to explain to Gabrielle that, owing to his reticence, she had never known who she was talking to. Gabrielle believed in personality types. She'd run tests for employers who wanted to find out what they had in their staff, what each employee's work habits and stress strategies might be, according to type. Gabrielle believed that how people took what happened to them depended on type. Bad had done Gabrielle's tests, for fun and from vanity. He was a politician, an extrovert, the tests said. Bad concurred, could see himself in the results. But none of it had helped his girlfriend, to whom he never gave his full history. What good did it do her to see a positive, politic, extroverted Brian and not to have pictured that same man as a boy who, despite teasing, was confident enough of his own judgment to step back off the platform at Dart Ridge? Bad had never told her about that. He hadn't said, "I was alone on a mountain path. Suddenly, utterly alone—though there was a girl behind me shaking a stone from her shoe, and a boy nearby jammed into a thornbush and hanging on for dear life." He hadn't said, "I'm still alone on the mountain path. I'm still looking at the air." Or: "I'm still alone at the foot of the crester run, staring at the black air above a waterfall at the top of a fifteen-meter pitch." It was too late to tell now, to explain, because he wasn't alone anymore, and the cave's system lay open to him now, an animated cross section, full of figures and lights. There were the cavers in the Salle de la Nef, shawled in sleeping bags, waiting for the water to recede. Dawn and Jacques Palomba were lying in a cozy cavern, full of paintings and candles. The rescue teams pushed their threads of light through dark tunnels, Gino with them, his face warm behind his cold lamp. The Pilgrim's Way was visible for all its length, vined with cable—speakers and monitors like fruit on those vines—crowded with pilgrims, the bishop at their head, in his purple and gold. Bad had found a different mountain path, too. A path that wasn't the work of alpine guides, Parks and Reserves, or the Department of Conservation and that didn't have a viewing platform above a glacier. It was a mule track, part of a network of tracks around the nexus of the Salt Route, the pass into Piedmont. Bad was standing on that path, watching a vampire, who was watching a soldier, who was watching a snake and watched by a butcher with a billhook. There was blood on the glacier still—but there was blood everywhere. Dawn's eye fell out, and she put it back in.

Gabrielle continued to cry, and Bad held her to his ear. He apologized again, then pressed the button that ended the call.

The day after the Blessed Martine's festival the bishop's secretary offered Daniel a lift to Nice. The bishop had returned to the city the night before, but like Daniel, the secretary had stayed on for a postmortem of the pilgrimage.

Daniel spent his morning talking with the secretary, the mayor and town clerk of Dardo, and the two priests from St. Barthelemy's. They sat in the sun at one of the tables now restored to the terrace at the wide end of the piazza before the church. They discussed safety issues and possible improved access. They talked about the maintenance of "a sense of the sacred"—a discussion Daniel regarded as necessary but uncomfortable, since neither town officials nor clergy seemed to want to distinguish between preserving the pilgrimage as a sacred experience and improving its *packaging* as such. Daniel, meanwhile, was making plans and forming his position for another talk, one he'd have with the bishop in Nice, about the small clutch of testimonies the parish had gathered—reported sightings, as it were, of further miracles he would be called on to investigate. Miracles attributed to Martine Raimondi opened doors for Daniel Octave—the doors of other people's homes, other people's lives.

Daniel listened to the talk and watched the dark space of the open basement below a house opposite the church. The basement was in use as a chicken coop, and three beige chickens were pressed against the wire in a patch of sun, making noises of broody contentment. Lunch was in an hour at the monastery where Daniel had spent the night as a guest of the brothers of a contemplative order. After lunch Daniel would catch his ride. In the morning he'd get on a train to Menton. Martine Dardo's funeral was at La Conception, in Menton's old town. He would light a candle for her.

His friend Father Neske would say, scornfully, "What's the use, Daniel, of lighting a candle when this pope has it that we're all to be judged and cleansed by some purgatorial process in the instant after we expire? The pity and compassion of those we leave behind has no part in that process. They haven't even had time to draw breath, let alone to pray, let alone to hold a flame to a clean wick. You see, Daniel, for God and His divine cleansing fires there is no duration. There is no *time*. And"—here Neske would give his characteristic lopsided shrug—"if that is so, then everything is settled already, and we are all either already damned or saved by predestination. So you see, Daniel, this pope wants us all to be Protestants."

Daniel remembered how he had answered the old man's

172 ~ Elizabeth Knox

arguments. He remembered that he'd managed to be at once dismissive of Father Neske's outrage *and* disloyal to the Church. He had said to Neske that the Church was only embarrassed by an untidy cosmology. Purgatory had always been something of a problem.

Neske was acid. Yes, purification *was* more "in line" with the Presbyterians and Pentecostals. And—of course—all denominations were having enough difficulty in trying to figure out where to put Hell on a map of the universe. But should the Church give countenance to the difficulties of other denominations?

Daniel's stomach rumbled. He placed his hand on it and looked down with humorous displeasure. But no one at the table had heard. The other men were getting up out of their seats, responding at different speeds to the sight of the woman who cleaned St. Barthelemy's coming down its steps, unsteady and bowlegged. She stopped and sat down, crying and calling out to the fathers. They hurried to her, and Daniel joined them.

She said that she'd been dusting the high altar when she noticed that the smaller reliquary was missing.

The fathers helped her to her feet and escorted her back into the church.

The brass brackets that clipped the smaller reliquary to the back of the altar were broken—or rather, two were prized open and two snapped off.

The priest of St. Barthelemy's said that he hadn't noticed the reliquary missing when he said mass that morning. He dropped his chin on his chest to think. He'd been looking up, he said, or looking at what he held in his hands.

"With the volume of people through the church yesterday—" said the bishop's secretary. But then he remembered that all the pilgrims had stayed on the other side of the rail.

"Who was in the church when we were in the caves?" Daniel asked.

There were police and paramedics in the piazza. And two technicians were in the crypt.

"I'll speak to them," said one of the parish priests. "I'll get on to it now." He went away, while his colleague soothed the cleaning woman and sent her home.

Daniel was late for lunch. The brothers had waited to begin because the younger two wanted to ask him about the occasions on which he had spoken to the pope.

While he ate, Daniel told the brothers about the sense of achievement he believed he shared with His Holiness—and others—at the mass to celebrate Martine Raimondi's beatification. "I was very proud to have worked with God," Daniel said, then laughed. "I think His Holiness could see that I was bursting with pride—of the right sort. However, the *first* time I was introduced to His Holiness, I was so overcome that my ears were ringing and I couldn't hear a word he said." Daniel didn't tell the brothers that he often had that problem. He often found himself shut in a bell jar of shyness. Because of his shifty mother, it was always a shock for Daniel to look into another's face. From infancy Daniel had sought to hold his mother's gaze—and hadn't been able to. By the time he was twelve Daniel understood that it was expected of everyone to look, if only for an instant, into other people's eyes when they were speaking. He had made an effort, and terror forced his eyes to flutter or squint or dart about. His focus trembled, and people imagined he was angry. People to whom he spoke supposed that they had somehow frightened or offended him. They were often at pains to make him see that if he was hurt, it hadn't been their intention to hurt him; they were being *misunderstood*. They would keep talking, defensive, into his burning silence. It made things worse. If ordinary, polite attention was too intimate, these pained reassurances were even more difficult for Daniel. Sometimes he would laugh and look away. Or he'd look at the ceiling and say his piece. When Daniel had his audience with the pope—in 1991, after the tomb in Turin was opened—he wasn't able to remember their mutual interest in the matter they were to discuss and he forgot the Vatican's long correspondence with the bishop in Nice. Instead, he was afraid that his eyes would start their startled dancing, their tics of fright. He made himself look— and was blinded by the haze of blood in his head. His ears rang and he barely kept his feet.

Daniel went on to tell the brothers about the missing reliquary. They were sympathetic, but one said he'd often wondered whether that particular relic was—he shrugged—more *appropriate* than *authentic*. Martine Raimondi hadn't ever held the match in her hand. It had remained in her grandfather's pocket. Her grandfather had preserved it—slipped it under the leather lining of his cigarette case.

"It commemorates a moment," Daniel began, then stopped—vexed—because the brother was *right*; a relic should be holy, not merely commemorative. Martine's grandfather's last unlit match was a stored moment, a moment from a sterile world that had split off from the world they were all now in—the world in which Martine Raimondi's prayers were answered. The unlit match was time cauterized, the means of a final human gesture in defiance of death, a splinter of sulphur-tipped wood. Its flame, if ignited, would have burned in a world in which Martine's prayers went unanswered, in which perhaps there was no God to take her hand and lead her through the dark.

"You're right," Daniel said.

The brother blushed.

"But of course the reliquary itself was valuable," said another brother.

"There were so many tourists," said the first. Then he amended, "Pilgrims."

With all that equipment, they could easily add a security

camera, Daniel thought. He'd mention it to the fathers at St. Barthelemy's. He asked the brothers if he could make a call. (There was only one phone in the monastery. One phone and one radio—usually tuned to sports broadcasts.)

Daniel was shown into the room with the phone. It rang just as his hand was approaching it.

"Excuse me," said the brother beside Daniel. He picked up the receiver, listened for a moment, then handed it to Daniel. "It's for you, Father Octave." He left the room.

The phone wasn't a cordless, and Daniel did what he always had and wound himself into its cord, tethered himself to the caller before he said a word.

It was the detective.

"You tracked me down." Daniel was surprised. "I thought I might see you at the funeral tomorrow."

"I don't have time to go, I'm afraid."

"Is there something further?" Daniel said.

"No, there's something *else*. Something you might be able to help me with."

Daniel heard a kind of menace in the detective's voice.

"Something has disturbed me," the detective said. "I'm not often disturbed. Genoa is a big city, with a steady supply of bodies, blunders, atrocities." The detective said that since the twenty-sixth—the day before he first spoke to Daniel—he'd been waiting for a body to be identified. The body was found on the twenty-fifth among the concrete piles of an open basement beneath a restaurant in Portofino. The basement opened onto a tunnel, which provided public access under a private beach.

Get to it, thought Daniel. He had no idea where the detective was headed. Two brothers went by the open door and waved to Daniel. One hesitated, seeing Daniel's expression—anxious, impatient. Daniel waved back, then signaled them away.

"There were rats under the restaurant, and the body was

in a bad way," the detective said. "No fingerprints. And no matches with the dental records of missing persons—"

"I can't see why you want to keep me in suspense," Daniel said. "Do you want to take me by surprise?"

"Father, I want to share *my* surprise."

Daniel had turned to the window, further involving himself in the phone cord's expanding coils. He saw the two brothers on their way down to the monastery's terraces, where they had spent the morning suspending nets from the lower branches of the olive trees.

"Fortunately," the detective went on, "the victim had a dental abnormality. He had very good teeth—a fluoride baby—and he still had all of them, including his *five* wisdom teeth. He'd had some orthodontic work, and his orthodontist had X rays."

"I can't imagine what you're going to tell me." Daniel closed his eyes. He was exasperated. He was curious. He stood so still, the air seemed to flutter around him.

The detective was saying, "When we got the records I thought, *Where have I heard that name before?*"

"Showman," said Daniel. It was an accusation and an acknowledgment of the detective's power.

"The body was of a male, twenty-two years of age. Death by decapitation. He was your Jacques Palomba."

Daniel lost everything for a moment, then found himself on the floor. He had pulled the phone off the desk when he fell. He lay, wound in its coils. The phone squawked: "Father? Father Octave?"

Daniel retrieved the receiver. He put it to his ear and pinched his numb lips between its mouthpiece and his teeth. "Yes?" he said.

Daniel had last seen Jacques Palomba—the boy saved by Raimondi's second miracle—four years before, with his family, at the pilgrimage. Palomba was on antidepressants, his mother confided. Jacques found life difficult and disappointing. Nothing else had matched "the event." "Not its excitement, nor its *significance*," Jacques's mother said. She said that her son was a restless, dissatisfied boy. "He goes about as if he's looking for something he's lost." She had fumed with anxiety. She wanted Jacques to have a nice life. (She and her husband had nice lives. They had an apartment in Monaco, where she was an oral hygienist and he performed hair transplants—he'd done Sinatra. Their children had yachts, club memberships, the means to play tennis on the coveted clay courts and to go skiing four times a year.) "What would *you* say to Jacques, Father? Should he do something different? Something *difficult*? Perhaps God doesn't spare anyone like that just so that he can lead an ordinary life."

"Father?" said the detective.

Daniel sat up and wiped his eyes. He told the detective that he hadn't seen Jacques Palomba for four years. Had the detective contacted Palomba's family?

"Not yet."

"You called *me* first?"

"Yes." The detective was silent for a long moment; then he said, "You see, Father, I don't understand. I read your *Life of the Blessed Martine Raimondi*, and I don't understand." The detective was embarrassed. "I don't mean God's will. I don't expect to understand that. Because of my work there are times when I've thought about God's will. Thought hard. But, Father, I don't understand the *coincidence*."

Two people from the saint's story were dead in suspicious circumstances, and it seemed to Daniel and the detective that a subsidence had appeared in the world, around the saint's story. The kind of subsidence that first brings a hidden cave system to notice, to light.

"I don't understand it, either," Daniel told the detective. He got up off the floor and disentangled himself from the phone cord. "Will you contact Jacques's family now?"

"Yes," the detective said. "I'm sorry, Father. I had to share it—the coincidence. My colleagues think it's creepy. And I was hoping it might mean something to you."

"In what way?" Daniel said. For how could he explain to the detective what it meant to him, who had always had the uncomfortable feeling that there were things in Martine Raimondi's life that were, not exactly false, but *wrongly attributed*? Daniel said to the detective, "Look—long after you've finished calculating the statistical probability of Palomba and Dardo having lost their lives only a few days and kilometers apart, you'll still be wondering, about Palomba at least, *Why does God not go on protecting those He's saved?* I pray that in time, and with God's guidance, I'll be able to help you with *that*."

Daniel heard the detective sigh. He couldn't tell what sort of sigh it was. He said, "I'll be back in Nice from tomorrow, at the bishopric, if you need to reach me. While I'm there I'll visit Palomba's family in Monaco."

The detective thanked Daniel, then hung up abruptly, avoiding any ceremony—like Father Octave's blessing.

Statistical probability. Daniel couldn't recall exactly what he had said to the young tourist on the train. Something about odd events and the normal curve. But what was the normal curve? A run of blind wall, in a maze, along which you could walk, seeing only a little of the way ahead, until, eventually, around a long corner, you came face-to-face with the Minotaur.

Chapter 11

A BAD CANDIDATE

*E*ve heard Ila and Dawn arrive at the Menton apartment in the early hours of the morning. She thought she heard her sister laughing and wondered what Ila—silent Ila—might have done to make Dawn laugh.

After breakfast Eve went out to Martine's funeral—at which she was the sole mourner, Father Octave having failed to appear. She followed her friend up to the Moskelute tomb, oversaw the interment, and received its key from the undertaker. Eve thanked him and the priest and pallbearers. She pocketed the key and walked down through the old town.

She didn't go back to the apartment but spent the rest of the day in a manner customary to other Mentonnais of her station. She went to a patisserie and had a pear tart and a coffee. She sat in the shade on a park bench, beneath the orange trees on the Avenue Verdun. She nodded or spoke briefly to people she knew and once went into a café to borrow an ashtray, into which she poured some mineral water to rehydrate a tiny

white-haired troll of a dog who had been left tethered to the
leg of a bench by its master, who was asleep but plugged into
a radio giving a running commentary on a bicycle race.

Eve was too late for the markets, so she went into a shop
opposite the entrance to her street, bought several overripe
tomatoes, a baguette, and a cylinder of soft goat's cheese
coated with ash. She took her time considering wine—since
she was choosing for Dawn and Ila as well as for herself.

When she left the shop she stood still for a moment, dazzled by reflections, the low, angled sunlight on the glossy
patches of old chewing gum plastered to the pavement, then set
off across the delta of roadway at the bus station. At the entrance to the steep street to her apartment block Eve paused to
let a car go by. It was a long car and swung out in order to make
the turn into the narrow entry. Its windows were mirrored, and
Eve saw herself in its beetle green glass, foreshortened and as
pale as a wraith. The car revved and ran up the hill.

Eve went slowly, stopping now and then to catch her
breath. She trudged up the Palais Lutetia's front steps. It had
rained in Menton while she was up in the Roya Valley, for
the recently trimmed red and purple bougainvillea on the
balustrade had sprouted fresh, questing shoots. Eve waited a
moment in the sun, panting and hitching her shoulders to free
the fabric of her shirt from the patch of sweat on her back. She
noticed the car that had passed her, stopped in the yellow-
painted turning space of the *palais*'s inadequate parking lot. Its
driver was still sitting in it. Eve had the impression he was
watching her. She squinted but couldn't penetrate the reflective glass to see who he might be.

Eve pushed herself up the steps and went into her building.

It was cooler in the lobby beneath the apartment's central
well, where stairs with marble treads wound up ten floors
around an elevator shaft fenced with bronze mesh. The
Moskelute apartment was on the second floor, but because it
was her habit when burdened by shopping, Eve went to the el-

evator. As she put her hand into the handle of its concertinaed door, Eve heard footfalls behind her. Someone was hurrying up the flight of steps from the outer door to the entrance hall. Eve glanced back over her shoulder and saw a shapeless shadow against the blue late-afternoon sky and the orange-tiled roofs of the apartments down the slope. The figure came into the light from the stairwell and Eve saw his enveloping coat, ski mask, shades, gloved hands.

She hauled the elevator door open and lunged inside. The elevator cage shook. She swept the outer door closed and heard its catch click. She slid the inner door into place and flung herself away from the hand that snaked through the two cages and made a grab at her. She hit the up button.

The elevator hummed and began to move. Eve backed against the cage's far wall. As the elevator went up, she stooped to keep her attacker in sight.

The figure moved swiftly. Eve could suddenly see the whole rectangle of light from the front door. She began to jab as many buttons as she could and, as she'd hoped, the Palais Lutetia's aged and temperamental elevator came to a stubborn stop. Eve looked up and saw boots, the swinging hem of a long coat. He was on the second floor before the elevator and at the call button. She heard the button rattle as he pressed it rapidly, over and over.

The elevator didn't move.

The wrapped figure crept slowly back down.

Sunlight came through the tall windows that gave a view from each of the *palais*'s landings through the rear of the building and back toward the east, where the sun was touching the top of the high barrier of the Maritime Alps. There was a patch of hard, hot late-afternoon sun on the first marble-tiled landing. The bundled figure edged past it, his masked and hooded head averted. He came back down the lower flight. He stopped in the hall, raised his head, and looked into the elevator cage at Eve. He seized the outer cage and shook it.

A booming echoed up and down the height of the building. The metal grated and complained.

Who was this? Eve thought. Then she thought: *This is Tom.* Tom Hilxen—her husband's biographer. At some point she had recognized his walk, his posture. She said, perplexed, "Tom?"

Tom Hilxen doffed his hood and pulled off his shades and ski mask. He stuffed them into his pockets.

Eve said, "If I'd known it was you I wouldn't have imagined you were dangerous. You frightened me. What *are* you doing?"

Tom rattled the cage again. He put a hand through the bars and began to grope for the buttons.

Eve was so startled by his persistence that she dropped her shopping. The wine bottle burst. Shards of glass shot out in every direction, and a gush of wine splattered onto the elevator floor and ran out its open walls.

Tom kept up his fumbling search.

Eve tried to remain calm. She said, "What are you *doing*, Tom? Where have you been? Why are you trying to frighten me?"

She didn't get an answer. Instead Tom Hilxen jumped onto the bars of the outer cage and began to rattle them furiously.

The racket of Tom's attack brought Dawn to the door of the apartment. Dawn was awake early, tousled and in a bathrobe. She looked around the door and saw the elevator caught between floors with her sister inside it. She came out and padded down the first flight, her feet making sticky sounds on the marble. On the landing she stopped, then sank against the wall, her eyes streaming. She couldn't look for long—the sun reflecting from the floor near her bare feet was too strong. Dawn tucked her feet beneath the hem of the robe, flung her hair forward across her face, then made a small parting with a fingertip and peered through it.

Tom finally spoke. He said—to Dawn—"*No.*" He wasn't prepared to see her.

"No?" Dawn said sweetly.

"*Yes.* No," said Tom.

"Binary is a bit too slow for conversation, Tom," said Dawn. She edged along the wall, then whimpered, dropped her head, and thrust her reddening hands into the wide ends of the robe's sleeves.

Eve told her sister to stay put.

At that moment a woman appeared in the hall behind Tom. It was Eve's upstairs neighbor, a straw blond, mahogany-skinned matron. She said, "*Pardon,*" to Tom, then, when he didn't immediately move, "*Permesso!*"

Tom shuffled out of her way, angled his body toward the ranks of mailboxes, hunched his shoulders, and hung his head.

"Madame Moskelute, is there some problem with the elevator?" Eve's neighbor asked.

"Um," said Eve stupidly. Then, "Yes. I'm trapped. Could you call the concierge?" The concierge was on-site; his apartment had its entrance at the rear of the *palais*.

The neighbor looked dubious. She watched the elevator cage drip into the elevator well. The hall smelled of machine oil and spilled wine. The neighbor lived on the fifth floor, and she was laden with shopping. She hefted her bags and looked pointedly at Tom. Perhaps this able-bodied individual might be prevailed upon to carry them?

Tom refused to meet her eye.

The neighbor sighed. She said she'd call the concierge. She began up the stairs, sighing and huffing. "*Madame,*" she said again, greeting Dawn in tones of deep disapproval. (The building did not like its tenants to appear in the stairwell—or even on their balconies—in nightwear. The rule was informal but its pressure definite.)

Eve, Dawn, and Tom remained frozen while the burdened

matron huffed up ten flights to the fifth floor. They listened to her key in her lock, then her door closing.

Tom moved toward the elevator again. He put his arm back into the cage and sought the controls. Eve shrank against the far wall, well away from him. She shouted that the concierge was coming. She looked over her shoulder, saw Dawn edging through the narrow strip of shadow below the landing window. "Why are you trying to scare me?" Eve yelled at Tom. She knew that Dawn and Ila had hurt Tom, but he had stayed with them for years and had seemed to forgive them. When Tom vanished they all assumed that he'd met with some accident, not that he'd intended to disappear.

Tom said, "Ila's fledgling killed our nestling."

"Who?" Dawn said. "I don't understand."

Eve looked over her shoulder again. She saw the sun passing out of the notch in the mountain crest above St. Agnes, the gap that had concentrated the last ten minutes of its hot light. She saw a filmy fan of shadows sweep upward from the windowsill and close the other fan of hazy golden air. The ray of shadow brushed aside the ray of light, and both transparent geometries were gone. The window was suddenly blue with twilight, and Eve saw Ila cross it, leaping, airborne, a weightless blur. Dawn surged up after him—but looked slow. The whole stairwell shuddered as Ila hit the angle of its walls with both feet and one hand and launched himself, twisting in midair, in an arcing leap, over the whole bottom flight. Eve shifted her focus and saw Tom move toward the door, then stop, his back arched and arms outflung. Tom grunted, then wrenched himself off the blade in his back. The cleaver in Ila's hand continued its stroke; it slit Tom's coat open and slammed into the floor, shattering a tile.

Eve shouted at Ila, "Stop!"

Tom bolted. Ila hefted the cleaver—one of Eve's cooking utensils—and sprang after him. Tom staggered, and Ila took a skid on Tom's blood. They reached the front door at the same moment—Tom flung himself through it and, arms over his head, sailed across the balustrade. Ila came up hard against the brightness beyond the door, down toward the sea, where glass still scintillated in the low sun. He took cover against the door, his colorless eyes pouring tears.

Eve heard a car start; she heard it laboring back and forth, making an uncoordinated hash of its turn in the *palais*'s narrow parking lot. Dawn rushed out past Ila but returned as the car squealed away down the hill.

Dawn took off her bathrobe and used it to wipe up the blood, followed the splashes to their source, and dabbed at that. She folded the bloodied robe. Eve watched her sister, her swinging, matted blond and brown hair, her muscled body, its white markings smooth and continuous with her pale skin. "The concierge may come at any minute," Eve said.

Dawn said she was almost done. She slung the bloody robe over her shoulders and came to the cage. She stretched a slender arm through it but couldn't reach her sister. "Are you all right?" she asked.

Eve said she thought she was—only she wished they would both get out of sight before the concierge appeared.

Ila went back up the stairs, carrying the bloodied cleaver upright, like an ice-cream cone. Dawn sprinted up after him. They shut themselves into the apartment.

Eve waited. She was trembling. She knelt on the wet floor to shake bits of broken bottle out of the bag containing the rest of her shopping—sorted herself out thus far.

The concierge appeared, preceded by a wafting stink of pastis. He stared at Eve blearily and swayed. He had Madame Moskelute push the elevator's buttons in various combinations and himself hammered helplessly on the call button. Then he shrugged and blew out his cheeks and trudged up twenty flights to the control room at the top of the building. Five minutes later the elevator jerked into action. It traveled up to the tenth floor, where the concierge let Eve out. He scowled at the mess of wine and glass on the elevator floor. Eve gave him twenty francs, then picked up her shopping and went back down the stairs to her apartment.

Eve unpacked her shopping. She rinsed and dried her hands and set to work at chopping board and stove top. Ila sat on a sofa, his feet tucked under him, and licked blood from the cleaver. Dawn wandered in and out of a bedroom, changing her outfit several times. Eve eyed her sister and thought that this was a rather strange manifestation of distress. Then she looked down at the frying pan, her wooden spatula chasing a pile of caramelized onions from side to side of it, and she realized that really she and Dawn, though upset, were behaving completely in character—she was cooking, and Dawn was trying on clothes.

Eve said to Ila, "Did you hear what Tom said right before you came out the door?"

Ila didn't answer her. He was busy grooming a dribble of blood from one wrist.

"Actually . . . why haven't you *asked* us what Tom said?" Eve left her cooking unattended and came to the door. The spatula dripped green olive oil on her apron. "And why did you just attack him?"

Ila threw the cleaver down on the couch beside him and peered at Eve through the starbursts of his white eyelashes. "They go away, and come back, and think *I'm* the fatted calf," he said. "If they come back they're always trouble."

Eve shook her head at him.

"Tom killed Martine," Ila said, reasonable. "And now he's trying to kill you."

Eve asked what made Ila imagine Tom had killed Martine.

"He answered the phone in Martine's apartment."

Dawn reappeared, stooped over, shook herself, and came

up again to show the hall mirror the smooth tops of her breasts pressed together in the slit neck of a green dress. She told Ila he was barking up the wrong tree. "Tom said, 'Ila's fledgling killed our nestling.' "

"Martine wasn't a fledgling," said Eve. Then she asked Ila whether Tom had been in Martine's apartment before or after her death.

"After, I believe."

"We don't know that Martine wasn't a fledgling," Dawn said. "And I'm only going by what Tom said. In Ila's nest there was only me and Martine. *I* haven't killed anyone's nestling. Hell, I haven't even ever *met* another vampire. Tom must have meant Martine. If he was in her apartment he might have only been trying to find her. Find her and ask her questions."

Tom had said "*our* nestling." Eve wondered who Tom had found, who he could tolerate well enough to live with. Proud Tom. Resentful Tom.

"It's Martine who is dead," Ila said to Dawn. "Who was killed."

"And Martine couldn't have killed anyone," Eve added. She said that perhaps Tom had only wanted to talk to them about it—Ila's fledgling, his nestling—his grievance, whatever it was.

"Intimidate first and talk later? Well, yes, I suppose that's like Tom," Dawn said. Then to Ila, "But you showed up, with the cleaver."

"Do you imagine Tom was only playing with Eve?" Ila said to Dawn. "Only pretending? No. Tom was always a bad choice. Not that he was mine. Not that I *had* a choice."

Eve's knife paused in its tattoo on the chopping board. Dawn stopped peering into the mirror. For a moment the only sound was of garlic and onions sizzling in the pan.

Dawn said, "This is the most we've heard from you in over a year."

"I talked to Martine," Ila said.

"Oh, *that's* right. Martine was your guru. Martine was your confessor."

"Dawn," Eve said, warning her sister.

Ila hung his head; he nodded at the rug, rhythmic nodding, as though he were jacked into some music inaudible to them. He said, "Eve? Is she *really* dead?"

Eve was gentle. She said, "Yes, she is. We'll go and say goodbye to her tonight. But I must make dinner first, since I'm at the bottom of the food chain."

Dawn strutted out of the room and came back a moment later in a red slip dress and carrying some black pumps by their tall heels. She dropped the shoes on the floor and mounted them, cocked her hip, and wriggled to show the mirror her small pouting belly and raised rump.

Eve asked her sister what she was doing.

"She's dressing for her new friend," Ila said.

"Something's burning," Dawn said.

Eve turned to the stove to chip at the place where the bacon's thready flesh had adhered to the pan.

Eve had answered Tom Hilxen's second letter, the one that arrived in 1979, two weeks after Jean had died. Tom offered his condolences and asked if he might see her. He had a grant to do some study, he wrote, to extend his thesis on Jean Ares. To turn it into a book. Eve acknowledged Tom's condolences and said she wasn't ready to meet him, wasn't ready even to consider decisions she had to make.

Tom Hilxen came to Europe and seemed to circle her. She would hear from one of Ares's sons that he'd met Mr. Hilxen. A daughter had a copy of Mr. Hilxen's thesis. Another daughter mailed Eve a copy of an obituary—from the *Denver Post*—with Tom Hilxen's byline. Apparently the family were all better prepared than Eve had been for Jean to continue his journey. *Downward,* Eve thought, remembering the smooth mechanism by which Jean's casket had sunk into its green baize–lined grave, a grave like a jeweler's case set in the dry white soil of the cemetery. Eve imagined a continuation of that smooth process. Her husband would go on down into the smelter of a first posthumous biography and emerge, bronze-dipped, sealed off from her in the shell of someone else's regard. Someone—this young American.

They did eventually meet. Eve sought a meeting after she read Hilxen's article about Jean's first marriage. He had interviewed Anna Beder, the photographer to whom Jean was married from 1927 to 1936. Their alliance was a famous one—famously difficult and dramatic—and it had been written about often, by art historians and memoirists. What Tom's article contributed to the discussion was a sensitive interview with Madame Beder talking for the first time about Ares in a tone that was both tender and *temperate.* She covered familiar material, but her interviewer had helped her rethink. Jean Ares was still a maddening monster of ego and appetite, but, Beder said, at the article's conclusion: "I'm sure that Eve Moskelute has a different story, and had a different Jean Ares."

Eve issued an invitation. She asked Tom to a lunch she gave each year, late September, at the house in Cap de Nice. At their meeting Eve was pleased by Tom's courtesy, his boyish courtliness. She liked his ardent interest in Ares and in all Ares's family. He paid attention to everyone and never appeared rushed or rapacious for information. She liked the way he carried plates, handed Jean's aged sister to her chair, retied a six-year-old grandchild's sash, and kicked a ball with the boys.

But, toward the day's end, his convivial attention to Eve became more of an approach. There were things he thought he should mention. He had read her book. He said they must have a talk, practitioner to practitioner, about the nature of his task. He said, "I welcome an opportunity to discuss *our* discipline, as well as *my* subject." He said things that Eve was sure

he believed she wanted to hear—for instance, the airy plati-
tude: "How can we know to write a life?" He clearly thought
she needed a sign of his respectful attitude to the compromises
and uncertainties of a biographer's art. Tom's pose was perhaps
meant to be reassuring but was a routine gesture of abdication,
of abdicated responsibility. It was like his courtesy: Tom figu-
ratively stood aside for Eve, seeming to say, *After you. You knew
him.* Seeming to say, *Informants first.*

Eve was annoyed that Tom had chosen this approach, that
he had chosen to coat his real passion for Jean's work with this
sugary plausibility.

Also at Eve's lunch was one of Ares and Anna Beder's
grandchildren, a boy of nineteen who regarded his grandfather's fame as a favor he could call in, and a chip he could cash
in, anywhere between Menton and Marseille. The boy was
very keen on Tom—an American biographer was just another
sign of his grandfather's specialness, a specialness that Eve
knew the boy secretly hoped would someday shine in him, too.
Though the boy hoped to profit by Ares and to angle himself
to reflect Ares's radiance, he also hoped to inherit his grandfather's energy and appetite, to find, as Ares had, a cataract at the
back of the cave of his character. The boy was enthusing to
Tom, in competent English, about Ares's work and the sort of
soul "from whose deep rose those rainbow monsters."

"Ah . . . but do we want to buy into the myth of the
Artist?" Tom said, with mealymouthed snubbing sophistica-
tion. He met Eve's eyes, complicitous.

A week after the lunch Tom called. He said that he was
sorry they had "got off on the wrong foot." Sorry they had
made a poor start.

"Start of what?" Eve said. Then, "What did you mean by
what you said? Were you letting me know that Ares's biography wasn't buying into Ares's myth? Or did you mean—and I
think you *did* mean—that you don't believe in the specialness
of artists? Do you think that it's only a sorry need we have to

suppose that an artist like Ares wasn't like you and me? Do you suppose that my belief that my husband was special is only a disorder of worship in a secular age?

"Listen," Eve said. She told Tom that she was one of those people who had *laughed* at half of Jean's paintings. "He liked that. I laughed because his paintings were maddeningly amusing, as well as beautiful. Sometimes I'd watch him work. I'd share his light and read. Or I'd just watch him, awed and appalled. And when he was done—I'd know because he'd clean his fingers—he would turn around to me, with the old turps-covered towel in his hands, and raise his eyebrows to ask me what I thought. I'm thinking of *one* occasion now. An example. I can remember asking him, 'Why that expression?' And he looked at the painting and said, 'Ah, I see,' and began to laugh. And I said, 'That man is going to lose the wrestling match because he's busy being shocked by the size of his opponent's feet.' Then we laughed harder, and sat, laughing, and wiping our eyes." Eve said to Tom Hilxen that she thought that the life in Jean's work came out of Jean. That all his canvases were mirrors he'd once looked into and which had taken a print of his positive attention. "His work was special," Eve said, "and there isn't any more of it. No more where that came from. Because, gosh"—she slapped her forehead, despite the fact that she was on the phone and the gesture would be lost on Tom— "his work came from *him.*"

Tom was quiet, listening.

"What's more," Eve said, "you're *not* like me. We can't indulge in talk about 'the nature of the task.' When I wrote about Chambord all I did was move the dust about. You're interviewing the family of the deceased. We're *the bereaved.*"

"I understand," Tom said.

"Good," Eve said, and hung up on him.

Later she relented. She didn't regret what she'd said, only discovered that she'd been wrong about one thing—that in writing about Chambord she'd stirred up more than dust.

192 の Elizabeth Knox

A scant month after the family lunch, Eve took her anonymous eighteenth-century illumination to a picture framer. She and the framer unpacked it together while they discussed how best to mount it. A calling card fell out of the packaging. The card said "Martine Dardo" and carried an address in Genoa and a phone number. Eve put the card in her pocket. Over the next few days she would take it out occasionally and brood upon it. Then she called Martine Dardo. They arranged a meeting. Eve was to visit Martine at her house one evening. The evening arrived, and Eve appeared carrying a basket of chocolate orange sticks from Geoff de Bruges. She found that Martine Dardo wasn't alone. In Martine's twilit living room there was a young woman standing at the window, a young woman with butchered brown and blond hair, a big-eyed, jittery young woman who, after a long bewildered moment, Eve was able to recognize as her twin, her sister—her dead sister—Dawn.

Tom Hilxen conducted his interviews with Eve in the last year of the decade in which she'd lived with Ares. As an interviewer Tom was scrupulous rather than sympathetic. He listened, leaning away from the black radiator of a big tape recorder, as stolid and as imposing as his machine. Tom's neutral attention imbued each interview with a sense of responsibility. They were doing vital, serious work. If Tom had been more eager, Eve might have felt that they were having a conversation, that she was telling her stories for the benefit of the person present, not just posterity.

Jean had been a very good listener, avid and responsive, and had trained Eve in intimate conversation. She could talk to Jean for hours and never feel like a broadcaster. Rather, she would feel like a helmsman of a boat on a river, negotiating a current, watching the riverbank and watched by it, traveling somewhere fresh and unexpected on the flow of her husband's

perfectly navigable attention. Talking to Tom—and his machine—exhausted Eve. She felt that she was giving blood (and
she knew about that, gave regularly, wrapped up with her lost-
and-found twin in a strange and more desperate version of
their embraces during the thunderstorms of their childhood).

Eve talked and relived her marriage. It was like talking to
an insurance assessor about what was missing after a theft or
fire and discovering just how irreplaceable it all was. She
grieved; she filled her wineglass too often and lost her temper
with the biographer, who was there, all ears—ears and not
much else—assaying every word, sorting the dross of her feelings from the heavier mineral of his subject's life. Eve cried
and insulted Tom, and he was finally moved—apparently
moved—because he put his arms around her and soothed her
by repeating, over and over, the name of one of Jean's famous
paintings—*Drunken Eve.*

Once Eve had lost her temper with Tom she began to enjoy
his company, rather than only submit dutifully to his project.
She found she was able to talk about him to Dawn in an
amused and disparaging way. To tell "Tom" stories.

"Tom's working on reconciling one Ares with another,"
Eve told Dawn. "For instance—Anna Beder's Ares and mine.
I spoke to Anna the other day and she said—and this is an
old woman's perspective—that Tom just doesn't understand
how much people can change over a lifetime. But I think Tom
knows full well, only Tom thinks Jean shouldn't have
changed—or, enjoying the kind of influence he enjoyed, Jean
should have been a better person, or possibly that the only
mitigating circumstance of Jean's criminally great talent
should have been an inhuman consistency. Tom *frets* about it.
He's been in thrall, imaginatively, to Jean for ten years and he
feels resentful. You see . . . Tom loves Jean, but Jean doesn't
love Tom."

"So is that why Tom's having an affair with you?" Dawn said. "His unrequited love for your husband?"

Eve laughed and said that she hoped Tom's biography was his love's consummation and that she and Tom were possibly only caught up in the excitement of a shared project. "But I like Tom, Dawn. And I feel as if he's the very last gift Jean has given me. I'm *grateful* for Tom."

"Grateful to Jean for Tom," Dawn said.

Eve told her sister that her general sense of gratitude to Jean Ares for everything—her life, his world—would probably stay with her forever and would, in time, include all sorts of other things that life brought her.

"Are you sure you're not just a fetish to Tom?" Dawn said. "Isn't that what fucking a great man's widow is usually about?"

"But we get on so well," Eve said, rather weakly—though it was true.

She and Tom enjoyed each other. She was the first person to read the manuscript of his biography—and had her say before his agent and his commissioning editor. Then the book was in production and he was back and forth between the States and Europe. Eve saw less of him, but they kept up a lively correspondence over the proofs. It was vital, Eve understood, for her to have an intimate relationship in the world, one at least, among all her many friends and acquaintances and Jean's numerous relations, for her to have someone near to her in the world *aboveground*. Because Eve, like Persephone, spent half her life in an underworld with Dawn and the two vampires of Dawn's nest. Tom's passions all had recognizable social faces. He was ambitious; he fought scholarly battles, had intellectual foes, was exacting, fastidious, and decorous. He wasn't ever to be found drowsy and fastened mouth-to-mouth with someone by dried blood.

On each of Tom's returns to Europe he and Eve would resume their affair. In 1983 the book came out, in several languages, and was widely promoted, so that Eve would encounter it often—its cover and herself as *Eve among the Arlesiennes.*

Tom stopped over on an author tour and took Eve to dinner. They went to a restaurant with no view and with a small menu serving only Niçoise cuisine. Eve was pleased to note that Tom had finally absorbed this one of her lessons on how to live in a place of high-volume tourism and passionate local epicurism. She watched him with the waiters and saw that he knew exactly how to behave. She was proud of him.

Over dessert he asked her whether she thought—honestly—that their relationship had any future.

Eve was careful. She said that she hoped that, like her, he was happy to go on as they were until things changed. "For instance," she said, "you find a new subject, or a job that keeps you in America all the time. Or until one of us becomes committed to someone else in a way that means we must end this." Then Eve asked Tom if there was someone else.

Tom shook his head. Then he said that he just didn't see any future in their relationship.

Eve remained calm. She considered the nine years between their ages. She said she was sorry, she wasn't very good at thinking about the future. "But you know that."

Tom nodded. "Yes. You lost your sister. And Ares was in his seventies."

How wonderful it was, Eve thought, to be so succinctly understood.

"It's the age difference," Tom said.

Eve was thirty-nine; he, thirty-one.

"You want a family?" Eve said.

"Well . . . that," Tom said, as though it *wasn't* that. As though the problem for him was that Eve was fading and depreciating in value. Eve knew that she was still rather beautiful. But she knew exactly how much ground she had lost between twenty-seven and thirty-nine—could see herself at twenty-seven whenever she looked at the lustrous Dawn.

"I see," Eve said. Then she told Tom that naturally she wouldn't hold him. But she'd thought they were having a marvelous time.

Tom took her hands. He said that he felt very privileged to have known her.

And Eve, looking around the restaurant, said, with only mild reproach, that she wished he'd waited till they were alone to have this conversation.

"I suppose it was cowardly of me," he said.

"A little."

"I didn't want any dramatics."

Tom didn't want dramatics, but he continued to come and go in Eve's part of the world, and when he was there he'd call up and visit her and would sit staring at her with mournful expectation.

In 1984 he was in Arles for several weeks, working on a documentary some American director was making about Ares. Tom told Eve, over the phone, that they'd been filming in the Roman Storehouse when the strangest thing had happened. "A woman appeared. A woman in white. She was watching us from a discreet distance, and I said to Pete that we should get a shot of her—a blurry long shot—and use it for *Eve under the Arches*. Pete said okay, but that perhaps we should ask first. So I approached her and—Eve—*she looked like you*. I was walking toward her, and the nearer I got, I kept expecting the illusion to dissipate. For there to be something different. Something *amiss*. But there wasn't. This girl—she's an Italian—she's a dead ringer. She even has your mouth—like she's looking for a fight. You know."

Tom was so excited by—as he saw it—this gift of coincidence. "So we're going to use her," he concluded.

Eve carried the phone to the limit of its cord. She picked up a cup, a gilt-rimmed teacup with a mustache protector—some old Moskelute thing. She stood in the hallway and threw the cup at Dawn's door.

"What was that?" Tom said.

Eve told him that her grandfather had tossed his teacup at her grandmother. "An incurable snob. German. Her father was Bismarck's undersecretary. She never let anyone forget it."

"Eve. They're not alive." Tom was pedantic and not at all playful. It was *his* turn to astonish *her*, and she should be listening to his story.

"No. But," Eve said.

Dawn's door opened and Dawn peered around it, tousled. She yawned and flashed her spines at Eve, then brushed the shards of porcelain with her toes.

"But," Eve said to Tom. "There are no coincidences. How can this girl just look like me? You stay away from her."

"Jealous?" said Tom, and Eve could hear his smirk.

" 'You are ambrosia to me,' " Eve quoted. " 'But in my mouth it is you who will become as a god.' "

Tom said, "What?" Then, "Oh . . . Chambord again." He was quiet, thinking.

Eve looked into her sister's eyes. Dawn had understood that it was Tom Hilxen on the phone and was smiling and twisting a lock of hair around one finger.

"So, what you're trying to say is that *you're* the real oil, not some dewy twenty-something look-alike," Tom said. "Oh, Eve. I have absolutely no intention of *sleeping* with this girl."

"All right," Eve said, tired.

" 'Absolutely no dramatics,' " Dawn said, quoting Tom.

Tom wanted to know if someone was there with Eve.

"Dawn is with me."

A pause. Then, "I see. The family ghosts. Sister, grandma, grandpa."

Eve asked Tom if he imagined that God loved him so

much that He would send him—and this director Pete—a prop made of flesh. Then she said, "*Dawn* looks like me at twenty-seven."

Dawn said, "I'll give him an 'age difference.' "

"Dawn is indignant on my behalf," Eve said.

"Oh, Eve," said Tom. "Is this one of those put-on multiple-personality things? You never struck me as the histrionic type." He sounded secretly pleased.

Eve told Tom that he was a fool.

The next time Eve saw Tom Hilxen he was lying, limp and pale, in Dawn's bed, his nipples surrounded by wide aureoles of fresh bite wounds.

Dawn told Eve that she'd quite like to keep Tom. But she didn't husband him, and Eve had to watch him become gradually breathless, hollow-eyed, and shuffling. When she couldn't bear to see more—or to have any part in what would happen—Eve went away. She went to Paris to stay with friends.

Martine told her later what happened.

Only Ila could "make" Tom. Dawn and Martine were only nestlings, too young to be infectious or to build their own nests. Ila, old, infectious, "a breeder," was the only one able to decide who would join them.

Silent Ila had been listening to what was said about Tom Hilxen—and he said no. He listened to Martine's arguments. She said that Dawn couldn't just let Tom go, because of the kind of man he was. "He digs and delves and tells people stories," Martine argued. "He's practically a vampire already—the way he latched on and fattened himself on Eve's Jean."

"*I don't want him,*" Ila said.

Dawn and Martine badgered Ila so he withdrew to Dardo,

to the house—his but in Eve's name—on the Rue Oscura. He went into hibernation—as Martine and he had lately been teaching themselves to do. "Sleep more; eat less," Martine said, like a mantra. It was a discipline at which Ila far excelled her. Martine could manage only a fortnight. Ila could hole up in July and not emerge until September.

Dawn and Tom followed Ila to Dardo six weeks later. The house was locked—but Dawn had a key. Ila's room wasn't locked, and Dawn had brought a heavy bolt and a padlock. She had Tom put the bolt on Ila's door, at noon, when Ila would be in his deepest sleep. At evening, when she woke, Dawn unfastened Ila's door and sent Tom into Ila's room.

Martine had worked out what Dawn was about when Dawn and Tom didn't appear one night—Tom was, by then, not fit enough for any purposeless excursions. Martine followed them to Dardo and arrived, shortly before sunrise, to find Dawn trying to reason with Ila through the padlocked door. Dawn was talking, saying again and again that Ila *owed* her. Martine could almost hear Ila's ferocious silence. "I'm here," Martine said to him, through the door, then, quietly to Dawn, "Ila might easily have killed him. Did you think of that?"

"Then he'd have done it—not me," Dawn said, her little lower jaw set and chin dimpled. "Tom was too far gone to think of it himself."

Martine could hear Tom in the room. He was crying, saying, "I'm sick. I'm sick."

Then the women heard sounds, cracks and smashes, timber breaking—not the door, oak and oak-framed, or the bolt, steel and two and a half centimeters in diameter.

Ila went out through the ceiling of the room and through the tiled roof—though the tiles were heavy slabs of the local green shist. The women spun around to see big black squares of tile falling past the east-facing window. The sun was barely behind the mountains, and the sky was blue. Tiles rasped down the roof and fell. Dawn shoved the key into the padlock, opened it, shot the bolt, and went into the room shouting at Martine to lock it after her.

Ila swung through the window, just as the sun appeared.

For the next moment he and Martine were busy, standing against the wall on either side of the window frame and gingerly prodding the shutters closed. Their coordinated effort was rewarded, and the sunlight was excluded from the room.

"The door is locked," Martine told Ila.

"There's a hole in the roof. She won't like that at noon," Ila said.

"I'll let them out before then," Martine said.

Ila fixed his eyes on the door.

"This needn't be farcical," Martine said. "You made him. He's yours now, too."

"He caught his death. He trapped it, and starved it out of its scruples."

Martine said that desperate times called for desperate measures.

"You've said that to me before," Ila told her. "About the soldiers in the Castel Abelio. I can still see them, and the broken keep full of steam from their opened bodies." Then Ila told Martine that he'd go to Dawn's room to sleep. Martine could deal with everything.

Tom was sick; then he got better and grew strong. He became a good vampire—cautious, self-controlled, apparently eager to learn how best to live.

For seven years—'85 to '92—Tom was a nestling in Ila's nest. Then, one day, he didn't come home. He had roamed a little before, so they waited. They waited because the caves at Dardo had flooded and Tom could be trapped somewhere remote and waiting for the water to go down. But after a month they gave him up—Martine and Ila gave him up for dead.

"He was caught out," Ila said. "It happens."

Eve began to cry then, because for the first time she could see a terrible possibility, that one day Dawn would fail to come home. That Dawn would be gone again—and without a trace, like Tom, like some unfixed photographic image when the darkroom door is accidentally opened during a delicate part of the development process.

"But Tom was still able to go abroad, wrapped up. He was still quite tolerant of sunlight," Dawn argued. "He'd be hard to catch out. How could he be?"

They all thought about it for a time. Ila moved to Eve's side and put his hand lightly on her arm. Eve blew her nose and looked at him, then at Martine, who was staring through the wall of the room—the main room of the house in Dardo. Martine wore the look of a seer, someone seeing some event happening a long way off, in another country, or in the future. Martine said, "He could be caught out in a boat. In a boat far from land."

On the evening of Martine's funeral Eve had her dinner. Ila and Dawn kept her company with a glass of wine each.

When Eve was in the kitchen doing her dishes she heard the doorbell. She dried her hands and went to answer it, expecting to see the entrance hall empty, Ila and Dawn having made themselves scarce. But they were both still there. Ila was on the sofa under her mother's portrait, and Dawn was at the door.

The visitor was Dawn's. It was the young man who, a week before, Eve had dispatched to Jean's house in Nice.

"Eve, I believe you know Bad Phelan?" Dawn said. She drew the young man into the room and helped him unbuckle and shuck his heavy pack.

Bad smiled at Eve and wiggled his eyebrows.

"And here's Ila, too, Bad," Dawn said. "I hope you don't

mind turning right around—after another glass of wine perhaps? We were all about to go out and visit Martine's tomb." Dawn was leaning against her friend and speaking too quickly.

Bad said to Eve that it turned out that the only coincidence was the poster on the garage pillar, Ares's portrait of her. The moment he noticed the poster was, for him, so vividly memorable that it was still in his head when something else reminded him of Dawn. Martine's hair. "Given only those things—the poster and Martine's hair—I was able to make connections and follow them. I made a rope by splicing other ropes, and I climbed down it. You see, *I'd been bitten before.*"

"So, here you are," Eve said.

Dawn turned to face Eve and Ila, her arm around Bad's waist. She said, more to Ila than Eve, that Bad wasn't just her friend; he was her *candidate.*

At dusk Eve parked her car in the turning bay by the gates of Menton's old cemetery. She had called the caretaker, and he was waiting for her. Bad watched from the back window. He saw money change hands. He saw Eve open the brandy bottle she carried, then produce a glass from the pocket of her swing coat. She poured the caretaker a glass, and he sat down on a low pediment at the foot of the steps to drink it. He left the cemetery gates open and his keys hanging in the lock.

Eve came back to the car and tapped on the window. The others got out and joined her. They went up the steps into the cemetery and the caretaker gave each of them a nod as they went by, even Ila, who had his face turned away.

They went up to the top terrace. The path between the graves was strewn with white peastone, into which Dawn's heel spikes sank several centimeters deep.

Eve stopped at the door of a large tomb. Its walls were canted slightly, the ground on which it stood subsiding. Its onion dome and walls were covered in faded tiles, set in a black lattice of mildewed grouting. Eve passed the brandy bottle to Dawn and fished two further glasses from her pocket. "We can share," she said.

Dawn peered at the bottle's label.

"I got it from the place that carries brandy for every year," Eve said. "Every birthday."

"Which birthday, though?" Dawn squinted at the smaller print. "Nineteen twenty-one or nineteen forty-four?" Then she complained that her eyes hadn't used to play up in this light.

Ila took off the steel-framed aviator glasses with which he'd hidden his eyes and passed them to Dawn. Passed them across Bad, who stood between them. Bad turned and stared at Ila. The vampire might be mistaken for an albino, but his color wasn't quite right:—more white blond and sand—in hair and skin—than an albino's sanguine pink and downy white. Ila's skin, in the cyanotic rose of the twilight, was simply too pale. His movements were quick and deft, but he was worn, looked dehydrated and as leached of living color as a dying man.

"Who am I sharing with?" Dawn asked her sister, then bumped Bad with her hip.

"Bad had nearly a bottle before," Eve said. "And now he can't control his big feet."

"Nothing for Bad," Dawn said to Bad, and bumped him again.

Ila had gone to the door of the tomb and stood with his palms and one cheek pressed to its greened bronze. "Is she really dead, Eve?" he asked again. "I didn't *see* her." He turned his head, swapped cheeks, as though he hoped to cool them on the metal. "I never do see them," he said.

"*Them.*" Dawn's voice was bleak, despite Bad's ardent nuzzling. "Us," she said. "Your series of lost loves. Of failed projects."

"Martine," Ila whispered, to the woman in the tomb. "My nestling."

"*My* friend," said Eve. She took the bottle from her sister. She filled the two glasses. "Let's do this properly," Eve said. She raised a glass. "To my friend Martine, who trusted me, and took me into her family."

Dawn raised her glass too, her slender arm twisted inward, like Liberty with her torch. "Here's to Martine, who was kind to me in Corsica, when I was lost." She put the glass to her mouth, swigged, and handed it to Ila.

Ila—the Island—came away from the tomb door to take the glass but said nothing.

Bad took the glass from Eve. "Me, too," he said. He was exultant. "Here's to Martine! I didn't know her, but I was able to do something for her. And I was repaid, ten times over."

"Is it ten times?" said Dawn. "Are you counting?"

Bad giggled. He put his mouth to the glass, sipped, and spluttered.

Ila tasted his brandy and then set the glass on the lintel of the tomb door. It fell off and broke.

"I bet you could have caught that," Bad said. He was disappointed. He gave his own glass back to Eve and stooped to collect the shards.

Ila turned his head down sharply. He inhaled and said, "You've cut yourself," to Bad—the first time he'd addressed him.

Eve wiped her eyes on the back of one hand, swung her shoulder bag before her, and raised its flap to take out a box. Bad saw silver, gold, and glass: it was the reliquary Dawn had stolen from St. Barthelemy's. Eve fumbled at the box. She sniffed and then sobbed.

"Oh, *Eve.*" Dawn put her arms around her sister, then removed the reliquary from Eve's grasp. She, too, tried to open it, with no more success.

"In case of fire, break glass," said Bad.

Dawn passed the reliquary to him and he carried it across the path and struck the crystal front against an arrowhead spike on the iron railing. The crystal cracked and Bad inverted the box, then fished inside. He held out his hand to Dawn, the match sulphur end up between his thumb and index finger. Dawn took it and gave it to Ila. Ila stepped up to the tomb, braced the brittle aged splinter with his finger, and struck its head against the door. He held the flame there, bright, in a halo of verdigris. He said, very softly, "When you stopped in the cave, you should have looked at this light, and not at me. I should have left you to God."

The match was old and dry. Its flame ran swiftly down into the valley between Ila's desiccated fingertips, where it flared, a bright point under its blackened stem's interrogative curl. Then it flared, shrank, turned blue, and went out.

Chapter 12

DANIEL IS GROOMED

*D*aniel missed Martine's funeral because Jacques Palomba's uncle, who was answering the phones at the family's Monaco apartment, was of the opinion that Father Octave should stop in that morning. It was not a suggestion.

Daniel caught an early train. When he got off at Monaco the dew of the 4:00 A.M. sprinklers hadn't yet evaporated from the flawless cut-pile lawns and flower beds of parks that were really only road islands. The municipal workers were out in force, and the streets looked scoured, then—as the sunlight reached them—steam-cleaned, as though fresh from a steriliz- ing machine.

Palomba's father and uncle were in a car, waiting to turn into traffic, paused at the nearly perpendicular entrance to the underground garage of the Palombas' apartment building. The uncle recognized Daniel and let his window down. They were on their way to Genoa, he said, where they had an appointment with the police. Jacques's father tried to get out of the car but couldn't open the door against gravity. Daniel helped him; he held the door, and let it down when the man was clear. Palomba's father looked ill, waxy and sweating. His hair gel had deposited a milky tidemark at his hairline. He shook Daniel's hand. He said that his wife was asleep, finally. She would want to see Daniel, but . . .

"I can come back."

". . . but the girls are up."

"The girls" were Palomba's daughters. One was in her late twenties, the other in her mid-teens.

"Well . . . you're here," said Jacques's father. "You should see them." His eyes grew red. His brow remained serene, his eyes wide open in their baby's-palm surrounds of cushiony pink skin. The man's face was frozen by some cosmetic procedure, but his voice seesawed with grief. "You should go up," he said. He turned back to the car. Daniel lifted its bank-vault door and Jacques's father dropped himself into it. Before the door closed, Daniel was caught in a frigid gust of leather-scented air—the Mercedes's big-pore pigskin seats. The car revved and moved, fell forward and upright, and swung into the traffic.

Daniel followed the building's curved facade and found its main door. He buzzed and gave his name and was admitted.

The elder sister sat with Daniel on a sofa, clutched his hand, and wept. The younger perched on a chair facing them, tilted forward as though ready for flight, or a high-impact embrace.

The sisters were not coherent. They would sob for long moments, then rush into speech together. Questions mostly: "Do you . . . ?" Or: "Why does . . . ?" They'd get no further.

The elder said, "Jacques was better." She said, "He did this," and touched the top of her head, lifted her tousled gold curls so that the skin on her throat slid upward and the angle between her jaw and neck grew shallow. Daniel watched her

gesture and looked for injuries. Then he realized she meant
her hair. "He was working," she said. "We didn't talk. The
music was loud, and he was dancing about behind my chair."

The younger girl asked Daniel if they could pray. They
stacked their hands, and Daniel prayed. He couldn't speak to
measure, so spoke to form. He was deaf to himself. He didn't
know who his prayer was for. Seven years earlier he had interviewed Jacques Palomba but had only heard and looked on
Jacques through the one-way glass of his story.

As Daniel was on his way out he asked Jacques's older sister if she recalled the name of the place Jacques worked—the
salon where he'd cut her hair.

"It was a spa, Father," she said.

"Where is it?"

"Genoa," she said, and gave him the name of the street. "It
has a white facade and gilded ironwork."

The following day Daniel caught the same early train and,
with a change at Ventimiglia, he was in Genoa by noon. The
spa was called Paradiso, and the woman at the reception desk
wouldn't let Daniel into its salon—Inferno—without an appointment. She said that lunch was a bad time and did Daniel
know what he wanted? What in the way of a haircut?

Daniel shook his head. He was wearing a crew-necked
shirt, not his collar. He kept his hand over his lapel pin—his
little gold cross. "I'll wait," he said. He took a seat. The receptionist fetched him a coffee and gave him the spa's current
catalog. She sat back down at her glass-topped desk, a devo-
tional figure between two candles, the tea lights under oil
burners.

Paradiso was really too steep for Daniel's purse. He didn't
have to account for *everything* but had already overspent on
train fares. This was the second trip he'd taken without the
bishop's permission. He hadn't been able to ask, hadn't even

been able to say, *The boy Blessed Martine saved has been murdered. His head was cut off.*

Daniel removed his lapel pin and put it in his pocket. He counted his money.

The receptionist answered her phone. She touched the tiny bead of the microphone before her mouth. She looked at Daniel, her irises human within the zone of her outlined, diagrammatic eyes. She told Daniel that the stylist could take him at 12:40.

They were playing trance on the sound system in the salon— an endless slippery chute of music.

The stylist slipped his fingers into Daniel's neat, wet-combed hair, pulled it up, and dropped it. The stylist listened to Daniel for a moment, then scowled and said he didn't *do* dry cuts. He wheeled Daniel over to a sink, positioned him, then tilted his chair. Daniel's head balanced on a point at the base of his skull, on the lip of the black porcelain sink. The stylist waved his apprentice away. He said he'd wash Daniel's hair himself. He leaned over Daniel. The stylist wore a sleeveless Lycra shirt and Daniel could see the man's armpits and hair like smooth weeds in a watercourse.

The stylist shielded Daniel's forehead with the blade of his hand. He aimed the warm stream of the shower behind it. Daniel felt heat cup his scalp. Drops ran into one of his ears, pooled, and cooled. A cap clicked, and the stylist poured a syrup of raspberry-scented shampoo into one palm, put his hands together, and lathered Daniel's hair. He leaned down, put his mouth by Daniel's ear. "You asked about Jacques," he said. "Are you the police?"

"No," said Daniel.

The stylist straightened; he went to work with his fingertips, and Daniel's scalp slipped about over his skull. The man inclined closer again, his thumbs busy above Daniel's temples.

"Are you another of Jacques's spooky friends?" the stylist asked.

"Tell me about them," Daniel said.

The man met Daniel's eyes, then picked up the shower-head again to rinse Daniel's hair. "Do you ever condition it?" he asked.

"My hair? No. I use whatever I find."

"In the supermarket?"

"In the shower."

The stylist clicked his tongue against his palate. He toweled Daniel's hair, then sat him up to apply an aromatic treatment. He stood behind Daniel and massaged his scalp.

Daniel closed his eyes. He was floating. The membrane of the moment ruptured, time revealed a capacity hitherto undisclosed to him and only breathed in. Time filled him up, and he was falling asleep for once *inside* rather than *beside* himself. Daniel made an effort; he roused himself. He said, "Jacques's family knew about the drugs."

The drugs were no big deal, the stylist said, only the usual—party drugs. They didn't suit Jacques, though, who was always down between parties. Depressed.

"Were these people—Jacques's spooky friends—something to do with the drugs?"

The stylist said Daniel was on the same false trail as the police. Jacques had left the spa five months before. The last time the stylist had seen him, Jacques had been less depressed, perhaps, but smug and secretive. "And he was with that woman, his client. . . ."

The woman—Jacques's client—had come in every two weeks to have her roots touched up. Red. She was prematurely gray, in her twenties, but silver, like Richard Gere, or perhaps white, like Steve Martin. "There's a gene for that," the stylist said. "Premature gray." Jacques had touched up her hair, tinted her eyebrows and eyelashes.

The stylist turbaned Daniel's head in a towel and got him

up, led him to a station before a triptych of mirrors, each a Gothic arch. On the granite-topped bench before the mirrors stood a white dish full of tea lights. By their radiance Daniel saw himself, his face boyish and unused, younger than his years, and poorly ornamented by his mother's cold, shy, inscrutable eyes. The stylist slipped the spike of a comb into Daniel's hairline and began to separate his hair into sections. He asked Daniel if he had thought yet what he wanted done.

"Nothing flamboyant."

"No? Well, it's too short to offer much scope, not without color. And it's good hair, a great color, true Tropic of Cancer black."

The stylist called out to an apprentice. He asked her to go find last year's appointment book. "There'll be a name and contact number for that woman," he told Daniel.

"Did you give all this to the police?" Daniel asked—and blinked as a fall of wet cut hair splattered down, brushed his eyelashes, and settled like scattered stamens on the backs of his hands.

"This was Jacques's last place of employment. He gave up his apartment shortly after he left his job. The police wanted to know where he'd been living, who with, and *what on*. They wanted to know about his drug taking. We"—the stylist indicated the serpentine line of mirrored stations and hairdressers busy with scissors, razors, foils, dye-covered brushes—"we weren't going to give them names."

"What *did* you tell them?"

"I talked about Jacques. How he seemed when I last saw him. Smug and secretive."

Daniel waited. He watched the stylist in the mirror. The man was frowning, testing the hair above Daniel's temple for length, running it up between his fingers. "Shorter," he said. Then, "Jacques *looked* really good. He said he was better off out of this—the spa—and that he shouldn't have followed his folks into the beauty industry. He said that he'd once imagined he was *better* than that. I found this remark a little insulting, and I told him, 'Jesus, it's only a job!' Then he said—and I remember his exact words, because they were weird—'But I'm *not* better, because my miracle was only a case of mistaken identity.' " The stylist lifted his scissors. "Stay still," he said, alarmed. He got a cloth and dabbed at the tip of Daniel's left ear—the pointed one, distorted by a bad forceps delivery. "You jumped and I cut you."

Daniel ignored this. He asked if the man knew what Jacques had meant by "his miracle."

The stylist shook his head.

Daniel told him about the flood in '92, the fourteen-year-old schoolboy who went missing, and his answered prayers. Then he asked the stylist if this story threw any light on things Jacques had said about himself.

"There must be light, because now I'm seeing shadows that weren't there before," the stylist said. He sprayed Daniel's hair with water and went back to work on it. He said he was sorry that Jacques hadn't ever spoken about his miracle. "Perhaps he thought we'd contaminate it," he said. He looked sad. "I didn't even know he was religious. And I suppose things can seem different to someone who is. I thought Jacques had become secretive. But I guess he always was."

"Did he seem ashamed?" Daniel asked.

"No, smug—I told you."

"Smug," Daniel mused. "And his miracle was only mistaken identity."

"Careful," the stylist said. "I don't want to let any more of your blood. Why did that shock you? That's what made you jump."

"Jacques's testimony is part of history."

"Oh . . . *history*." The stylist was dismissive, as if, to him, history was only hearsay. Then he said, "There." He put his scissors back in their cylinder of disinfectant and showed Daniel a tube labeled "Polish." He squeezed a clear, bubble-jeweled drop into his palm, rubbed his hands together, and ran them through Daniel's hair. Then he held up a mirror so Daniel could inspect the back of his own head. Daniel looked—and felt alarm and embarrassment. It was the best haircut he'd ever had, and it had the effect of making his face look, to him, interesting and attractive.

"Do you like it?" the stylist asked.

"I think I look very handsome," Daniel said, unable to hide his dismay.

The stylist laughed. "It'll wear off," he said. He conducted Daniel to the salon receptionist, the cash register, and the appointment book. The apprentice had found last year's book and had left it there for the stylist. Daniel counted out cash, gave it to the girl, and then bent over the book. The stylist was looking at pages, stroking the columns, the different hands, crossings out, mended entries. His fingers stopped and tapped the book. He gave Daniel a piece of paper and a pen. He said, "She always paid in cash. Like you."

Daniel wrote down the name: "Grazide," and the number of a mobile phone.

There was a yacht between the horizon and the shadow of the mountains that lay like a net slung between Cap Martin and Capo Mortola. The vessel wasn't new, one of those sculpted white yachts, topped by whipping aerials. It was of an older vintage and had a black steel hull and single raked-back funnel. Even at a distance, its varnished deck and rails were aglow.

Daniel watched the yacht's progress with the same expectant attention he might give to a shot in a film. He waited as though for the story to begin. He waited for the arrival of a protagonist. At that moment Daniel felt that he was not, himself, a protagonist. He felt that the view from the top terrace of the old cemetery in Menton was something he was being shown, that he was as passive as any other member of the audience and didn't have to say what he thought or to turn in his copy. He felt that there wasn't a thing he had to attend to after the lights came up.

These were not feelings Daniel normally had. He wasn't usually this detached or this self-conscious. He was, he had always thought, a busy, interested creature, burrowing his way through the world, deeper than some (because, as a priest, it was his business to consider morals and mysteries) and more myopic than others (because he had renounced the world, except where the Company asked him to involve himself on behalf of the Church). Yet as Daniel sat on the raised lip of a dry drain, beside a tap, on the top terrace of the old cemetery in Menton, he felt that he was waiting for a word—for *something* from *someone*. As he waited—in reality for the caretaker to come past and roust out the last visitors before closing the gates—Daniel scraped up a few marble chips from the freshly strewn path and tossed them from hand to hand, winnowing stone from stone. His hands were dirty. He was listening with all his fluent, viscous attention to the clack and splatter of the pebbles and looking at everything before him—the town, its sunny kindness, even with the sun gone; and the bay of Garavan, its vivid water streaked and cape haloed with smooth patches of current. Opposite Daniel, among the rank of graves at the edge of the tall terrace, was a tomb sealed by a statue. The statue was a little bigger than life-size. It was of a coffin— lid springing up as though lifted by a gale—and a woman, whose white marble limbs were wrapped in wind-whipped, billowing marble draperies. The woman was sailing forth from the coffin with her face turned to the heavens. She was great and buoyant and didn't have a glance to spare for the lovely hospitable landscape that lay below her, seeming to dare her to look down.

Daniel scattered another handful of stones and stared at the statue. He thought, *Look back. Look down.* He put out a dusty hand to touch the faded tiles on the wall of the tomb beside him. They were still warm from the sun. He got up and dusted his hands, careful of his black suit, and turned from the view to the Moskelute tomb. It was imposing, dilapidated, exotically tiled and domed. Daniel had caught a train to Menton that morning—the day after the funeral—and had asked at La Conception where Martine Dardo was interred. The priest who had conducted the service told Daniel that Martine Dardo was in her friend Eve Moskelute's family tomb. Daniel heard from the priest how, at the beginning of the previous century, a consumptive Moskelute, a countess, had lived in Menton, the warmest port on the Côte d'Azur, in order to prolong her life. Her family had purchased property—a villa, and an apartment in one of the speculative developments that sprang up shortly before World War I. The ailing countess built herself a mausoleum. She declined and died. The war came, then the revolution in Russia. The family dispersed or disappeared. The villa was sold, but the apartment was retained by the countess's nephew, Eve Moskelute's paternal grandfather. The tomb was real estate the family had in perpetuity, and Eve's own twin sister was laid to rest there in 1969, the last interment before that of Martine Dardo. Eve had been the only mourner at her friend's funeral, the priest told Daniel, but later the caretaker told him that Madame Moskelute and three handsome young people had visited the tomb on the evening after the funeral.

Yesterday evening.

Daniel put a hand on the stone frame of the bronze door. He leaned closer to look at a smear, a sooty flare on the bronze, a small mark in the shape of a black leaf, its stem excised.

Daniel considered this mark. It wasn't candle smoke, the plush soot of wax. He considered the mark with his eyes rather than his mind. To give himself more light, Daniel stepped back—then saw something glinting above him on the sill of the door's marble lintel. It was a silver box, its seams sealed with gold. Daniel grabbed it and saw the broken crystal panel, the red velvet interior, the notch, empty, and the tiny square imprint of the missing match.

Daniel stood for a long time, his thoughts circling, like Noah's raven, looking for land and finding only a shifting mass of water.

He was disturbed by the sound of footfalls on the peastone walk. He turned, expecting the caretaker. But it was a man with white hair, a fine-boned face, and dry, pale skin. The man wore aviator glasses, and Daniel couldn't see his eyes. The man stopped before Daniel and held out a hand, palm up.

Daniel looked down at his own hands, then offered the man the reliquary. "Careless to leave it," Daniel said.

The man's parched fingertips brushed Daniel's hand as he scooped the reliquary out of it.

"The reliquary is quite valuable in itself," Daniel said. He had recognized the man as the person he'd spoken to briefly on the mule track above Dardo.

"I've undertaken to put it back," the man said. Even his voice was dry, an atonal whisper.

"Back in St. Barthelemy's?"

The man nodded. Then he moved past Daniel and inclined against the door of the tomb, pressed his ear to it, and stood still, as if he was listening.

"All quiet?" Daniel said—against every civil instinct he had.

The man didn't answer him. He only turned his face and swapped ears.

"Will you talk to me?" Daniel said.

The man pushed himself off the tomb door. "I'm going to light a candle for her now," he said.

Daniel took that to mean he should go with the man—who was already walking away.

The man went down the steps from the top terrace, two at a time. He was quiet and moved as if his body had volume but not mass. Daniel was hard put to keep up—except that the man stopped at the gates to give the caretaker a twenty-franc note.

Daniel lost the man again on a curving downhill flight of shallow steps. He caught him up at La Conception, at the altar of the Virgin, where there were real candles—no art worth preserving from the smoke—instead of a coin slot and light-bulbs in the shape of flames.

Daniel and the man lit a candle each, and Daniel said a prayer.

The man removed his dark glasses and hung them by one earpiece from the perishing ribbed-cotton neck of his worn but clean long-sleeved T-shirt. Daniel looked him over, saw good running shoes, old Levi's, white eyelashes, and eyes, in the candlelight, as pale as candle flames.

"Martine was ill," Daniel said. He waited. "I was told that she was in correspondence with people about it. A support network or—"

"You're just fishing," the man said.

"Yes," Daniel said, then, "Martine had books on cellular biology. Medical texts with color plates. She told me that she even studied English in order to read some of them." He was thinking of those patient, passionate self-taught scientists, the parents of Lorenzo Odone, who took up the study of chemistry to save their son.

The man was looking straight at Daniel, into his eyes, and, after a moment, Daniel realized he wasn't shaken; he hadn't shied away.

"I'm wondering what you're thinking," the man said. He sounded surprised.

"I'm thinking about the people who find medicine unprepared to save those they love, so learn everything medicine knows about their problems in order to solve those problems themselves."

"Yes," the man said.

"Like Martine," Daniel said.

"Yes. But it wasn't just medicine. Martine liked those stories. And *other* stories about how some things that science and rationality have made their own originally sprang from spiritual desire. Like Alan Turling's heroic spiritual desire."

"I'm afraid you've lost me." Daniel thought the man's voice had taken on a familiar quality—he sounded like those people who testified about miracles to the Congregation for the Causes of Saints.

"Alan Turling was a British mathematician. The father of the modern computer. He came up with differential calculus." The man gave a small speedy flick of his head. "Martine liked to say, of inventions and discoveries, that people *came up with* them. 'We bait our hooks,' she'd say, 'but it's God Who brings fish to our lines.' Turling made a machine that used differential calculus to break the Germans' codes in the last war. He also thought about artificial intelligence. But he didn't think about it first because he wanted to build machines that think and speak in math. He thought about it because a friend he loved died and he needed to understand what a mind was, apart from a body. He needed to know if mind was distinguishable, separate, separable, and might survive the death of the body."

Daniel stood, his mouth open, so amazed by this man's oddity that he felt that the tiers of candles had curved up over him, as bright as stadium lights.

"Martine liked her computer. And she'd say, 'To think that computers are the children of lost love.' "

Daniel wondered how he came to be hearing about souls when he'd wanted to ask about sickness.

But Martine's friend came around to Daniel's subject himself. "Martine liked her computer," he said. "And when she got the Internet she could search the sites of the big teaching hospitals in America. She searched libraries of images. Images of cell samples. She was finally able to distinguish what she saw through the eyepieces of her microscope from what she *should* be seeing. It was a process of elimination, she said to me."

Daniel tried to pay attention but was distracted by the man's eyes, which must be a very pale blue, their coolness canceled by golden candlelight. They appeared colorless, like the eyes of a silver-coated weimaraner. Daniel felt that he wasn't being seen, that the eyes were blind, wouldn't absorb light, and couldn't take in an image. Daniel thought, *I'm invisible to him.* But, of course, the man was in mourning and, despite his distracting oddities, wanted simply to talk about his friend. Daniel could be anyone, a handy ear.

When Daniel had sufficiently soothed himself with these thoughts he found he was more prepared to hear what was being said to him.

Which was this:

Martine had identified a parasite in her body. It wasn't a case of its cohabitation; it didn't sleep, as some parasites do, in her gut or encapsulated in her reproductive organs. No, it was everywhere, percolating throughout her entire system. It was everywhere, and it looked exactly like the cells at each site, performed the same functions, acting in the liver as the liver, in the muscles as the muscles, in blood as blood. It was a mimic. Only *its* cells were immortalized, like cancer cells. But unlike cancer, its cells weren't all-consuming or monstrous.

"Immortal, but not monsters," the man told Daniel, and smiled. He went on to say that Martine had surmised that the parasite had its factory in her gut. There it converted human genetic material—not its host's, however, but what its host ate. Her stomach didn't digest, she explained, but filed off engine numbers, changed license plates, and applied a coat of new paint—so to speak. The parasite's aim—if the machineries of nature could be said to have aims—was to colonize its host by making *a copy.* Sooner or later the parasite would reach great enough concentrations in its host's body and its host would become infectious. The parasite's human host's instinct for intimacy would carry it—the parasite—into other humans, further hosts. " 'Intimacy,' Martine said, 'is another thirst.' "

This was mad stuff. Daniel's mother had collected and organized data to shore up her sense of being failed, or abused, by the world. Daniel was familiar with *that* kind of thinking and wise to it. But *this* was different. These delusions required more than the misinterpretation of facts; they required invention—and an exercise of faith.

Daniel asked Martine's friend how long she'd been telling him these things.

"Five years. Since she first found what she'd always imagined was there. Since she proved her hypothesis. She had always looked at the places on her body where the pigment was wholly gone, looked, and wondered, because they appeared where she'd been injured. Martine was once a chemist, so she was equipped by habit to ask the right questions."

"*No,*" said Daniel, distressed. "I hope you didn't just listen to her. I hope that—as a friend—you did more than listen."

"I did what she told me to do. What *she* did," the man said. He said that Martine had hoped to remain *herself*. She'd tried to retard the parasite's progress. She'd resolved not to feed it. Or to feed it as little and as seldom as possible.

Daniel covered his own mouth, stifling something. He looked at the floor, its undulating tiles, and pushed his knuckles against the seam of his clenched teeth. He thought, *She didn't eat.* The poor, deluded woman saw her illness as an invader and had tried to starve it out.

The man was still talking, telling Daniel about his dead friend. His light, hoarse voice wasn't wholly unemotional, but the emotion was wrong. He was enthusiastic about his friend's thinking and full of praise. He told Daniel about another thing that had interested Martine: the treatment of diabetics before the discovery of insulin. In the early part of the twentieth century diabetics were kept alive on a high-fat diet. The diet prolonged their lives. There were sanatoriums full of hyperglycemic patients, kept conscious and living by their total avoidance of carbohydrates. They ate fat and starved more slowly. They and their families, and their doctors, knew that a cure would come, and so they existed, in big, silent spas, where they crept about like ghosts, supporting themselves on rails rigged around the walls, while only their doctors and nurses walked *through* rooms, in the middle of the floor, in their full vigor.

"Martine would talk about that," the man said, "and how she hoped to keep herself—an essential tissue of herself—alive, till science was able to save her. She was afraid that while the parasite could copy her human capacity to learn, it couldn't reproduce what she *had* learned, her memories. She was concerned for her soul. Would the parasite replace her soul with its own? Would her soul simply steam away with each cell the parasite replaced? Martine had a grandmother who'd been paralyzed, then struck speechless, by strokes. She'd think about her grandmother and wonder whether it was possible that a soul could go to God piecemeal. She was a little girl when her grandmother first fell ill. She'd watched her grandmother and had wondered if God already had her grandmother's voice and gestures with Him in Heaven. She'd say to me that she hoped her own soul was going to God like a slow vapor, like the mist lifting as daylight comes."

Martine Dardo had never been very thin, only bleached and sere, like this man. *He* didn't look starved, Daniel thought, only ill, prematurely aged, damaged. Daniel asked the man whether he had the same illness—or allergy—as Martine. He asked, "Were you in Martine's support group?"

The man laughed. "No. She was in mine."

Daniel frowned. "Meaning?"

"Martine was my nestling," the man said.

Daniel didn't understand. For a moment he imagined that this was what it was like for non-Catholic laity on first hearing a term, doctrinal or otherwise, used by the Society of Jesus.

Daniel felt that he was in the presence of a member of some other order, whose names, terms, and rules he didn't know. He wanted to ask questions: *What's a nestling? To what extent did you humor poor Martine?*

The man said, again, "I'm wondering what you're thinking," his former surprise replaced by wistfulness. "But it's all rather a lot for you to digest, Father Octave."

"You know me," Daniel said, "but who are you?"

"Lou Ila."

Lou Ila. In Provençal: the Island. *A dust devil who dances forever.*

"Wait," said Daniel.

"I can do that," said Ila.

Daniel had to sit. He turned around and fumbled for the end of a pew—swung himself into it. He fanned his face, waved away the questions he was too confused to ask. Ila squatted beside him and asked for a pen. "You should visit Eve," he said. He took Daniel's wrist in one dry hand, unbuttoned a cuff, and pushed up Daniel's sleeve. He twisted Daniel's wrist over to expose the paler blue-veined surface of his inner arm. There Ila wrote three phone numbers. He said, "Eve moves about, between three houses she has." He released Daniel's wrist and slipped the pen back into Daniel's pocket.

Ila stood up and moved away. The candle flames flowed, flickering in the breeze he made passing quickly out of their air—before settling again, motionless and stretched on their black wicks.

Chapter 13

ANEMIA

After a time Bad noticed that whenever he talked about his family Dawn would leave the room. He'd find himself turning to her sister to finish his sentence. He and Dawn didn't talk much when they were alone, or if they did she'd tell him stories. He would lie, groggy, watching her face, if she had left the lamp on, or, if not, staring at the tiny orange running light on the plug-in insect repellent, its citronella a catch in the throat of the night that had swallowed him.

When he bought the plug-in, Bad said to Dawn that he'd let *her* have him but not the mosquitoes. He would lie in her arms, looking over her shoulder at the light, which moved in and out of focus, so that sometimes it was a blob of crosshatched orange, sometimes a proper tiny, bright point. Bad would think about mosquitoes as Dawn paused in her story to make grazes on his chest—to taste, not feed. He thought about the thin fiber in a mosquito's mouth pumping anticoagulants into capillaries a millimeter under his skin. Then he might provoke Dawn to bite him. "Deeper," he'd say, his hand on the back of her neck, like a man more normally greedy, directing some obliging woman. But Bad wanted Dawn to pump something into *him*. Her venom was a neurotoxin, Eve had explained, a local anesthetic, and a neurotoxin loaded with endorphins. Eve said, "Whenever I have to go to the dentist I get Dawn to bite me."

Under the venom's influence Bad would feel exultant, then soothed and sleepy. But no matter how much water he drank before retiring he'd wake up in a dry fever with his lips stuck to his teeth, the lining of his cheeks patchy with pinhead ulcers and transparent tatters of peeling skin.

He and Dawn were always in bed before sunrise. Bad would take his watch off and put it under his pillow. Time was excluded from the room. Dawn would fall asleep when Bad was ready to be awake. Bad would listen to the traffic swell on the Avenue Sospel as the people who slept in Italy but worked in France arrived for the day. Or—a step up—those who slept in Menton but worked in Monaco got into their cars and made their way onto the autoroute.

At night there were infrequent trains, and Bad had time between them to wonder and fantasize about their destinations, particularly those that crossed the rail bridge with no alteration in speed, the long-distance trains that only stopped at the principal stations.

Once, when Dawn had subsided into silence, Bad turned to her to wonder. "Where is that one headed? There are so many possibilities," he said. "I keep thinking that—if I had time—I could walk from here to Capetown, or Finland, or Manchuria. The trains cross the bridge and I hear all those land miles. It's a different kind of distance. It's not what I'm used to. It's not an impossible distance. If Capetown was home, I could walk home." Then he said, "Of course I'm forgetting money and food and shoe leather. But a vampire could do it."

"If the vampire were old and wise enough to have mapped out every cave or old cellar along the way," Dawn said. "But Ila says that dynamite put an end to all that. Explosives and earth-moving machines. A vampire can no longer rely on anything dug in to stay put. And I can remember Martine saying that, for her, one of the few tolerable things about her sainthood was that it might generate one or two protection orders from historical societies. Then Ila said that sanctity itself wasn't much guarantee of things staying put. And he talked about the churches destroyed during the Revolution." Dawn laughed as she did when she was slowing up, a sound between growl and gurgle.

Ila's memories, reported by Dawn, were for Bad a kind of equivalent to Europe's land miles. They were so different from what he knew and treasured, the stories handed down through his family in a generational relay, stories that were journeys because—ultimately—they contained journeys and great chances taken. Bad's aunt was "doing the family tree," searching genealogical databases and hiring researchers in Kent or Jersey or County Cork to look at the parish records—marriage and birth certificates—or passenger manifests on ships that sailed from London or Southampton or Galway. *Sea miles.* Ships like cocoons. Lives transformed.

Dawn said that Ila had kept a *face*, a face smacked off a statue of Saint Benezet the bridge builder by some anticlerical vandals, during the Revolution. The face had been knocked off whole, a marble flake with a forehead, eyes, nose, mouth, and most of a chin. The statue had stood in a roadside shrine on the island of Barthelasse. It was stained green up to the lower rims of its eyes by the waters of the flood of '21. "*Seventeen* twenty-one," Dawn said. "The flood that was slowest to fall. Eve wants Ila to restore it to its body," Dawn said, "which is now in the museum attached to the Palace of the Popes in Avignon. Ila was born on Barthelasse, the island in the stream of the Rhône. He hasn't used his real name for a long time. He's 'the Island.' If you want to know why he took me to Corsica, Bad, then ask him why he's called the 'the Island.' "

Bad listened to Dawn grind her teeth, plucking at her spines with her lower incisors—a squeaky rustle. He dozed then and dreamed about the train he heard in his sleep belting across the bridge over the Avenue Sospel. In his dream he was on that train, which didn't cradle him or rock like a train on tracks. Instead it quivered, like the tip of a flexible rod shaken in the air. Bad woke in his dream and put up the train's—the *plane's*—beige plastic blind to see the lavender smoke of ocean far below him and the orange of a sunrise that had chased them all night and was still chasing them as the sun came up and the plane descended toward the Hauraki Gulf.

Bad woke, his eyes stinging but tearless, a band of pain across the bridge of his nose, his face cut in two as though he were Ila's stained saint. Dawn was comatose. The light of the plug-in insect repellent had shrunk back to its proper size and pallor, and there was a glow on the ceiling above the screen that stood between Dawn's bed and the window, a curtained, double-glazed window, with a seal like an air lock, so that when Dawn closed it for the night Bad's ears would pop. The light came through the external shutters, their slats sun-blasted and coated with flaking gray paint. The sun was full on the front of the apartment. Behind the pall of citronella was the smell of morning coffee. Eve had been to the market and had put out coffee and pastries on the table on the terrace. In the sun. Where Bad would join her.

There were times when Bad went to bed in darkness, alone, fell asleep listening to the trains and thinking, *Florence, Strasbourg, Lyon, Turin, Barcelona*, and picturing the capable hands of an attendant making up a berth. Bad would fall asleep, Dawn's saliva in his blood, stiffening his joints. Dawn would join him shortly before sunrise, smelling of someone else, of cologne and cigarette smoke, or *stinking* of the men who slept in the open air, on salvaged sofas, on the Chemin du Peyronet. The men who existed on stale baguettes and blistering rosé decanted from plastic flagons in the market under the rail bridge. "They'll be gone by the high season," Dawn would tell Bad. "The mayor of Menton has the police see them all off, up the line to Nice." Dawn spoke as if she had to make the most of these tramps while they lasted. She sounded like Eve, unpacking her shopping and remarking that they'd best make the most of the *fevettes*, the baby fava beans, while they were in season. Dawn, sated and happy and missing Bad, would come to bed without having washed, her skin impregnated with a stink as thick as coal tar, of rancid sweat, piss, stale wine, and the greasy smoke of burning rubbish. She'd have wiped her mouth and chin so that she could be seen in the street, but her neck would be tattooed with blood splashes, her shoulders printed with bruises where the men had held her—not believing their luck or the severity of their sensations—down on her knees before them. The hair around her face was set in stiff quills, a glue of dried semen. Bad would know that, at the moment of crisis, her head had moved, had made another— illicit—outlet in the tramp's body, one that spurted red. Bad had taken note of the white freckles—scars—that speckled Dawn's inner thighs, as thick as scales along her branching arteries. And he'd had that attention, her tandem attack. First she'd tease him by numbing him, tease herself by grating his skin with her bristles as she sucked, so that the blood oozed. Then, when he came, finally, despite her venom numbing him, she'd turn her head to bite his thigh. He would feel one foot tingle and grow cold, feel her hunger drawing heat right out of his heart.

"Why don't you wash?" Bad said once, and Dawn told him that she wanted him to *know*, wanted him to join her. "There's no *harm* done. The man wakes with a thick head and finds his

228 ~ Elizabeth Knox

fly open. He says to himself, 'The crazy bitch bit my prick.' Ila
used to go into the clubs carrying his needles, and cannula, and
plastic flex, and a powerful Valium derivative used in dentistry—
a pretty poor substitute for the drug in his mouth. He'd pick up
people who would wake up in their own beds with no memory
of the night before, feeling hammered and ill, and with a bruise
and puncture mark in the crook of one arm. Imagine what they
imagined, and what they feared."

Bad repeated, "You should have washed."

And Dawn: "Come on, enjoy it." Inviting him. "I want you
to *know*. I want you to join me."

He joined her. But then he wouldn't surface again till the
late afternoon, so hungry he'd wake retching. He'd find Dawn
fastened to his arm, her barbs in him and her tongue idly lapping to keep his wounds open and seeping.

In the third week of June Eve asked them all to go with her to
Cap de Nice. She meant to make the most of Jean's house before it opened to its summer public. Besides, she said, since
Dawn and Ila were wide awake and hungry it was better to
move nearer to Nice and its bigger population.

As usual, on waking, Bad went to find Eve. He closed every
door behind him, left the darkened wing, and wandered down-
stairs and through the great rectangular rooms of the Musée
Jean Ares. The marble was cold beneath his feet. He walked
toward the light, through a final barrier of a floor-to-ceiling
curtain—hung to protect the paintings in the room that gave
onto the long, deep terrace of the house. The curtain was yellow silk, its hem weighted so that it would only billow open at
its seams, the silk bulging and the corner weight raised an inch
or two, before each gust let go and the weight dropped to the
flagstones, connecting with a tiny *clink*. Bad went through the

curtains and found Eve on the terrace, at a table under an umbrella, drinking coffee from a ceramic cup made to look like
crumpled paper. Eve had been waiting for him. She had another cup and a brioche. She poured coffee and gave him the
International Herald Tribune. She was reading *Nice-Matin*.

Bad ate, sipped coffee, and read a feature about lemon-
cino—he daydreamed about lemon groves in Sicily, where he
and his girlfriend, Gabrielle, had planned to go. Bad's day-
dreams were exactly the same as his night ones—they began
with land travel, some destination he could reach by train, but
would jump their tracks and drop him somewhere distant
and silent and wintry—home, on the green Whanganui River,
his landing softened by a morning mist rising from its cold
surface.

"I can't seem to stay awake," Bad told Eve. He finished his
coffee and used his warmed tongue to groom the lacerated
place on his arm.

"You should wash," Eve said. "You smell of homeless
men."

Bad told Eve that Dawn was like a baby who dozes off with
a bottle in its mouth. "You know—you see them, asleep, but
giving an occasional slurp." He recalled that his sister had told
him that babies shouldn't be put down to sleep with bottles.
He told Eve, "It's no good for their ears, apparently."

"Hmmm?" Eve said. Her noise was casual but her expression engaged.

"My sister works in child care," Bad explained, then
looked aside, anxious. For a moment he had imagined Dawn
was with them and that he'd driven her off, out of the room
again, by mentioning his family.

"What's your sister's name?" Eve asked.

Eve's interest primed Bad's pump, and in the following
forty minutes he told her about his family, about Pops, who
had paid for his schooling, about his final year in high school,
the outdoors adventure course, and Dart Ridge. Then he

found himself trying to describe the Riwaka Resurgence. Bad was remembering its deceptive depth, the clarity that made it seem shallow. He was thinking about what it was that had hooked him on caves and had brought him to Dawn and to this moment, his conversation with Dawn's sister on the sunny terrace of a villa on the Côte d'Azur.

Bad hadn't ever been in a cave before he met his first pot-holers in the Yorkshire pub where he'd worked in the bar. But it wasn't the potholers who turned him on to caves, not their charm, their conviviality, their games for rainy days—the "table traverse" they'd do around the pub's pool table, going right around it without ever a putting a foot on the floor. It wasn't even their stories about tight spots, heroic rescues, and unseen wonders. It was something Bad had seen before he met them, before he went to England. It was the Riwaka Resurgence.

After Dart Ridge, Bad went on the road trip with three other survivors to visit the families of their dead friends. When they were in Nelson, he and his friends took the minivan along the gravel road that ran around the base of the Takaka Hill to take a look at the Riwaka Resurgence, the place where the Riwaka River reappeared from underground. They left the van in the parking lot and went along the track, Bad and the boy who had jumped carrying the boy in the wheelchair and guiding the girl whose eyes had given her trouble ever since the accident. They reached the place and stood on the bank above the welling green water. It came up quietly but in volume—the river's surface piled in pouring humps of water directly above the place it reappeared. It was beautiful, and none of them had seen anything like it. They stood there for a long time, long enough for something startling to happen. There appeared in the powerful, quiet, welling water a thread of bubbles. Then a gout of bubbles. A ray of light lanced up through the water, waving like a feeler, and a man slid out of the cave in the press of water. The man wore a wet suit, air tanks, a helmet, and a lamp. He was followed by another man. It was, to Bad, as if the mountain had given birth to twins. The cave divers surfaced, unmasked their eyes, unplugged their mouths, and said predictable things like "Hi" and how long they'd been down in the dark.

Bad fell silent. He watched a powdery gray lizard scuttle along the balustrade, in sharp relief against the white grit of Eve's garden terrace, a terrace surrounded by dry-voiced date palms, whose leaves trapped rippling shadows, like eels in coral. A path went down through the date palms, turning into steps through a stand of spiny aloes and prickly pears—some autographed by tourists as far back as 1980. The steps went on down to the sea, today a calm, transparent turquoise.

"I'm so light-headed," Bad told Eve. "I keep losing myself. One moment I'm here; the next I'm at home. I feel as if I'm in a holding pattern." He made his hand tilt and turn in the air. "I can't seem to come in to land."

Eve said that she was making them roast chicken, stuffed with *finocchio* and flambéed in pastis. "I'll put it on now," she said, pushed back her chair, and went indoors, through the yellow curtains.

Before Daniel Octave phoned Eve Moskelute, he finally had his postponed talk with the bishop.

He sat in a chair set squarely before a massive desk in the bishop's somber audience room—perhaps the least Niçoise of any room in Nice. He kept his hands clasped so that he wouldn't fidget. He told the bishop what had happened to Jacques Palomba.

The bishop listened, then asked a few questions pertinent to Daniel's revelation. Then he inclined his head against his high-backed chair and asked Daniel when he had last spoken to his confessor.

"The week before I left Rome." Daniel's confessor had

asked, as he must, the ritual questions: "Are you happy in the Company? Do you still pray every day?" Questions to which Daniel had returned his usual affirmative answers. But the bishop was not a Jesuit, and it wasn't these questions that concerned him.

"This is difficult," Daniel said. His hands escaped him, and he found his thumbs caressing the big rivets that fastened the upholstery to the arm of his chair, smooth in the velvet's nap, like the round pads on the paws of a cat. He put his hands together again and stabbed his thumbnails into their opposite palms. "Nonsense always appears to me as a vile imposition. I take it too personally. And there is nothing more nonsensical than spurious connections."

"You *are* going to explain, I hope, Daniel," the bishop said.

Daniel said that, in the investigation of miracles, it could be said that the testimony of witnesses was never fully complete—couldn't be complete—till those witnesses were dead.

"Do you mean to take Jacques Palomba's life—subsequent to the miracle—and his death as further *testimony* from him?"

"No, Your Grace. Because a miracle isn't conditional."

The bishop nodded. "Then . . . where is your trouble?"

Daniel said that at one point in his original investigation he had suspected that Martine Raimondi had had a child—that her namesake, the Dardo woman, who'd had Raimondi's letters, was that child.

"Did you air this suspicion?"

"It was short-lived," Daniel said. "Alberto Vail's testimony removed any doubts I had about the Blessed Martine's virtue."

Daniel said that when he learned that Palomba had been murdered he remembered, however, something *else* Vail had told him. Vail had said that, two days before the Germans caught Martine Ramondi, he'd visited her, where she was laid up, sick, in a house above Tende. "Alberto told me that she'd expressed fears for the future of the men preserved by her miracle."

"And, thinking of Palomba's fate, you recalled her fears?" the bishop said. Then, compassionate, "Daniel, these are *your* doubts. This is *your* test."

"No," Daniel said, then found that he wasn't able to tell the truth. To tell what was tormenting him, a series of spurious connections—indecent, unreasonable connections. He didn't tell but backed off into cover, a hide made of light, not shadow. He offered the bishop an ethical argument. He said, "We're all invited to partake of events, to respond morally and emotionally to things that haven't happened to us and that we witness only remotely, usually on television. We're asked to regard current events in the light of history. We're given examples—I have my own, the Jesuit fathers who resisted Vichy and the Nazis. I have asked myself—as we're encouraged to ask ourselves—in their place what would I have done? It's the wrong question. And what equips us to ask the right ones? We're always being asked for our opinions—our tastes—or to imagine ourselves in other lives. We watch films or read stories and see our surrogates, because that's the way stories sell themselves to us. I wrote a book about Fathers Fessard and de Montcheuil and Chaillet and I still haven't found a way to *think* about them. Some way that isn't polluted by that vain question: What would I have done? What I've learned about Fessard and de Montcheuil and Chaillet isn't finished till I can either answer that question or learn not to ask it. Yet if I say, 'I haven't finished learning,' I'm still putting their lives in the wrong perspective, as if these men are something made by the past to be revealed to the present—to *me*. As if their lives exist to provide examples. All I can *honestly* think is that I can't leave the Company because, unlike Fessard and de Montcheuil and Chaillet, I haven't been tested."

The bishop blinked at Daniel. Then he said, "Are you thinking of leaving the Company?"

Daniel raised his hands and rubbed his temples. "No," he said. "But Jacques Palomba shouldn't have had his head cut off. And yet what happened to him isn't something I should regard as a test of my faith. This isn't about my doubts. Yet it must make me go back to the evidence I've gathered and look harder at Martine Raimondi's doubts." After a long moment Daniel looked up at the bishop. The man had waited, had kept quiet, but Daniel saw that the bishop's face wore a most extraordinary look—that love and pity and admiration were shining out of the bishop's rather ordinary, heavy, sallow face. The bishop said, "Your mentor, the man who first brought you back to the Church when you were a boy, the Supplician, Father Gaston Groux, who was killed in El Salvador, wasn't his head cut off?"

Daniel turned his face sharply, as if from a blow. "Yes," he said. "Yes. I'd forgotten."

"There's no sense we can see in what has happened to Palomba. But there's sense in your distress, Daniel."

No life was a closed system—Daniel knew that. A car is a closed system. A car with engine trouble can't contaminate the one parked beside it so that it, too, won't start. But Jacques Palomba's and Martine Dardo's lives should have been a little more like closed systems than they were. The two shouldn't have anything more in common than that they both had parts—great and small, respectively—in the Blessed Martine's life. Daniel *could* accept the proximity in time of their deaths. He didn't like it any more than the detective, from his side, liked the fact that he found himself investigating the deaths of two people who had been interviewed by Father Daniel Octave in connection with one saint's story. But Daniel had begun to think about other interviews and had remembered Vail saying that, before her arrest, during her illness, Martine Raimondi had expressed anxiety about the future of the saved men of St. Barthelemy's. Daniel had called the nursing home in Breil where Alberto Vail now lived. Like a good investigator, Daniel checked his facts, his quotes.

"I never said that, Daniel," Alberto told him. "That was

your interpretation. You said it, and I didn't even nod my head. *I* said that Martine was troubled. Her trouble hurt me because I knew her faith was all-important to her. We had argued in the past. We were young, always rushing about and trampling the green wheat in each other's hearts. I had wanted Martine to see the light—socialism and . . . not atheism, but pragmatic unbelief. Because I admired her I wanted her to see things my way. But she was very sick, and I was concerned for her morale. So when she said to me, about having led the men of Dardo to safety through the dark, that she had prayed to God for help and God had sent her a devil, I was unhappy. I am still unhappy that it's the last thing I heard her say."

Daniel felt hurt, disappointed. He said, "Why didn't you tell me this, Alberto?"

"Because it still makes me unhappy!"

This discovery wasn't good. But there was worse. Daniel thought he should see Eve Moskelute—because he had missed Martine Dardo's funeral and because Eve and Martine's odd mutual friend had said he should. Daniel had a reflex respect for scholarship. He never liked to be on the back foot with other scholars, so whenever he planned to meet one he made sure he read some of what they'd published. Eve Moskelute's biography of Guy de Chambord was years out of print, but Daniel acquired a copy of her translation of Chambord's *Lumière du Jour*. He read it at one sitting. Near its end Daniel found this passage: *I was trapped in a pit, a narrow place in my life. I prayed to God for help, and God sent a devil to guide me. A beautiful devil, whose dusty incoherence I was able to see only by the daylight she shunned.*

Eve finished putting on her chicken and went back to the terrace. She had wine and a bowl of figs. She split a fig for Bad, put it down before him, where its perfume would rise to his nose.

Bad looked dazed. His eyes floated above purple cradles of bruising. It was as though someone had punched him. He picked up the fig and Eve watched him eat. She broke several more and gave them to him—hand-fed him. Then she poured him a glass of wine and took his free hand and held it, fondled it. His fingertips were tacky from the fruit and his knuckles from other juices. His hands were heavily callused—from rope, he said when she asked.

Eve remembered the first time she had taken Tom Hilxen's hand in her own. They were at a concert, and she picked up his hand and drew it into her lap to hold. She inspected it, fascinated by the dappled bark effect of his freckles and the sandy hair on his knuckles. She would know this hand, she thought. They would be lovers, it was inevitable, and her taking his hand was their affair's first premeditated move. But Tom's hand wasn't Ares's and, as Eve enjoyed the sensation of its weight and warmth and latent mobility, she also understood that it wouldn't make much of a print on her; its warmth wouldn't make her malleable again in that place Ares's had printed forever by troweling smooth again—the place she'd been injured by the loss of her sister. Ares, the old man, was the love of her life. Eve understood that. Ares was dead and she was young, and yet for her he'd have no equal, no late rival. When she took Tom's hand into her own Eve felt intrigued but not tender. She held his hand firmly, excluded all the air between them. He was a graft she hoped would take. Her sap should still be rising. Ares was gone, but Eve had her sister back, and her sister's beautiful friends, yet she could only accept the attentions of this clever young American as an inheritance, something else Ares had left in her care.

Eve put Bad's hand back down on the table and gave it a few friendly pats.

"I might go for a swim," Bad said. He rubbed his hands down his shirtfront, not to clean them but as if he were checking his own substance.

"That's a nice idea," said Eve. She touched her own throat, the place tears were pressing.

Bad looked at her. "Ila," he said. "Dawn says that if I know why he's called the Island I'll know why he took her to Corsica." He waited, then said, "He has a story. They all have stories."

"All right," said Eve.

Chapter 14

CHAMBORD AND GRAZIDE

is given name was Agricol, an eighth child—
fourth son—born on that saint's day. His family
lived on Île de la Barthelasse, the green, sparsely wooded, low-
lying island in the stream of the Rhône. The island over which
the twenty-two arches of Saint Benezet's bridge had once
marched. The bridge was all but gone by Ila's day, and the people would travel by ferry from the island to Avignon.

His family were farm laborers, but despite his name Ila
didn't like the life, and at fifteen he crossed the river to the city.
He spent the little money he had on a water carrier: a harness
and canvas-covered container, with a padded belt, a tap, and a
cup fastened by a chain to the container. The man he bought
it from sported a flat place on his shoulders that corresponded
to the shape of its yoke. Ila took over the old man's territory.
He carried water from the Fountain of the Innocents, around
a fanned segment of streets. He cried, "A 'leau!"—perhaps his
first words of French. He climbed the stairs with the heavy

container, topped up jugs in third-floor households. Like the man from whom he bought the water carrier, Ila might have spent his days in that work and his nights sharing the straw with other plow-shy peasants, if it wasn't for a conversation he had with a man who painted signs.

The man was employed mending a painted panel. The panel belonged to an order of sisters who ran a hospital at the edge of the parkland behind the cathedral. The painter had carried the panel outside, into the street and sunlight, so he could see what he was about. He was puzzling out his main problem when he noticed Ila passing with his hollow, slopping burden. The man was thirsty, so he called Ila to him. He paid his coin and unhooked the chained cup himself and turned the spigot on the tap. Ila looked at the panel and could immediately see the painter's problem. The picture was a Madonna Misericordia—the Virgin with a crowd of people sheltering under the spread tent of her mantle. Someone had gouged out the Virgin's eyes. Her painted sockets were scored and empty, raw chisel holes in the wood. Ila asked the painter how he was going to fix it. The man wondered whether clay from the brickworks by the river might do the trick. Ila frowned and pondered, then told the man that he had once used wax to stop up a hole in an attic floor where some very enterprising ants would come through, in great numbers, to eat his bread. He had used a little beeswax—in fact, he'd broken the bottom off a small votive candle in the nave of the Chapel of the Gray Penitents. Tallow wouldn't do, he said; the ants would only have eaten it. "You could paint a pair of eyes on paper or cloth, then set them in wax."

The painter put the cup back on its hook and said yes, he would try that.

Ila didn't see the panel again, but he ran into the painter some weeks later, at work on the sign for a tavern—the Silent Woman (she was headless). The painter said that the eyes in wax had worked. He climbed down from his ladder and began to clean his brushes while Ila admired his sign. Then Ila asked if he could use the paint the man still had on his palette and borrow a brush. He wanted to decorate something. He gave the man a drink and showed him the canvas sling in which his copper vessel rested. Ila had just washed the sling and he thought, since the padding on his yoke was embroidered, a little decoration elsewhere wouldn't go amiss.

The painter passed Ila his palette and brush. He leaned into the tavern to call the landlord out to inspect his work.

Ila sat down on the cobbles with the vessel and its clean canvas sling between his feet.

The painter, who had accepted part of his payment in wine, hunkered down on the tavern's step with a bottle and watched Ila paint. There was a blob of fleshy pink on the palette, with black and white, red, and yellow. The painter thought that, at best, he would see a clumsy female figure appear under his borrowed brush. Or, more likely, a decorative sun and moon and stars. But instead he saw the boy had begun, with the brush dipped only in the white, to draw the shape of an animal—white on the yellowed bone color of the canvas. After a time, Ila dabbled the brush in the marbled border of the black and white paints and mixed an even gray. With this he outlined his animal—a calf, its head turned back over its shoulder.

The painter offered some advice—where the line was too thick, on the calf's flank, the boy could scrape some paint off with the brush handle. Ila did so, then picked up a rag and wiped the brush's bristles. He dipped in black and painted a cow behind the calf, framing its white body. This animal, too, he outlined in pale gray, made gray nostrils in her black muzzle, and gray long-lashed cow eyes. After that Ila quickly and carefully made a thin carpet of red trefoil flowers on which the cow and her calf were standing. He stopped and looked up at the painter, who gestured with his bottle. "Please, go on. There's paint left on the palette."

Ila mixed red and gray and yellow to make a donkey brown. With this color and the black and white, he painted a rabbit, its ears back, sniffing at an arrow that lay on the canvas ground. The rabbit was clearly in the foreground and in proportion to the calf and cow. Though the picture had no perspective, its proportions imagined perspective.

The painter took another swig of wine and cleared his throat. "I'm no master to take on an apprentice," he said. "I travel about with all my tools in this." He patted his scratched brass-bound box. By way of apology he uncapped a jar of blue and spread a dab on his palette.

Ila added red to his brown to change its tone. He painted a tree, mixed blue and yellow to add green leaves, and outlined each leaf in a yellower green, which made them seem to shine. He painted red apples on the tree and at its base another rabbit, ears at a clock's five-to-one, up on its hind legs with one paw resting on the tree trunk and the other before it and bent at the wrist.

"It's *alive*," the painter said, somewhat drunkenly. He offered Ila the bottle. "You're going to regret that." He pointed at the painting. And when Ila raised his brows the painter said, "It'll take a day—more—to dry. Ah, but you're in luck. Tomorrow's the Sabbath."

Ila carried his water vessel back to his attic lodgings. He was careful of the decorated sling and turned it to the wall to preserve it from the dust of chaff that spilled from the disintegrating pallets in the room where he slept. The painting was dry by Monday.

A few days later the painter found Ila, at midday, refilling his vessel at the Fountain of the Innocents. The man persuaded Ila to come with him. He took Ila to an enameler's workshop in the Place du Change and had Ila show the enameler his cow, calf, apple tree, arrow, and rabbits.

"He did it, without a pattern, right before my eyes," the painter said.

The enameler pursed his lips and kept his counsel. He was a prosperous-looking individual who wore clean, decent clothes under his leather apron and arm guards. The painter was shabby and itinerant—the two men were clearly not of the same station in life.

"He's a clean boy," the painter added.

"A water carrier must be clean," Ila said. "At least where the dirt will show."

"I'll give him a trial," the enameler said to the painter. And to Ila: "I'll feed you today and tomorrow and see how your hand is with enamel, plain stuff, and some fancy work on base metal. Let's just see how you do."

"And I'll come back the day after tomorrow," the painter said, as though reminding the enameler of a bargain they had made.

"As you wish," said the enameler, acknowledging no bargain.

Then the enameler took Ila through from shop to workshop, and Ila left his yoke and vessel in a corner and turned to learning a trade.

He was good at it, of course. He had a good eye and a steady hand and was a quick study at things he didn't know—about different metals, the temperature and consistency of enamel, how different pigments behaved.

After two days the painter came and collected a finder's fee, and the enameler took on an apprentice. Ila had a clean—if fumy—workshop to sleep in. Later he slept in the shop, behind the counter, guarding the premises at night while the enameler's family slept above. In a year's time there was a bigger workshop and shop—an expansion rather than a move—and Ila had a room he shared with another apprentice.

Ila gave his yoke and water vessel away to another strong country boy he met at the Fountain of the Innocents.

•　•　•

Three years later, when he was eighteen, his master called Ila in one autumn evening from the workshop to take a look at a design a customer had brought in.

Ila's master had a paper spread on his counter, held down by a silver serving spoon. A spoon with a deep bowl—flat at the bottom—and steep sides. On the paper the same spoon was pictured, in a larger scale, its bowl decorated by a chase—hounds, a tattered, distressed man, and the goddess Diana, a horned moon over her head. On its handle were entwined naked figures.

The customer was a lady, wearing black, her pale gold hair lightly powdered. Ila looked at her hair and thought of a filmed gold sheen—mist over the river at sunrise.

Ila's master said to him, "How long will it take?" Then to the customer, "My journeyman has a better hand than mine."

"How many colors?" Ila asked. He knew his master would prefer him to plan that but wanted a hint—was the commission worth his taking pains and doing his very best?

"The motto is black on white," the customer said. "But I'd like the picture to be as natural as possible, without abusing the materials, of course." She put out her hand—it appeared under Ila's gaze, which was directed at her design. (The motto was worrying Ila; the letters were shapes he could copy but not interpret. He wanted to know what it *said* to help him with its illustration.) The woman's hand was fine-boned, smooth-skinned, white. She wore a ring on her middle finger, a clear crystal set in gold; under the crystal was an eye cut from a miniature, a glaring authoritarian eye. The customer had put out her hand to touch the gorget Ila wore. A crescent-shaped cavalryman's steel gorget that Ila had bought from a pawnbroker and had enameled with a picture of Saint Benezet and his bridge, the walls of Avignon, and the towers of the Palace of the Popes. Saint Benezet stood above the bridge, in the heavens, not on clouds but on the backs of a flock of sleeping lambs.

"Is this your work?" the woman said.

"Yes, and the saint is my own design. The saint and his sheep. The city is copied from a map."

"The hill behind the Petit Palais is still bare, of everything but windmills," the woman said. Then, musing, "I remember." She withdrew her hand and told Ila's master that he'd do very well. She'd return in three days. "At evening," she said, "so be sure to remain open."

Ila's master wrote her a receipt for the spoon, and she went out and got into a sedan chair waiting at the door.

"Who is she?" Ila asked.

His master replied that he didn't know; the receipt had her initial only. But she had mentioned that the spoon was a gift for her friend the Marquis Guy de Chambord.

"Chambord has a château just over the river on the road to Lyon. Some years ago I decorated the stocks of the marquis's pistols—with bears in arms. The marquis is a traveler. He collects curiosities." Ila's master bundled up the spoon and the plan and gave them to his journeyman. "Begin tomorrow," he said.

Ila asked what the motto said, and his master had to retrieve the plan to read: " 'Many people are rather wicked, even those who hate pleasure.' " Ila's master shook his head. "She's not an honest woman, I fear, for that's not an honest sentiment. However, it is honest work for you."

Ila thanked his master.

Three days later Ila's master received a letter that asked him to send his journeyman with the spoon if it was finished. Madame G. would wait for an answer, then send a chair.

"The lady has taken a liking to you," Ila's master said, teasing him.

Ila was eighteen and handsome—black-eyed, broad-shouldered, and narrow-hipped.

"Tie your hair," said Ila's master. "And be circumspect—I

don't want to lose a customer, not this woman, or the marquis."

The spoon was finished, so Ila wrapped it in a velvet cloth and climbed into the sedan chair. He was carried through the city to the west, to a narrow house in the shadow of the town wall, near the Porte du Rhône. When Ila arrived at the door of the house its shutters were only just being put up. Ila dismounted from the chair and watched a fresh-faced girl, her breasts resting on the sill as she leaned out—an iron rod in one plump hand—to lever the top shutter up. The girl withdrew, and the window was empty, its shutter now the lid of an unwinking eye. Ila imagined that Madame G. had just returned home, and, indeed, he found her in her robe, her thick hair still clotted with powder, dull, and as tangled as the aerial roots of some parasitic creeper. She called him to her as he came into her hall. He crossed an image on its flagstones—in low relief the face and supplicatory hands of a woman, the marble so worn away by traffic, so clouded, that her figure looked leprous.

Madame G. took the package from Ila and unwrapped the spoon. She advanced on Ila, her eyes still lowered to her hands and the spoon, and pushed against him, shoulder to shoulder, propelled him to the window and the light—light from the sky, blue above the shadowed street. Ila gasped. The lady was close, not pressing, but he could smell her hair—grease, wood smoke, starchy powder. She held the spoon between them and tilted it to the light.

"I see that you've turned my lovers into wrestlers," she said.

Ila didn't answer, couldn't think how.

She glanced up at him. "Do you suppose my feelings for my friend are martial?"

Ila muttered that it wasn't clear from her sketch that they were lovers—then corrected himself, that *the figures* were lovers. (He had looked, long and hard, wondering whether the one with his back to him had a more rounded bottom and was, perhaps, a her. But the figure's hair had seemed masculine, locks escaping from a ribboned queue.) Ila waited for the customer to say he'd ruined the spoon, to send him back to his master with a bill for the price of the silver. But the woman smiled and raised the enameled spoon to run its cool bowl gently along Ila's collarbone. "I think your wrestlers might be lovers," she said. She turned the spoon and used its handle as a pick to pluck Ila's enameled cross from his shirt. It hung out from his chest, swinging slightly, and she regarded it, cold and assessing.

Ila's cross wasn't quite a crucifix—though it did incorporate the figure of Christ. Ila's Christ wasn't crucified, but on the horizontal arm He was dead in His tomb, half-shrouded, with sunken ribs and gray skin. On the vertical arm He was risen, robed in white, His pierced hands raised before His chest and His haloed face serene.

"What were you thinking?" asked Madame G.

Again Ila was at a loss how to answer.

The woman drew away from him. She gave him the spoon and its velvet wrapping and told him to wait. She told her maid that she would want her carriage in half an hour. "Give this man something to eat and drink. Sit there," she said to Ila, and pointed at a chair by the window. She gathered her robe and nightgown in her hands and climbed the stairs.

The girl fed Ila. As she was pouring wine she whispered, "My mistress bathes in cold water. She sleeps all day. She never dines at home. This is my fare."

"Is she kind to you?" Ila whispered back, then, "Decent?"

"Generous and fair," the girl said. "My family live nearby. If I didn't see them every week I'd be rather lonely. She never has guests. There's only me and the groom. He drives her to the château, then eats with the marquis's servants and sleeps on the floor in the marquis's carriage house. *He* sees people. My mistress sleeps almost every hour that she and the marquis are apart."

"I see," said Ila, in a worldly way.

The girl smiled at him. "Have you botched her gift?"

"I hope not. I think not. There were no instructions on her sketch." Ila made a scribble in the air with the tip of one finger, mimed writing. "And the lady is only a fair draftsman."

The lady was on the stairs watching them.

The girl put the bottle on the tray, bobbed, and hurried away.

"Come with me," said Madame G.

Ila retrieved the wrapped spoon and followed her to her carriage. She settled herself opposite him and asked him to please clip down each one of the heavy leather blinds. There was only a single candle burning in a fan shell sconce above her head. She tapped on the ceiling and the carriage moved off.

Ila felt the road dip down from the city gates, the cobbles become rutted mud. He heard the driver negotiating with the ferryman. Once they had reached the island, Ila put his finger into the join in the blind and parted it. He applied his eye to the gap and saw trees, a curve of road back toward the river, and thousands of sparks of silky floating seed drifting over the river's brown water.

Madame G. said to Ila, "Leave that."

Ila sat back in the gloom.

"I'd like you to show the marquis your cross," the woman said—then was quiet for the remainder of the journey.

It was dark when they reached the château. Very little of it was visible—some lit windows and two encircling arms of an external staircase that mounted to a terrace before its door. There were torches burning at the edge of the terrace, whose fluttering light dabbed at things in the distance; a lawn appearing as jets of green flame, the gleam of water edged with reeds, a white boat tethered in their furry shadows, and the trunks of plane trees, as smooth as some material poured into a mold.

Ila followed Madame G. and a servant through rooms with many candles magnified by mirrored crystal. He stopped once to stare at an infant preserved in a jar, its skin as blanched as a shallot in white vinegar, its soft wrists and ankles encircled by bracelets of coral beads. There were other jars, a shelf full, like a larder of horrible fruit.

"Come along," said Madame G.

Ila stopped dead at the door to a room full of paintings. The woman took the package from him and put it into the hands of a man who had come forward to meet her—a man in brocade and lace and silk stockings and silver-buckled shoes. The two came together in an eager, enraptured way.

Ila was meanwhile peering at a big murky canvas, focusing on the bony verity of Christ's bleeding knees. He heard the marquis laugh. He looked at another painting, small, old, exact in every detail, of the beheaded saints Damian and Cosmo, whose heads rolled on the road, their rolling facilitated by round halos. Their calm faces were visible through the thin, sweated-on linen that shrouded their severed heads.

Ila heard steps approaching, soles of stacked leather on a rug—wealth that made another simple thing possible: stealth, a quiet tread, the footfalls of someone nearer to angel than ox. Ila didn't turn to the marquis; he was still snatching sights—a painting of the Virgin in a garden, blown, drowsy roses by her drooping head. Ila opened his mouth the better to breathe. His eyes went up the walls from painting to painting till he felt that his body had begun to follow his gaze, felt his fizzing, avaricious, untaught hands climbing the air. He saw a chase through a forest, nymphs in diaphanous robes and rampant satyrs with pricks that were pointed and tapering, like those of dogs. He saw a still life with an almanac, *Apollo Anglicus*, a seal, sealing wax, quill knife, quills, watch, and combs.

The marquis and Madame G. stood before him, both looking at his rapt upturned face. Ila finally looked down at them. He was panting, as if he had been running. He thought—of the Virgin's roses—*White on the edge of each petal.* He said, "I see how."

"Nothing is too good for you," the woman said—to Chambord.

The marquis picked up a chair and set it behind Ila. Ila sat down and the woman crouched at his feet, with her hands resting lightly on his knees. The marquis squatted, too, and his brocaded robe settled after him, sighing. The marquis was grizzled and dark-eyed. His eyelids drooped at their outer corners; he looked pensive or possibly tired. He held the spoon in his hand. "I see that the handle's end is sharp, and its stem is grooved all the way to its bowl," he said in an aside to Madame G.

"Yes. I chose its shape. It's a spoon and a bloodletting instrument. And I chose its motto and design. This journeyman chose only to substitute wrestlers for my lovers. But, Guy," she said, "look at his cross."

The marquis fished the cross from Ila's shirt.

"See how he's solved the problem of precedence," the woman said. "The risen Christ doesn't overlap the dead, nor the dead the risen."

"The Dutch are responsible for that heretical picturing—Christ in the tomb," Chambord said. "Holbein," he added.

"I don't know it," she said.

The marquis asked Ila, "This medal you've used to mask that difficult join—the place where the dead and risen overlap—why is it what it is? Where did you see it?"

The medal was another of Ila's rabbits sniffing an arrow.

"It's just something that came to me—the first time I had a brush in my hand," Ila said. "I *do* know what I intend it to mean." Ila hesitated and blushed. "The rabbit is so innocent that it doesn't know someone has aimed an arrow at it. It is so innocent that it doesn't understand the Grace of its escape. It only wonders whether the arrow is good to eat."

The marquis looked at his mistress and returned her compliment. "Nothing is too good for you," he said. To Ila he said, "Please take a look about." The marquis got up, went to the door, and gave instructions to a servant.

Ila floated up; he drifted, only anchored by his eyes. He picked up an ivory ball, a symmetrical knot of rats, a surface of slick backs and whippy tails. He rolled the ball against his mouth. The marquis gave him a glass of wine. The glass had a gold rim, the first metal Ila had had in his mouth that had no impure tang. Nothing bloody. Ila sipped the wine and sighed. He looked down into the eyes of the man who had served him—the marquis, his better—and who intended *who knew what*. Ila decided that whatever the marquis wanted he would give; he would give for time here, for the freedom of the house, for the white on the edge of each rose petal, for *knowledge of how*.

They fed him cakes that glistened with a film of clear honey. The wine tasted of raisins and shriveled the skin on the inside of his mouth. Madame G.—Grazide—led him to a deep couch, with curtains and bolsters, like a bed, a better bed than Ila had ever occupied. She had him sit in its muffling cloth cavern. Grazide sat beside him. Chambord refilled Ila's glass, then sat beside Grazide. She turned her back to the marquis and lifted her hair off her neck. He unfastened the gold lacing at the back of her dress, loosened its neck to bare her shoulders and upper arms.

Grazide said to Chambord that he would now see what else she could offer him.

Ila put his head back and drained his glass. He was on fire with sugar and liquor, hot already, happy to be touched. He didn't much care that he was in the room with a woman and her lover. *He liked the room.* He lay back and looked at its carved ceiling. "Wood, not stone," he mused aloud. He turned his head to smooch his cheek across the silk-lined fox fur rug that draped the daybed. He told the couple that the room was like the Chambre du Camier in the Palace of the Popes, where he'd gone to mend the enameling on a medallion, on a lamp, on an altar. Ila spoke with drunken exactitude. His ears were full of fur, it seemed—fur's dry warmth was deafening him. He told them that the Chambre du Camier reeked of fire. But the fire was three hundred years cold. Its smell had outlived the people who had extinguished it.

"Yes," said Grazide. She lisped, as though something in her mouth was restricting the movement of her tongue. "You'll see," she said, promising. "You will see more of that."

"*If* I see he's not harmed," Chambord said.

Grazide lay back beside Ila and raised one leg. Chambord took her little shoe by its heel and removed it; he stroked her calf, his stroke gathering the end of the stocking so that it rolled to her ankle. He peeled her stocking off. He bared the other leg, too. Grazide turned to Ila, her face fair and clean in its frame of the woody tendrils of her dirty powder-clotted hair. She pressed against him, ducked her head under his chin, and bit him.

The marquis and Grazide were talking like angels. They spoke in Provençal, as Ila's family and neighbors had. But Grazide used words Ila had never heard. Their conversation was musical, a measured dance, formal and courtly. They spoke about God, Grazide saying to Chambord that there was a good God and an evil God. That souls belonged to the good God and bodies to the evil. She said the world would not end till every soul had left it.

While she talked, she stroked Ila's chest. Ila lay turned to them. He could see how Chambord still rested in the cradle of

Grazide's arms and thighs, his head on her shoulder. Grazide's mouth and chin were dark with dry blood, and blood was smeared in a thin, sticky wash on Chambord's cheeks. Ila knew that it was his blood, only it didn't seem to matter. All he minded was his shyness—he didn't dare to nestle closer to them, not just look and listen but touch.

After a time Chambord and Grazide uncoupled, with a whimper of wet skin parting. They rearranged themselves, came to lie on either side of him. The marquis tilted Ila's chin and looked at the wounds on his neck, then put his mouth to the place and kissed it, as a man might kiss the ring of the Papal Legate, a seal of authority. Grazide pushed her fingers into Ila's hair and ran her hand through it, pulling, moving his head so that the scabs on his neck split and oozed. She told Chambord that she'd buy out this journeyman's remaining time. She'd pay his master more than he was worth. "I'll keep him with me as he changes, and bring him back to you once his own weapons have formed, and are primed. Then you shall feel what I have felt—night's venomous electricity. You will join me, and when I'm old, and have forgotten who I am, you can teach me my own grammar, and remind me who I love."

Chambord's hand was up under Grazide's skirts and Ila could see tendons in the man's sinewy arm roll across his arm bone as his fingers worked. Chambord said to her, "How much do you love pleasure?" His other hand found Ila's fly, which was still buttoned, and pulled hard so that the buttons popped, one by one, from their frayed holes. Grazide got up and shrugged off her dress, stripped off her stays and under- skirts, and mounted Ila, naked, shining above him, her flesh rosy with blood like black wine in a porcelain cup. Her skin was pale and dappled with white reptilian markings. She rocked and rose to the rhythm Ila helplessly, reflexively took. Chambord watched them, his eyes sleepy and his small mouth slightly open. Once he touched them, to move one of Ila's hands from Grazide's breast and jam its heel into her gasping mouth. She bit the hand, and again Ila experienced a rush, his body melting and spilling beyond its margins. He felt hot liquid dribble down his arm and drip from his elbow onto his flexing stomach.

When the birds had begun their chorus Ila was given chocolate. Beside the daybed was a table with a solid silver top, decorated with figures in high relief, too high for Ila to put his hot cup down. He burned his mouth trying to spare his hands.

Madame Grazide dressed. She put on the cloak she'd come in, a cloak with a deep, enveloping hood.

Ila shuffled off the bed and put his empty cup down on the marquis's rug. He tried to put himself in order. His fingers were numb and clumsy with his buttons. He couldn't fasten them, so left them, gathered the flaps of his fly together under the tail of his shirt, and wove his way to Grazide's side.

But Grazide moved away from him, fled through the door like a shadow pursued by torchlight.

"Come," said Chambord. He grasped Ila's arm above the elbow and drew him out of the room. Ila took one stupid, covetous look as he left—at a mantelpiece they passed, at a brass clock with automata. The clock was chiming and angels had appeared from its workings to parade before an enthroned Madonna and child. It was Death who struck the bell. Ila stumbled through the door and onto a landing. He saw the hall and the staircase, a fleet black shape hurrying down its sweeping curve. Then Grazide was gone—and an instant after she vanished the sun appeared, in a gap between the horizon and a pall of mist.

Ila stopped. He said, "What was that? What's that sound?"

The staircase banister was of iron, and when the sun came a corresponding filigree of shadow appeared on the wall, sharply black in clear gold light.

"What sound?" said the marquis.

Ila tripped on the sagging legs of his trousers. Chambord turned to him, tucked his shirt in, and buttoned his fly. Then Chambord's hands were still, though he still held Ila by the buckle of the belt he had just finished fastening. For a moment they stood, their heads hanging, cheek to cheek, their mouths so close that their breath made one ghost in the sunlight on that cold landing.

Then the marquis shook his head and tugged at Ila's arm.

They continued on down. The door was open, and Grazide's carriage was standing at it, its curtains closed fast.

Chambord released Ila and went through another door, beside the main entranceway. He walked away from Ila into a chapel, where he cast himself facedown on the floor before the altar. The marquis lay prone, his forehead to the flagstones. He flung out his arms. Thick pillars of altar candles and the altar's gold seemed piled up over him.

Ila went down to the carriage. The sun had risen into the mist, and more mist was coming up in stealthy wisps from oak and plane trees and the leads of the château's roof. Ila got into the carriage. It was dark inside, and for a moment the space seemed to be inhabited only by shadows; then Grazide's face turned back to him—she'd had it pressed against the far wall. "How thick is the mist?" she asked.

"It's becoming thicker, I think."

Grazide stopped the carriage on the Island. She made a tiny crack in the leather concertina curtains—their pleats as thick as the flanks of a forge bellows. She poked her gloved fingers through the gap and peered at the day. Then she opened the carriage door. Her groom, startled, was too slow off his box; his mistress had already jumped onto the road and was walking away from the carriage, her cloak dragging over the damp white grit. Ila followed her. The day was cold and bright, the world without borders and severely limited. The mist entered Ila's body; with each intake of breath he felt himself grow heavier.

Grazide stopped beside a roadside shrine. It was a landmark Ila knew from his childhood but had scarcely spared a glance. The shrine held a figure of Saint Benezet the bridge builder. Grazide raised her gloved hands to draw her hood up more securely and turned her back to the pearly part of the white mass of vapor around them—the screen behind which the sun was hiding. She told Ila to look at the stain under the saint's eyes. Floodwaters had once risen to the rims of Benezet's eyes. He had looked out over flotsam and treetops. The big trees fell because the ground liquefied and couldn't hold their roots. Mortar melted and coffins floated out of the crypts of the churches, then out of the ground itself, birthed like bubbles. Grazide had been asleep in a crypt, she said, and had floated out, riding on a coffin. "By daylight," she said. "I was young, and could still endure it for a short time." She said that she'd survived by cocooning herself in mud, by making a statue of herself until the river fell and she could cross to the city, which was sodden but solid.

Grazide put her arms around Ila and stood on her toes so that she took his face into her hood. She said that Chambord believed he couldn't be pleased, but Ila would please him. "You can couple with him as I can't. I can't because I'm a breeder— not of babies, but of my own kind." She made a face. "I have made you into what I am. Your attentions to Chambord will be *my* attentions. Your mouth will be *my* mouth—but young and clean. You can give him a taste, and then you will dance for me, dance naked on your back, for me. We will show him what he can have, to give as well as take. Pleasure. His pleasure and mine." Her eyes gleamed.

"I heard the sun," Ila said.

Grazide raised her eyebrows.

Ila said that when he was on the landing the sun had come with a sound like a flare of gas on a marsh in the stillness of a hard frost, the flame that comes with a whisper and stands as straight as the candles at Mother Mary's feet. "The air is alive, and a blue flame springs with a hiss from a muddy vent."

Grazide sighed. "You mustn't speak to the marquis like that. I chose you because you're comely, and unafraid, and ignorant. You be that. Continue to be that. Be *bloody*. I'll keep you full. Full and satisfied. You will ache with use. You can look all you like at what he owns, but Chambord is mine, *my* library, scholar, seer, magician, confessor. My lover. You will keep your mouth shut except to bite him—do you understand?" Then Grazide kissed Ila and took his tongue into her mouth and showed him what she had there.

Grazide kept Ila at her house while he changed. When she went out she locked him in. She brought him the few things he owned—she'd paid the enameler so handsomely he'd not be asking questions. Ila might like to visit the man again—once he had learned a little decorum—in order to allay any remaining fears the man had.

Ila sickened and altered—then grew well again, well and hungry. His eyes watered and his skin stung in sunlight, so he learned to avoid it. Grazide took him out in the city at night and let him loose on drunks and beggars. She never spoke to him but to issue instructions. And she never used his name. He was "boy"—"my strong bloody boy."

A month passed; then Grazide took Ila back to the château. This time he was allowed into the marquis's bedchamber. He watched the marquis and his mistress making love in the candlelight, on a bed of clean linen sprinkled with sprigs of lavender. And, as he was instructed, Ila joined the couple fully clothed, only to bite Chambord's shoulder when the marquis was in the throes of pleasure.

"'Of *pleasure*,' Ila would emphasize when he told his story. This story I've put together from what he's told Dawn, and me, and Martine," Eve told Bad. "He said that he couldn't know what he took from Chambord when he first bit him—other than blood. But he later came to see that he did take another, everyday, thing—pleasure the Church would say was unsanctified. Unsanctified, but natural—natural carnal pleasure. For once Ila had put his spines into Chambord, and the man's body began its prolonged, ecstatic spasming, had its fit of joy, Ila felt that he had brought the man down, that he had sunk his teeth in the muscle of Chambord's shoulder, and had felled him as a lion fells an antelope. That, while Chambord came back to consciousness, he had, in fact, died then."

Afterward Chambord put up an arm and drew Ila down onto the bed, scooped Ila and Grazide together beneath him. Grazide, displeased, hissed at Ila.

But on later occasions they went further—Grazide and Chambord—inspired by the receding horizon of their ecstasy. Ila would join them in the bed and would bite Chambord as Grazide was biting *him*. And Ila, incited by her venom, would lose all restraint and would bite and bite, for the pleasure of sinking his barbs and pumping venom—his mouth itched and tingled with its bounty. Chambord would howl, then lie limp, moaning and stuporous, his chest like a pricked piecrust, its holes running with warm red juice.

That winter Chambord dismissed most of his servants and shut up much of the château. They nested through the cold months, the three of them. Ila had the freedom of Chambord's house, and the marquis gave him a box of inks, thick paper, brushes, and pens. Illumination was a clear step up from enameling and, Chambord said, Ila's talent was decorative, his eye untrained in perspective, in seeing what was *really there*.

The marquis and Grazide read and talked and lay for hours, face-to-face, looking at each other in the firelight or at something they shared, something invisible to Ila.

Ila went out at night, through the château's parkland, and followed the trails of hearth smoke to villages. It snowed, and he forged through the snow with the energy of a wolf. The days were short, each only an island, standing dry but diminished in a flooding river.

It became apparent that Chambord was exhausted. He shivered if he left the warm rooms. The skin of his lips turned a soft mauve in shade and was puckered by dry patches. Grazide would bare his skin, kiss him, and beg him to *let* her. To let her *finish* him. Let her take him.

Chambord said no, wait.

The spring came; the snow melted; the fields were muddy, then suddenly green. Ila found that there weren't enough hours in the night, after he'd ranged to feed and walked back along his wet, difficult pathways. He shut himself in the château's longest gallery, closed the shutters against the dawn, lit candles, and made his pictures.

One morning at the end of May, when Ila was at work in the long gallery, he noticed that there were people in the house. Figures crossed the light from the landing, men moving to and fro, carrying trunks. Ila heard them laboring, burdened, down the stairs. He wasn't able to go to the window and look through the curtains, couldn't see if there was a carriage at the door. But he heard them arrive—carriages—heard the flinty strumming of iron wheels on gravel, a thud of hooves, the clink of harness, and a carriage's springs graunch as it stood and took the weight of luggage.

The spring sun loomed like a wave above the château. It was nearly noon. Ila retired to the daybed and loosed the cord that held its curtains open. They swung together and he was in the dark. He lay back and shut his eyes.

Later there was a sound, a discreet creak of skin on paper, the flap and settle of sheets picked up, then put down again. In the silence between each little sound Ila heard attention. He knew that someone was taking a good look at his illuminations.

The curtains opened and the marquis sat on the edge of the bed. He had pushed back the shutters in the room, for the triangle of light in which he sat lapped like molten silver in a crucible.

Chambord inclined into Ila's cave and put his hand on Ila's shoulder. "You're the one I knew," he said. He withdrew his hand.

Ila couldn't move; his eyes had closed. The sunlight came through them, though, a pink haze divided by the smear of Chambord's shadow.

"I want you to tell her this," Chambord said. *"I still know the difference between a treasure and a curiosity."*

Ila heard the marquis speak but didn't hear him go. He never did pass on the marquis's message, because when he woke in the evening the room was cold, though there were flames in the fireplace. Flames with green and blue and violet tongues. Ila's illuminations lay, in a collapsed stack, in the hearth, on the coals of that morning's blaze. They had caught and were burning. Ila jumped out of bed and rushed to the fireplace. He pulled them out. Each sheet was brittle and edged black, their jeweled surfaces browned by heat. Ila took in this damage, then put them back and watched as the fire consumed them.

He heard a door close and went to the window. Grazide's cloaked figure emerged onto the terrace in the soft impression of the firelit window. Ila saw her pause, notice his shadow against the weak light on the ground at her feet. She glanced back, then hurried on.

The next day people came and draped all the château's furniture with dust sheets. They came early, and Ila was able to hide himself. It was the first time he'd slept crammed into a tight space—not a tenant or occupant but like vermin in a house. The servants nailed the shutters closed and left the château. Ila stayed with the phantoms of mirrors and tables, chairs and paintings and wardrobes. He waited for one of them to come back—Grazide or the marquis.

They didn't come. Ila was lonely and hungry. He left the château to look for Grazide in Avignon and found her house deserted, so went back to the Island and his mother's house. He was the ailing son come home to recover or to die. He lay on a bed by the stove in his mother's house and shunned the daylight, covered his head against the long pool of sunlight that spilled across the floor from the door at evening. Those sisters and brothers who still lived at home seemed to catch Ila's sickness, though not his sensitivity to light. Their neighbors watched as each sibling grew pale and vague, drawn, and blue about the mouth. It was remarked upon that their elder brother didn't appear at their funerals. Then his mother was seen at the market, shawled and shivering in the hot summer weather. The rest of the family convened and made a decision. They went to the house and dragged Ila out of it. He slumped in the yard, his hands over his streaming eyes. They prodded him till he got up; then they drove him away, shoving him before them along the road. They stood behind him in a close cluster, puzzled and fearful, as he walked into a water-filled, cress-covered ditch at the roadside and scooped mud from its bank to lather on his neck and face and hands, further spoiling the yellowed linen of his once fine shirt. He looked at them—

uncles, cousins, neighbors—out of his glistening gray face. The sun was hot and steam rose from the drying mud—his head and hands smoked. Then he turned and walked away from them into the forest.

"Despite everything he had heard Grazide say, despite her long assault of temptation and Chambord's scrupulous refusal, despite all that going on around him, Ila had not taken in the salient fact. He followed his instincts, the instincts that came with his appetite, and tried to have his family join him. He tried to keep them. He tried to turn them into vampires. And all he was able to do was kill them slowly, stifle them with anemia."

Eve inclined against the hot back of her wrought-iron chair. She felt its rigid lace through the cotton of her shirt.

Bad sat slumped. His whole posture was leaden. His face was so softened by exhaustion that he had a hint of jowls, a sling of flesh gathered under his jaw. "Okay," he said, "I get it. Dawn can't make me. She's too young."

"Yes. She's trying to force Ila's hand by making you fade, as his brothers and sisters faded. Did she ask you to ask him why he took her to Corsica?"

Bad nodded.

"Ila took Dawn to Corsica because he knew she'd not be able to stop trying to take me—not just her sister, but her *twin*."

Eve watched Bad muse, saw the tremor in his head—a vibration of denial. She said, "Dawn persuaded Ila to take Tom fifteen years ago. She tricked Ila into it, and tricked Tom, too, really, who after months of her attentions was so anemic that he wasn't mentally competent. And Ila doesn't like the way Tom turned out."

Bad thought about this. Eve watched him thinking. It was like watching bubbles rise through syrup. Eventually he asked her what had happened to Chambord and Grazide.

"I know from my research that when he left his château in 1771 the marquis went straight to Marseille, from where he sailed to Naples. Chambord never returned to France. He died in Sicily in 1788. And Grazide is known to history only as a fictional character, the heroine of Chambord's romance, *Daylight*."

Chapter 15

TOM'S INVITATIONS

*E*arly that evening Eve was rolling ripe figs into clingy strips of fat-striped prosciutto. The table on the terrace was covered in dirty glasses. Eve had just filled two flutes with Gioioso, a sparkling white, and with a deliberate, slightly unsteady hand had dribbled into each a measure of *crème de framboise*. When the phone rang, Bad hadn't yet touched his glass, was still studying with drunken appreciation how the red liquor had formed billowing clouds on the updraft of bubbles. Bad heaved himself up, settled the damp towel around his loins, and went to get the phone. He carried it to Eve. "It's Father Octave. I told him we'd been drinking all afternoon. But that I'd been for a swim."

Eve took the phone. She said, "Bad's been for a swim and I've basted my chicken twice." Eve listened to the phone, then said to Bad, "Father Octave gathers that this isn't a good time."

"Tell him we are at cruising altitude."

Eve did, listened, then said to Bad, "He says that he senses that there is little he could say at the moment that would be regarded as improper or trespassing." Eve enunciated very deliberately. "He says he's tempted to pursue his inquiries anyway, though it feels like taking an unfair advantage."

"You're good at that," said Bad. "Quoting. I admire you for that. I want to be like that when I'm old."

"So, I'm old," said Eve. "*I* admire Father Octave's frankness." Then, softer and only audible to Bad, "His manipulative, Jesuitical frankness."

"Tell him we're having a golden hour," said Bad.

Eve conveyed this to Father Octave. She listened, smiled, and said, "Yes. Please do," and ended the call. "He says he'll call again in the morning when we're less burnished and more tarnished."

Bad laughed and slapped the tabletop. The glasses rattled.

"He said he has something to tell me. Something about Jacques Palomba."

"Who?" said Bad, then, "Oh, right. The boy Dawn saved."

Ila appeared on the twilit terrace and settled in a chair, moving as though he was subject to a lighter gravity. He reached across the table and brushed the back of Eve's hand with his withered fingers. Eve told him that Father Octave—the priest who'd written the *Life of the Blessed Martine Raimondi*—wanted to visit.

"Good," said Ila. "I can ask him what he thinks about the brainless people. And clones."

Bad saw that Eve was astonished—though it was bleary astonishment. She said, "What?"

Ila said he'd been reading that there were people who didn't have brains but only a cerebellum, cranial fluid, and a thin layer of cerebral tissue lining their skulls. This thin layer kept them fully functional, did all the work of walking, hand-to-eye, speech and memory, reason and feeling and self-consciousness. No one knew how many of these brainless people there were since they were only ever discovered when they suffered a head injury requiring an X ray. Their whole selves were stored in a tiny deposit of matter. It took only so much to house a self—of sorts. "And then there are clones," said Ila. "If I cloned you, Eve, where would your soul be? Does God sublet souls?"

Eve was thinking. She pulled faces, pressed a thumb against one eyebrow, and held her eye wide open. Then she took Ila's hand and held it. "Dear, do you want to meet Father Octave? It's a little risky because you're a little odd. Odd, and old. Do you want to discuss your soul with him?"

Ila told Eve that he'd met Father Octave already, on the mule track above Dardo and in the cemetery at Menton— where he'd told him about Martine's research and the parasite.

"Oh," said Eve.

Bad tried to think of something to say, a protest about secrecy and Dawn's safety. He opened his mouth but only produced a spiritous belch.

"When you talked about the parasite, did Father Octave understand you?" Eve said, coaxing.

"He listened."

"Did you mention to him that you're a vampire?"

Ila frowned. "I don't remember. I do remember that he was unhappy to hear about Martine's state of mind."

Eve slapped her chest; she practically bounced in her chair with a mixture of relief and ebullience. "Good. You told him about Martine's discoveries, and he thought you were telling him that she was delusional." She'd lit up, seemed younger, lighter—dry and jittery, not at all like someone who had been drinking since noon.

"No," said Ila, "I told him what Martine thought. I reported her findings. I was serious, and he listened." Ila said that, besides, Father Octave couldn't imagine that Martine was mad and killed herself, because Father Octave had cause to believe that she'd been killed. "It was he who told me that Tom was at Martine's house and had answered her phone."

Eve now seemed fully sober. She said that, just because Tom had answered Martine's phone, it didn't mean he'd killed her.

Dawn slipped through the gap in the yellow curtain and strolled onto the terrace. She was wearing a satin slip, and the ends of her hair were still damp from the shower. She flipped the switch that turned on the outdoor lights. The terrace became a room, the rising moon pale beyond its lights. The Ligurian tree frogs stopped trilling, perhaps wary, perhaps busy shuffling around to put a tree trunk between themselves and the electric light.

"Daniel Octave wants to come and speak to me," Eve said to her sister. "And apparently Ila has been talking to him."

Dawn caressed Bad's salt-stiffened curls. She said to Ila, "I thought you weren't speaking to anyone." She stooped to touch Bad under his ear with her mouth.

"*Now, now,*" said Eve. "Bad has to eat."

"So do I."

"Bad's a nursing mother," Eve said.

Dawn kept her head by Bad's ear—he could feel her breath misting its polished curves. She said softly—and Bad at first thought she was speaking only to him—"I know what you're doing." She straightened. "I know you've been quietly chiseling away at Ila about Bad, behind my back."

"Oh, Dawn." Eve was exasperated.

"I found someone I want to keep. Is that clear? This decision is none of your business, Eve. Ila has to be guided by me in this matter. He can't think straight. He's starving himself!"

Ila said, "It's not *myself* I'm starving."

Dawn put her bunched fists to her chest. "I'm choosing for our nest." She was speaking only to Ila now. Pleading with him. "There aren't enough of us. I can't keep you alive—even if you're as little trouble as an Eskimo grandmother. Our nest can't be just you and me with Eve to look after us—no matter how much money and goodwill Eve can muster. And Eve's not getting any younger."

"Stop," said Ila. "Stop now. I won't take *anyone*, Dawn. I'm finished with that."

Dawn looked skeptical. "We'll see," she said.

Daniel Octave dialed the number from the hairstylist's appointment book. An answering service said merely that he should leave a message. He gave his name and the number of the mobile Martine had bought him—then had to dig it out of his luggage. It told him that its batteries were low, then promptly switched itself off. He attached it to its charger and plugged it in.

Daniel tried to read, to catch up on some work. An hour passed. Then, when his mobile was charged, he used it to call Father Neske in Montreal.

Father Neske said he was sure Daniel didn't want to hear about his sciatica, but it was kind of Daniel to ask about his health. "Or is it my heart you're asking about?"

"Your heart?" Daniel was alarmed. "What's wrong with your heart?"

"Or my soul, perhaps," said the old man. "But let's hear about *you*, Daniel. How's your work? If I ask you about that, you'll find something to say."

"My work? Well . . . I'm absorbed by it."

"And absolved of yourself, I trust."

"No," Daniel said. "Not anymore."

There was silence on the end of the phone. Then, "At last," said Father Neske. "A crack."

Daniel thought of the cave system at Dardo, the Pilgrim's Way, and the black mouths of its unlit, funneling side passages. He said to Father Neske that, for years, since the novitiate really, he'd been so proud of his intellectual attainments and what he'd thought of, complacently, as his spiritual progress. But he had only processed other people's wonder, had let it pass through his hands.

"Daniel," said Neske. "The trouble with you is that you have no desires. Or you've made them small. You've let your fears and former miseries digest them—you've ground desire down with miseries like gizzard stones."

"There *was* something I wanted. That I knew I wanted."

"What was that?"

"A blessing." Daniel said he didn't mean a ceremonious blessing—those hadn't ever been in short supply. It was some other kind he wanted. When he'd played hockey in high school—and had been regularly trampled—his coach would check his cuts and say, *"You'll live."* That was as good as communion.

Daniel told Neske that when he was a boy of about twelve—it was shortly after his mother had been taken in hand by the Welfare people—he'd come home and walk past the ramparts of stacked newspapers (Welfare hadn't quite got around to that) led by habit through the darkness to the kitchen and his mother. Father Groux had told Daniel to give his mother some time every day. Daniel would get himself a glass of milk and would sit and listen to her for a while before making his now foolproof excuse, "I have to do my homework." His mother might be washing clothes at the sink and he'd have to remind her about the washing machine. She might be talking about the woman from Welfare—the smell of detergent on the woman's clothes: "That dreadful chemical smell that's in everyone's backyards." She'd say that she supposed the woman from Welfare was considered pretty. "But she's just another of *those*," she'd say. "Daniel, you should know that there are women who like sex and women who don't. And the women who don't like sex use it to get what they want out of men."

Daniel told Neske that every day he'd open his illustrated Bible at a certain page. The picture showed women fetching water at a fountain. He would dip his fingers into his milk and would dab it on his forehead, where first it was cool, then, much later, dry, the milk forming a thin glaze that would stiffen if he frowned. It stayed there, as if someone were touching him lightly. It stopped him from frowning—was a kind of biofeedback. It reminded him of the picture. The way the woman in the foreground had balanced a full jar on her shoulders. The way that, when he looked at the picture, he'd begin to float and imagine that anything he touched, of any weight, he could carry. But even as he floated up he'd be *thinking*; he'd be nervously pleased that he was a boy, not a girl, and wouldn't be obliged to choose—to like sex, like his mother, who wasn't a prude and was neglected, or to be squeamish and scheming and *successful*. "I don't know why I believed her," Daniel said. "I guess I tried to follow her thinking, and it began to seem real."

Daniel became impatient with himself. He said to Neske, "But you'll think I'm talking about sex."

"No," said Neske. "You're saying that you were discouraged from being fully alive in your senses by the squalor of your mother's house, and by what she claimed for herself. You're saying you were alive only in one spot, where the milk dried on your forehead, where you tried to give yourself a blessing."

Daniel shut his eyes. He was mute with love. How he loved this man—if gratitude were love—for understanding him. When he found his voice, however, it was merely polite and gracious. He said thank you. Then he went on to explain that the Bible illustrations were Twenties aquatints. The water in the fountain had looked sweet. Daniel told Neske that he had wanted to carry it up to wash everything. He had lived with that; the water he hadn't been able to carry apparently piled above him, behind its dam. The water came from a river that—he now knew—had carved its way out of a cave, out of the dark of God's imminence. "For ten years now the Pilgrim's Way under Dardo has been, for me, a place where I know God is. Where I know I can find Him."

"But?" said Father Neske.

Daniel pinched his temples. He squeezed his eyes shut. He tried to stop himself. "But it isn't God," he said.

"Tell me what happened."

"My life with my mother equipped me to follow irrational thinking. To give it a fair hearing. I've been hearing some strange stories, some alternate evidence. That's how I know that it isn't God in the cave. It's a puzzle, and a horror."

"Daniel?"

"I know it is."

"Daniel, listen to me," said Neske.

"I know it is," Daniel said again. He was thinking of Jacques Palomba, the boy preserved by his prayers to Martine Raimondi and the man who'd been found, eighteen days before, in the open basement of a beach café, his neck nearly severed and his hands pressed to his head. ("As if he was holding it on," the detective said.)

"Daniel, you have to tell people when you're having trouble. When something is too much for you. You're not providing cover for your crazy mother. That habit has never helped you."

Daniel told Neske to please stop playing psychologist.

"Ask for help, Daniel. Tell me what it is that you feel you have to cover up."

"I'm only trying to get to the bottom of something."

"Talk to your confessor. Have you any idea the high regard in which you're held? The time and attention that are there for the asking, for you? Within the Company—"

"I'm trying to get to the bottom of something whose bottom is invisible to me. My rope isn't long enough, and I'm at the end of it. You, Father, being you—not going soft on me—should say, 'Then let go.' I should be able to rely on you to give me that advice."

Father Neske laughed unhappily. "But, Daniel, I *am* soft on you." Father Neske said he'd talk to the Superior of his house, who would call Daniel's confessor in Rome to report that Father Octave was having a spiritual crisis.

"But this isn't despair," said Daniel. He thought of Martine Dardo in a boat without engine or oars. "I *have* to let go. To get to the bottom I have to fall. I must have faith that my faith won't be destroyed by what I find."

"Don't do everything alone," Neske said, pleading.

"But I do," said Daniel, surprised.

When he finished the call his phone chirruped. He dialed its mailbox and was told by a man with an American accent—the man who had been in Martine's apartment—that he would like Daniel to meet him, two days hence, at ten in the evening, in the Chapel of the Gray Penitents, on the Rue des Teinturiers, in Avignon.

In the small hours, Eve, parched and hungover, took a similar call.

"Let's parley," said Tom.

Eve heard "party." "*Pardon?*" she said, then, "Tom."

"English, Eve."

"You want to talk?"

"To meet. To talk. Ila's nest and mine."

Eve wormed her way up in bed, out of the stew of damp bedclothes. "Tom, you don't have a nest." Tom was being grand and managerial.

He gave her directions, an address, the time of a rendezvous. He didn't argue with her.

"Where have you been?" Eve said. "Your publisher told me you're still banking their royalties. And I saw your essay on Anna Beder in the *New Yorker* last year."

Tom said, "Well, what do you expect? I was a *whole person*, a mature human being, a man of the world, when Ila made me."

Eve asked Tom why he'd attacked her in the elevator.

"I wanted to see how many of you there were, how many would come to your assistance. I was counting—one, two. Also, I was very upset. I thought you must all know—but you don't, do you? You still haven't realized that Martine was a murderer." Then Tom said it was hot inland, in Avignon, and that Eve should remember to pack her support hose.

"That's beneath you," said Eve.

Tom sniggered and hung up.

Dawn was still awake, intertwined with the pallid, stuporous Bad in her shuttered room. When Eve finished telling her about Tom's proposal Dawn thought for a bit, then told Eve to take Bad by train. "Today. I'll drive Ila tonight. First I'll hit the clubs and gorge, then feed Ila. Make him eat. I'll tell him that I'm not going anywhere near Tom unless he's up to full speed. I'll remind him that Tom's not scared of being caught out. But, Eve," Dawn said, "it's beginning to look as if Martine did harm someone of Tom's. Why would Tom turn up only to lie?"

Eve shook her head. She just wanted to see Tom, who she'd imagined had met with an accident and whom she'd mourned for years in a bitter, misshapen way. She came closer to the bed and put out a hand to test the temperature of Bad's cheek. It was cool and clammy.

"I didn't bite him," Dawn said. "He's only hungover."

Eve gave her sister a sharp look and went out.

Dawn was shaking Bad. He tried to push her away, but she persisted. He made an effort to wake up enough to tell her to leave him alone. That was hard; it was like climbing a giant sand dune.

Dawn was saying that she had to leave him. They were all going to Avignon, and she had to feed herself and Ila tonight if she'd be traveling most of the following night. Eve had agreed to meet Tom Hilxen in Avignon. Eve needed to learn what Tom knew about Martine's death.

Dawn said, "Bad, before we drag you off to Avignon, and *involve* you, there's something you should know. About Tom Hilxen."

Dawn told Bad that when she'd first met him in Le Lien Vert she'd been with Tom and that she and Tom had quarreled.

Tom had asked Dawn to a party. She'd understood him. Had understood what he meant by "party." There were things she and Tom did together of which Martine and Ila would not approve. Tom thought it false to have changed and yet find himself living by the same rules he'd been *obliged* to follow in his former life. Obliged by the practical rules of kindness and civil behavior. Tom argued that he'd been armed with a performance-enhancing drug and he should be allowed to enjoy it. To Tom, enjoying it meant making conquests, having a variety of bodies in ecstasy under him. It was simply a matter of taste, he said, how one treated one's donors. He liked each donor's astonishment better than their subsequent slavish anticipation.

Dawn had gathered from things her sister said that Tom was perhaps a little disappointing as a lover. That what Tom had was all *up front*—so to speak. He was attractive and seductive but not sensitive or imaginative. Tom's bite more than made up for the discrepancy between his image and performance, but his habits as a lover had already hardened, and it was his habit to view the desire of others as a demand, an imposition.

Tom began to hold "parties." He'd pick up whole groups

of young vacationers and would throw money about—Eve's money. He liked to have Dawn present to bite him, to jack him up. At first Dawn enjoyed the parties. They were more comfortable and leisurely than her nightclub hunting yet hadn't any of the complications of an attachment to one person.

"There always were people I'd return to, people I'd toy with taking and keeping. People I'd idly size up—proto-candidates, really. I wanted to fall in love, so would leave them reluctantly. I'd endanger their health, then feel bad about it."

Tom's parties had helped for a time. At the parties Dawn hadn't imagined she'd fall in love, yet they weren't like the nightclubs, the homeless men—bleak, purely hungry encounters. Tom's parties were happy and nutritious.

Tom helped Dawn see certain things. He liked to call Martine a "virtual flagellant." He said that Martine wanted to deny them all their simple sovereign pleasures. Martine was teaching Ila to mortify his flesh, Tom said, when it was clear from Ila's stories—when Ila had enough blood in him to tell them—that Ila and Martine had once been lovers. "Remember how he told us that he'd hide under the dry earth in the olive groves waiting for Martine to bring soldiers she'd lured, as many as they could manage. In '45 and after the war but before demobilization. Remember him talking about Martine, her body, like an idol covered in libations, moonlight glistening on the sticky rivulets of whiskey on her throat." It was clear, Tom said, that Ila had loved Martine with a passion and that he'd now joined her in a mutual pact of self-denial. Martine had rejected Ila, had found him and herself horrible, so that he, too, had rejected himself and his natural needs, and was being mummified alive by self-starvation.

It was all true, Dawn told Bad. Everything Tom said was true. But his rejection of Martine's way gave him too much license. If Martine hated herself, she did, nevertheless, love others. Tom loved himself and never really cared for others.

Before he'd changed he was a charming and ambitious man—people, those who were somehow useful to him, were part of the inner landscape of his ego. People never ceased to surprise him, because he seldom bothered to find out what they were thinking.

Bad asked Dawn what Tom did, what *happened*. How did Tom finally show himself?

After Tom's parties, Dawn said, there was often someone a little too cold and blue about the mouth. She would tell Tom, "We must be more careful!" Tom would say yes, but it was probably just a matter of practice, of experience. He joked—perhaps they should conduct a physical on each potential partygoer. Perhaps he should invest in a stethoscope.

That day, July '92, in the cave, near the exit to the Pilgrim's Way, Tom had a party, to which Dawn went along. The other partygoers were speeding, drunk, off their heads, and happy. But Dawn saw Tom go out after a time, and she followed him to make sure he was all right and to see that he didn't take a wrong turning and get lost—Tom didn't know the cave system as well as she did. She saw him *purging*, sticking his fingers down his throat in order to vomit. Then she watched him go back to a young woman to whom he was paying particular attention. Tom sometimes used Valium derivatives as well as venom—"for different results" he'd say, "and to practice for when I'm infectious and will have to." The woman to whom he was being particularly attentive was drunk, dazed, and compliant. He had bitten her, so she was amorous, too, but unable to please herself efficiently or to follow the action. Tom had a cannula in her, and after he'd purged he returned to her and his drinking straw. Dawn saw that Tom had made these arrangements in order to get far enough from her body to watch her face as the blood left her.

Tom liked to watch the life leaving people, Dawn realized. "I simply reacted," Dawn said. "In disgust. I didn't want to hear him put up an argument. I picked up a fist-sized stone and shoved it in his mouth. I was stronger than him then, as he was still very young. I dislocated his jaw and the stone stuck there. The partygoers took off, uphill luckily, and I fled. I ran till I was sure I'd lost him. I found what I thought would be another way out—through the caverns with waterfalls. I wanted to get to Ila first to explain—as if he were our parent. As if Tom and I were squabbling siblings. But, as it was, I didn't have to explain, because Tom disappeared. Ila and Martine thought he'd been caught out and was dead. I kept insisting that we'd see him again—because only I knew he'd had reason to leave."

"And reason to hate you," Bad said.

"Yes. Tom's dangerous. You should know that before you go to meet him."

Chapter 16

AVIGNON

ad slept through most of the train journey. Sometimes he woke because the train made a noise like a carbide lamp lighting, a soft *g'dunk*. He'd open his eyes expecting a cave's walls, somewhere familiar, Nettlebed or Profanity or The Birthday Series. Instead he'd see, through the carriage window, a plowed field, with big geometrical clods of glossy red earth; and, after St. Raphael, a great reddish escarpment, long, layered, tilted, a mountain going down into the flat countryside like a ship sinking, stern up.

Once Bad woke as color came through his closed lids. The cave of his skull filled with yellow. He opened his eyes and looked at the field of sunflowers.

Beside him Eve said, "If you stay with Dawn you'll be giving that up."

●　●　●

When they reached Avignon and got out of the train Bad asked Eve what was the date? The day?

She told him.

It was the second week of July and he was in Avignon, in the lull before the festival, as his girlfriend had planned. He and Gabrielle had a room booked at a two-star hotel.

Bad steered Eve toward the city gates. "I'm sure it's near the station. Le Magnan."

"It'll be on the street beyond this gate," Eve said. "Portal Magnanen."

"I'm going to take my room. I won't lose my deposit. That's a first, on this trip."

Eve tucked her arm in his and went along with him. Bad knew she was worried about him and cheered by signs of decision and forward thinking.

Le Magnan was on the corner of two streets, wide and narrow. Eve took a room on the quiet side, overlooking its central courtyard, where breakfast was long cleared away and plastic chairs were tilted against plastic tables, between two fig trees and a pink oleander.

Bad's room was one floor above the narrow street and the cacophonous reverberations of a scooter, another scooter, then a group of young men shouting at one another in Arabic. Bad's bathroom was poorly ventilated, the shower stall slow to drain. Bad took a long shower, finished it standing up to his ankles in water. When he moved, water slopped on the floor. He realized that he'd showered in the dark—so put on the light to shave. He got into bed. His mattress was covered in plastic, upon which the sheets had an unreliable purchase. Before long Bad had bulldozed the sheet, ripple by ripple, across the bed and onto the floor. He got out and lay on the nylon bedcover, which stayed still by virtue of its weight. He slept for eight hours. Dawn woke him by licking him, then lying on him, her body heavy and greasy, her hands and mouth impatient and avid. She had come from the street, through the open window.

She didn't bite him. But she asked him to put his tongue out and touched its tip with the tip of her own tongue, pushed tip to tip in time with his pulsing. But Bad was exhausted and couldn't stay hard, so Dawn positioned herself near him, groin to groin and not quite touching, till he grew toward the sustaining moisture and was rewarded. They slid over each other. He could see her, skin glistening, sex wholly wet in the diffuse streetlight that came through the open window.

Later a thunderstorm arrived and rolled across the city. There were sharp cracks over the roofs of the nearby streets. The hairs in Bad's nostrils prickled. Then it rained; drops trickled, then splattered, then roared. After five minutes it was over; the eaves dripped onto the reverberating street with a sound like people standing below Bad's window and clapping out of sync.

Bad slept fitfully and woke finally, fully, feeling as though he were coasting into recovery from the fever of a flu. He was tired but not groggy. For two nights now Dawn had abstained from biting him.

Bad felt better but found that, overnight, he had adhered to the bed. His lower legs were on the bare plastic mattress protector but were less gluey than the rest of him.

Dawn was hot and damp, her arms plaited with his. He untangled himself, bare skin parting with the sound a piece of bread makes when picked up after falling honey-side-down on a smooth floor. The nylon cover was stuck to Bad, and the tacky agent had dried. Bad parted from the bedding with a rasping sound. His body hair pricked and stirred. The shutters were closed and Bad switched on the light to get dressed. He saw the patches of watery blood dried on the bedcover and on his body, wiped and troweled into a textured wash by Dawn's touches. Bloody fingerprints circled his nipples, and when he drew a sharp breath they cracked, crazed, and flaked, so that he felt her touch again, a residual caress.

Bad put on the bedside lamp and saw that his lover's chest was covered in joined pinpricks of sweat, droplets of blood-tinged moisture. Her eyes sat shallow in their sockets, fine lines wholly smoothed away. Her lips were fat, their skin as fine as the membrane formed on warmed milk. Dawn lay with her face turned from the fastened shutters. Bad pinched the lobe of her exposed ear, tested it for ripeness. It was rosy and jutting, and he could feel her pulse moving it, making it shrink and tumesce infinitesimally with each beat of her heart.

This was Dawn gorged. Gorged and giving, for her throat was encircled with a lacy necklace of bloody perforations. She had been enjoyed by Ila, in an intimate, unbusinesslike way, and Bad knew that when she came in the night before and coupled with him and made him come and come without biting him, her sweat as thick and oily as the slick of clay, she was jacked up on Ila's mouth, on his hundred-proof, contaminating venom.

Bad went and showered, stood shivering in the warm water, his head resting against the wall of the stall.

Eve had left a note for Bad at the desk. He collected it as he went past and left his key.

I didn't really expect to see you at breakfast, but we must get together this afternoon to "walk the course," so to speak, before the event. Ila and Dawn won't have time to find bolt-holes before the meeting. Tom has been very careful not to allow for that, so we must cover for them. I'll be in again at two, and will expect to see you. Eve.

Bad had a late breakfast, or an early lunch, and dragged himself about the sights. He was too tired to take much in or had lost the use of the senses on which the tourist most depends in order to know which way to point his camera. Bad wasn't carrying his camera. He had forgotten he owned one, forgotten he meant to collect memories—photos and souvenirs—reminders, proof.

It was hot, and Bad kept clear of the terraced piazza before the Palace of the Popes. The piazza was paved with halved oval stones, all of a similar size, and these brown cobbles gave out more heat than the sandstone of the side streets, some of which had surfaces so polished by foot traffic they were like indoor flooring.

Bad wandered over the remaining arches of the bridge, an audio guide pressed to one ear. He peered into the Chapel of St. Nicolas and tried to find a sinker—something seriously impressive—to carry his attention to the depths of the day. Everything was foreign—of course—and the antiquities before which he paused, shoulders rounded and upper back bowed and trembling, didn't bring him to his senses, to themselves. Everything was foreign; even the English in his ear was a well-modulated nonsense. Wind skimmed along that stretch of the Rhône and idly tried to sweep all the tourists off the bridge. Children shrieked, their voices vibrating like fluttering ribbons.

The wind was in the town, too, making clangs and thrums in the scaffolding of stages. The trees were letting go, and some doorways looked like old graves stuffed full of brown blown leaves. Nothing showed signs of last night's rain.

It occurred to Bad that this was the mistral in which he had once been so interested. It occurred to Bad that his legs ached and had begun to tremble.

He went back to his hotel.

It was 1:00 P.M. The desk was empty but for a cat, which saw Bad coming and flipped over, to snake its head crown-down along the counter. Bad made kissing noises and scratched its chin. The hotel proprietor heard him and darted out from behind a curtain. The man seemed pleased to see Bad. He had some good news. Bad concentrated to follow him. He was told that his girlfriend had arrived—as planned—and had checked in. The proprietor had given her Bad's room key, so Bad should—and the man balled his fist and rapped eagerly on the air.

Bad was baffled. He went up to his room, left the DO NOT DISTURB sign on the door. The sun was on the balcony above the enclosed courtyard. The carpet on the balcony was soggy where someone had watered the begonias in a hanging pot. The sunlight coming under the eaves was knee-high on the door, and the door was unlocked. Bad cracked it open quickly and slipped inside. Dawn would be hammered to her bed by the sun. Bad didn't turn on the light. He wanted to touch her without having to see her varnished, blood-plump body. He crossed the few feet between the door and bed, put his hand down, and found Dawn. The air in the room smelled meaty, ferrous, of animal fermentation. There was another smell underlying Dawn's red perspiration, something fresh and familiar to Bad. And he wondered whether Ila had found his way into the room somehow, despite the daylight.

Bad moved around the bed, his hands following Dawn's curves—she gave a growling sigh—and his feet encountered another fleshy solidity. He stooped and touched. Someone was lying on the floor beside the bed.

As Bad bent over the person he identified her, recognized the soft, solid body, and the scent, as belonging to Gabrielle.

Bad recoiled. He blundered back across the room and turned on the light.

Gabrielle was pale and limp. She lay with her knees splayed, her dress open to the waist, and her head forced back and jammed to the eyebrows under the sill of a bedside cabinet.

Bad crawled across the room, put her ankles together, and pulled her free. She had a deep pink crease on her forehead, and she had a patch of dark perforations at the top of one big, soft breast, marks as discrete and black as the holes in a saltshaker. The skin was bruised there, too, from the speedy force of Dawn's penetration.

Gabrielle's breath caught and her palate vibrated. She snored and moaned. Bad jumped over her and straddled Dawn. He slapped her, shouted in her face. She whined. Her arms were sluggish in assuming a guarding position, forearms and fists together, but were at once powerfully locked in place. Bad rolled off her and wrestled Gabrielle up and walked her into the bathroom. She went down on her knees, so he clamped her chin onto the edge of the basin and turned on a tap. He splashed cold water on her face.

Then Dawn was in the bathroom doorway, droopy, shambolic, dull-eyed. She said that the woman had disturbed her. The woman had stood in the doorway with sunlight pushing in behind her and had said something. Had said, "Brian?"

Dawn bit her, bled her, put her down.

"You can't do this!" Bad yelled at Dawn.

Gabrielle snorted, and her limp arms twitched, then rose vaguely to fumble at Bad and at herself.

"What do you mean I can't do this?" Dawn said, irritated. "You've been with me for weeks. Which side of the line do you think you're on now?"

Gabrielle whimpered. Her eyes were open but rolled back. Bad eased her down onto the bathroom floor. He got up and faced Dawn and told her to get out.

"I can't get out," she said—but her "out" was more of an "ow," since her spines had risen and were pressing on her tongue.

Bad exploded. He shoved Dawn and shouted, called her all the standard names enraged antipodean men used, and each time he struck her he felt her body, hot and heavy and drowsy, until she stopped him, fell forward with an arm raised, a bar across his throat. She fell onto him and carried him to the floor so that his head was pillowed on Gabrielle's hip.

Dawn bit him under his ear. But it was as though her

appetite and his blood volume were at different unequal pressures. He was too much for her. She pumped in only a little venom, and he was scarcely moved, felt only a tingle of delight, before she wrenched herself free and vomited on his shoulder, a pint of maroon liquid, blood and blood clots.

Bad burst into tears. He wrapped his arms around her and held her hard, his murderous vampire. "I love you," he said, desperate. "Please help me."

It was late afternoon when Daniel Octave ran into Bad Phelan and his slovenly, drug-dazed female friend. They were sitting on a low wall at the entrance to the garden behind the cathedral, he perched, she slumped. There was a pack beside them, smaller than the one Daniel remembered Bad carrying. If memory served—and it generally did—Bad's was festooned with coiled nylon rope and steel climbing equipment.

Bad seemed to be watching the children pedaling their sulkies—pedalcars, low to the ground, with a bobbing horse in front and shaded by fringed canopies.

Daniel stopped before the couple. "Have you never seen these?" he asked.

Bad looked up. "Father Octave," he said. He didn't seem at all surprised to see Daniel.

The woman wore a baggy T-shirt over a very attractive pleated skirt and sandals. There was a fresh blood spot on the shirt, over one breast. She sat, knock-kneed, with her head resting on Bad's upper arm.

Bad introduced her. "This is Miss McKone. Gabrielle. She's sick and I'm trying to find her a hotel room."

"Not a doctor?"

"The hotel can find a doctor. Don't they always have doctors on call?"

"I wouldn't know. Can I be of any assistance?"

Bad was very grateful. He said that they'd traipsed about

asking, but it was proving difficult. He didn't have his phone or guidebook, so they were just asking at places they passed. Gabrielle was tired. They had to find somewhere soon. Bad said he wondered if it might be possible for Father Octave to sit here with her in the shade while Bad covered ground and found a place. Then he'd be back to take her off Father Octave's hands.

Gabrielle stirred, said, "I thought we had a room."

"We don't." Bad met Daniel's eyes and shook his head.

There was some story here, Daniel thought, something about unreciprocated love, the woman not letting the man go.

"Where are you staying?" Daniel asked Bad.

"Oh . . . it isn't suitable."

"She really does seem to need a doctor, as a priority."

"It's not as bad as it looks, Father. She's just having one of her turns."

He got up and took Daniel's hands, set them on the woman's shoulders. Daniel sat beside her and put an arm around her shoulders—took her weight.

"I won't be long," Bad said.

"Just a minute. First tell me where you're staying."

Bad blushed. He said he was taking turns in the back of someone's van, in a camping ground outside the city walls.

"And how are you getting on with your investigations?" Daniel said. He could see that Phelan had been living rough—and only *drinking* with Eve Moskelute. Bad had lost condition, was pasty-faced and bruised under the eyes. But at Daniel's question Bad lit up and laughed.

"Father, there's always more than one solution to a problem. Let me tell you a little story. How I solved my Rubik's Cube.

"My dad loves puzzles, and he's good at them. When the cube came out he couldn't wait to impose the bugger on us— me and my brother—and we were just little fellas. Me, I've always hated puzzles, with answers built into them, puzzles at which you have to look and look. My gaze would always wander, even when my hands were fiddling, working the creaking plastic, twisting it this way and that. I wasn't getting anywhere with it, and Dad was teasing me, and I didn't want to be beaten. So do you know what I did? I steamed my cube and peeled off all its little colored squares and glued them on again so that it had all six planes the same. Solved! And as far as I was concerned I *had* solved the real problem, the problem of appearances. I hadn't wanted it to appear that I couldn't solve the cube."

"Have you been saving that up for me?" Daniel asked. Then, "I suppose I deserve it, after my albinos."

"That's right," said Bad, then, scornful, "*Statistical probability.*"

Daniel lifted a hand and waved to Bad. "Don't be gone long," he said.

The sun moved on and Daniel and the sick woman lost their shade. Daniel checked his watch every so often and squinted down the cobbled slope at all the tourists. After forty minutes Daniel concluded that Bad wasn't coming back. He'd bolted, leaving Daniel holding the baby.

Daniel asked the woman whether she was well enough to walk.

She began to cry. She was clearly exhausted.

"I'll take you to the nearest hotel. We can find a doctor."

The woman said she wasn't sick. She'd been attacked. Why had Brian attacked her?

Daniel didn't press for further details. Nor did he ask if she wanted the police. Instead, he picked up her pack, strapped it on, and wrestled her up off the wall where she'd been slumped. He walked her across the square. He told her that they would go in the first place, take the first vacancy—never mind the expense. He assessed her—her jewelry, jacket, shoes, pack, all good quality. She could afford it. He wanted to be rid of the woman and her delirious complaints.

Gabrielle told him that there was someone else in Brian's room. "She stabbed me."

There was blood on her blouse.

"I bashed my head on a table," she said. "When she pushed me over. She held me down on the floor."

Daniel spotted a five-star hotel, situated between the Palace of the Popes and the river. Daniel asked her could she afford this—short-term.

She said she could and, furthermore, from now on she'd do things *her* way, not on the cheap to humor men who made a virtue of having no ambition.

Daniel ushered her into the hotel lobby. She was immediately in her element. She fished a credit card out of her money belt and slid it across the granite counter. The gesture was self-possessed—but once she'd completed it she stood sobbing. She told Daniel that, from now on, she was sticking with her own kind. "The girl Brian had in his room—she stabbed me. What kind of person does a thing like that?"

Daniel told the man behind the counter that this young woman would want a doctor and might want the police.

The woman seemed to be feeling a little better—more indignant, less unhappy. She said to Daniel and the hotel proprietor that if a man tells you he loves adventure you can be sure it means that one day he's going to go off with some head case. "I think the woman in Brian's room stabbed me with the pocketknife I gave him for his birthday. It was perfect, a Marmout, with all the tools."

The hotel proprietor made noises of sympathy.

"Brian likes to think he's a hero, but he's just a thrill seeker," she confided. "Well—I've got his number."

"Will you file a complaint?" the proprietor asked.

She shook her head, ground both fists into her eyes—bawling, touchingly babyish. She said to Daniel, "When you see him next—"

"I scarcely know Mr. Phelan. We met twice, on a train and at the pilgrimage in Dardo. He only entrusted you to me because I'm a priest."

The woman looked astonished, took a step back, and looked at Daniel. She said, "Oh."

"Please get her a doctor," said Daniel to the proprietor.

"A doctor and a room," she said. "I smell of the cleaning stuff in the carpet." She began to sob again. "He made me admire him and he's mad."

The proprietor tutted, tapped a bell to summon the bell captain, and gave Bad's girlfriend forms to sign.

Daniel wrote out his mobile number and offered it to her. "I must go."

She thanked him, said, "If you do see him, tell him . . ."

"Yes?"

"Oh . . . tell him that it just isn't acceptable."

Daniel nodded, said all right, he'd convey that to Mr. Phelan should they meet again. "Take care," he said.

"You bet I will," she said. "I've learned my lesson—real men are really unreliable."

At dusk Daniel found his way to the Rue des Teinturiers. Its cafés were crowded, its clubs only just turning on their lights. The street was packed, narrow, the sky overhead a crooked black crack. The activity was confined to one side of the street; on the other, a stream ran through a stone-lined channel, tamed by masonry, and driving waterwheels, the turning blades of perpetually wet timber reflecting the strings of colored lights on the awnings of the cafés and purple fluorescents outlining the entrances to clubs.

The Chapel of the Gray Penitents was part of Louis the

Thirteenth's spiritual capital. It was built to pay penance for a massacre some hundred years before. Daniel recognized the stark, simple fresco of kneeling figures, the penitents in cassocks and hoods, only their eyes visible. The iron gates were open—iron like pulled strands of burnt toffee. Daniel went through them, challenged only by cicadas that studded the trunk of a plane tree, small vibrating shadows. He crossed the bridge and entered the building.

Daniel found a series of chapels leading into the main nave, all at angles to one another—the whole building a complicated piece of jigsaw shaped to fit among older buildings and along the channeled stream. Daniel passed through the first chapel, a long gallery whose walls were painted to look like stone with fat shallow veins, through the Chapel of the Vignerons, and into a larger domed hexagonal room. All the rooms were empty. When he entered the main nave its wooden floor complained loudly. This room, too, was empty, though a haze of bluish incense smoke hung near the ceiling, a layer of pollution between Daniel and its roof, a starry firmament. The church was well lit but somber. Daniel paced the aisle slowly toward the gilded ironwork gates before the main tabernacle. The gates were closed, though candles burned beyond them. Above the tabernacle was a huge gilded, carved plaque, of storm clouds, and a sunburst, cherubim sporting in its breaking light.

Behind Daniel the floor stirred, with a soft, rustling crackle, as though someone were moving in a wickerwork chair. He turned around. There was no one near him, but he saw a figure he hadn't noticed before, a man sitting in a pew with both arms spread out along its back. Daniel approached him. "Are you the man I spoke to on the phone? The man in Martine Dardo's apartment?"

"Have a seat," the man said. He was American.

The man didn't move, so Daniel perched on the pew at arm's length and faced him. The man didn't even turn his head. Daniel said, "I was given a name at Jacques Palomba's last place of employment. The name and number of a woman. Was it you who answered *her* phone, too?"

The man smiled, leaned toward Daniel, and put out a hand. "Tom Hilxen," he said, and gave Daniel a firm, collegial handshake. His smile was wry. "I suppose this all looks a little cloak-and-dagger. The fact is, this was where I planned to be. I have another appointment here, later tonight. Like most novel places of rendezvous it's a choice dictated by sentiment—nothing sinister."

He tucked his chin in and looked at Daniel from under his eyebrows, a gleam of amusement in his eyes. "I hope you're not disappointed."

Daniel asked Tom Hilxen how he had known Jacques Palomba.

"How? Intimately." Tom's smile was positively scintillating. "I hope that doesn't offend you, Father."

The man didn't seem at all disturbed by the murder of someone he had known intimately. Perhaps he didn't know any details. Daniel told Mr. Hilxen how Jacques had been found and how the detective—disturbed by the coincidental relationship between Jacques Palomba's murder and the accidental death of Martine Dardo—had called Daniel. Daniel explained his connection to both people—that he was the postulator who had written the Process.

"Yes, I did know all that," Tom Hilxen said. He slipped his hand into his jacket pocket and produced a flat silver flask. He shook it at Daniel. It made a high-pitched slopping sound.

"No, thank you."

"Please. I find it difficult to talk about Jacques. I have so many regrets. I find it distasteful even to describe the company he got into, latterly. I'd taken that boy under my wing. I undertook to teach him to manage his talents. I told myself that he was only adventurous, and lacked imagination. That it was only a matter of stimulating his imagination to teach him a little more caution. But what a folly it is—don't you think?—to feel you can pass on experience. Our talk conveys nothing to the young. They think we're telling stories to entertain them. They take it as flattery. Flattering attention. We think we're imparting something that might save their lives, but all we are really doing is whiling away an hour or two. Please," Hilxen said again, and proffered the flask. "Join me."

Daniel took the flask. His cooperation would please the man. The man wanted a show of conviviality. The man wanted Daniel to see him as wise and weary, patient and disillusioned. A friend and guide to young Jacques Palomba—who had disappointed him. Disappointed him by dying. Daniel decided that he would humor Mr. Hilxen, would put up with his cold-hearted pomposity, in order to discover if this man, who had known Jacques, had any idea who had killed him.

Daniel unscrewed the lid of the flask. He took a swig. He expected scotch, but it was amaro—bitter and medicinal.

"Good," said Tom Hilxen. He motioned to Daniel that he should keep the flask for now.

Daniel asked him if he was a friend of Grazide—Palomba's client at the spa.

"Yes. I expect her to join me soon. We arranged to meet some people here. Under the mark of inundation." Hilxen pointed across the nave. "It's on that column there. A line scored on the stone, as though some giant stood its child there to measure the progress of its growth. It marks how high the waters rose in the flood of 1821. Few French churches have timber floors—have you noticed? This floor is timber so that they can cut through it to let the water in, so that the water won't float the building off its foundations."

Daniel asked who Tom and his friend Grazide were meeting and whether it had anything to do with Jacques Palomba.

"Yes, it does. But, Father," said Tom, "why don't you fill me in on what you know, so that we won't cover the same ground twice?"

Daniel replaced the flask's cap and heard how it grated on the sugar in its threads. The liquor hadn't seemed sweet enough to leave a sugary deposit. "I hate to seem ridiculous," Daniel admitted to Tom Hilxen. "I've been pussyfooting around my concerns for weeks now."

"We all do," the man said consolingly. "We hate to seem ridiculous, and there's nothing more ridiculous than desire—don't you think? Even if it's only desire for the truth."

Daniel told Tom Hilxen about the detective's call and his trip to Genoa, to the spa where Jacques had worked. He told Mr. Hilxen about the name he was given—Grazide—and how, in comforting Palomba's family, he had missed the funeral of his friend Martine Dardo. He talked about Martine's connection to Jacques. About the Blessed Martine Raimondi. He told him how he had arranged to meet Martine's friend Eve Moskelute. And how, in preparation for that meeting, he had read Ms. Moskelute's translation of Chambord's *Daylight*. How he had discovered that the heroine of *Daylight* had the same name as Jacques Palomba's client, Grazide. Chambord had said that, in his hour of darkness, God sent him a devil as his guide—a dusty incoherence. And Martine Raimondi—the saint to whom Jacques Palomba prayed when he was lost in a flooded cave in 1992—her very last words to her partisan friend were to the effect that when she prayed for God's help in the caves of Dardo, God sent her a devil.

Daniel said all this without embarrassment, without feeling ridiculous. He found that, lacking these feelings, he felt unexpectedly serene. Calm, and careless. At last he felt that he could talk about all this—to himself or to anyone else. The improbable connections—between people in the past, the near and distant past, and the present—which had been a torment to him, were no more. The whole problem seemed rather remote. He looked up at the wavering light of the candles in the red glass of the lamps hanging on either side of the tabernacle. The light stirred. The shadows fluttered—not like the bodies of insects behind glass, but like the distortions on an LCD screen on a computer when it's touched. The chapel, its opulent gilded carving, its cherubs and sunburst, all seemed a projection, an image made of many bits, like 256-bit color. Someone was lightly pressing Daniel's view of the chapel, here and there, so that the light distorted, and the images in the light, as though bending around invisible dabbling fingertips.

Daniel put his hand to his head. He placed the flask down on the pew between himself and Mr. Hilxen. Mr. Hilxen was smiling at him. A gentle, expectant smile.

Daniel tried to gather his thoughts, to remember what he'd meant to ask. He hadn't yet asked anything, had only laid out the pattern of his paranoid connections. All he could think to say was, "How does all that strike you?"

Hilxen relaxed and spread his arms along the back of the pew again so that Daniel could feel one, warm against the top of his shoulders. "It seems like a code that lacks its key." Hilxen turned his head and smiled again at Daniel, proprietorial. "Can you imagine what its key might be? Perhaps it's only one word."

Daniel didn't bother to shake his head. A moment before he had needed to know, but he found he was losing interest in knowledge. It was hard to care about something that made his head hurt. Though his head wasn't actually hurting. It felt more stuffed, muffled. He watched Tom Hilxen put a hand into a jacket pocket. Tom produced a piece of coiled plastic tubing. Daniel wondered what it was for. Tom Hilxen put the tube down on his knees. From the other pocket he produced a flat plastic Ziploc bag containing several small instruments Daniel was unable to recognize. Tom shook one of these out of the bag and put it between his teeth to free his hands. He picked up Daniel's now very heavy hand, the nearest, and turned it over to unbutton the shirt cuff.

"What?" said Daniel. He heard "wash." He noticed that breathing out had become more difficult than breathing in, that the air he expelled was a weight on which he had to press. His saliva was thick and sticky, filling his mouth like honey.

Tom loosened the cuff buttons and slid Daniel's sleeve up his arm. Daniel watched all this, mesmerized.

Mr. Hilxen opened another sealed packet, like the moistened towelettes airlines hand out. Tom produced an alcohol wipe and stroked it, cool, across the skin in the crook of Daniel's arm. Then he took the instrument out from between his teeth and uncapped it, closed a hand around Daniel's arm just above the elbow, and squeezed. Daniel watched his veins rise and saw Hilxen slide the needle of a cannula into the place where the veins forked in the crook of his arm. Daniel was curious but unconcerned. He wasn't in pain, and though he knew he was in danger, he was happier somehow with this kind of danger than all the things he'd been anticipating, the things he'd thought he would learn.

Tom Hilxen clipped the plastic tubing to the end of the cannula and put its end to his own lips and sucked. Daniel watched his blood run through the transparent tube. It was as if someone were writing with red ink in the air, making a signature, a series of dark loops. Daniel was drawn out of himself. He had hoped to talk. He had hoped someone would tell him. He had dreaded that someone would tell him. He watched the urbane American drink his blood. It was done with delicacy, with no great show of appetite. Mr. Hilxen had the appearance of a therapist or craftsman. There was no naked interest or possessiveness in his posture. He was polite. He sipped. But he didn't stop. He went on, long after Daniel had slid down the seat and he had raised his eyes from his neat work to meet Daniel's gaze to watch, with unconnected interest, the process of Daniel's loss of consciousness.

Bad didn't tell Eve about Gabrielle. He found he couldn't. He was ashamed of Dawn. More so when he saw her that evening—she'd been out early and had eaten again, had topped up, and was engorged, her eyelids puffy and mouth throbbing red. Ila was, for once, fully fed. His crepey skin was smooth, his stiff, guarded gait easy. He glowed, looked all of eighteen years old, and as refined and pale as a spirit.

In the evening they walked the streets near the Chapel of the Gray Penitents. They found bolt-holes, a round, iron inspection hatch leading to a vertical shaft full of cables—phone and fiber-optic—and a narrow north–south running alley, sealed off by gates and shaded by deep eaves.

Ila produced a chisel from his pocket and squatted on the street and inserted its flat head into the slot on another drain's inspection hatch. He prized the cover up, slid it to one side, and peered into a shaft, the deep stone-lined drain. "This is by far the best place," he said, then pushed the cover back and had Dawn try to open it. She, too, could manage. The final, *nearest* bolt-hole was behind the waterwheel and under the bridge at the door of the chapel. But the depths of that darkness were visible to people along the street and leaning over the wall, and it was always possible that the public—being public-spirited— would set out to rescue an unhappy vampire who took shelter there during the day.

They came out into a main street, thronged with people, through which the occasional car moved, yellow fog lamps igniting eddies of parched leaves. Heat still radiated from the cobbles, and Bad felt he was wading up to his knees in warm water. They turned back in their tracks, checking again, then went on into the Rue des Teinturiers, where Eve asked them to stop—to wait a minute.

Eve said she'd stay outside for a time. She'd keep her eye on the street.

Dawn was baffled. "You made this appointment. It is you who's been determined to find out what Tom knows about

Martine. Do you think you can you trust Ila to ask the right questions?"

Eve said she hoped to join them shortly. She just felt it would be a good idea to leave someone posted in the street.

"Bad can do it," Dawn said.

"Bad might not know a vampire if he saw one."

Dawn seemed to accept this.

"Besides . . . I'm not in any hurry to have Tom condescend to me," Eve said.

"All right," Dawn said. They left her. She watched them pass through the gate onto the bridge that crossed the channeled stream. They passed through the chapel's door, under the fresco of hooded, kneeling flagellants.

Eve caught the eye of a dreadlocked waiter. He took her order, for tea—it was after 2:00 A.M.

Her tea came, and Eve sipped it and watched the street.

Perhaps twenty minutes later Eve saw a vampire, a slender woman with gnarly ropes of artificially vivid red curls, who walked carrying a round slab of steel before her—a manhole cover—held out from her abdomen to spare her elegant linen dress. The woman was watched by everyone on the street, but it was only a week before the festival and the town was full of theatrical performers, technicians, productions setting up, and the watchers clearly supposed the manhole cover to be some prop. Eve knew it was not. She knew it belonged on the nearest bolt-hole and was the inspection hatch over the node of underground cables. Eve watched the woman carry the slab to the coping of the stone channel, just upstream of the waterwheel. The woman rested the rim of the manhole cover on the wall, then tipped it into the water. Several people near her, who'd witnessed this, attempted to speak to her. But she brushed them aside, flicked her shoulders, and pushed her grimy palms at them, without actually looking into their faces or listening to what they had to say. She had seen Eve—had *recognized* her. The woman crossed the street and climbed over

297 Daylight

the café's low barrier of fairy lights. Eve looked up into the woman's eyes. Aqua eyes, with an unstable iris that slid as she glanced to either side, her iris slow to follow the glance. The woman was wearing colored contact lenses, Eve realized. Eve saw that the woman's part and hairline were pure white, as though her hair was thinning and it was her scalp that showed.

"Will you please join us in the chapel?" the woman said to Eve.

The tongue on the lock of the gate at the bridge into the Chapel of the Gray Penitents had been fastened back into its groove with black gaffer tape. Bad had stopped to finger the tape. "This makes me uneasy," he said. "This technical savvy."

The first two chapels were empty, the main nave nearly so. A tall fair-haired man waited by a pillar, under the mark of inundation—1821. His eye sockets were hollows of shadow, most of the light in the chapel being cast down, reflected from the spotlit vaults of its ceiling.

"Ila. Dawn," the man said.

"Gidday," said Bad, looking for acknowledgment. He waved a hand—and was ignored.

"Where have you been, Tom?" Dawn said.

"We're starting there again, are we?" Tom said to Dawn. "With how could I have thought to leave so *fine* a nest." Tom's voice dropped a degree with each word. "Where have I been? *Not in the same world as you.*"

Dawn's jaw jutted with anger. Her eyes were all pupil; she had a mist of sweat on her forehead and neck, each little bead bearing a pink tincture of blood. There was a pink patch on her shirt where it had adhered to her chest.

"Talk," said Ila. "Tell me about Martine."

Tom said he thought they should wait for his friend. And he had expected Eve.

"It's too late for Eve; she's *getting on*, you know," Dawn said, tense and not taking any trouble to sound convincing.

"Yes. And I'm sure Ila—inconsistent as ever—has respect for Eve's gray hair," Tom said. He looked Bad over, and Bad felt that the man was assessing his body mass index, fat to muscle. "Is this your latest candidate, Dawn?"

"This is my only candidate, my first candidate." Dawn was fierce.

Tom's smirk twitched and froze.

"My fledgling killed your nestling," Ila said, prompting Tom.

"Wait," said Tom.

"I can do that," said Ila.

Dawn linked her arm with Bad's, pulled him to her, held him like a pledge. Bad began to say something, but Dawn gave him a sharp shake, shook the breath out of him. He looked at her and she frowned. Bad was silent. Dawn and Ila were, too. Flames fluttered behind a red glass of the lamps suspended above the tabernacle.

Tom couldn't stay quiet. He had to talk, it seemed. He said that when a vampire walked into the salon in Genoa where Jacques Palomba worked he'd practically poured himself into her lap. "His nine years of longing had been freeze-dried by his middle-class Monaco family. He met my friend and he ran with desire. She guessed he'd been bitten before. She listened to his story and even had the grace to let him know by whom he'd been bitten. She gave him his whole truth; then she gave him to me—so that I could taste him. Could assess his candidacy. He was a lovely boy, eager and compliant—" Tom broke off and peered at Bad. He asked Bad, "Are you eager and compliant?"

"For a start, I'm not a boy," Bad said. He'd pitched his voice low with disgust, and it came out well in the reverberant space of the nave, wide-voweled, scornful. "Nor a hairdresser," he added. "And I never had to be rescued." Which wasn't quite true.

"Yes, of course. You're a bit more *meaty*," Tom said. Then he continued. "We told Jacques about Martine."

"And Jacques was so infatuated with his own past, and his story, that he went to find her," Ila said.

"Oh, I see. What would be curiosity in *you* was only vanity in my nestling?" Tom said. "Next you'll be telling me that he attacked Martine."

The door creaked open—the door padded with cracked leather that stood between the hexagonal room and the main nave. Eve came in, followed by a red-haired woman. Eve hurried to Ila's side, the timber floor crackling and complaining at this unaccustomed vigorous impact. "Tom," said Eve.

"Tom's nestling was Jacques Palomba—the boy I saved in '92. The boy in the Blessed Martine's story. Tom told Jacques about Martine and he went to find her," Dawn said to her sister, filling her in. "Tom's a first-class, A-one prick," she added, as if this, too, were meant only informatively.

Eve said to Ila that she was worried about their bolt-holes. She spoke softly and—Bad thought—seemed a little dazed. He put a hand on her shoulder. He inclined toward her and whispered to her that Tom really was a big swinging dork. He hoped this would help her morale. It helped *him* to see that Tom Hilxen was pompous and managing and hadn't been able to wait out Ila's negative, uninflected silence.

"Martine was a hypocrite," Tom said.

"Oh, Tom, you always think people hypocritical when they're only inconsistent," Eve said. "For heaven sake, you thought *Jean* was a hypocrite!"

"Martine said we mustn't eat except when absolutely necessary," Tom said. "She said we mustn't impose our strength, or the narcotic in our mouths, our mind-bending means to satisfy our bodily appetites. She said we mustn't take pleasure in the power and freedom of our exile—exile from our lives as citizens, from our ability to be parents, from daylight. She said we must renounce the world, *and* the underworld. She said, 'Don't take.' She meant, 'Don't touch.' She was a nun. She became a nun because she was a cripple. She rejected sexual love before it could reject her. She mortified her flesh because she hated it; she hated it even once she was able to roll up a rock face like thistle seed. But Jacques walked in—a good Catholic boy—and worshiped her, appealed to her, as he'd appealed to the Venerable Martine Ramondi. She bit him. She thought she could just cheat on her diet, that she'd get away with it, like that Australian guru who told people she got all her nourishment from light yet would sneak food with such accomplished secrecy that several of her followers had to die before she was unmasked. Martine thought she could get away with it—but she hadn't realized she was fertile. She'd been so busy living on charity—I presume—only biting Dawn, then preaching to Dawn about curbing her appetite, no doubt."

"She wasn't like that!" Dawn said.

Ila said, "Let him talk."

"Martine bit Jacques and made him," Tom concluded. Or, at least, he paused.

"But *you* meant to make him, anyway," Eve said. "He was your candidate."

"For the rest we can only imagine what happened," the red-haired woman said. Her English was slow and oddly cadenced, as though her first language was one that employed tonal modulation in its grammar, like Mandarin.

"Grazide," said Ila.

Grazide turned to Tom, tilted her head back to look up at him—she was nearly a foot under his lanky height. She met Tom's eyes and pointed at Ila. "Is this who I hate?"

"Yes," said Tom.

"I need Tom to remind me," Grazide said to Ila, her voice

sweet and reasonable, "because I've forgotten." She stroked
Tom's arm, then dropped her eyes, coy. She said Tom was gal-
lant. He'd seen her through her change of life. He was sufficiently interesting to keep her talking, to help her retain her
grammar. She favored Eve with a gracious, grateful nod.
"Thanks to you, madame, I know a little of what I've forgotten." She sighed but didn't seem sad; it was more a pose of
formal melancholy. "My history has evaporated," she said.
"Leaving only myself—a powdery residue."

Bad thought that she was fishing for compliments.

"My fledgling killed your nestling," Ila said to Grazide. "In
Tom's testimony so far Martine's only *made* Jacques Palomba."

"Is Palomba dead?" Bad said.

Tom didn't answer Bad but Ila. "We must imagine that,
having made Jacques, Martine decided not to let him live. Or
even *eat*—she was so very against eating."

"Jacques's head was cut off," Grazide said.

Ila shook his head. "No. It wasn't Martine. It just sometimes happens. Astute humans do it. Jacques showed himself,
and was killed. If Martine was at fault, her fault was not providing guidance."

"She killed him, then killed herself," Tom insisted.

"She was *caught out*," Ila said.

Eve put her arm around Ila and he flinched away, blurred,
then was several feet off, Bad's eyes having failed to follow him.
Eve dropped her arm. She said, "Ila, I think Martine did kill
herself." She glared at Tom. "Not, however, because she murdered Palomba. Martine simply couldn't face being fertile."

"There's no point in these recriminations," Tom said, "if I
can't persuade you. Ila, Grazide believes you will take responsibility for your fledgling. She just won't credit that it was
Martine who really ran your nest, and called the shots." He
looked at Grazide. He said that Grazide had something to tell
Ila. He said that when he—Tom—and Grazide met, she was

shedding her last old skin, so to speak, and was afraid, thinking that what she was about to lose was what mattered.

Ila detached himself from Dawn and Eve and advanced on Tom and Grazide. He seemed bewitched. He stopped before Grazide and put a hand to her face. He set his fanned fingers on one cheek and brought his thumb slowly in toward her eye. She didn't blink. She let his thumb come to rest on the ball of her eye—he slid the lens from her iris. The plastic gathered, green, under his thumb, and popped out onto her cheek. The revealed eye was garnet, a red jewel. Ila looked into her eyes and laughed happily. "Stop-and-go," he said, of her eyes. Then he said something in a language Bad didn't know.

"What did he say?" Grazide asked Tom.

Eve said, "He's speaking Provençal. He just delivered a long-delayed message from Chambord to you: 'Chambord said to tell you that he could still tell the difference between a treasure and a curiosity.' "

"Chambord's proud powers of discernment are now all only air," Grazide said. "His fame is your work, madame, a mask you choose to wear over your own art. Who would care what Chambord said—had ever said—if not for you? This man, who, I'm told, like me, knew him? Perhaps only this man. Love, like every other impurity, has left me. What is God's has gone to God—leaving my *self*, whole and utterly happy. Perhaps I'm the first inhabitant of a world that has split off from this one. A world that will replace this one if fledglings don't kill nestlings, and nests breed and increase, and grow older, and forget, and become fully themselves, as I have."

Bad took a few steps backward and sat down on a pew. His joints ached—had for days now—and he was running a low-grade fever. Eve put it all down to iron deficiency. Without the aches he might have felt tranquilized and uncaring. But the pain kept him alert enough to notice Eve, who had seemed dazzled by Grazide—starstruck—shake herself and glance at her watch. She checked her watch and the window, where, Bad saw, the darkness was growing grainy.

Grazide was speaking to Dawn now, making an offer—in the spirit of friendship, she said. Ila was reluctant to become a father again, a father to this fine young man of Dawn's. She—Grazide—could deal with him. She moved toward Bad. Bad got up in a hurry, but Dawn had interposed herself, a hand up to halt Grazide. Dawn was perhaps more possessive than protective, but Bad was grateful. He didn't like the look in Grazide's exposed, bloody eye, where her pupil seemed to float like a small black seed.

Grazide shrugged and stepped away, back into the port of Tom's arms.

Tom told Ila that Grazide had some good news for him.

Eve gave a snort. Then she said, "Ila."

Bad followed her gaze. The windows were no longer grainy black but gray.

"Now that I've changed fully," Grazide said, "I can stand the sun. All you have to do is wait another eighty years, and keep eating; then you, too—"

"He doesn't believe you," Tom said.

"He really is very simple," said Grazide, in the tone of someone who has had a report confirmed by her own observations. To Ila she said, "You can stay up to watch me if you like. See for yourself, through your blistering eyes, me, standing in the sun."

Eve said *she'd* watch Grazide. And Tom said, "How typical, the writer always putting herself forward as a witness." He shook his head: "Eve, Eve, Eve." His tone was tender, and he moved toward Eve, put his arms around her, paternal and consoling. Then he turned her face-forward in his arms, gripped her hard, and bit her.

Normal human reaction time—and it's the same for all normal humans—is three-quarters of a second. Bad had seen

Dawn move faster than that, and he'd *failed* to see Ila, who could move faster than Bad's brain could follow him. Bad saw a series of movements without having time to move himself. Ila and Dawn went to Eve's aid. But not before Bad saw Eve's face soften, her lips part, head loll back, neck arch. He was looking at himself—Dawn's spines in him—both swooning and stiffened by joy. Purely chemical joy, without discernment. It was sad and obscene. He didn't want to see any more or know any more—or *choose*. He'd had enough. He saw Dawn and Ila separate Eve and Tom, quick but careful, and he guessed that it was possible that if Tom withdrew too swiftly, he would leave some spines in Eve. Bad backed away from them all, obliquely, across the aisle.

Ila picked Eve up and carried her to the pew where Bad had been sitting and set her down. Dawn moved to follow Ila, but Tom and Grazide caught her, their actions so coordinated that they seemed moved by one mind. Tom folded Dawn in his long, sinewy arms and both vampires nuzzled into her neck, on either side, where it joined her shoulders. Dawn cried out, her cry cut off. The vampires were drinking, noisy, like children sucking juice from oranges. Dawn was rigid and trembling, her arms outflung. Bad saw the fat veins on Dawn's splayed hands shrink, sink down flush to her skin, her tendons show instead, and each knuckle grow white. Then Tom and Grazide released Dawn, and she teetered for a moment, then dropped onto her knees. Tom and Grazide moved away, in unison, fast, and left the chapel. Again the door slapped to and fro, showing its padded exterior and cold nicotine brown twilight through the skylight on the dome of the hexagonal antechapel.

Bad had backed up against a barrier. Something was digging into his thigh. He looked over his shoulder and saw a shiny black shoe, black-trousered legs, a body sprawled face-up along a pew. Bad saw pallid brown skin, glossy black hair, the line of white showing under Daniel Octave's eyelids. He saw stillness, the abandon of the abandoned. Bad saw a corpse. He saw the corpse of Father Octave—and he fled the chapel.

Eve looked up at Dawn, who was stroking her cheek. Dawn was white and wilted, her cheeks hollow. "Are you all right?" Eve asked—then answered *Dawn's* question, which was identical. "Yes, I'm all right."

Ila said, "We should be gone." He lifted Eve; he took the sisters on either arm and steered them to the chapel door.

"Wait," said Eve. She'd seen something, someone lying on a pew, one black-clad leg cocked, one arm trailing on the floor.

"I'll wait tomorrow night," Ila said. "No more waiting tonight."

Eve nudged Ila and Dawn sideways till they, too, saw the man—who lay, a blood-crusted cannula sticking out of the skin in the crook of his arm and twitching in time to his heartbeat.

Ila said, "It's Father Octave." He gave Eve to Dawn and crouched beside the priest, plucked the cannula out of his arm, pushed the rolled sleeve down over the bloody hole, and bent the arm, set Father Octave's hand to his shoulder to stop the bleeding.

Ila touched Daniel Octave's cheek. "He's cold," he said. Ila took off his jacket and draped it over the man.

Even woozy, Eve was intrigued. Not by Father Octave's presence—Tom, always a thorough researcher himself, wouldn't on first instinct rebuff anyone who came asking questions—no, what intrigued Eve was the fact that Father Daniel Octave wasn't white. She hadn't expected that. She saw Ila's very pale hand on Father Octave's brown skin and felt disoriented. Martine had never mentioned that Father Octave was Indian. It made Eve wonder about Martine—about how much else there was she hadn't been told and should know.

Dawn was plucking at her. Eve looked at her sister, who

was looking at the window and moaning with fear. Eve saw blue sky. "Ila," she said. She tugged at his shirt. Ila's hand lingered on Daniel Octave's face, then let go.

Ila and Dawn left Eve behind. She crossed the hexagonal chapel hard on their heels but only saw a door swinging on the Chapel of the Vignerons. By the time she reached the main door she could only spot Dawn, just rounding the corner in the street.

Eve found Bad leaning over the rail of the bridge, beside the waterwheel. Bad was sobbing, his face white with shock. Eve pulled at his arm and asked him to hurry. He came after her. Then, after a moment, he caught on and took off, sprinted up the street ahead of her.

There was a car, a battered four-wheel-drive, a big vehicle with a wide wheelbase, parked over the manhole. Parked as Bad had observed cars in Italy, in no-parking zones, not parallel to the curb but at an angle, as though coy about their intentions, as if to say, *I'm only stopped a moment and don't really mean it.*

When Bad appeared, Ila was at the back bumper, braced to push. But his hands slipped. He dropped to his knees and struck his chin on the bumper.

Dawn screamed, plucked at Ila, then hauled off and ran at the vehicle, jolted it with her shoulder—a rhino blindsiding a safari truck.

The vehicle rocked and its alarm went off.

Eve arrived behind Bad. Dawn rushed up to her sister, sobbed, "Eve! Eve!" like a child, hunched over, her fists clenched. She cowered behind her sister.

Bad pulled his jacket off and wrapped it around his fist. He punched in the driver's window, thrust his head inside, let the hand brake off, and put the car in neutral.

The car whooped, bugled, and whistled.

Bad ran around the car to Ila. He realized Ila had removed his jacket and the chisel was gone. Bad looked at Eve. Eve was no help. She stood, her arms around Dawn, Dawn's face pressed into her chest. Eve was watching the sun come, its light lapping at the tops of the roofs.

Bad ran back to the car window, leaned in, and found the button that popped its hood. He rushed to the front of the car and slipped his hand under the hood, found the catch, disengaged it, and heaved the hood up. He was after the lever that held the hood open. With his free hand he jerked it back and forth but couldn't snap it off. Then Ila was beside him. Ila had the rod; he twisted it. The metal torqued, turned white in one place, and came apart like a snapped licorice stick.

Bad dropped the hood and put his shoulder to the grille. Ila joined him—for a moment they were touching, face-to-face. Ila's flesh was cold, and his eyes were closed against the daylight and streaming tears.

The car rolled backward. The manhole appeared beneath Bad's feet. Ila opened his eyes to bend the rod at its tip, to find the slot, insert the rod, to lever, lift, slide the cover.

Eve hustled her sister over to the hole. Dawn was stumbling and stupid with terror. Eve prized herself free of Dawn's embrace and forced her to look down, down at the darkness.

Dawn gave a small grateful whimper and jumped into the drain. Ila jumped after her and looked up out of the hole, his hand on its lip, keeping him suspended above the drop. He motioned to Bad to push the cover into place.

The rim of the sun appeared over the roofs—to Bad beautiful, instantly warming. Its light hit Ila's fingers; the white skin went red, then white again with blisters. Ila let go of the lip of the drain and dropped into the dark. Bad repositioned the rod and hauled at the cover. The iron grated over the cobbles. But before its dull circle eclipsed the black drain mouth, Bad looked down and saw water gleaming, Ila lying in the wet curve of the pipe, and Dawn, standing, craning up to the opening, her face tearstained and desperate. She raised her hands, reached out to the daylight, and to him.

The drain cover fell into place with a blunt clang. Bad straightened and dropped the bent steel rod. Beside them the car flashed and howled. It was impossible to speak over its noise. Bad looked at Eve—and Eve saw things breaking in him. Then he turned and walked briskly away from her and the car, looking about, checking, patting his hair down, a smooth, practiced criminal hastening from the scene.

Chapter 17

A BOAT,
FAR FROM LAND

he bishop sent a car to fetch Daniel from Avignon. The priest who drove was young, barely out of the seminary, an attenuated giant whose Adam's apple and round wristbones seemed to have burst out of the confines of his suit's collar and cuffs. The driver perhaps had an overactive thyroid, which contributed to his air of pop-eyed wariness. The skeletal story the driver had about his charge had inclined him to treat this Father Octave he'd been sent to retrieve as a reprobate rather than an invalid. Father Octave wasn't ill, hadn't "collapsed"—though the bishop said he had. The word in the ranks, however, was that the bishop's favorite annual visitor, the austere Jesuit historian, had been found in the Chapel of the Gray Penitents, unconscious and stinking of *Branca Menta*.

Daniel slumped against the restraint of his seat belt. He was aware of the driver watching him in the rearview mirror.

He was conscious that for a time this doubtful scrutiny would be his lot.

Daniel, who had never tired easily, was exhausted. He wanted his room in the convent in Nice; he wanted its narrow bed. If he kept quiet, kept his eyes closed, all the way back, perhaps he'd be allowed to rest before having to explain himself. Daniel's desire for respite was the nearest he had ever come to a feeling of homesickness. He had "come home" when his grandmother was alive and in her kitchen, creating a gravitational field of comfort, the only one whose pull Daniel had ever felt or fallen into. Since his grandmother had died, Daniel had obediently gone where he was expected to be— from school and into his evening and weekend incarceration with his mother and her fears—then, from the seminary on, he went wherever he was sent. He was scarcely ever sorry to leave a place or glad to arrive. Now, retrieved by the bishop, wanting his bed, Daniel for the first time felt bleak about the fact that he didn't belong anywhere.

The bishop already had a full account of how Father Octave was found, semiconscious, in the Chapel of the Gray Penitents, by the priest and altar boys who had come in for the six o'clock mass. Father Octave was wearing one jacket and was covered by another. When roused he'd insisted on retaining the other jacket and had also retrieved some bloody instruments—pieces of plastic, the priest reported—from the chapel floor. He'd squirreled them away in the pockets of his own jacket, with a knife or a screwdriver from the pocket of the other. Father Octave's breath smelled of drink, but his dreamy disorientation had worried the priest because it wasn't like drunkenness. He was very pale and had one blood-soaked cuff. They delivered him, under protest, to an emergency room— where he napped on a gurney in a cubicle for half an hour before anyone came to see him. He allowed the doctor to take his blood pressure but refused a blood test. The priest of the Gray Penitents took him back to the rectory and phoned the bishop in Nice.

The bishop repeated this story while Daniel sat before him, slumped, in his crumpled suit and with his blood-browned shirtsleeve. Daniel considered how best to play himself—calm, contrite, forthcoming. He said he'd been trying to find out who had killed Jacques Palomba—he'd pursued what he thought were leads, though he knew it was really a matter for the police. "But I'd been told some things in confidence," Daniel explained.

"Confidence isn't the sanctity of the confessional, Daniel. And keeping things to yourself is a habit you have." The bishop said he'd been speaking to Daniel's friend Father Neske.

Daniel protested, impatient, that *everyone knew about him.* Because the bishop did know about his parentage, his mother's troubles, and Gaston Groux—the bishop knew *enough*, at least.

"We know as much as you know, Daniel," the bishop said.

Daniel was surly. "Meaning what?"

"You're possibly the least self-reflective person I know—of those who have any intelligence, or habit of reflection." The bishop spread his palms. "So I ask you, do you know what you've been doing?"

"I've been trying to find out why Jacques Palomba was murdered."

"Don't you mean *who* murdered him?"

Daniel scratched the back of his neck. He felt like hitting someone—not specifically this man, but someone.

"If 'why,' then I imagine you've prayed for guidance," the bishop said.

"All right, *who*, then," said Daniel, impolite. He said that he'd got a woman's name and number from a coworker of Palomba's. He had a rendezvous with a man—a friend of the

woman he was looking for. They met in the Chapel of the
Gray Penitents. The man had a flask and Daniel joined him in
a drink. The drink was drugged. "But, as you see, here I am,
alive and intact."

"So . . . no harm done," said the bishop, dubious.

"And *contrite*," Daniel added, annoyed.

"Do you think I want contrition?" the bishop said. Then
he told Daniel that he'd been recalled to Rome. The bishop
had spoken to the Father General himself that morning.
"What I want you to do right now, Daniel, is to phone the detective in charge of the investigation and give him names,
numbers, descriptions. Then you can have something to eat
and get some sleep." The bishop got out of his chair to push
the phone across the desk.

Daniel called the detective. He surrendered everything—
except Tom Hilxen's name. He said, "He didn't give a name."
Daniel gave the detective a description but neglected to mention that the man was an American. The bishop watched
Daniel tender his story. Daniel was worried that the bishop
would hear his omissions as the beat of silence in a badly
spliced tape. So he told the detective more. He told the detective how the drug felt.

"Rohypnol," the detective said, in a pause, "the 'date rape'
drug."

Daniel gave an account of the cannula and the tube and
how the man had siphoned off his blood. The detective
seemed less surprised than galvanized by the description and
Daniel thought, *He's encountered this before.*

When Daniel got off the phone he stood up, without having been given leave to go.

"Daniel," the bishop said.

Daniel stopped, but stayed half turned away toward
the door.

"Why didn't you tell me? Why let me stand here and hear
it all secondhand?"

"I think it's not, strictly speaking, secondhand if you're listening in," Daniel said.

"Please stop making these hairsplitting distinctions," said the bishop. "Daniel, that man *assaulted* you."

"Yes. I suppose so."

The bishop waited.

"I'm tired. I need to sleep," Daniel said.

"Will you please, just for a moment, do me the favor of looking me in the eye?" said the bishop.

Daniel steeled himself, then turned to stare, blandly, at the bridge of the bishop's nose.

"What can we do for you?" the bishop said.

"I need to sleep," said Daniel.

"Daniel, I know that you've borne real suffering as mere discomfort for a sizable and formative part of your life, without giving anything away—and yet, right now, I can see that you're suffering. I want to help you."

The thing about sleep, Daniel said, that was both good and bad was that no one could go there with you.

"What are you saying? I don't like the sound of that."

Daniel sighed. "I'm saying that I refuse to think anymore about what has happened to me till fortified by rest. That's only sensible. It's like putting an ice pack on an injury to reduce the swelling. It'll be less of a crisis if I postpone it with sleep."

"Very well," said the bishop, and Daniel could hear that he was upset—upset that Daniel had rebuffed his offer of help—and unwilling to let Daniel out of his sight. But, "Very well," he said, and let Daniel go.

Sleep spat Daniel out hours before dawn, and he got out of bed to pace his small room, sometimes slapping the wall as he turned, like a prisoner in his first mad hours of solitary confinement.

At sunrise he showered and dressed in his other suit. Then he left the convent and walked down to the bus station, where he sold his watch for a third of its value in grubby cash.

Two days later, Daniel sat indoors in a restaurant, opposite the high gates of Eve Moskelute's Ventimiglia house. Daniel had ordered the set menu and could park himself for hours. He grazed his way through six courses. First the frittata, then stuffed zucchini flowers, then baked baby salmon, spaghetti *frutti di mare*, roast duck, and crème brûlée.

The restaurant was full and Daniel well concealed behind a window curtained by wisteria and by a party of Austrians at the long table on the terrace.

Halfway through his meal, Daniel took his jacket off. It was hot, and the lunch was hard work, and the jacket pockets were full. Daniel had the mobile phone Martine had given him, and he had *evidence*—a clear plastic tube with deposits of dried black blood flecking its interior and a sculptor's chisel with the name Ares burnt into its wooden handle.

In the late afternoon Eve felt a migraine coming on and went to lie down in a darkened room. She got into bed, closed her eyes and, for a moment, was rewarded with blank darkness. Then the darkness filled with bright lines, then with facets, glowing geometries like the insides of clustered soap bubbles.

The pain waited, wasn't yet on the wing, was a treeful of roosting birds. Eve closed her eyes. The birds exploded into the air. They made a tree above the tree, turning together, a pain that billowed, but that had a shape and was still confined.

Eve felt a cool, dry hand on her forehead.

The birds alighted again, the shadow of a tree sinking back into the tree's green branches.

Eve told Ila she had a migraine; she had to stay in the dark.

He lay down beside her and stroked her softly between her eyebrows.

"I'm trying to keep the birds in the tree," Eve said. "In the tree they're soft. If a flock flies apart it's shrapnel."

Ila pushed the ball of his thumb between her eyebrows. Eve's aura grew tattered, and a few more tatters came to settle.

Ila said he'd once had a nestling who was afraid of the dark.

Eve hadn't heard this story. She was intrigued, distracted, so surfaced from her aura and its logic. It was like passing from one world to another. She opened her eyes and saw Ila's hand above her face, its weight depending only on its thumb. Because of the migraine it seemed bigger than an ordinary hand; it was a room, too, a white ceiling, the spotlit vaults of the main nave of the Chapel of the Gray Penitents.

Ila said that Montulet was a soldier of the empire. "The first empire. My first nestling." Ila found Montulet lying in one of the narrow canyons of old Genoa, on a night with no moon, when every household was barred to the street. Ila scented blood and found the man by smell and touch. He felt the soldier's triple row of silver ball buttons and the leopard hide on his helmet, the static warmth of ostrich plumes. "His throat was slit. He'd been set on in the street," Ila said. "I bit him though his blood was flowing already. Because there was no reason not to bite. Because I didn't know I'd become fertile. My bite saved his life. It made him." Yet because Montulet had met his assassins in the dark he was henceforth afraid of it. He always carried a lamp. Many times Ila and Montulet had sat together through the night, in the summer on the steps by the green reservoir, in the garden of a house Ila had, with a lamp between them.

"Montulet did what I think Martine must have done. He waited up one night to see the sun. We'd been talking, and I remember that he quoted Callimachus: 'I wept when I remembered how often you and I had tired the sun with talking and sent him down the sky.' "

Eve asked Ila why he was thinking about his first.

"Because my bite was to his benefit, but he didn't turn out well. Because I was thinking that none of them turned out well." Ila found another place on Eve's forehead and applied gentle modulated pressure with the ball of his thumb. "I'm waiting for Martine," he said.

"I know. And I'm waiting for Jean. Loss is backward anticipation."

Ila asked Eve to tell him—once more—how Ares used to see God.

Eve said that Jean got migraines, too, and there were times when he said he had the feeling of being stripped down to his innermost skin, but in beautiful balmy weather. Then, sometimes, the world at which he was looking would turn transparent, or seem to, as if someone were applying terrific pressure, pointing at one place with the tip of a powerful finger—from *the other side*. In the place that was pointed at, Jean would see what was *there*—a raft of cloud or a flowering bush—but these things would say what God says: "I am."

"But," Eve said, "Jean got migraines, with beautiful auras. And Jean was an atheist. So he had to conclude that what he saw was a pathology. He said to me that Dante wrote that there was a place in Purgatory for those who believe but don't profess. 'Well, this is professing,' Jean said, 'but am I only deceived by my spectacular brain chemistry?' And he said that the experience, the religious experience, was more real than his doubts about it. The doubts were characteristic, he said, when he doubted he was *himself*—but the experience was more real than everything else outside it, including his experience of himself."

Again Eve felt the flat of Ila's dry palm smoothing her brow. Ila said, "I like that story."

● ● ●

By six the restaurant was empty of everyone but a couple of old men having coffee and grappa with the waiters. One waiter came to stand in the doorway. He threw up his hands and exclaimed over his shoulder to the others about the weather, "The valley is gone!"

Daniel looked and saw nothing much. Eve's house, its iron gates, salmon-colored plaster walls, and orange-tiled roof, were in sight, the roof glistening as if frosted, the whole building and street lit by a strong, diffuse white light. Then Daniel saw mist begin to pour across the roof and off the eaves, like dry ice off the edge of a stage. The line of the roof was erased, the courtyard filled, and mist strained out through the gate's bars and crept across the street. What was solid smudged— smudged and dulled—as though the view were furred with a pale mold.

The mist only tempered the July heat. All the same, Daniel unhooked his jacket from the back of his chair. He found his wallet and put fresh notes on the tray, the check parked under the bowl of brown sugar lumps. The waiter smiled and swooped.

The door of Eve's house opened. A pale figure craned out, appeared to test the mist, as people put out a palm to test the grain of rain, coarse or fine. The figure's hair was white—so it was Eve's friend Ila. Ila stepped out, shut the door gently, then pulled on a hooded sweatshirt. For a moment, clothes rucked up, he showed a flat, adolescent-looking stomach. The sweatshirt's cuffs covered his hands; his face vanished into the deep hood. He walked to the gate, sloped shoulders rounded. The gate slid open. Ila darted through, then turned back to watch it close.

Daniel put his jacket on. He waited till Ila set off, then followed.

Ila moved quickly through the wide streets, then slowed in the Piazzetta della Fontana. Daniel waited at the head of the street, his back to the wall. He saw Ila stoop, free a hand from his sleeve to scoop water, and splash his face. Then he went on. Daniel hurried after him. In passing, Daniel looked at the splashes on the stone and discerned a deliberate handprint on the cheek of one of the spurting-mouthed faces and on the muzzle of the lion above them.

Martine's friend had greeted the fountain's statues.

Daniel took a piecemeal tour of the town, straining for a glimpse of the man he followed. Ventimiglia was sober and grubby. Its mist smelled of soap powder, of laundry on lines high overhead. Daniel followed the sound of footfalls through a street with sunken, uneven paving. He crossed another piazza, past a church whose facade was riddled with bullet holes, old scars, almost the same color as its mildew-spotted walls. He was led into another dark street, where he met a dog, pissing boldly and copiously on the ground between two water-filled plastic bottles, placed to discourage dogs.

Martine's friend took the darkest, narrowest route downhill. Following him, Daniel passed doorways that were blind arches. He went down streets that were tunnels, lamplit, their walls painted with pitch. Damp streets, their gutters full of silt as slippery as spilled polenta. The last arched tunnel mouth had only brightness beyond it, a pearly filter of sun-suffused mist. When Daniel reached this opening, Ila was nowhere in sight. Daniel edged out onto black asphalt. He crossed a broken white line, then reached a low barrier, white-painted posts with chain looped between them. There was one gap in this fence, so Daniel went through it. He found himself on a rough path, a mule track, shallow steps going down through a stand of broom that still smelled buttery from the sun.

Daniel could hear the town behind him now. He heard a truck on the road, in low gear, crawling through the mist. He heard boys playing soccer, a plastic ball twanging on pavement, bunting on a knee or head or boot. He heard a television, and someone calling from house to house.

The track went on through a thicket of prickly pear and a stand of nodding hibiscus. The mist filled with smoke, funneling up the track, thick, lazy smoke mixed with water vapor. Daniel came upon a pile of burning cuttings. The fire was unattended, banked down. It had been bigger; the small smoking pile stood in a footprint of greasy blackened earth. The cuttings were grubbed from several cleared terraces and, two steps down from the fire, Daniel came upon the headless body of a snake. A viper. Daniel stopped and stared at the snake's short, oiled body. The fire hissed behind him, sap sizzling in green branches.

Daniel didn't hear Ila. He simply coalesced in his pale clothes—out of the mist. His face, in the hollow of the hood, was smooth, fresh, and transparently pale. The dry lines in his skin were wholly gone. His eyes, between long white eyelashes, were rosy gray. Ila said to Daniel that "that soldier"— the soldier in the saint's story—had also stopped to look at a snake. Though in Daniel's account he only "stopped short of the dark place under the cypress to look at something on the path." "It was a grass snake," Ila said. "A black trickle in the dust, like a libation." He made a pouring motion with one hand, shaking it free of his sleeve to do so. His cuffs were wet from the fountain. He touched the viper with the toe of his boot. The headless body moved weakly, a low swell of muscle running its length. "The soldier went"—Ila spread out his palms, open and upturned by his hips—"as if he were giving a blessing. But it was a show of gratitude. He was happy about his girl, and the snake, so he said, 'Thank you.' I was waiting for him, lying on the terrace behind a stand of artichoke flowers. I knew the butcher was waiting, too. The butcher was a local—I left the locals alone. Afterward I thanked the butcher for the soldier by giving him a chamois I caught. For which the butcher gave thanks to the men in the hills. But when the soldier gave thanks for the snake, he thanked God, Who was there, too, on the hillside." Ila smiled. "If that story was a song, it would be a round. A round of gratitude."

Daniel fished in his pocket. His fingers had gone numb, but his hand gathered the chisel's general shape. He produced it and showed it to Ila.

"I carried that from Eve's house in Nice," Ila said. "Eve is so guilty about having abandoned you in Avignon that she's thinking of making a big donation to the Congregation for the Causes of Saints. That's you, isn't it?"

Daniel nodded.

Ila said he was going to the marina. For a moment he watched Daniel, waiting for a response; then Ila stepped backward, two steps down, and turned and submerged himself slowly in the mist.

Daniel thought about what he'd been told. But his thoughts couldn't seem to hold on to the signal—the past and the story he knew. The present interfered, substituting itself object for object, mist for moonlight, a dead viper for a living grass snake, a priest who bore false witness for all the story's other people—the characters and props of a pageant Daniel had loved—soldier, butcher, cypress, billhook. Only two things remained the same. God was here, too, in the present as in the past, as much in the cold, flickering tongues of mist in Daniel's nostrils as in the sun above the mist and a whisker above the mountains. And the vampire was the same—in the present as in the past. The vampire Ila, like God, was a witness Daniel hadn't yet been able to interview.

Ventimiglia's waterfront reserve wasn't groomed like its counterpart just over the border in Menton. Here the same sea came in against little workaday breakwaters. Daniel, counting these breakwaters, came upon the sign for the marina. He crossed a parking lot and went past the radar-topped harbormaster's office and along a concrete jetty. At first Daniel thought the jetty was a continuation of the road; then a first squat mooring post appeared from the mist and, after that, the stern of a launch—*Kembali*, port of registration: Nice.

From the mist ahead, out to sea it seemed, there came a sound, a metallic grinding.

Daniel walked on past *Marbruck* of Constantina, *Nina* of Jersey, *Woodpecker* of Poole, *White Lady* of Saint Peter's Port, *Allegrina* of Basel, and *Luca* of La Rochelle.

Ila was crouching, balanced but seemingly suspended out over the water. He was busy working a ring free from a bolt in the wall of the jetty. A skiff was chained to the ring. The boat was new; it had a fiberglass hull with a light fiberglass cover bolted onto it. The cover was smashed, and visible through the jagged holes were a fluorescent yellow life vest and the varnished timber of an oar blade. The bolt was loose already, and, as Ila continued to work it, it began to inch free, the thread of its screws scabbed with grains of cement.

When the bolt was fully free, Ila yanked the skiff to him by its chain and used the long cement-encrusted shaft of the bolt like an ice pick to further shatter the fiberglass cover. Then he climbed gingerly from the jetty and into the boat, placing his feet in the holes he'd made. He began to work on the locked catches of the cover, to wrench them this way and that.

Daniel glanced back over his shoulder. He could see only the nearer moored boats and the damp concrete of the jetty. There was no motion in the mist. The mist was a negative presence, not an element. It appeared that the shore had simply faded, like an unfixed photographic image.

Ila tore the cover free from its fastening. He tossed it into the sea. It drifted bumping between the skiff and the nearest launch.

Daniel remarked that the harbormaster's station must be unattended.

Ila shook his head, then pulled a syringe out of one pocket of the sweatshirt. He showed it to Daniel, then flicked it into the water. From his other pocket he produced a length of transparent plastic tubing and the same kind of small Ziploc bag that Tom Hilxen had carried.

Daniel flinched back.

Ila dropped the tube and bag into the water. Then he sat down on the rower's seat and threaded the oars out from underneath it. The oarlocks were hanging on the oars already, so Ila had only to set their posts into the holes in the skiff's side, then touch the oars' grips together to balance them. He clapped one oar gently to the skiff's side and shot out the other to prod the jetty, to propel the skiff away from it.

Daniel gasped. He gulped down the mist—a thin gruel. He took a step forward, hesitated an instant, the inflexible soles of his black dress shoes seesawing on the brink. Then he jumped. He landed in the boat, sprawled across the vampire's legs.

Ila made a thoughtful noise and picked Daniel up, one fist gripping the bunched front of Daniel's jacket. Ila set Daniel upright on the stern seat.

Daniel straightened his jacket and smoothed his hair. He shook his hands, trying to ease his jarred wrists.

Ila reached back, found a life vest, and dangled it in front of Daniel. Daniel took it and put it on.

Ila hunched forward, put the blades of the oars in the water, and began to row, a steady swing and draw.

The oars dipped, making big circles on the silky gray water, then raised and dripped, the drips making smaller circles. Daniel looked over his shoulder and watched this tiled path recede.

Ila rowed for a quarter of an hour. He put the boat in the current from the river and let it drift. He shipped his oars. The mist grew creamy, lit by the smothered sunset, then it drained of warmth and turned milky blue.

Ila sat with his eyes closed. Didn't open them when Daniel explained that he was here because Tom Hilxen had put a needle in him. "It felt like a protracted blood test," Daniel said.

"No, it didn't," said the vampire.

Ila was right. It hadn't. It had been an assault, an outrage, but Daniel had long ago learned to spin so fast, so smoothly on his axis, that he had seemed to stay still, deflecting every outrage. He'd always thought his guardedness was merely a manner, a matter of long habituation—and useful. But he was all shield, only shield, and he didn't feel the things he should—like hurt, when harmed.

"Tom is a poseur. He is a boy borrowing his father's razor to shave the down on his girlish cheeks," Ila said.

"He held me down," said Daniel.

Ila's eyes flashed. They were so pale that when his pupils contracted the iris seemed all white. "No, he didn't," Ila said.

"All right. He didn't. He drugged me."

"The effects won't last," Ila said. "You weren't bitten, so you won't dream about it, or long for it." Ila was explaining technicalities. He was patiently reassuring Daniel. "But I do wonder—since Tom didn't bite you—why you jumped into the boat with me." Ila studied Daniel, speculative, then asked him to please look under that seat for a lamp—they might want one later. "To tire it with talking," the vampire said.

Daniel looked—the skiff was well provided, had its own small tackle box with fishing gear and flares, and one of those chunky buoyant marine flashlights. Daniel gave it to Ila, who said he had imagined an oil lamp, its yellow light softened by the soot in its glass chimney.

"Sorry," said Daniel. "Do you know how to work it?"

Ila frowned. He said he'd kept his capacity to learn. In that respect he was as young as he looked. But, lately, he'd been too tired to take new things on. He'd hibernated and starved himself while Martine stayed awake to look for a cure.

"She hoped to cure herself of herself," said Daniel.

Ila smiled. "I told Eve you were listening."

It grew darker. The mist spilled off the mountains; it thinned and dissolved on the sea. The coast appeared: the lights of Ventimiglia and Menton-Garavan. The two capes were sketched by their sparser settlement. The moon came up and Daniel was no longer forced to check their distance from shore by the magnitude of various lights.

Daniel switched the lamp on. Its cold fluorescent bulbs shone out from panels of faceted plastic. Ila looked at his hands in the light and tucked them back inside his too-long sleeves. He began—unprompted—to tell Daniel a story, his and Martine's.

"I left Marseille after having to dig myself out of the rubble of its old town," he said. "The Germans had demolished the streets with high explosives in an attempt to ferret out the resistance. I burrowed my way out of a collapsed cellar and gradually, over weeks, made my way to where I knew I'd be safe. I went back to the caves. I had learned, long before, to regard soldiers of any invading army as fair game—though I was always more parasite than predator, preferring to bleed people and leave them alive. Preferring not to bite them because, once I had become infectious, to bite someone meant taking their life into my hands.

"The Grotto of the Hermit looked out over Dardo on its spur of rock, and over the river. I liked to sleep there, at the back of the cave, because I knew how far the sun looked in at every season. I knew that it only put one foot through the door in early June.

"I knew the country, the walking distances between each village, a safe summer night's run for me. I knew the grottos, the houses whose roofs were fallen but whose fireplaces were deep enough to hide in from daylight.

"I made it a point of honor—and practicality—not to trouble the people among whom I lived. There were always enough travelers in the mountains. For centuries there were soldiers. The coastal towns and mountain villages had always changed hands between the Savoyards, the king of Naples, the Lascaris, the Grimaldis, Napoléon, even the Templars of Segovia. I knew how I should live. My habits followed my learning—I spoke Provençal, then French, Ligurian, then Italian, Catalan, then Spanish. I knew what lay underneath time's alterations."

Ila said, "Eve's angry about the euro; she's not looking forward to fumbling her change like a foreigner. But the nations of Europe are inventions. It's all new. I remember Grazide looking at an old map I'd copied. In my map the hill behind the cathedral in Avignon was bare of everything but windmills, and Grazide said, to herself, 'I remember that.' I hope you understand what I mean."

"Yes," said Daniel.

His word was echoed by a splash, a fish jumping in the black water beside the boat, attracted by the light.

Ila's eyes glowed, irises silver, pupils pulsing with every alteration in the intensity of the light, with every tilt of the boat on the gentle swell.

"Tell me about Martine," said Daniel.

The Grotto of the Hermit had a view to the east of the mountains and the sky. When the sun was past its zenith, Ila had liked to go there to watch mowers in the water meadow or ravens skimming the rock face of the Col de Baus, the view in a frame fringed by fangs of stone.

One day, when Ila was wedged comfortably in a shadowy crack at the back of the grotto, a young woman in fawn and white came up the passage from the crypt of St. Barthelemy's. Ila was surprised—he had only just arrived and hadn't heard the Germans breaking open the grate.

When she knelt where the hermit had—long before Ila's time—Ila recognized her habit: a young nun.

She knelt and prayed. She said not "God, save us," but, "God, save *them*." Her voice quivered. "God, save them, or if You won't save them, give me the courage to go with them into the dark." Her hands seemed to be washing themselves, moving continually, slippery with sweat. "Please, Father," she said, "let me not be tempted to save myself. Give me the courage to go with them."

The nun stopped praying, or perhaps went on in silence. The grotto wasn't like the dry depths of the cave proper; it wasn't perfectly quiet. Ila could hear the village—goats bleating, a truck engine turning over, heaving and backfiring and dying.

Ila made deductions. The grate had been removed by the Germans, the ones who'd put it up in the first place. The Germans were going to imprison some people in the caves. And, he deduced, this woman wasn't necessarily among the condemned. Ila would have been surprised if the Germans were killing nuns. But this particular invading army had surprised him already. They did things with—it seemed to him—unique dispatch. He was wary of them.

The nun was weeping, her hands locked together as though wrestling. She jumped when Ila spoke, spun around, and fell onto her hip—the hip that she had held higher than the other when she'd first come limping up into the grotto.

Ila said, "I can't give you courage, but I can save you. I could lead you safely through the dark. Because it's my dark." Ila unfolded from the crack in the grotto's back wall. The nun—Martine—stared at him. And in her stare Ila saw how much he'd changed. He could bear a casual scrutiny—but not this. He had become like one of those things Chambord had kept in spirits—leached and changed.

She said to Ila, "Will you?"

He said, "I will."

She said, "Will it cost me?"

He said, "It will." Though he hadn't thought till that moment to make her pay, to make any claims. It was her question that made him want to keep her. Perhaps, as she thought, she lacked moral courage. But she was fatalistic. And fatalism was a flavor Ila liked. He'd had many rapt surrenders but few sober ones. Martine felt she was being asked to bargain, so Ila made a bargain with her.

She went back down to her grandfather and the other villagers, and Ila whispered after her as she went. He said, "I won't let them see me. You take the lead."

And, indeed, Ila was as invisible as God.

Martine led the men into the cave. She carried a lamp, a jar full of oil with a floating wick. Its flame was a stunted bud. Martine wasn't trembling anymore; she kept the lamp steady, didn't swamp its seed of light. The way was rough enough and she had a limp, but she kept the lamp steady.

Ila walked backward. Only Martine could see him, the dim smoke of his face and hands at the very limit of the lamplight. Ila used the light, too. He couldn't see in the dark, but there had been times when he'd crossed from the high entrance to Dardo without light, and he knew the way by touch, by the degree of the slope, the architecture of the tunnels, the temperature and purity of the air.

The villagers lit a second lamp. They hurried. When they reached a larger chamber they paused to nurse the flame, which was failing. Ila moved closer to them while they were all busy looking at the light, its clear gold sinking into clear blue around the black matter of the wick.

The lamp went out.

Ila heard the people panting with fear.

Martine's grandfather lit a match. In its light the walls glistened. The men and woman were like the translucent

328 ~ Elizabeth Knox

flowstone of the cave. Their breath gave the match a halo. The match went out. But there was another. There were others. To Ila the people looked, in the light of each, like a church picture, like a gathering of saints.

By the light of the second-to-last match Ila beckoned to Martine. She said to the others, "Come on." The people went on, without light, and Ila took Martine's hand in his. He led her, put her hand to touch the low places in the roof, guided her feet over the rough places on the floor, kept her from side passages, dead ends, and openings onto the rest of the system.

As they came near the exit, Ila asked Martine if she could see the light—it was evening. "No," she said. And, "No," again, later.

Eventually Ila asked did she not *want* him to leave her? And a moment later she said she could see the light. She sang out to her grandfather and the other villagers. Ila stuffed his dusty self into a hollow in the passage, and the men blundered past him. Their figures made a jumble of thick shadows against the grainy dark of night. Then they were out. But Martine had waited. She stood with her hands by her sides—as later Ila heard she had stood before the irresolute guns of the terrified men of the firing squad. She waited for her guide to take his payment or to tell her what it was to be.

But Ila had decided to let her go. When he was younger her certainty would have provoked him. He'd have wanted— as Dawn wanted when making Tom—to make Martine see that the world worked differently than she believed it did. That the world wasn't populated by souls that were either safe or imperiled and there weren't devils everywhere, like hot spots of bacteria in a culture, a growth medium that was God, or God's creation—everything else inside Him and dependent on Him. The younger Ila would've been provoked by her fatalistic complacency, but Ila was feeling uncertain and short on knowledge himself. He wasn't up to the pedagogical exercise of teaching this young woman.

"I wanted to be rid of her," Ila said.

Daniel saw that the vampire was regarding him as though he were a resource. That is, Ila was planning to use what he knew Daniel would know in order to make himself understood. When Ila had first spoken to him, in Menton, Daniel had thought, *I could be anyone.* He'd thought Ila was like his mother, to whom Daniel had often appeared only as a mask between two apparently cocked ears. But it was clear to Daniel now that Ila was talking to him—to Father Daniel Octave— and that he wouldn't have spoken in the cemetery if he hadn't found himself faced with a priest.

Ila said that he imagined that Daniel, in his line of work, often came upon people at prayer. "If I walk into a church I expect to see people praying. I mean, I don't see them. It's too everyday. Martine came into my cave with her prayer. When people pray they do so out of the thick of themselves. If they make modifications to their feelings it's only to better direct the flow of those feelings toward the person they imagine God is. They try to please their idea, but they don't pretend, as they might do to friends or family. Martine came into my cave and brought herself, her life and times. I preyed on them—people. But I was like a naturalist in his hide; I watched them, too.

"Eve says I don't draw people because she thinks it hurts me to try to. If I was to draw you, Daniel, I'd draw the way you're sitting, your clothes—but without head or hands. As I became older and more retiring it became impossible for me to look closely enough at people to want to draw them. I focused on their apparel, not their faces. It was a kind of tenderness. I'd look and feel lonely, not touched but bruised.

"Martine came into my cave with her limp, her distress, her moral dilemma, her circle of frightened firelit faces, and her thin, Gothic hands. It clawed at me, and I wanted to be rid of her."

Martine Raimondi came back to the caves, transformed, wearing boots, trousers, a patched shirt, and a leather jacket. She carried a flashlight. She walked a distance in, calling, trying to raise her demon. Ila came to see what she wanted. He didn't want to see her get into any more trouble. She said she wanted him to help her. Had the Germans restored the grate between the crypt and caves? If so, could Ila shift it?

They had, and he could.

For some weeks Ila kept her from harm by carrying messages to the confessional in St. Barthelemy's—from partisans in the hills to those in the village. She asked Ila to guide men with guns through his cave. He refused. She asked his price. He told her what he was. He was a vampire—an immortal. What could his price possibly be? He told her that she was asking a wolf for the use of his lair.

Martine was with the partisans for four months. During that time she came to value their struggle more highly than her own vocation. She came to believe that she should use this devil God had sent her. And she did see Ila as a devil, a cannibal, a murderer. If he sometimes seemed meek, he was only trying to deceive her, she thought. She made it abundantly clear to Ila that that was what she thought. Martine wanted what Alberto Vail and his friends did, what the Maquis over the border wanted—the watch on the pass removed, that platoon and the radio in the ruined tower of Castel Abelio. She'd seen Ila wrench the grate from its bolts, and she imagined his hands dripping German blood.

She said to him, "You're a killer; kill them for us." She tried to tempt him: "Imagine the feast you could have."

Martine was whispering to him in an olive grove—one night when the new moon gleamed in its hollow socket of shadow. "Fifteen men," she said.

And Ila asked her, "Do you think that if you use me as your instrument, you haven't got blood on your hands?" He was thinking of the tongs used by priests to give plague sufferers Holy Communion.

"The moment I met you I gave myself up for lost," Martine said. She was shaking, as she did when moved, this time to anger.

Ila asked her, "Who do you think is making these decisions about us? Do you think I'm a demon you raised, that you're damned already, so you might as well use me?"

"Yes!" Martine was fierce.

He pointed uphill: "That's *my* cave, and I chose to help you through it."

She pushed him then; she shouted at him, "You're a monster! Be a monster!"

Ila tried to explain. He opened his mouth to talk about the butcher and the soldier, why the soldier had stopped, what the soldier saw, the gesture he made, that it was the soldier's gratitude to God for the sight of the snake—a little trickle of fluid darkness—that made Ila want to help her and the condemned villagers. He hadn't saved the soldier, true, and had drunk from him and thanked the butcher for killing him, but it seemed to him that, whatever its outcome, the gratitude, all of it, had belonged in a different world from the condemnation, and Ila had wanted to live in *that* world. But Martine hadn't let him talk. She lost her temper and struck him in the mouth.

He walked off, sucking his split lip. He went back into his caves.

It was weeks till he saw her again. He stopped her on the mule track that came down from Castel Abelio to Dardo. There was a full moon, and he recognized her at some distance by her painful rocking gait. He followed her, closed the distance gradually till he was able to warn her: "If you go any closer to Dardo you'll be putting yourself in danger."

Martine stopped and waited for him. She said she'd been looking for him. She'd been calling at the high entrance for two days now, and he hadn't come.

"See," he said. "You can't conjure me."

Martine began to shake again and Ila kept his distance, supposing she was angry. She eased herself down to sit on the path.

He said that it was September and he could range farther; the nights were longer now. She couldn't expect to see him.

Martine told him she'd been ill. She held out her hand and unwound a bandage and showed him the gash on her knuckles. It looked fresh, uninfected. When she'd hit him, she'd cut her hand, she said. It hadn't healed or changed, and she'd been sickening. She said, "I thought your vampirism was a curse. I thought it came from some kind of carnal connection—or from some sin, or weakness. But now I think it's a disease, and that I'm infected."

Martine told Ila that she'd studied pharmacology at the University of Turin. She was a pharmacist—a scientist. She'd thought it all through and it seemed to her that what this was, was some kind of disease.

"It usually takes quickly," he said, "from a bite. I didn't bite you, so perhaps you'll fight it off. If it's a disease."

She nodded. She was swaying with exhaustion. She said to Ila that she'd thought he was dead. A walking corpse.

"But you've held my hand," he said. "Felt my warmth."

"I'm going to keep to my bed till I'm well," she told him. "Shall I show you where I'll be?"

Ila put his arms around her shoulders and under her knees. He picked her up and she let him carry her to the house in the mountains above Tende.

Five days later Giesen's men found Martine at the house

and took her back to Dardo. She was already under a sentence of death, so she didn't need any further processing. She wouldn't tell Giesen how many others had escaped—of the men he'd sent into the caves. She was asked about Alberto Vail and wouldn't say anything. They sent a priest to her, a father from Tende. He heard her confession, and when he tried to console her with the idea of her martyrdom she said that she'd rather live on and fight.

She was executed. Mother Pauline of the Order of the Daughters of Grace, who saw Martine's body before her coffin was sealed, said there was only one wound, in her chest. The firing squad had aimed wide—all but one. Giesen had unclipped his holster but hadn't drawn his gun. He hadn't put its muzzle to her skull. In the end that was too much, even for him. The doctor who examined her body—held upright against the pole by the belt around her middle—found no pulse in her neck.

By the time Ila discovered what had happened, Martine's body was already on the train to Turin. He'd gone to the house above Tende and found it empty, its door hanging by one hinge. He asked after Martine the next night, after the late mass at St. Barthelemy's. (He'd broken the grate again. Giesen had only just had it restored—he hadn't thought of it till the nun made her reappearance.) The villagers at the mass took Ila for a partisan. They told him that Martine Raimondi had been arrested and shot. Hadn't he known? Word had been sent to Alberto Vail before the execution, but no one had come to save her. The old women clutched at Ila, crying about the Raimondis and Martine's poor grandfather.

Ila stopped speaking. Daniel watched Ila pause to brush at his own arms as though at hands holding him. Then he brushed them off, those importunate phantoms, those black-scarved, bandy-legged, distraught old women from fifty years before.

Ila said that he'd run out of the church, through the town, and up the mule track. He went up the mountain, all the way to the Castel Abelio. They hadn't time—those soldiers—even to think to shoot at him before he was over the lowest part of its broken wall. They opened fire. They were frightened and, without thinking, they followed him with their guns. He ran around the top of the wall, then down its side, around the hollow tower, his momentum keeping him on the wall, running at a ninety-degree angle to the ground. One circuit, moving diagonally down, so that the man at the machine gun, following him, felled a number of his own friends before he had time to take his hands off the trigger.

"I tore them to pieces," Ila told Daniel. "I think Alberto Vail's men can't have looked closely at what they found. It was all over in a minute, maybe. A minute of screaming mayhem. The dogs rushed about, demented with fear. I remember tripping over a dog, then catching them all, and lowering them by their legs, snapping and writhing, into the dry well. I remember peering in at them when it was finished. They were mad, seething over each other, howling and biting. They had lost all fellow feeling in their terror. But after a moment they noticed me; then they all cowered down, and began wriggling on their bellies, as puppies do to their fathers. I remember that. And I remember looking around at the radio, shedding solid orange sparks, and the smoke hanging in the air—smoke and steam from the opened bodies. Then I left the fortress. When I'd been gone a moment the dogs began to yammer. It was the dogs, by their homage and then by their howling, who told me what I'd done, and what I was.

"I never knew," Ila said. "I hadn't understood. I hadn't exercised my abilities. I was proud of my *knowledge*, my memory—I was a farmer's almanac, a hundred-year tide table, a library of maps and plans. That's how I was able to save Martine. The old women in the church knew where Martine's order meant to take her—Santa Maria della Fiori, in Turin.

The order let the right people know where she was. They were cultivating a cult. They had their eyes on the prize from the moment she was executed—a martyr and a miracle worker. I knew the church, Toronelli's double-walled dome. I have pictures of plans stored in my mind. That's my talent. I remembered pictures even when I was still living on bread and cheese and wine. It was the talent I was born with.

"Martine was hungry when I found her. She'd been being obediently dead. She'd kept still, listening to the voices of her sisters, their prayer vigil. She was waiting for God to get to her—supposing he was busy with the war. She said sometimes she imagined she'd died in the cave, and that the sound of my digging was explorers, in the future. She said she was worried the explorers were in for a nasty surprise.

"I made a hole, wriggled through it, and took her in my arms. I bit my own wrist and suckled her."

Ila stopped speaking again. He looked bleak. Then he took up the oars and began to row. He moved so briskly that Daniel nearly lost his seat. The lamp fell into the bottom of the boat. Daniel retrieved it and hugged it to him. He looked back to see a wake, the boat jumping forward in spurts and the water rushing in behind it. The lights of land were far away. Daniel felt in his jacket for his phone. He wondered who to call, who could help. He decided to call Eve Moskelute, who could at least offer some advice or talk to her friend herself. He produced the phone and pressed a button—its keyboard lit up green.

Daniel felt the phone leave his hand and heard a splash as it hit the water. He found himself looking at a red afterimage, the phone's digits overlaying his empty hand. The vampire's hands were still on the oars. It was as if Daniel had thrown the mobile away himself.

"Now you'll have to row back," Ila said. "You should have kept it hidden."

Ila rowed for fifteen minutes, then set one oar in the water, and the boat slewed about, so that Daniel faced the lights of land and Ila was facing east. He shipped his oars.

Daniel asked how Giesen's body came to be in Martine's tomb.

Ila burst out laughing. Daniel could have sworn he saw the vampire blush. "Well," Ila said, then laughed some more.

Daniel told him to please stop it. At once.

"Well," Ila said again. "You were so persistent—in a pussy-footing way, Martine said—about the matter of her mother-hood. I mean, *Raimondi's* motherhood, *Dardo's* provenance. You'd managed to get her to promise you a DNA sample, to compare with what you found in the tomb. The tomb was empty, of course. Martine wasn't running any risk in making you that promise. But—you see—when you got permission to open the tomb, we knew about it. We had a date: March 1991. Giesen was Dawn's idea. She knew the caves nearly as well as I did by then—and for years she'd been flipping a salute to Giesen's mummy, in the dry funkhole where I keep things. Jacques Palomba would have seen Giesen if we hadn't moved him by then.

"We packed him into one of those big plastic bags with a zipper that people use to carry suits. He was flat enough for that—sunken and desiccated.

"Dawn and Tom Hilxen and I took Giesen by car to Turin, a couple of weeks before you people opened the tomb. We carried him into Santa Maria della Fiori on a quiet morning when there were only a few tourists in the church. We took the top off the sarcophagus—there were three of us; that was enough—and put him in for you to find."

Daniel squeezed out the breath he had been holding. "You're going to burn," he said. It was a cold certainty. He held on to the idea; it focused his mind, as certain painful disciplines of the novitiate had—an hour's kneeling or a spiked chain worn wrapped around one thigh. "You'll fetch up float-

ing facedown in a slick of your own fat," Daniel said. "Like
Martine."

Ila inclined toward Daniel and opened his mouth. No
speech came out of it, but Daniel saw a row of thin white
spines of cartilage drop from the roof of Ila's mouth and beads
of milky, faintly luminescent substance appear on their tips.
The venom dripped onto Ila's pink tongue. Then Ila shut his
mouth and sat back, the muscles of his jaw bunching as he
pushed his tongue up to quell the spines.

"I'm surprised it's taken you this long," Daniel went on,
"to do the decent thing. To despair, and do the decent thing."
Daniel turned his head and looked at the eastern horizon with
an expression of keen anticipation.

There was a band of lemony light above the sea. Daniel
pointed it out to Ila and smirked. For several minutes Daniel
sat, with his arms folded, glaring and gloating by turns. Then
his curiosity got the better of him and he had to ask Ila how
Giesen got into the caves.

"I carried him off from his hotel. I got into his room by
breaking through the tiles on its roof. He was unconscious
when I left him in the caves. I went to Turin to find Martine.
When I thought of him again and went looking I found his
corpse. I'd forgotten to take his gun." The vampire pressed the
tips of two fingers to his temple, then made the sound of a
gunshot. He said, "Giesen woke in the cold, muffling dark. No
one came when he called."

Daniel had come to an end. He had wandered in his maze,
or followed the thread of his suspicion. He had dropped down
a dark shaft, had released the rope's end, and had fallen free.
He'd found out, finally. There were no miracles. And he was
sitting in a boat opposite the monster at the heart of the
maze—his Minotaur.

But, because he was thorough, Daniel finished checking
his facts. He said, "You rescued Jacques Palomba, too?"

"Dawn did. She was injured. He helped her recover. She kept him warm and hydrated. I left him where he'd be found. But Jacques had been bitten, and had an unfulfilled longing. When he met a vampire again he knew he'd found what he felt he lacked."

"Jacques found Martine and she infected him?" Daniel said.

"Yes. Jacques found Tom and Grazide, who told him about Martine. Jacques went looking for her. She'd finally become infectious. Tom says she infected Jacques and killed him, and then herself."

Daniel nodded. He said she'd mentioned finally infecting someone as a reason for casting herself adrift. "She called me on the phone she gave me. The phone you just threw into the sea. She called shortly before the sun came up. When the sun came up she broke the connection. She said she'd finally infected someone—infected, and killed."

Ila was looking at Daniel with amazement. "You were there."

Daniel said yes, in a way. But he hadn't known what to say or what he was being told. He only understood that she'd done something that was intolerable to her. Then he said, "Row back, Ila. Do it now. You might make it."

Ila shrugged this off. "That's why Tom was so angry— Jacques was Tom's candidate. As Bad was Dawn's."

"Was?"

"Bad's gone. He saw enough." Ila said that when he and Martine were nesting in the space between the double-walled dome of Santa Maria della Fiori she said to him, "I prayed to God for courage and God has given me a life that requires courage." Martine had imagination, Ila said. After all, she'd only seen him saving people, not gorged, dangerous, and indiscriminate, as Bad had seen Dawn.

"You came and got her out of her grave," Daniel said. "Imagine what she imagined."

"Martine and Dawn." Ila half-closed his eyes and stared past Daniel at the purple, orange, and browns of the east. The few clouds had fanned rays of shadow rising from them into the pale sky. Ila's skin and hair were clear, reflective surfaces, and he glowed with the colors of twilight. "Tom still has his credit cards and his zip code," Ila said. "He didn't give everything up."

"He gave up daylight and kept his credit cards." Daniel laughed and shook his head.

Ila was still looking east. He said he wondered how it had happened. Had the burning killed Martine? Or had she drowned herself because of the pain? She shouldn't have been alone. He was here now, but it was too late.

"Don't die," Daniel said.

But Ila didn't hear him. He was saying, "I miss Martine. We were together for so long. I can't wait for her. I can't live waiting."

"Look at me," Daniel said. He had an idea or feeling or an itch. He felt he was being pushed to do something he couldn't fully comprehend, something foreign to his nature. So, he was being pushed; it was outside him. He was its instrument. He wanted Ila to tell him about Chambord. About 1771 and everything since, even if everything amounted to glimpses through a window at night, of a living room, figures in a frame, like an illumination: people, their apparel, their artifacts.

Daniel must have said something—asked for a story—because Ila answered him. He said, "There isn't time." His voice was mild and wondering. He was shining, a screen; his refined pallor had turned transparent. He was a frosted glass into which someone had poured the twilit air. Yes—Daniel thought—Ila was a mark that showed how high the flood came, an unlit match in a reliquary; he was something put by, something for later, for an unforeseen contingency. He was *God knew what*. All the apparent coincidences had led Daniel to a nest, a *conference* of vampires. A conference like the one

Daniel had inferred from the fourth albino he met on his walk through the Marais. But this vampire—long-lived, contemplative, feeling—didn't belong finally to any conference. This one was *a sign*, like Daniel's third albino, and so belonged to God. *God* knew what Ila was, and what he was for.

Daniel stood up in the boat. He was saying, "Look at me." The boat rocked. The bilgewater had a skin of light on it, the white dawn sky in a tilting reflection. Ila looked past Daniel at the east. He opened his mouth and screamed with rage and terror. He howled at the sun, the igniting daylight.

Ila leapt to his feet and flipped the boat. Daniel was thrown into the water, its cool glassiness turning from gray-bronze to green as Daniel went down. The lamp drifted up past him. Submerged, it was no longer an unpoetic object. It rolled upward, casting rays of light through the water, a light-house rotating on an odd axis in a green fog. Daniel followed it up, the life vest apparently plucking him up into the air. The sky had regained its high dome; the back of every wave was burning; the sun, halved by the horizon, was coming up in an audible chorus. Daniel shook water out of his ears. He was sure there was a sound he should hear. An oar tapped against his back, then floated away. Daniel swam, pushed past the floating light. He saw the sleek plastic skin of the upturned boat. Daniel swam to it. He grabbed its side and pushed himself down under the water—with the vest it was like lifting a weight.

Ila was curled into the carapace of the boat. Daniel came up beside him, in the narrow space between the hull and the water, where the tackle box floated, bumping.

Ila opened his eyes and looked at Daniel. "Get out of my air," he said.

Chapter 18

A SEA RESCUE

*G*ino had been home for some time. He had just come off his shift, the graveyard.

Bad sat on the air mattress, his hands hanging between his knees. He heard Gino come in and watched lights come and go on the polished marble floor, the yellow light from the landing as the apartment door opened, a faint lightening of no color as Gino opened the shutters, a white fluorescent from the fridge interior. Gino came and offered Bad a bottle, a genie of grainy vapor creeping out of its uncapped top. "Still not sleeping?" Gino said.

Bad had imagined that leaving Dawn would be like a withdrawal. He'd been so deeply immersed in the experience of being with her, so lost to the life and values he understood, that he'd thought that leaving her would be like giving up a highly addictive drug and a life formed around feeding a drug habit. Bad had little experience of withdrawal from the inside. His experience was confined to the low dose of amitriptyline he'd been on after the bomb blast, to ease his neck injury and help him sleep. He hadn't liked it; it made him feel—he told Gabrielle—like a Glaswegian looking for a fight on Saturday night. When he took himself off it he was awake, night after night, awake and in pain till exhaustion reasserted his normal sleep cycle. Leaving Dawn should have been like coming off a very effective drug. He'd expected insomnia, agitation, indigestion, general pain. He'd made a bad choice, had been entrapped; he'd got into something he wasn't able to handle. Bad represented his predicament to himself in this way, in language he'd learned in high school health lessons and at a rudimentary counseling skills course he'd attended at the police college.

For five days Bad had abstained. He'd thought that his suffering should be the pain of enforced abstinence. He took walks to keep fit. He set out to get on top of his longing. But he discovered that what he felt was less longing than loss.

Bad took the bottle from Gino, swigged, and said, "I have to go home."

Gino said yes, he'd looked at Bad's itinerary and had talked to Bad's mother and grandfather. He put Bad's phone down on the bed between them. "You should check your messages."

Gino began to talk about knowing your limits. He said that there were some experiences that were too big. Those ones would, you'd think, stretch a person, make him bigger, if all out of shape. But instead, he said, they made a person get smaller. Gino measured out a centimeter of air between thumb and forefinger, then found the word: "Shrink," he said.

Gino told Bad why he didn't go cave diving anymore. Gino said that if he was asked why, he'd just say that it wasn't an acceptable risk. But it wasn't only that. Cave diving was like having your heart stopped just to see what would happen next. On Gino's last dive he'd been with two others. The three men were very deep, in a system they thought hadn't been explored. The man in the lead was the most experienced. Gino and the other man were just following the rope. As they fiddled with the gas mix and performed mental tests, making different demands on themselves, he and the other man moved farther apart. The man moved ahead of Gino, perhaps trying to catch up to the leader. The man was confused, cold, disoriented by mild nitrogen narcosis—but he went on, faithfully following the rope. The *duplicitous* rope—for there were two in the passage. Other divers had been there on an earlier occasion. The man would have been able to see the light from the leader's lamp, for although the passage branched, the wall where it branched was honeycombed with holes for a further thirty meters. He could see the leader's light, so he didn't notice that he'd strayed. The current was stronger in the passage he was carried into, he was tired, and it was easy to drift along the length of the wrong rope. He wouldn't have known till he reached its frayed end.

Gino eventually came within sight of the man and, from his vantage point in the passage above the branch, saw his friends reaching out to hold hands through a hole in a wall of rock. He saw the waving fronds of the frayed rope. Gino took the old rope and braced his feet to reel his friend up. But the man wasn't holding the rope, only the leader's hand. Gino saw the leader urging the man to grab the rope, to let Gino pull him up. And he saw the man would not, was holding to his friend's hand stubbornly, his grip the last task his exhausted, baffled brain could grasp. He could do only that, hold on. But he was too tired to do that for long and eventually let go, and Gino watched him drop away, down, illuminating the clear water as he went. Gino saw the man's face through his mask, his eyes, and knew that the man knew he was going. The man looked back, but he didn't struggle. The current carried him away and down. "Beyond assistance," Gino said. "And beyond imagination."

Gino told Bad he'd realized that, whenever he told that story, he told part of it from the point of view of the man who'd died. "That moment he reaches the frayed end and realizes he's on the wrong rope." Gino had wondered why he did that, then came to understand that he was following his friend as far as he was able. Gino said, "We imagine how they felt because they can't tell us. We go with them, as far as we can."

Bad bumped Gino's shoulder with his own—to say thanks.

Gino bumped back and touched the top of his bottle to Bad's to encourage Bad to drink.

On the bed between them, the mobile began to ring.

Eve had been woken by her phone. Or she thought it might have been the phone. She'd become conscious and listened to the silence where some alarm had just finished sounding. She got up, went to get a glass of water. The light was on in the kitchen, and there was a drawing on the table. A black-and-white ink sketch. It was of an empty boat, a lamp on its stern seat, and the sun, its disk halved by a sea horizon. The sketch was Ila's, his picture of what Martine may have left behind her when she left the world.

Eve thought, *This is a suicide note.*

The phone call was Eve for Bad. "I need your help," she said.

It was two hours by the autostrada to Menton, where Gino had a friend with a good boat—a diving instructor at the Centre de Plongée. Gino called ahead. He didn't launch into any exhaustive explanations, didn't have to, any more than Bad had had to when he came off the phone to say that Eve's other friend—who had the same problems as the woman they had fished out of the sea cave at Riomaggiore—seemed set to follow that woman's example. "Eve thinks it's too late to call the police," Bad told Gino. "She thinks she knows where we can find him. She just wants him found."

Gino said all right, a recovery, not a rescue. And Bad could see Gino didn't quite believe it—thought that Bad's new friend Eve was being pessimistic or private, was just trying to save her friend the trouble of a police prosecution and the shame of a psychiatric referral.

But Gino went along with Bad.

It was still dark when they left Genoa. The sun came up when they were in one of the tunnels between Bordighera and Ventimiglia. Gino's car came out of the tunnel and Bad looked to his right at the terraced foothills, which a moment before had loomed dark and immediate and now receded in intricate sunlit detail. The phone was ringing when they left the tunnel. Bad answered it.

Eve was in tears. It was hard to make sense of what she said. She'd hoped, she'd hoped, but it wasn't him. The call that woke her wasn't him. She'd checked with her service, checked the caller identification. It was Daniel Octave—but she had no idea what he wanted at 3:30 A.M. She'd hoped it was Ila. She'd been down to the marina and there was a boat missing—a skiff. The harbormaster had been on his hands and knees across his doorstep vomiting when she arrived. She'd put him in a taxi. It was too late—she'd known it would be—but how terrible to watch the sun come up.

"I thought Daniel Octave was dead," Bad said. Then, "Is Dawn home?"

"Yes. Don't come here," Eve said, firm although she was still crying. "She's asleep. I haven't told her."

"Do you have binoculars?" Bad said. Then, "Wait—tunnel."

He held the phone to his chest for the duration of the tunnel and then put it back to his ear to issue instructions. Eve was to go to where she had a view of the sea—one of the elevated places in the old town that looked seaward—and she was to look for the boat. "Take your phone and call me," Bad said.

The diving instructor's boat had a high bridge, and a cabin below the deck. The diving instructor motored out of Menton's harbor at the maximum legal speed while Gino and Bad changed into their wet suits. The morning was warm already, and Bad left his suit unzipped, its arms knotted above his waist. Gino passed him a flotation vest, and Bad put it down on the deck. Gino put his on—the one with the radio clipped to its shoulder. Gino switched the radio on and checked it with his friend, who was at the wheel, his legs planted, leaning back as if the little ripples juddering the boat as it picked up speed were a steep sea. The instructor turned around and gave Gino a thumbs-up and spoke at his own shoulder. Bad heard Gino's radio cough and splutter and a short conversation in two languages, mostly *si* and *oui*—or rather the *she* and *way* of the Rivieras. Gino signed off and scratched his nose on the radio's stubby aerial. He said his friend had wanted to know the protocols of this operation. "I told him *maintenance of confidentiality.*"

"Thanks," Bad said.

Gino said the boat had a marine emergency medical unit. It had oxygen, a defibrillator, airway ventilation equipment, a Stryker cot—better than a nasty old Stokes basket—and vac suction. "And body bags," Gino finished.

Gino wanted Bad to tell him what to expect.

Bad told Gino that he couldn't tell him how many minutes it was after the event. But did Gino remember the blisters on the woman? That was photosensitivity. The guy they were going to find had the same allergy. He had gone out in a boat to expose himself—not just to jump into the sea.

Gino closed his eyes. He turned into the sea breeze and it twitched his cropped hair. He said he understood why a person would release himself from suffering or trouble. But when he was called out because someone had set himself on fire—

"Yes," said Bad. "Wanting not just to die, but to suffer."

"I hate that," Gino said. He said that his friend also had budgeting concerns.

"No problem."

Eve called again. There was a haze of early-morning condensation over the sea. A thin veil. She could make out three small boats through it. But only one boat was still; the others seemed to be going places.

Bad had her sight off Capo Mortola to work out roughly where the motionless boat was. "You should be able to see us now," Bad told her. A moment later: "Please, Eve, you have to pull yourself together."

Gino was looking at him. Gino thrust out his lower lip and drew a line down his cheek from the corner of his eye.

Bad nodded—yes, she was crying.

"Tell her to look for a person in the boat. He may have kept his options open and got under cover."

Bad passed this on. And he mentioned the diving instructor's budgeting concerns.

"I can pay," Eve said. "That's my one perpetually open option."

A moment later Bad told her to stay on the phone, then said to Gino, "She can't make out much through the haze."

Gino talked on the radio to his friend at the wheel. He and Bad leaned out either side of the boat and faced forward.

The haze was scarcely substantial; it only seemed to soften the horizon. Bad could smell it, though, a notional layer of freshwater above the salt. He tried not think of Ila, then had him in his head, vivid, slight, silent, dry, deadly. "God!" Bad said, to himself and Gino. "This will finish me off." Then he laughed. He put the phone to his ear—asked if Eve could see them and how near they were.

"You'll need to turn right a bit."

"Starboard," Bad said.

"Yes, starboard, maybe five degrees," Eve said, catching on—a quick study. Bad heard her saying something to someone with her. He asked, "Who is that?"

She didn't answer at once, then explained it was a concerned neighbor. "I'll cry quietly now," she said.

The instructor shouted down to Bad and Gino. He pointed with one hand, his other moving the wheel. The boat turned. Gino came across to where Bad stood, and they craned together. The haze became visible once they could see what it had previously obscured.

The white hull of the upturned boat seemed to slide out from under the place where the sky's blue was just a little smeary.

The instructor closed the throttle right down and the launch coasted slowly on toward the upturned hull.

Bad heard a voice. A croak. Someone calling.

Bad pushed his arms into the sleeves of his wet suit, left the vest, and dived into the water. He struck away from the launch as it turned to idle, its bow wave following him and washing up the back of his neck. Bad stretched out into his fastest crawl. He swam around the boat and stopped, treading water.

Daniel Octave was wearing a life vest. He was afloat, with one palm flat against the water-beaded plastic of the hull.

Bad said, "I thought you were dead."

The launch cleared the boat, coasted around, and stood off only a few feet, its engine making Bad's whole body buzz.

Gino leaned over the side and said, *"Buongiorno."*

Father Octave was clumsily trying to get a grip on something he had under his hand.

Gino told Bad to get the guy to swim to him and they'd bounce him into the launch.

Bad moved closer to Daniel and saw the end of the plastic tube that Daniel was holding against the side of the upturned boat and clear of the water. It was the same sort of tube that had been hanging from the crook of Daniel's needle-pierced arm when Bad had discovered him unconscious on a pew in the Chapel of the Gray Penitents.

Bad went right up to Daniel, touched his tired face, and said, "Hang on, just a moment."

Bad dived, turned over in the water, and saw Ila, under the boat, the other end of the tube in his mouth, his hair transparent, skin red and blistered in some places, his form framed by a glistening skin of trapped air.

Bad surfaced. He swam back to the launch, fixed his eyes on Gino, and asked for a body bag. "There's a body under the boat."

Gino stared at Bad, his face totally blank. He was making a great effort to understand.

The diving instructor left the bridge, clattered down its metal stairs, and began waving his arms in Daniel Octave's direction.

Bad ignored him.

Gino asked, carefully, if it wasn't the usual practice to get the survivor out of the water first, then recover any bodies? To recover them and *then* bag them?

"Yes. You know that as well as I do," Bad said. "As well as he does." He pointed at the diving instructor. "Nevertheless, give me one of the body bags."

Gino pushed past the diving instructor and found a body bag. He dropped it down to Bad. Bad held it over his head to unzip it, then swam back to the upturned boat. He told Daniel that he could let go now.

Daniel dropped his end of the plastic tube and pushed away from the hull. He swam slowly to the launch. Bad saw Gino lean over the side and put out a hand to Daniel.

Bad dived. He submerged the body bag, wrestled the air out of it, and carried it under the upturned boat. The plastic tube, full of water now, drifted down past Bad.

Bad spread the body bag as much as he was able, holding

350 > Elizabeth Knox

it open for Ila, who pushed down from his nest of trapped air and swam into the bag. He did it with dexterity, didn't fight it or tangle in it, but let it envelop him. Bad wrapped Ila, then turned in the water and swam down another few feet to find the zipper and draw it up.

Bad had to breathe. He kicked up, the open end of the bag clutched in one fist. The weight of the bag—its deadweight—delayed him. The surface hung above his face for long seconds; then he broke it, took a breath, and put his head back down to see, to close the zipper.

Bad dragged the body bag the few feet to the launch. He turned the body feet-down and head-up in the water and, as he'd been trained, bounced it until Gino and the instructor were able to haul it up.

Bad scrambled on board unassisted. He dropped down onto the body bag and its contents, lay across Ila until he could muster some speech.

In the short moments he lay there Bad felt the black plastic heat up in the sun.

"I'll take him below," he said to Gino and the instructor.

He saw that they were looking at him fearfully, Gino distressed, the instructor disgusted. Bad waved them off. He got up and began to drag the bag. Daniel Octave came to his assistance. Together they dragged Ila down the steps—*bump, bump, bump*—into the cabin.

Daniel Octave sat down on the floor, in a puddle of seawater, and struggled out of his life vest. His brown skin had a green tinge—he was exhausted.

Bad knelt on the cabin's bunk to pull the curtains across the windows. The light came yellow between their regular pleats.

Bad hunkered down beside Daniel and unzipped the top of the body bag.

Ila raised himself on one elbow from the seawater puddled in the black plastic. His hair sizzled as water ran out of its thickness. His eyes followed Bad as he pushed back on his heels and staggered to his feet. "Thank you, Bad," Ila said.

Bad backed off. His feet hit the bottom step and he climbed up it. He ducked his head because of the low ceiling but still stared at them—Daniel and Ila.

They were watching him with very different expressions. Ila looked grateful. Daniel seemed to want to say he was sorry for something.

Bad told them to send him a postcard from Corsica. Then he turned his back and went on deck.

Eve walked slowly away from the sea and along the Via Appio to her house. She kept the phone pressed to her ear.

Bad asked about Dawn, and Eve, without any insulating civility left to her, could only tell him what it would hurt him to hear. She told Bad that Dawn thought he'd come back. Dawn hoped, like those in exile hope to be allowed to go home.

Bad told Eve he'd come to understand that, in Dawn, he'd found the right woman. He thought for a while it was her glamour he loved, her life, her intoxicating stories and lovemaking. He was in awe of all that. Her life seemed to prove things he'd felt he'd needed proven. He was in "the hero business"—as his girlfriend would say—because he wanted to cheat death, to intervene, to defuse time when it began to tick down toward bloody calamity. He'd seen Dawn go over the edge of a fifteen-meter pitch and had felt the thud when she hit the bottom—then, eight years later, he'd run into her, *running*, like a deer. It filled him with awe. But, in the end, Bad had fallen in love with Dawn Moskelute herself, her nerve, her sense of fun, her warm heart.

He couldn't choose her life. He'd thought he could and had begun grieving, for the big things, like his family; for the little things, like plans he and Gino had to go into business together—*Industrial Abseiling: for those hard-to-reach places.* He had begun to mourn for the things he couldn't even imagine giving up, like the sun he was sure cast its light into every corner of his consciousness. Whenever he thought about *that* he realized that in choosing Dawn's life he would, in fact, be choosing to become one of another species.

"That's just too weird," Bad said, rather weakly.

Eve walked on through the still, clinging air. The sun seemed only to have warmed the water vapor, not dispersed it. The air felt like the possibility of autumn, a hint of it, in high summer.

But it wasn't just that—Bad said—the things he'd have to give up. It was the thing he realized he'd have to accept—the possibility of being a murderer. "I'm not especially ethical," Bad said. "Only forewarned. Those kids, those classmates of mine, died violently. I saw what that meant. I saw the blood, and I saw their parents afterward trying to live with what had happened, and to live without them. I can't sign on somewhere I might cause deaths. In the chapel, when I saw Father Octave lying so still on that pew, I thought Tom Hilxen had killed him. It hit me then—I mean, *I saw it all.* I can't put myself in that position. I'm probably a bloody pacifist, too," he finished. He sounded exasperated.

Eve stopped at her gate and rested her head on its bars. She told Bad that if she repeated all this to Dawn it would probably only make Dawn love him more.

"I don't want her to love me more. I want her to be all right."

Eve thought Bad was crying. But then he laughed and said, in a muffled, embarrassed way, that he was wrong about Daniel Octave anyway.

"I know. He was coming around when we left him," Eve said. "Poor man."

"Yes—well—I think you might find he's come *all the way* around," Bad said. Father Octave went out in the boat with Ila. It was he who'd kept Ila alive. Bad could see now that he and

Father Octave had been traveling in the same direction for a long time—he had got there first, but Daniel Octave got there finally. Daniel Octave was a better candidate. He'd already renounced the world and was—Bad said—part of a secret society already, so eminently suited to joining a secret family.

"*I* wanted to," Bad said. Eve was sure he was crying now. Tears of grief and frustration. "I loved you. Dawn and you. Both of you."

Eve told Bad he could come back and be *brotherly;* he could try that.

It wouldn't make any difference, he said; he couldn't be with them. Being with them meant accepting the possibility of being a murderer or—if he was only brotherly, as Eve was sisterly—being *an accessory* to murder.

Eve said, "You're being all-or-nothing."

"This *is* all-or-nothing. Some things are."

Eve listened to him weep. It seemed to hurt him physically. He didn't know how to do it without a wrenching struggle. After a time he said, "Give Dawn my love," then, deep and swallowed, "my *sunshine.* Yes—give her my love," he said. "After all, what am I going to do with it?"

"Industrial abseiling?" Eve said.

He laughed. Then he told her, "Goodbye," quiet and tender, and ended the call.

Eve was sitting by her sister's bed when Dawn woke. It was early for Dawn, and she fought her way out of her sun-induced stupor, moaning and thrashing. She'd clearly sensed that something was wrong. She broke out of sleep and sat bolt upright, blinking at Eve. She said, "What's the matter?"

Eve asked her sister to lie down again and then told her everything. That they had nearly lost Ila. That he was waiting out the daylight in a body bag in the cabin of a boat moored at the marina in Menton. He'd meant to be caught out but hadn't been able to go through with it. Or he'd been prevented, because he wasn't alone; he'd taken Father Octave out with him. Bad had rescued both of them—Ila from under the upturned boat.

Eve finished her explanation and sat staring at her sister. She felt shattered.

Dawn shuddered; she shook herself. She said, in a little voice, that she needed Ila to live.

"I know. I thought I'd lost you both. Or he'd condemned me to having to watch you blunder about making terrible mistakes and having no means to make a nest. *God*." Eve was shaking, too. "*I* want Ila to live. Martine didn't deserve him. She didn't deserve him to die for her."

Dawn said, "Yes, that's right. Though," she growled, "I won't be biting any goddamned Jesuits. No more bodiless, body-hating celibates. No." Dawn took a deep breath and subsided. She stroked Eve's arm and made a soothing sound, a motherly humming. She said, "The trouble with you, Eve, is that you think everything is over for you. Ares is dead and so you're only an unhappy spectator in matters of love. You think you're all in the past. You've been taking comfort in Ila because he's like the past, like an archive; even his appetite is archived. But you've just discovered that you don't want Ila to actually be in the past. And then there's Martine. You've been so worried about how Ila feels, having lost her, that you haven't considered how you feel. How *mad* at her you are. How, basically, she's left you holding the baby. Well," Dawn said, "this is what I feel about Martine. This honors her, and might help you. I'm not like Martine, and Ila, and you. I can't think about my soul. I have to be a pilgrim, and simply set out walking. I've set out after Martine, *with* you, and *with* Ila. And with Bad—because he'll come back." Dawn's face, pillowed on her glossy variegated hair, was glowing and serene. "I do know you don't want him to come back," she added. She squeezed Eve's hand.

"No, I don't. I want him to be a better man in a more ordinary life. That's what I want to see. Except I won't see it. I
just have to have faith that it will happen without me there to
witness it."

"He'll come back," Dawn said. "That's fate, not faith. How
can he be better than our story?"

Bad was late for his flight. He'd spent some time at Heathrow
changing his tickets for the second leg of his journey. When he
came down the aisle at the rear of the plane it was already
pushing back from the gate and the cabin crew were closing all
the overhead lockers.

Gabrielle had spread herself out and had a stack of magazines on the empty seat beside her. She looked up at Bad, and
her jaw dropped. Then she collected herself, gathered the
magazines, and gave Bad room to sit down. She said, "I did
wonder whether you might turn up and take your seat."

"How are you?" he said.

"What do you care?"

Bad kicked his bag under the seat in front of him and
clipped his belt closed. He raised his hands and surrendered
himself to a flight attendant's momentary inspection.

"But I suppose since we've a long journey, I should try to
be civil," Gabrielle conceded.

"I'd appreciate it," Bad said. "Anyway—cheer up; at least
you lose me at LAX, where I'm changing from Qantas to Air
New Zealand."

Gabrielle smirked as though consoled by some gaffe he'd
made. "I *wondered* what you were going to do next. Now I
know."

"That's what I'm doing *first*, Gabrielle. I'm going home.
Next I'll set up in Auckland, near home, but still an outpost of
the world."

"Set up what?"

"A business, I hope."

"In Auckland?" Gabrielle clearly considered this some sort of defeat. Or she meant him to. She opened one of her magazines, cracked its gleaming pages over her lap. She asked him if he had something to read. "I don't suppose you kept my book?"

Bad's birthday present, the motivational book, was in Dawn's bedroom in Menton, propping up one leg of Dawn's bed. One night, when he and Dawn were tussling, a caster broke off a leg of the bed and Bad had produced the book to wedge beneath it and bring the bed back to level.

"Actually," Gabrielle said, ingenuous, "I had a nice, long, enlightening talk with your grandfather—about you, and what you need. He told me things *you* should have, Brian. He told me about Dart Ridge. And do you know what? He thinks you should get over it."

Bad didn't reply to this and, after a moment, Gabrielle plugged in her headset and put it on.

Bad considered the obstacles in his life. Should he get over them? He thought that, at least, the obstacles gave his life a topography. They were like the mountains flanking the Roya River seen from the spur at Dardo, peaks that made it possible to measure distance, that sectioned the sky, differentiated space in a void, that invited any observer on a journey. If Bad imagined his obstacles—fearful loss, puzzling loss, sad loss—as mountains, then he could imagine a mountain path. A path like the Salt Route, that went by the cemetery gates, that passed through the darkness under the old cypress, that climbed on beyond Castel Abelio and its ghosts.

Bad was pressed into his seat. The jet tore upward, rocking slightly in the current of its climb. He shut his eyes and said a prayer. The jet banked, and he opened them again to look out the window on—to his eye immeasurable—sun-suffused blue air.